releasing me

JEWEL E. ANN

RELEASING ME

BOOK TWO

JEWEL E. ANN

This book is a work of fiction. Any resemblances to actual persons, living or dead, events, or locales are purely coincidental.

Copyright © 2013 by Jewel E. Ann

ISBN: 978-1-955520-46-1

All rights reserved.

This book is a work of fiction and is created without use of AI technology. Any resemblances to actual persons, living or dead, events, or locales are purely coincidental.

Without in any way limiting the author's exclusive rights under copyright, any use of this publication to "train" generative artificial intelligence (AI) technologies to generate text is expressly prohibited. The author reserves all rights to license uses of this work for generative AI training and development of machine learning language models.

Cover Designer: Jenn Beach

Formatting: Jenn Beach

For everyone who took a chance on me.

AUTHOR NOTE

Dear reader,

The thoughts and dialogue of these fictional characters do not necessarily represent my beliefs. They are representative of my perception of the world and the diverse opinions and language of humanity at the time of writing this story. Please understand that interpretation of words and beliefs change over time, as does my writing to reflect those changes and improve my craft. However, it's not realistic to continually edit a large and ever-growing backlist of titles. Thank you for understanding.

PROLOGUE

"Addy, I know this isn't how we imagined the start of our future together. But I love you, and I believe years from now it won't matter how or why we ended up together. All that will matter is that we ended up together. I'll live anywhere you want to live, I'll look for a job that gets me home by five, and I'll be yours on the weekends. You are my best friend, my love, and I want you to be my forever. Addy, will you marry me?"

"Yes ... yes, I'll marry you, Malcolm."

CHAPTER ONE

Quinn

"H**E COULD WAKE** up at any time, but he's going to feel groggy and possibly disoriented. Even when the anesthesia wears off, he may have trouble staying awake. We're giving him some strong medication for pain management and he'll want to sleep."

"Thank you, Doctor."

Addy? What happened? Where am I? God, I feel like shit. Why can't I open my eyes? Is this a dream?

I couldn't see my beautiful girl, all I could do was hear her voice.

That voice, the one that feels like home, is so clear, like she's right here with me, but I can't open my eyes. Why can't I see my beautiful girl?

"Addy, dear, you should go back to my hotel room and get some rest."

Mother? What are you doing here? What am I doing here? Where am I and why can't I open my eyes?

"I appreciate your concern, Elena, but I can't leave him, not until he wakes up."

"I wish you'd reconsider, but I understand. I'm going to have Chase get you something to eat, then."

"I'm not hungry."

"You need to eat, my dear, so if you're not going to go get some rest at the hotel, then you need to at least eat something. I won't take no for an answer."

"Fine, but just a salad or some fruit."

I felt her hand on mine. I couldn't see her face, but I knew her touch: warm, delicate fingers tracing familiar patterns over my knuckles, palm, and wrist. It was intimate, kind, and healing. I knew everything about her, at least everything I needed to know. I knew it that fateful day we met.

I WAS in Milwaukee visiting my latest investment, an eco-friendly hotel that had recently opened. Driving through the lakefront business district, I turned my head to take in the great view of the lake. Thankfully, I returned my eyes to the road just in time to honk my horn and slam on my brakes. That was when I saw her —long blond hair parted into pig tails. The first thing I thought was, "Seriously? A grown woman in pigtails?" She reminded me of Pippi Longstocking.

This insane woman stood in the middle of the

street with her arms stretched out, twirling in circles, and I jumped out of my Range Rover. My next thought: Julie Andrews as Maria in *The Sound of Music*. No one, outside of my immediate family, knew I'd seen just about every musical ever made, but not by choice. My mom insisted I watch musicals; it was her way of feeling less guilty about planting me in front of the television while she took care of my younger siblings.

Was Pippi Longstocking suicidal, drunk, high, or just flat-out crazy? Then she looked at me. The most beautiful, ocean blue eyes I had ever seen almost knocked me off my feet. We exchanged a few unpleasantries laced with sexual tension, but those eyes ... they were the warm sun, a gentle breeze, a glimpse of forever.

MY EYELIDS WERE LEADENED. I was so tired. The bright light stung my eyes when I managed to force them open.

"Quinn?" That's all she said, but it was like an angel beckoning me to Heaven.

I tried to speak but each word cut like a razor along my dry, burning throat.

"Here, drink a little water."

She held up a cup and I took a small sip.

"Addy, w-what ... happened?" The words clawed their way up my throat.

"I'm going to get the doctor." She kissed my cheek and hurried out the door.

A few moments later she returned with a doctor, nurse, my mother, and Chase.

"Quinn, I'm Dr. Muñez. You had a climbing accident and were airlifted to the hospital. You had a ruptured spleen that was causing internal bleeding. We successfully removed the spleen, but you still have a fractured rib and pelvis. We're going to monitor you over the next couple of days. Then you will need another surgery to repair your pelvis. Depending on the outcome of the surgery and your progress, I'm estimating two to three weeks before you can go home. In the meantime, we will have you on pain medication which will make you drowsy. You need to rest and keep visitors to a minimum. Do you have any questions?"

I fell? I remembered Addy climbing, but not me.

Internal bleeding, ruptured spleen, fractured bones? This must be a nightmare.

I needed to wake up! Broken and speechless. That couldn't be my reality.

Euphoria. I remembered that feeling. Her huge grin. Greedy eyes raking over my bare chest. Warm sun on my back. My fingers gripping onto the sharp edges of the rock. Tears falling from her eyes. Muffled voices. *Fuzziness —the pieces don't fit. How could this have happened?* Addy wouldn't have dropped me, and I knew how to take a fall.

The nurse took my blood pressure, checked my IV fluids, and asked about my pain level. She handed me a button to self-administer more pain medication as needed. Then she proceeded to tell me that I had a catheter inserted as she checked that bag as well.

Fucking great! The woman who referred to me as her Latin sex god gets to watch my piss bag fill up.

"Quinn, sweetie?" My mother kissed my cheek then caressed her hand over it. "I'm glad to see you're awake. We were so worried when the hospital called and said you were in surgery."

"Wh-why call Ad-dy okay—" *Damn narcotics!* Jumbled thoughts. Sluggish speech. A complete idiot. That was what I felt like. I wanted to ask why the hospital called. *Had Addy been injured too?*

I looked at my beautiful girl standing a few feet behind my mother. She chewed the inside of her lip. Something was off, but my brain refused to let me figure it out. Surrendering to tired eyes and heavy lids, I let memories of the first time I saw her do that carry me away.

After my first encounter with Addy, I spent the afternoon at my hotel in Milwaukee. A business acquaintance of mine was speaking at a luncheon in one of the meeting rooms. I decided to listen in for a while after lunch had been served. Addy made her unforgettable entrance while I stood at the back of the room. Offering my hand to her, she paused for a moment and chewed on the inside of her lip. Her nervousness was rivaled only by her embarrassment. She gathered her senses and found her feet without my help. Her stubbornness only intensified her sexiness.

As she walked to the front of the room, I drank in her subtle but sexy confidence: shoulders back, chin up, hips swaying. I had been to countless fashion shows, with half-naked women parading up and down the catwalk in front of me. They were sexy and desirable, and more often than not, one of them ended up in my bed by the end of the night.

Addy was different. She was unquestionably sexy and hot as hell, but there was something about her—a mix of magnetism, intrigue, and sadness. The dick in me, and the one on me, wanted to find the closest bathroom and fuck her over the vanity until the image of her in those naughty schoolgirl pigtails was erased. But another part of me, one that I wasn't as familiar with, wanted to fold her in my arms and squeeze the sadness out of her until all that was left was a beautiful woman.

<hr>

"I'M GL-AD YOU-YOU'RE HERE," I told my mother. "Talk to Ad-dy a-lone?"

"Sure, sweetie, we'll be right outside."

Chase patted me on my arm. "I knew your wild streak would come to an end. I bet you were showing off too much for your girl." He laughed because the Cohen boys were too manly to show genuine emotion toward each other. Our father had set that example.

I forced a smile. "Probably."

After they exited the room, Addy sat on the edge of the bed and held my hand. Eyes red and glassy, her brave mask wavered.

"Baby, I'll be f-fine."

Those four words broke her open, and the biggest tears fell down her face. Her body was still as she held her breath to keep from sobbing. I wanted to reach up and wipe away her tears, but I was too weak. Moving any part of my body was a challenge and any attempt caused pain.

"Come here," I whispered.

She hesitated at first then leaned into me until our foreheads touched. It was an intimate gesture that we had between us. It acknowledged our unspoken emotions, even if we weren't ready to share them. Addy had a lot she wasn't ready to share.

THE FIRST TIME I rested my forehead on hers was the moment I realized I wanted to take the pain away from her past. It was the moment I knew she was more than sad; she was broken.

It didn't take much for me to find out *The Sage* belonged to her. The first few people I talked to were reluctant to share information, but eventually I found a young guy who worked at the marina and was willing to share all he knew for a few extra bucks. Yes, I deceived Addy, and I should have been direct with her about the boat, but I wanted her to open up to me in her own time. Mentioning *The Sage* was my way of giving her the perfect opportunity, but she didn't take the bait. Instead, she distracted me with sex—not difficult to do. She was nervous, which made her anxious. She wanted me to take her fast and forget about everything else. I told her how beautiful I thought she was, but I don't know if she knew I wasn't talking about anything I could see on the outside.

The next morning I left her; not because I wanted to, I just couldn't stay. She was broken and hiding her feelings about her past from me and everyone else. Sex was a physical outlet for her emotions. When I realized that my own emotions were in uncharted territory, I knew I needed to leave. It felt like we were on a course headed for destruction. I worried that I could break her even more, in an effort to save myself.

HER TEARS FELL to my face. As if I wasn't already in enough pain, hers broke my fucking heart. I tilted my head up just enough to kiss her cheeks. The salty taste of her tears familiar as I'd kissed them away so many times before. They came in waves. Every time they surfaced I gave her another piece of my heart like a bandage to her soul.

"I love you, Addy. Just tell me."

I feared the worst. Maybe she needed to tell me that she dropped me, that she was responsible for my accident. I didn't have to think twice about it; I knew I would forgive her. She wouldn't even have to ask, but my fear was she would never forgive herself. Just another thing to add to everything else she carried around from her past, and I didn't want her to have that on her conscience or on her heart.

"I'm so sorry, Quinn." Her words were barely audible.

"There's no reason for you to be sorry."

She sat up and my bed started to move. The pain that shot through my body was excruciating.

"Ah ... ah ... fuck!" I yelled.

"Oh my God, oh my God!" Addy screamed as she scrambled.

The nurse rushed in the room. Addy had accidentally pushed the button that controlled my bed. The nurse lowered me back down as I yelled again. Then she administered another dose of my pain medication.

Maybe it was the pain, the medicine or a combination, but I passed out. I dreamed of Addy. She had been responsible for some of my most painful and embarrassing experiences of the previous year.

<hr>

ADDY HAD the genius to rival any renowned scientist of the 20th century, but fate worked in everyone's favor when she ended up in a kitchen. There was little doubt in my mind that she surely would have blown up or destroyed any sort of laboratory.

My first sampling of her chef's special was a hurricane of a green smoothie all over both of us. She laughed and so did I, eventually. She ran a two-for-one-torment-Quinn special that day. I never did find out if the *RAW girls taste better* T-shirt was intentional or an accident. After I arrived back in Chicago, I picked up some bottled water from the market, went by the bank to sign some papers, then met some buddies from college at a local sports bar.

I could only imagine what people at the bank thought of the millionaire businessman from New York showing up wearing that shirt. Of course no one said anything, but I wished they would have. It might have saved me from the ultimate embarrassment of having it brought to my attention by guys who knew me before I wore tailored Armani suits. I came close to indulging in a beer just to make it through all the crap I received. Admittedly, I was ten percent pissed and ninety percent turned on. All I could think about was finding out if the RAW girl from Milwaukee tasted better.

Addy won her Oscar when she played the role of Quinn's dirty little secret on Christmas with my family. She was anything *but* that to me. However, that was how I made her feel that day. I took the award for biggest prick when I let it go on for as long as I did.

Addy's heart broke when she saw Olivia. My mom's heart broke when Addy told her I was opening an escort business. Her out-of-nowhere story reeked of revenge but when she stood to leave, the pain in her eyes brought me to my knees. I would have chosen death over letting her leave without my family knowing the truth.

The car. My precious Lamborghini still has a tattoo in the form of a rear fender dent, compliments of the love of my life and her beater car, Karma. Addy insisted on paying to have it repaired, but I was never ready. Every time I looked at the dent, I'd get an instant hard-on, remembering the best fucking blow job of my life. I went from intense agitation to absolute ecstasy in a matter of seconds. She didn't even hesitate; it seemed instinctive. After that day, I intentionally parked closer to Karma. I figured it would only be a matter of time before Addy would be on her knees again making amends, not to mention giving Tom a new security tape to watch over and over again.

THE PAIN MEDICATION did its job, for the most part. The following two days vanished, with flashes of light and snippets of sound, as I drifted in and out of sleep. I stayed awake long enough to eat a little food, but that was short-lived, as I was given only fluids before my second surgery. I never woke up alone. My mother, Addy, and Chase rotated shifts, keeping post by my bed. The morning of my surgery, they waited near the door as the nurses did some final tests before prepping me for surgery.

My mother held Addy's left hand, inspecting the

ring I gave her. They whispered something, but I couldn't hear them. My mother occasionally looked at me with an approving smile.

BUYING a ring for Addy was like buying a winter coat for a polar bear. She didn't need it, and in some ways it looked out of place on her finger. She was the epitome of "simple but elegant." However, I couldn't resist buying her something that symbolized how beautiful and unique she was to me.

I don't remember when I fell in love with Addy. My heart knew it long before my head. Over three months passed after purchasing the ring before I got up the nerve to ask her to marry me. I wanted to ask her the same day I picked it up from the jewelers, but I waited until I knew she'd say yes. Of course I never imagined it would take so long. Even when I packed it for our trip, I didn't know for sure if Spain would be the right time.

My decision to propose happened a split second before I said the words. Everything felt perfect. The problem was I'd been carrying around a ring waiting to find the perfect time, but just as unplanned and unexpected as the day Addy came into my life, the right time for forever found us on a moonlit beach in the Canary Islands.

How did I get here? Fluorescent lights. Sterile white walls. Sad faces. Why can I still feel the sand under my back and her naked body pressed against mine?

Addy wouldn't look at me. Her apology left an emotional barrier between us. I felt it, but I didn't understand it. Wrapping my head around the possibility that she'd dropped me was too difficult. The nurses let me have a few minutes alone with my family before taking me to surgery.

"I love you, my beautiful boy, Godspeed." My mother cradled my face and kissed me before exiting the room.

"See you on the other side ... I mean, well you know, after surgery." Chase fumbled his words while he squeezed my arm.

It was then only the two of us. Addy stood several feet away as if someone had given her a restraining order. After the bed incident it was possible the nurse did. I reached my hand out. She hesitated a moment before closing the gap and taking it.

"Addy, about the other day—"

"Shh, don't." She shook her head. "I love you and that's the last thing I want you to think about before they put you under and the first thing you remember when you come to. Okay?"

Once again her body went rigid, and I knew she was holding back her tears. Were they tears of fear or tears of regret? I hoped they were mostly tears of love.

"No matter what happens—"

"Shh, please don't." She swallowed and blinked away her tears.

I squeezed her hand and pulled her closer until she rested her head on mine. "No matter what happens today, tomorrow, or any day after that ... don't ever forget you are the love of my life."

She nodded against my head, then kissed me, as the nurses came in to take me to surgery.

Addy stepped back and forced a smile. "Bye, babe."

I shook my head as they wheeled my bed out. "Never goodbye."

CHAPTER TWO

Addy

IT FELT like Quinn was in surgery forever. When Dr. Muñez came out to let us know the surgery was a success, we all breathed a sigh of relief. He told us it would be a while before we could see Quinn, so I decided to go back to Elena and Chase's hotel. At bare minimum, I needed a shower and some clean clothes. It also gave me a chance to call Mac in private. I hadn't talked with her since the accident, just texting. I knew she was worried and desperate for more information.

"Addy, how's he doing?" Mac answered her phone with an emotionally-choked voice.

"He's out of surgery and the doctor said it was successful."

"Thank God. You don't sound very happy?"

"Mac, something happened."

She hesitated before responding. "What do you mean? What happened?"

The truth hurt in the most crushing way. I took a deep breath then shared the pain in my heart with Mac.

"When he was climbing I ... I let it slip that I'd been married." My voice broke as the tears fell.

"Addy, you weren't going to be able to keep it a secret forever."

"Oh God, Mac, it's not that." I wiped my face and sniffled. "It's when he fell." A sob escaped as my heart ached with the memory of his bloodied, limp body.

"I don't understand, sweetie. What's when he fell?"

"As soon as the words slipped out of my mouth, he fell. Mac, I'm the reason he fell. I'm the reason he's broken and in the hospital." I sucked in two quick shaky breaths.

"No, Addy, it's not your fault. Don't you dare take this all on yourself. I'm sure Quinn doesn't blame you."

I didn't respond but the silence on the line said it all.

"Mac, he—"

"Jesus, Addy ... he doesn't remember, does he?" Mac's words were a cautious whisper.

"No."

"Are you going to tell him?"

"Yes, of course. I tried a couple of days ago, but then I accidentally pushed this button and his bed started to move and he started to scream. Then the nurse came in and—"

"Addy! Slow down. You're starting to ramble."

"Sorry. I'm nervous, scared, confused, and … and just freaking out. I don't want to lose him."

"You're not going to lose him. He knows you have a past."

"Mac, I'm no longer asking him to accept my past. I'm asking him to accept my past forever changing the course of his future. You didn't see it, Mac. He would not have fallen in that spot at that time. And even if he would have, I know his instincts would have been better. It was as if he didn't do anything to protect himself."

"Addy, you don't know that, and he's going to be fine."

I pinched the bridge of my nose and shook my head. "They used plates and screws to piece his pelvis back together and he no longer has a spleen. It's not like we were created with a bunch of unnecessary organs. 'Hey, Quinn, sorry about your shitty immune system. A spleen would sure come in handy about now.'" I laughed at my own dramatic reaction and at the same time more tears fell to my cheeks. "What if he never walks without a limp? What if he never climbs, snowboards, or jumps out of a plane again?" A tight sob broke free. "What if … he never looks at me the same way again?" My voice was a strangled whisper.

"Addy, I'm getting on a plane as soon as I can to—"

"No, Mac, don't do that. We'll be home in a few weeks and you can fly to New York then."

"Addy, I don't want to see you go down that path again."

"I won't tell him until we get home."

"And if he remembers on his own before then?"

I wanted to believe that nine years later I was a stronger person, but since Quinn had picked up so many pieces of my broken heart and claimed them for his own, I wasn't so sure.

"Then you can get on a plane," I conceded.

BY THE TIME I returned to the hospital, Quinn was out of recovery and in a private room.

"Hey, Addy, he just fell back to sleep. Chase and I are going to grab some food. Did you eat?"

"Yes, I grabbed something at the hotel." I lied because she had enough to worry about; I didn't want her feeling responsible for me. I wasn't hungry, but I understood her motherly concern.

"Okay then, we'll be back in an hour or so. Call if you need us."

"I will. Thanks, Elena."

Elena and Chase hugged me before leaving. I sat in the chair next to Quinn's limp body in the hospital bed. The once chiseled edges to his muscles appeared softer, not quite as defined; the image before me was different than the naked, Latin sex god I used to stare at for hours. His face was pale and his eyes looked sunken in.

The main reason I couldn't eat was because of the guilt that sat like dead weight in the bottom of my gut. It was unlikely that Quinn's dissociative amnesia would last forever. I needed to tell him before something triggered his memory. I reclined the chair and closed my eyes. Overcome with exhaustion, I fell asleep.

The sun had set leaving a dimly lit room when I awoke. Dark eyes met mine, and I sat up in the chair.

"Hi," I whispered in a sleepy voice.

Quinn gave me a weak but loving smile as he opened his hand. I put mine in his, and even in his injured state, I was reminded of his strength as his large strong hand enveloped mine.

I looked around the room.

"They went back to the hotel. I told them not to wake you." His voice was raspy.

He had major surgery just hours ago yet he looked out for my well-being. My heart constricted.

"Are you in pain?"

"Not too bad. I think they have me on some pretty strong stuff."

"Dr. Muñez said the surgery went as good as could be expected. Given your age and health, you should make a full recovery." I spoke the words aloud to Quinn, but they were meant to convince myself more than him.

"I'm sure naughty Nurse Addy will have me *up* in no time."

It was faint, but I saw a sparkle in his eyes. I needed that more than he could ever have known.

"Hmm ... are you thinking white uniform, cleavage, miniskirt, and garter belt?" I lowered the pitch of my voice and slid my tongue along my upper lip.

"Dear God, yes please." His smile grew for a moment, but it was short lived as he winced.

I stood, stepping closer to him. "Are you OK?"

He exhaled a tight breath. "Yeah, just a reality check."

He pushed the button that controlled his pain medicine. It only took a few minutes for his eyes to get heavy again.

"I'm going to get a snack from the cafeteria. You get some rest. Okay, babe?" I leaned down and kissed his dry lips.

He didn't speak, he just gave a slight nod before his eyes closed.

I didn't go to the cafeteria. Instead, I went outside and walked around the hospital. The cool, evening breeze felt nice, and the fresh air helped clear my mind. I wanted to stay focused on Quinn and getting him better. We would talk about the other stuff once he was home and on the mend.

***

QUINN SPENT two and a half weeks in the hospital. Dr. Muñez wanted him to stay for a few more days, but Quinn insisted he was ready to leave. The physical therapist worked with Quinn, and he was able to get around with the aid of a walker. I had already made arrangements for one of the best physical therapists in New York City to come to our place and work with Quinn for as long as he needed.

Elena came back with us as well. She said she had some things to go through at her house anyway, but I knew Quinn was the real reason for her decision. She also insisted we start planning the "big" wedding. She thought it might cheer Quinn up and persuade him to work harder if he had a goal. I didn't argue with her, but the wedding had fallen off my radar. Quinn and I had too many obstacles to overcome before a wedding.

It was a relief to be home after the long flight. Elena went to her house to get settled while I made dinner for myself and Quinn.

"Nice to see you eating something again," Quinn commented as I shoved a fork full of pasta into my mouth.

I smiled, slurping the last piece that hung from my mouth. "Not to sound conceited, but this tastes so good. Overripe bananas and mushy apples from the hospital cafeteria took their toll. I probably lost ten pounds. My clothes feel baggy."

"You're looking too thin."

That comment was quite ironic coming from a guy who dated anorexic looking models.

"I won't for long if I keep making comfort food like this."

After dinner, Quinn rested on the couch while I

unpacked our suitcases. His eyelids fought to stay open by the time I came back downstairs.

"Do you want me to help you to bed, or would you like me to help you shower?"

Quinn laughed but it was more like a sarcastic grunt. "So this is how it's going to be for the next so many weeks or months? 'Quinn, do you need help with this? Quinn, do you need help with that? Quinn, do you need help with everything?'"

He looked out the window, not at me. I tried not to take it personally, since he didn't know how much it really was *my* fault, but the words still hurt. The depression and self-pity were expected, but I wasn't expecting it to start on our first night home.

Maybe I needed to tell him, lay it all on the line. The idea of getting it off my chest felt liberating, and I thought maybe Quinn needed someone to blame.

"Quinn I—"

"No, Addy, I'm sorry. I didn't mean it that way. I know this isn't going to be easy on you either, and it was a shit thing for me to say."

Tell him! No ... don't kick him when he's down.

He looked at me with so many mixed emotions: pain, anger, pity, but also love, compassion, and sorrow.

"I really need a shower, and yes, I would appreciate your help."

I helped him shower and it was the first time we were both naked together without an impulsive hunger for each other. He was in too much pain and so was I, but mine was a different sort of pain. After he hobbled his injured body to the bed, I put an herbal healing salve on his wounds and a clean dressing.

When I stood to put the supplies away he grabbed my arm. "Thank you."

"Please don't thank me," I pleaded with a painful smile.

"Addy, what's wrong?"

I pulled away from him and walked toward the bathroom.

"Did you drop me?" It was a faint whisper, but I heard him.

I froze. I couldn't turn to look at him. The time had come for me to tell him. I knew it would be a turning point in our relationship, but I feared it would be in the wrong direction. My breath was strangled, my heart constricted, and all words escaped me. I shook my head and kept walking. It wasn't a lie. I didn't drop him.

He didn't ask me about it again, and I was a coward. Every time an opportunity presented itself to tell him, we were either interrupted or I lost my nerve.

The following month was treacherous. Quinn made great progress during his physical therapy sessions, but not without pain. He defined *no pain, no gain*. It exhausted him, but he refused to sleep much during the day. He had his laptop in front of him almost constantly, working to keep his business deals moving forward. His assistant stopped by several days a week to have him sign papers, and he used video conferencing in place of traveling for meetings.

I felt like a helpless animal that had been attacked. Guilt ate me alive, and I wasn't sure how much longer I could take it. Elena was a lifesaver. She stayed with Quinn while I ran errands. Neither she nor Quinn ever asked me where I went or why I was gone for so long. When Quinn wasn't focused on his pain, he was focused on business. Elena tried to plan a wedding that didn't have a date or location.

Avoidance became my method for survival. I went to yoga then jogging in Central Park. One day I even went to a matinee by myself. The guilt consumed me, and I looked for any excuse to escape. Quinn struggled to deal with his injuries, but he didn't want my help.

I even avoided Mac by not answering her calls and giving short vague responses to her texts. She wanted to come visit, but I couldn't face her until I told Quinn the truth. However, every day it managed to elude me.

Alexis was in town for the weekend so Elena wanted to spend some time with her. Quinn and I were alone for two days without interruptions, or in my case, without an escape.

I sat at the kitchen table looking at my computer while Quinn worked on his at the couch. He closed it and set it aside.

"Come here, baby."

After shutting down my computer, I sat next to him. "Do you need something?"

He put his hand behind my head and pulled me to his lips. He kissed me slow at first, but then slipped his tongue into my mouth, deepening it. My body immediately responded. We had shared some cautious cuddling at night and chaste kisses before bed, but other than that, our relationship felt more like roommates than lovers.

He pulled away. His eyes held that look that I hadn't seen since the accident.

"Yes, I do need something." Bringing me to his mouth again with one hand, the other slipped under my shirt. He pulled down the cup of my bra releasing my breast. I moaned into his mouth as he cupped my breast in his large hand, kneading it while rubbing his thumb over my erect nipple. Leaning in closer to him, I put my hand on the arm of the sofa to help support my weight. I wanted to straddle him and feel him between my legs, but I thought it would be too much.

My body craved him. He released my breast and slipped his hand under the waistband of my leggings. I turned completely toward him, kneeling on the couch beside him to support myself. My tongue danced with his as soft needy moans escaped my chest. He slipped two fingers inside me.

"Quinn—" I tilted my head back as he moved his mouth to my neck.

My brain fought with guilt and shame, but my body was too desperate to be distracted by such thoughts. I moved my hips into his hand as his fingers plunged into me. He circled his thumb over my clit, and it didn't take long before I was panting through the waves of an orgasm.

"Oh God, Quinn."

I moved my hand down over his pants, but he grabbed my wrist.

"Don't."

I looked at him confused.

He released a breath. "Too many medications."

I'd considered things like addiction and liver damage, but I never stopped to think about the possibility of erectile dysfunction. "Then why did you—"

He gave me a quick kiss then brought my hand to his mouth. He pressed his lips to my palm. "Because I wanted to."

I sat down next to him with my legs curled under me. "I don't want you to do that."

He laughed. "Could have fooled me."

I bumped up against his arm and laid my head on his shoulder. "You know that's not what I mean. If you can't ... *you know*, then I don't want you to feel like you need to pleasure me."

"I don't think I *need* to pleasure you." He held my hand and interlaced our fingers while he turned my ring from side to side. "I *want* to pleasure you. I love you. I love touching you. And I especially love listening to the sounds you make when you lose all control."

I brought our entwined fingers up to my lips and kissed the back of his hand. "I love you too."

OUR INTIMATE MOMENT on the couch was incentive for Quinn to cut back on his pain medications. His X-rays at two months looked good, but his doctor recommended he avoid weight bearing activities for another month. Quinn moved from the couch to his home office in our condo to do his work. Aside from going to the doctor, he refused to leave home. He said he felt like an old man hobbling around with a cane.

Each day was unpredictable. Some days were good and Quinn breezed through his therapy. Other days were awful. He tried to hide it, but I could see the pain nearly brought tears to his eyes. He took just enough pain medication to take the edge off, but some days it didn't seem to have any effect.

Mac texted me that she and Evan were catching a flight to New York for the weekend and she wouldn't take no for an answer. That was all it took for me to finally call her.

"Don't even try and tell me it's too soon, Addy. I should have been there for you in Spain. There's no way I'm waiting any longer."

"You're right. I'm sorry, I've just been—" I let out a deep sigh. "Out of sorts."

"I'm sure you have been, but I think it's more about you avoiding me because you haven't told Quinn. And you're afraid of what I'm going to say."

"Mac, it's not that simple."

"No shit. Nothing about you and Quinn has ever

been simple, but the longer you wait, the worse the outcome will be."

"I know, I know! But I'm not going to tell him until after you leave. If I tell him now, then you might as well not come."

"Fine, but the second we leave on Sunday you'd better tell him. Deal?"

Whether she realized it or not, Mac started the countdown clock to Quinn leaving me, or more accurately, kicking me out. I was in a no-win situation.

"Whatever, just promise not to say anything about it while you're here."

"Yeah, yeah, we'll see you Friday afternoon."

I pressed *END* just as Quinn made his way to the great room from his office. The grimace on his face told me it was not a good day.

"Can I get you anything?"

He couldn't even speak until he stopped at the kitchen counter and leaned into it.

"Fuck!" He keeled over like someone stabbed a knife into his stomach.

The agonizing cry still ripped at my heart, but I no longer rushed to his aid. My pulse quickened, jaw clenched, and fingernails dug into my palms. The only thing more excruciating than his reaction to the pain was his reaction to my help. The rejection cut deep. Some days were good and some days were bad. This was his new "normal" on those bad days, and I hated feeling so helpless.

"It hurts like a motherfucker to sit, or stand, or

walk, or lie down." He rested his elbows on the counter and pulled at his hair in frustration.

Silently waiting it out with him was all I could do. I got him a glass of water, his pain pills, and a slice of banana bread to eat with them. After I unloaded the dishwasher, I noticed his empty glass and plate, but the pills were still on the counter.

He was collapsed on the couch with one arm stretched out to the side and the other draped over his face.

"Mac and Evan are coming in Friday afternoon."

He didn't respond.

"I'm going to ask your mom if they could stay with her."

"Why?" he mumbled.

"If you have a ... difficult day I just don't want—"

"You don't want what? Me cursing up a storm in front of them? Me being such a fucking downer?"

Dealing with Quinn on those days became the ultimate mind game, but I usually held my own. I grabbed one of his finance magazines off the counter and sat in the chair next to him pretending to read it.

"Yeah, pretty much. Well, I mean, not so much the cursing, that would make Mac feel right at home, but the 'fucking downer' part is the main reason. Would it kill you to try and be a little more hospitable? Every time someone comes over, all you do is sit on your ass and wait for me to answer the door, invite them in, and offer them a drink. You never want to play twister or join the conga line."

Quinn lifted his arm just enough to peek over at me. I held back my smile.

"I'd hate you if I didn't love you so damn much." His voice was strained in pain.

"Back at ya, babe." I grinned.

CHAPTER THREE

QUINN INSISTED I pick Mac and Evan up from the airport instead of sending a car for them. He declared it a better day and claimed he could "wipe his own ass" for a few hours. The physical therapist, Patrick, was scheduled to be there shortly after I left. Some days he was more capable of dealing with Quinn's "shit" than I was.

I took Mac and Evan to Elena's to drop off their bags before we went back to the condo. Elena welcomed them. She knew firsthand how uncomfortable it got when Quinn had a bad day. I had chased after her more than once when Quinn's pain-induced, foul mouth sent her running to the door.

"Hey, babe, we're here," I called out as we walked in the door.

"In here," he replied from his office.

"Make yourselves at home. I'm going to go check on him before I start dinner."

"Will do," Mac replied.

Quinn sat in his desk chair, looking out the window, with his back to the door.

"Shut the door."

"Um ... okay." I complied. "How was therapy?" I walked up behind him and sat on the edge of his desk.

He spun around in his chair to face me.

"Good. Where's Mac and Evan?"

His quick response to my question and curiosity to Mac and Evan's whereabouts was odd.

"They're in the great room. Why?"

"I think cutting back on my pain medication is finally paying off." He flashed me a conspiratorial grin.

"I'm not following."

He motioned with his index finger for me to come closer. I stood and leaned into him with my hands on the arms of his chair. He kissed me then I pulled back.

"Still not following."

He kissed me again, but that time it was more intense. He grabbed my hand and placed it between his legs on his growing erection.

"Mmm," I hummed into his mouth as I stroked him. "Welcome back." I raised my eye brows. "Later we'll have to see what we can do about this ... situation that has recently come *up*."

"Later? Are you kidding me? There might not be this *situation* later," he pleaded.

"We have guests out in the other room. What do you want me to do?"

Quinn smiled then bit his lip as he looked down at his arousal straining against his pants.

It wasn't that I didn't want to please him, because I did. I just had trouble blocking out the sound of Mac and Evan's voices in the other room. Quinn apparently didn't have the same issue.

"You're a desperate, kinky bastard, but fine." I dropped to my knees as he pushed down the front of his jogging pants.

"Keep talking like that. It only makes me harder."

I wrapped my hand around him and stroked the bottom of his shaft while my mouth worked him from the top. He ran his fingers through my hair.

"God, yes, like that."

His hips started to push up toward me and that's when I heard him suck in a quick breath through his teeth. I looked up at his face twisted in pain, not pleasure. His erection faded as quickly as it appeared.

He yanked up his pants.

"Are you okay?"

His face was still pained and he wouldn't look at me. "I'm fine just ... go. I'll be out in a few minutes."

"Quinn—"

"Just go, Addy!"

I hurried out hoping Mac and Evan hadn't heard Quinn raise his voice with me.

"Quinn's finishing up something then he'll be out. I'm going to start peeling potatoes," I announced after leaving Quinn's office.

"Want some help?" Mac asked.

"Sure."

"What can I do?" Evan questioned.

"Stay out of the kitchen," Mac deadpanned.

Evan frowned a pouty face as she blew him a kiss.

"So is Quinn feeling okay today?" Mac asked as she grabbed the knife and cutting board.

"Uh, yes, I think so, but things can change quickly," I answered honestly.

I had no idea what personality we would see when Quinn came out of his office.

"Well, I'm guessing he'll act fine around us no matter how he's feeling, but you just give me a wink or something if you think it's time for us to leave. There's nothing worse than trying to act like you're feeling fine when you're really not."

A few minutes later Quinn made his way out of his office.

"Hey, guys, nice to see you again," he said, forcing a cheery tone.

"Quinn!" Evan jumped up and shook his hand while giving him a pat on the back. "Good to see you too. Can I help you?"

"No, I'm fine, just a little slow."

Mac walked over to Quinn and gave him a gentle hug and kiss on the cheek before he lowered himself onto a dining room chair. "We were so worried about you. I'm glad to see you're going to be fine."

"Yeah, I'm getting there." He used his smile to hide the grimace that bending to sit down always elicited.

We ate dinner and kept the conversation centered on Mac and Evan. Quinn and I barely exchanged glances. We made tentative plans to go to Chicago to take *The Sage* out for the first time as soon as Quinn felt up to it. Quinn had suggested months ago that I bring her to New York, but her home wasn't in Manhattan and neither was mine. I knew, or at least hoped, in the near future we would end up in Chicago.

After dinner we gathered in the great room. Mac and Evan finished the second bottle of wine, while Quinn sipped his usual glass of water and I had tea.

"I haven't told my mom and dad about your engagement yet since they haven't met Quinn. Maybe you two could share the news if you make it to Chicago next month," Mac said.

I squinted my eyes and pursed my lips at her for steering the conversation in that direction. She flipped me an innocent smile, as if she was oblivious to my reaction.

"We'll see. It's going to depend on Quinn." I'm sure he thought I meant his health, but I was more concerned about his reaction to what I had yet to tell him.

"I'll be fine." Quinn's answer was short, and I could tell from his voice that he was tired and most likely in pain.

I winked at Mac and it took her wine-relaxed brain a minute to process my signal, but eventually she did.

"Oh yes, well, Evan, we should take off. I don't want to barge in on Elena too late."

"I'll drive you." I stood.

"Don't be silly. We're quite capable of hailing a cab," Mac insisted. "Maybe tomorrow Evan can come keep Quinn company and we can go check out some wedding dresses. I bet Elena would love that too."

"We'll see. I think finding the right dress sounds like a daunting task." I rolled my eyes.

"That's what you said the last time … uh, I mean—"

The room fell silent. My back was to Quinn, but I could see from the expressions on Mac and Evan's faces that he was not happy. I closed my eyes and shook my head.

When I opened them, her grimaced face pleaded with me for forgiveness, but I had none to offer at that moment. She looked at me the way I knew I would look at Quinn once I got up the nerve to turn around.

"Mac, let's go." Evan grabbed her arm and pulled her out the door.

There were no goodbyes or any further talk of the next day. Within a few brief seconds they were out the door and I was stuck in my own silent Hell.

I turned around. "Quinn—"

"You used to climb, with *him*, before you were … *married.*"

I had read everything there was to read on dissociative amnesia, and the thing that haunted me was the "trigger" that could bring it all back. It had been a race to see if I would get the nerve to tell Quinn before something else triggered his memory. I lost.

Quinn looked at me, but it felt more like he was looking through me, past me, to our past. His voice was calm and monotone. "That's what you said to me, when I was climbing. I remember."

"Quinn, I wanted to—"

"No! Jesus, Addy! Don't you dare try and tell me you wanted to tell me. That's what you're going to say, right? You wanted to tell me, but you couldn't? There is *nothing* about your past that you have *ever* wanted to tell me. Everything I know about you has been dragged out of you, piece by agonizing piece."

Tears flowed freely, rolling down my face. He was right, and I had nothing to say.

"That's what you meant in the hospital ... when you apologized. Isn't it? I fell. You didn't drop me. I fell when you told me that and you feel responsible. Don't you?"

I sobbed and wiped my tears as I started to move toward him.

"Don't." He held his hand out to stop me. "Go to bed, Addy. I can't talk to you about this anymore. I can't even look at you right now."

"But, Quinn—" I sobbed again.

"Go. To. Bed!"

I ran up the stairs and collapsed onto our bed, then cried myself to sleep—alone.

I LOST track of how many times I'd awakened in that condo with red, swollen eyes. I wondered if it was a sign. My pounding head declared war with my every move, but I made my way downstairs anyway. I expected to see Quinn asleep on the couch, but it was empty. Padding to his office, I found him leaning back in his chair. I stopped cold in my tracks, but not from the dark menacing glare he gave me; it was what I saw in his hand.

"What's in the glass?" I asked.

Quinn held it up and swirled it around before taking a drink. "Scotch."

"You don't drink." My voice was even and calm.

"No, I *didn't* drink, but I do now," he said in a condescending voice. "Who knew it would numb my pain better than those other stupid pills? Guess I should have tried it to begin with."

"Have you taken any pills today?" I was knowledge-able about the dangers of mixing alcohol with narcotics, but I wasn't sure if Quinn was.

"Nope. Figured I'd save that concoction for your next big reveal."

I wanted to take the glass from his hand and throw it through the window. I wanted to scream at him for being so stupid and weak to start down the same road his father had, but I couldn't because my problems were bigger, and I was the reason his life was so miserable at the moment. Nothing good would come from getting upset with him, so I surrendered.

I walked over and sat down on the edge of his desk facing him. As I thought about my next words, I expected tears to sting my eyes, but they didn't. I was all cried out, and I, too, felt numb, although not from alcohol like Quinn.

"His name was Malcolm. He was Mac's brother. She introduced us my freshman year of college. I was a virgin and so was he. Six months later, we had sex for the first time over Christmas break. We didn't fuck, we made love. He loved me and I loved him. It was painful, awkward, and fast; but it was also special, heartfelt, and beautiful.

Together, our wealthy families put on the biggest, most extravagant wedding Chicago had seen in years. Malcolm was older and graduated before me. He bought us a house and promised me the world—a fairytale. Fast forward a few years and the fairytale turned into a horror film. My parents died ... correction, my parents were *brutally murdered* in what was believed to be a home invasion. I found them. One ... body part ... at a time."

"Addy—" Quinn set his drink down and leaned toward me.

I held my hand out to stop him from moving any closer to me. "No, this is my story. My *big reveal*. Let me finish. Six months and thousands of dollars' worth of therapy later, the nightmares started to disappear, but that's when my story took another unexpected turn. It was around three o'clock in the morning when we woke to the sound of our fire alarms going off." I paused to think about my next words, but I couldn't find all of them quite yet.

"I made it out, but Malcolm ... did not. I didn't speak for the next week, until after the funeral, when Mac found me at the airport purchasing a one-way ticket to nowhere in particular. She boarded the plane with me and we did not return to Chicago for twelve months. When I left, I wanted to die; when we arrived home the following year, I no longer wanted to die. I still didn't care if I lived or not, I just no longer *wanted* to die."

I reached down and grabbed Quinn's glass of Scotch. His eyes followed my every move. Holding it up in the air, I said, "So here's to your shitty life, and mine." I emptied the rest of it in my mouth, wincing as it burned all the way down my throat, then slammed the glass down on his desk before walking out.

***

Moments later, I packed a bag and called Zach.

"Hey, Addy. How's our pain-in-the-ass patient?"

"He's drowning in self-pity and Scotch."

"He's drinking? Are you serious?" Zach asked, equal parts skeptical and horrified.

"I'm serious. Listen, Zach, I need to leave for a few days. I've messed up and I need some time to straighten myself out before I can deal with Quinn.

Can you help keep an eye on him? I'm going to let Elena know too, but Quinn on a bad day can break her down too easily. so she may need some backup."

"I'm sorry you're having a rough time, but don't worry about Quinn. I'll look after him."

"Thanks. I'll let you know when I'm on my way back here."

"Addy?"

"Yes."

"He loves you."

I blinked back a few tears. "Bye, Zach."

I contemplated writing a note to Quinn, but I decided to text him after I left. Just as I opened the door to leave I heard his voice.

"Where are you going?"

Deep breath ... I am peaceful, I am strong.

I couldn't turn around and look at him. "I'm leaving for a few days."

"You don't have to leave." His voice was soft and comforting, which made leaving that much harder.

I stared at my hand on the doorknob. "Yes, I do. I can't ask you to forgive me until I can forgive myself."

"Is there anything I can say to make you stay?"

I swallowed the lump in my throat and shook my head. "Goodbye."

I opened the door and a split-second before it closed behind me, I heard the two words that always led me back to him.

"Never goodbye," he called out.

CHAPTER FOUR

ON THE PLANE I composed two emails: one to Mac and the other to Elena.

Mac,
Take that amazing husband of yours
and go home. Continue to fill your
hearts with love and your home
with beautiful babies and cherished memories. You've held my
hand through the worst times of my
life, but last night I realized
you need to let go. I know you
left feeling guilty, and I'm sorry
I let you feel that way for a
single moment. I should have told
Quinn weeks ago. I'm leaving town
for a few days to straighten

myself out so I can hopefully have a chance at happiness with the man that I love. I'll call you when I get back and we'll set a date to go sailing and do things that normal friends should do. Have a safe flight home and give Evan my love.
Addy

Elena,
Thank you for so graciously welcoming Mac and Evan into your home. I'm leaving for a few days because I messed up horribly with Quinn. I awoke to find him in his office sipping a glass of Scotch this morning. Zach is going to help keep an eye on him while I'm gone. I love your son beyond words, and when I get back I'm going to do whatever it takes to make things right for him—for us.
Addy

As soon as the plane landed I sent the emails. After renting a car, I mindlessly drove to my destination and parked next to a large maple tree. Before I opened the door, my phone chimed. It was a text from Quinn.

> Why do you run? Please come home.

Quinn had to wait. I turned my phone off and tossed it on the seat before climbing out of the car. Closing my eyes, I stopped at the black iron gate. My ears filled with vibrating whispers from the leaves on the mature trees as the wind moved in rhythmic gusts. Birds chattered and I sensed the occasional rustled scurry of squirrels racing over the ground and up the broad tree trunks. I opened my eyes and proceeded through the gate, surrounded by green grass and rows of carved stone.

It had been eight years, but I still remembered— three rows to the north and ten stones west on the south side. Lowering to my knees, I traced the engraved name on the first one and then moved to the next. My stolen life that wasn't meant to be, laid six feet under me. The setting sun bathed my left side in warmth as I closed my eyes and inhaled a slow breath.

"Hi, Mom. I miss you and I think about you every day. I wonder where you are. I wonder if you found your pearly gates or if your beautiful soul has graced a new body. I think about Daddy too, especially lately. I remember how much he loved and adored you. I remember thinking no two people could ever love each other as much as you and Daddy did. I didn't have the same love with Malcolm, and I knew it the day I agreed to marry him. It was the right choice at the time. I took your advice and bloomed where I was planted. My proverbial garden was growing all around me in spite of losing the two people who loved me most in this world. But then..."

I wiped my tears "...but then that life was taken from me too. Did you know that? Did you and Daddy know about the fire? I lost every—everything, Mom. I hated God. It felt like He reached down and ripped my heart out of my chest and tore it into a million pieces ... but it was still ... beating. I prayed to Him, I prayed to you, I prayed to Daddy; I prayed to anyone who I thought could help me. I just wanted to be taken, too. I couldn't stand the sound of my heart beating ... alone."

Wiping my tears, I closed my eyes until my sobs subsided. "Now I've met someone and he's ... everything. We have the love you both had. It's beautiful, passionate, all consuming ... epic. But I've hurt him so badly, and I don't know how to make it right. I don't know if he'll ever know he's the reason my heart is still beating."

I lay on the ground and watered the earth with my tears, imagining my mom's arms wrapped around me, holding and comforting me. Eventually, darkness descended upon me, and the cooler breeze chilled my skin. I took one last look at my past carved in stone, then slowly made my way back to the car.

The next morning I checked out of the hotel and drove to a large lakefront estate. It looked beautiful— just like I remembered—massive shade trees and bordering perennial gardens. I wondered if the same family lived there. I sold it to a surgeon and his wife, who were expecting twins at the time. After finding the remains of my parents' severed bodies, I wanted the whole place leveled. I thought destroying it would erase the terrible memories from my mind.

My therapist talked me out of sending a wrecking ball though the front door of the restored 1870s nine million dollar mansion and instead finding a buyer that symbolized a new beginning, one that symbolized life. Imagining eight–year-old twins running around the perfectly manicured yard or swinging from the oak tree in the back reminded me that life goes on, even in the event of the most unimaginable tragedies. The living still go on living.

I SPENT the following three days visiting every place that held a significant memory in my heart. Buildings had been painted, old trees died and newer ones had matured. Even some things that hadn't changed looked different to me because I looked at them differently. It was a poignant reminder that my life was different and I needed to start looking at it that way.

After packing my bag, I got an early flight back to New York. I thought if Quinn could love me and forgive me my past, then so could I. Before boarding the plane, I called Zach. He gave me the heads-up that Quinn wasn't doing so well, but he didn't elaborate.

Before I opened the door, I reminded myself that no matter what I saw on the other side, the man I fell in love with was in there ... even if it took me a while to find him.

"Hello?" I called out.

"Oh, hi, Addy. I'm so glad you're back," Elena answered.

Her hands were immersed in dishwater and she had a tense face with a forced smile.

"What's wrong? Where's Quinn?" I dropped my bags and walked toward her.

"He's upstairs. He hasn't come down since you left."

I nodded. "I'll go check on him."

"Addy, wait."

I turned.

She grabbed her purse and embraced me in a big hug as she whispered in my ear. "I love you like a daughter and I want nothing more than to see you and my son together but—"

I squinted, cocking my head to the side. "But?"

She released a concerned sigh. "But I should not have stayed, and if it gets worse, neither should you."

I was still confused when she left, wondering what she meant when said she shouldn't have stayed. I couldn't imagine Quinn had been that awful to her in such a short amount of time. But then I reached the threshold of our bedroom and saw a scruffy, passed-out Quinn on the bed, surrounded by empty alcohol bottles. Then I knew.

Lucas. Elena was talking about Lucas.

I picked up all the bottles and opened the blinds. Quinn looked like he hadn't showered since I left. I liked Zach, but if that was his idea of keeping an eye on Quinn, I questioned his responsibility.

First, I checked for a pulse, then sat in the chair by the window and waited. Two hours later, the beast stirred. His painful moans sounded like a combination of a hangover and the numbness starting to wear off around his healing bones.

"Motherfucker! Who opened the goddamn shades?"

It was gut-wrenching to watch, but I waited in silence for him to sit up. He put his hand over his eyebrows and squinted at me. "Addy?"

"Quinn," I responded in a flat voice.

"Shit! I need a drink," he groaned as he wrapped his arms around his stomach in agony.

"I bet your liver begs to differ. I'll fill up the bathtub." I started toward the bathroom.

"I don't need a bath."

"Hmm, now I beg to differ." I kept going and turned on the faucet.

I grabbed Quinn's shampoo, soap, and razor from the shower. It was ironic how I used to think he looked sexy all scruffy, but at that moment he just looked dirty and hungover.

"Hobble your hungover ass in here and get your clothes off," I yelled over the running water.

When I peeked out the door, he was perched on the edge of the bed, hunched over.

I grabbed the hem of his shirt and slowly pulled it over his head. His face tightened as he raised his arms. I wrapped his arm over my shoulder and helped him up. Then I walked him to the bathroom and slipped his shorts and briefs down. He held my shoulders as he stepped out of them.

I helped him sit on the edge of the tub. He kept his head down as I grabbed his toothbrush and toothpaste. Tilting his chin, he relaxed his jaw enough to allow me to brush his teeth. I used our rinse cups to give him water with one and let him spit in the other. After he eased into the tub, I shut off the water. He leaned his head back and closed his eyes.

Kneeling down beside the tub, I laid my head on my crossed arms resting on the edge. After a while he still hadn't made an attempt to move, so I squeezed some shaving gel on my hands and lathered his face. With each stroke of the razor, I waited for his eyes to open, but they didn't. Grasping the bottom of my shirt, I pulled it over my head and removed my bra. Then I slipped my capris and panties down.

Nothing.

Quinn remained motionless. My heart ached for him, for us.

Carefully stepping into the tub, I kneeled between his outstretched legs.

Nothing.

I squirted shampoo in his hair and massaged his scalp.

Nothing.

Soaking up water with the washcloth, I rinsed out his hair, but he didn't so much as flinch as the sudsy water flowed down his face. Emotions threatened, but I pushed them away. Quinn couldn't take care of himself, let alone deal with my insecurities.

Using the soapy washcloth, I scrubbed over his neck, arms, chest, and abdomen, stopping to gently run my fingers across his scar.

Nothing.

Setting the washcloth aside, I rubbed his feet and worked my way up his legs, massaging his inner thighs with my thumbs. I felt his penis briefly graze my hand as it twitched. He didn't open his eyes, but there was a slight tensing to his face. He had a semi-erection and I contemplated touching him there, but I didn't.

Certain that Quinn was miserable, I stood and stepped out of the tub. With my exposed backside to him, I reached for a plush, gray towel and hugged it to my chest.

"You are so damn beautiful," he muttered in a raspy voice.

After pausing for a moment to let his words sink in, I wrapped the towel around myself. Turning around, I avoided his gaze as I pulled the plug to let the water drain. When our eyes met, I melted. It had been too long since I had seen love in his dark brown eyes. It was food to my starving soul.

"Here," I said, as I held out his towel.

He grasped both sides of the tub and cautiously worked his stiff body to a standing position. He rested his hand on the wall as he stepped out, taking the towel from me. After putting on my robe, I stripped the bedsheets and put on new ones.

I turned around and almost ran into Quinn, who was standing just inches from me, with only a towel wrapped around his waist.

"Jeez, you scared me," I gasped.

"Sorry."

He had me trapped in his heated gaze.

"Uh, do you want me to fix you something to eat?"

He shook his head as he untied my robe.

I swallowed my pooling saliva. "Quinn, we should talk."

He pushed my robe off my shoulders. "I don't want to talk." His voice was a gravelly whisper.

He feathered his fingers down my arms, leaving a wake of goose bumps. Then he removed his towel, letting it fall to the ground. He was fully erect, and just the thought of feeling him inside me had my body on high alert.

"Do you?" he asked.

I sat down on the bed and scooted back, resting my head on the pillow. My knees were bent and parted. He crawled up the bed to me, and I noticed only a slight tensing of his brow. His lips hovered over mine as he inched into me. He closed his eyes and released a plea-surable moan.

He opened his eyes and kissed me. "I love you."

My body craved the sensation of him moving against me, but I resisted the urge to encourage him. I didn't know where his pain and pleasure threshold was, so I let him control everything. His tongue grazed my teeth, and I opened up to him. As his tongue slid across mine, his hips pushed his hardness into me. He paused before he pulled back, then slid into me again. His pace was lethargic, but as long as he kept filling me with his firm erection, I didn't care.

He leisurely slid in and out of me until I felt engorged and hypersensitive, desperate for my release. I bit my lip and tried to hold back my instinct to meet his hips with more force, more friction. Then all of a sudden I didn't feel him in me anymore. I tried to look down but he smashed his mouth to mine as his fingers moved between my legs. He rubbed circles over my swollen clit until I broke our kiss crying out his name.

He cautiously rolled to his back beside me. The moment was awkward, and I hated that the part of us that had always been so perfect had become our silent challenge.

He didn't orgasm. He couldn't sustain his erection.

"Quinn—"

"Why don't you go make something to eat?" He cut me off.

He stared at the ceiling as he pulled the sheet over his waist.

"It's okay if you can't—"

"Jesus, Addy! Just go make the damn food!" he yelled.

I grabbed my robe and hurried down the stairs. It amazed me how he could whisper words of love to me then essentially kick me out of the bedroom ten minutes later. I fixed myself something to eat and waited for him to come downstairs. It was nearly forty-five minutes later before he made his way to the kitchen. I worked on my computer, making no attempt to look in his direction.

"I thought you were going to make something to eat?" he asked.

"I did."

"Where's mine?"

"In the refrigerator," I stated in a flat tone.

I heard him open the refrigerator door. "I don't see it."

"That's because you haven't made it yet."

Quinn slammed the door and went to his office. "I don't have the patience for your stupid mind games."

My thoughts exactly.

AN HOUR later Patrick showed up for Quinn's physical therapy, so I took the opportunity to get out for a while. I went to the local shelter and had some puppy ther-apy. There were ten new puppies that had arrived since my last visit, and they were exactly what I needed after my emotional roller coaster ride with Quinn. After I got in my car to leave the shelter, I noticed I missed a text from Patrick.

Sorry, Addy. Couldn't work with Quinn yet again. Call me tomorrow if he's sober.

I marched through the door and straight to Quinn's office. He was semiconscious in his chair, holding a half empty bottle of Jack Daniels. I grabbed it from him and poured the rest over his head before slamming the bottle down on his desk.

He jumped out of his stupor. "What the fuck?"

"Get your shit together!" I warned.

I left as quickly as I came. Barely making it through the doorway, I heard glass shattering as the empty bottle connected with the wall. I froze but didn't look back.

Deep breath … I am peaceful, I am strong.

"I'm not cleaning that up," I calmly said before I continued to the kitchen.

Quinn didn't come out of his office the rest of the evening. I checked on him before I went to bed. He had moved from his chair to the black leather couch by the window. I opened every cabinet and drawer in his office, looking for his booze stash. I found two bottles in his office, and then I proceeded to the kitchen where I found three more. I finished by stripping the bar of all alcohol. My assumption was we would not be entertaining anytime soon.

After every bottle was emptied, I went to bed. The man I loved was broken and so was my heart. I'd made it through one day of drunk Quinn, but I didn't know how many more I could take. I'd hoped that with all the alcohol thrown out he would sober up and we could talk.

The next morning I was brought out of my sleep by the sound of cabinet doors slamming and Quinn yelling. I rushed downstairs.

"What are you doing?" I asked.

"What the hell did you do with everything?" he growled.

"Everything?" I tapped my lower lip with my finger.

He grabbed me by my arms to the point of pain. "You know damn well what I mean."

"Quinn, you're hurting me. Let go," I pleaded as tears pooled in my eyes.

He released his grip but his dark eyes still pierced mine as he stood tall over me, teeth gritted, chest heaving.

I pushed back my fearful emotions and replaced them with my own anger.

"If you *ever* touch me like that again we are over. Do I make myself clear?"

He didn't respond.

I brushed past him and started to put the kitchen back together when I heard the words that had been looming in the shadows.

"You did this to me," he whispered.

I took a deep breath and exhaled as I turned to face him again.

"Keep going. Get it all out now." I challenged him.

"You should have told me. If you would have I ... we ..." He paused.

"We what? We wouldn't have been together? We wouldn't have been climbing there? You wouldn't have fallen? You wouldn't feel so much pain or feel broken? You wouldn't be drunk? You wouldn't be abusive toward me?"

"Don't!" he roared. "Don't try and make me feel bad for what I've done. You don't have any idea how much goddamn pain I've been through!"

"I know it's monumentally inadequate, but I'm sorry, Quinn. I should have told you before you ever proposed. I will live the rest of my life knowing that I am responsible for your injuries. But I can't ... I *won't* let you treat me this way. I won't stay and be your punching bag. I won't watch you drink yourself to death. If all you see is pain and regret when you look at me, then I shouldn't be here."

Quinn looked down at the floor for a few moments. Then he grabbed his keys and left. I didn't try to stop him.

IT WAS agony waiting for Quinn to return so I called Elena. She insisted she come over so I wouldn't be alone when he came home. I told Elena about Malcolm and the reason for Quinn's fall. I told her about my trip to Chicago to visit my parents' graves and everywhere I went while I was there. I talked about Quinn's drinking, and she shared her emotional stories about Lucas. Elena treated me and loved me like a daughter. I wept for my mother when Elena hugged me because I had longed for years to feel that kind of embrace again.

The day passed, and our concern for Quinn became unbearable. He had been gone for over six hours. I tried calling and texting him. Elena called Zach and I called Quinn's office, but nobody had seen or heard from him.

We waited another two hours. Elena was in Quinn's office trying to contact other people or places he might be. I sat on the couch, a total wreck, when the door finally opened. I jumped up and headed to the door but stopped in my tracks, like a bullet to my heart.

Oh. My. God!

I remembered back to Christmas when I arrived unannounced to his intimate family gathering. It was like everything was in slow motion, including my brain. It took my mind a few moments to fully process what my eyes saw. Quinn, with a bottle of booze in one hand and his other arm draped around the shoulders of a tall, thin blonde. They both stumbled in the door. Neither one saw me and I was completely speechless. I watched my house burn down and my life being destroyed all over again.

The door closed and she leaned back against it pulling him by his shirt. He took a pull of the amber liquid in his bottle then kissed her. She ran her hands up the inside of his shirt and his free hand cupped her breast over her black spaghetti strapped miniskirt dress.

"Quinn!" Elena shrieked.

I didn't look at her, unable to peel my eyes off the nightmare in front of me.

Quinn kept his body pressed to hers but turned his head. "Mother," was all he said.

"You live with your mom?" The clueless girl giggled.

Elena wasted no time shoving Quinn away and kicking the girl to the curb.

"No. He lives with his *fiancée*. Now get out and don't come back!" Elena hissed.

At that moment, Quinn caught sight of me, with his glazed eyes and shit-faced smirk. He didn't bring home another woman for sex; we both knew that. There was only one reason he brought her home—to hurt me.

Mission accomplished.

Nodding to acknowledge that he had made his point, I grabbed my computer, phone, and purse and walked to the door where they stood.

"You're wrong, Elena." I slipped my ring off and set it on the entry table. "Quinn doesn't live here with his fiancée, because he doesn't have a fiancée."

"Addy, don't—" Elena started to protest, but I shook my head to stop her from saying anymore.

"Dammit! Say something, Quinn! Don't you dare let her leave," she pleaded with her son.

Quinn stared at the ring on the table, and his eyes met mine. His smirk was gone and even though he had trouble staying focused on me, I finally saw a twinge of pain in his eyes. I didn't try to hold back the tears, I let them flow freely.

"I love you ... I'll always love you," I said with a shaky voice, as I wiped away my tears with the back of my fingers.

"What about your things?" Elena asked with a broken voice. She, too, had tears falling down her face.

I continued to look solely at Quinn. "There's *nothing* here I need anymore."

It was a lie. Everything I needed stood before me. My heart screamed for him to stop me. One word ... one syllable, was all he would have had to say. Every cell in my body begged for him to say it. Just one, small, word—*stay*.

Nothing.

He gave up on me ... he gave up on us.

I opened the door and turned my back to both Quinn and Elena. "Goodbye."

I heard Elena sniffling, but Quinn said nothing. There was no "never goodbye" because we both knew it was our forever goodbye. As soon as the door shut behind me, I let out a strangled sob. When I got in Karma, my phone chimed. It was a text from Mac.

> Hey, sweetie. My heavy heart is
> thinking of you. Eight years ago today
> we both lost so much. Hope you and
> Quinn are better and you're finding
> comfort in each other's arms. Call me.
> Love, Mac.

CHAPTER FIVE

"So where are we going, Addy?"

"I don't know, Mac. Anywhere but here. I just need to feel something outside of myself."

"It won't hurt like this forever."

"I know ... because I won't live forever. But right now my heart is bleeding out and if I stay I won't—"

"You won't what?"

"I won't survive."

NUMB. That's what it feels like to have your heart ripped from your chest. I trusted Quinn to catch me, and I found myself face-first on the ground. I gave him too much, but I didn't regret it. What I experienced was worth it. *He* was worth it. Lost, hopeless, and insignificant were the only feelings I recognized through the tingling numbness.

Before I left Quinn's, I turned off my phone. Then, like a leaf sailing on the waves of the wind, I found the open road and drove. With each passing mile, it became harder to breathe. I wasn't ready to let go of Quinn, but it wasn't my choice. We had been hanging by a thread, and he broke it. The love I used to see in his eyes was tainted with so much anger, I no longer recognized the man I loved. Forgiveness happens in the beat of a heart, forgetting takes a lifetime.

Headed for destination unknown, I was completely alone. Taking each intersection with the randomness of a coin toss, I drove until I just couldn't drive anymore—found a hotel and collapsed for about six hours. This was my routine every day for a week, until I instinctively made my way back to Milwaukee.

It was late, and the streets looked abandoned. I parked Karma in her old spot and grabbed what few belongings I had acquired over my week's journey. The air was stagnant and muggy, and the cricket chirps were amplified by the stillness. The familiarity of my loft embraced me. Everything was just how I'd left it. I'd thought my return would be to move everything to Chicago ... with Quinn. Instead, I found myself doubting if I would ever move back, if I would ever see Quinn again.

The next morning I realized I had two choices: waste more precious time grieving a love that wasn't meant to be or move on. I was familiar with the former, so I chose the latter. A long run followed by yoga and meditation brought out the strong and peaceful Addy I hadn't seen in the mirror for quite some time. The dull ache in my heart was still there; it was a constant reminder of how much I'd lost, but also how much I'd loved.

"Surprise!" I yelled out as I walked into the Café.

"Well, I was, when I saw your car out back this morning." Jake smiled as he walked toward me.

"Missed Karma, didn't you?"

He hugged me, leaving my feet dangling in the air. "Karma? No. You? Definitely."

I rubbed his head. "Chrome-dome no more? I like it. Copper blond reminds me of my dad."

He set me down and ran his fingers through his short, stubbly hair. "Less menacing."

"Since when do you want to be less menacing?"

"Since I started getting more satisfaction from the kitchen and less from the fighting ring."

"Mmm, I'm glad to hear that. I'm starving. Why don't you show me your latest masterpiece?"

"Absolutely. Have a seat and I'll be right back."

Jake returned with a plate of lemon-blueberry pancakes, topped with cinnamon-infused maple syrup.

"These look amazing, but I'm pretty sure I didn't run far enough this morning to eat all of them."

"You look thin, too thin. Don't get me wrong— you're beautiful, but thinner than I remember."

I smirked and nodded my head while I shoved in a large bite. "Fair enough," I murmured with a full mouth.

I had unintentionally lost weight since Quinn's accident. All my focus and attention had been on him. When Mac and I left for a year after the fire, I lost a lot of weight. Some people eat when they're stressed or grieving, but not me. I couldn't think about food until someone forced it down me.

"I've had too much on my mind to think about food." A painful smile etched my face.

Jake leaned back in his chair, lacing his fingers behind his head. "A chef who hasn't had time to think about food, huh? Sounds troubling."

"You could say that."

"I take it you're not here just to check up on me." He winked and flashed his boyish grin.

Savoring the delicious lemony sweetness in my mouth, I contemplated how to answer. "I left Quinn ... or he left me. I'm not sure, but we're no longer together."

Just as quick as I gained back my appetite, saying those words aloud robbed me of it again. I knew we were over, but that was the first time I acknowledged it since I'd left New York. I could barely swallow the bite I had in my mouth.

Jake looked at me with wide eyes and a slack mouth. The silence between us confirmed it.

"Hey, I'm going to go shower. I'll take the rest of the pancakes with me and bring the plate down later. If that's ok?"

"Addy, I don't know what to say."

"I just don't want them to go to waste, so I thought—"

"I'm not talking about that."

I stood up and rested my hand on his shoulder. "I know you're not. You don't have to say anything. There's really nothing to say. I'll see you later."

Jake nodded. I didn't want his pity, and I sensed he knew it.

AFTER I SHOWERED, I turned on my cell phone for the first time since I'd left New York. I had more missed calls from Elena and Mac than I could count, but nothing from Quinn. A pang of grief clenched my heart for a second, but I pushed away the looming feelings of bitter regret. I may have been the one who walked out the door, but he asked me to leave the moment his drunk ass crossed the threshold with that floozy.

I called Mac before the search party showed up at my door.

"Adler Sage Brecken, where the hell have you been?" Her voice was pure anger.

"Nice to hear your voice, too."

"Well, you don't just break off your engagement and go AWOL for a week without pissing people off with worry!"

"Pissed off with worry?" I laughed. "Now that's a new one."

"Stop it, Addy! You don't get to humor your way out of this."

"Who told you?"

"What?" Mac sounded confused.

"Who told you I broke off my engagement?"

She hesitated for a moment. "Quinn. Well ... technically Elena."

"I'm not following."

"I called looking for you after three days of leaving messages on your phone."

"You called Quinn or Elena?"

"Quinn first, then Elena. You should have called me, Addy. Does our friendship mean that little to you?"

"No, Mac. It's because our friendship means *so* much to me. *You* mean so much to me. I feel like I take away a part of your happiness every time I show up on your doorstep needing to be pieced back together. I knew you'd have insisted I drive straight to your house, but I needed time."

There was silence on the line. I figured she was processing. "So where are you now?" she asked in a calmer voice.

"Milwaukee."

"Oh, sweetie. You should come home."

"I am home. For now, this is home."

"I miss you."

Her whiny voice made me smile. "I miss you too, and I'll come visit soon."

"Addy?"

"Yeah?"

"Are you going to be okay?"

Of course she couldn't see me, but I nodded to myself as I closed my eyes and focused on my heart.

"Eventually."

EVERY DETAIL of the following month stayed etched in my head, but it wasn't because of my gifted memory, it was because time passed so slowly. I volunteered at The Sage Leaf Café most days, and found myself hanging out with Jake in the evenings. He shared his less-than-tragic breakup story. Jessica abruptly packed up and moved to California to follow her dreams of acting. Jake suspected it had more to do with her high school sweetheart, who paid a visit to her a few weeks before she decided to leave. He said he never really loved her and that she was more of a distraction than a lifetime commitment. That brought back memories of Quinn and his "distractions." It amazed me how men found it so easy to use women like that.

Jake and I did everything: movies, dining, rollerblading, dog walking, volunteering. I even tagged along to one of his fights. It was my first underground fight experience, and after it was over, I declared it was my last. Jake emerged virtually unscathed, but his opponent's bloodied body was hauled away on a stretcher. Jake insisted it looked worse than it really was, but I wasn't so sure. It was the first fight he'd had in months, and I was hopeful that someday he would give it up completely.

It was close to midnight by the time he dropped me off at my loft. He parked his Harley and removed his helmet as I removed mine.

"I'll be fine. You don't have to walk me to my door." I smiled.

He grabbed my hand and led me up the stairs. "Yes, I do."

When we got to the top, he turned to face me. Jake was not as tall as Quinn but still had several inches on me.

"Why?" I asked as I grazed my thumb over the small cut above his eye. It was his only mark from the fight.

He put his hand over mine pressing it to his cheek. "So I could do this."

His lips brushed mine. I started to pull away.

"Jake," I whispered.

"Shh." He kissed me again, lingering a bit longer, before stepping back with a sexy smile.

"Goodnight, Addy."

He jogged down the stairs and straddled his bike while fastening his helmet. My fingers brushed my lips as I stood frozen, watching him drive off. Jake was almost ten years younger than me, and my head was ready to explode with confusion. I finally opened the door to my loft, nearly stumbling inside, and plopped down on my couch.

I searched for every reason why kissing Jake was a catastrophically bad idea, but in the grand scheme of my messed-up life, I couldn't think of one good reason. As soon as I came to that conclusion, I packed a bag and drove to Chicago.

"ADDY!" Mac yelled, as I grabbed my bags from the backseat.

I walked toward her, then dropped my bags to hug her.

"Hey, Mackenzie! I've missed you."

She pulled back to look at me. "Well, you should not be missing me. You should be making my neighbors an offer they can't refuse on their house, so you can move in next to me."

"Chicago ... someday, but not yet."

We walked into her house.

"Evan and I are holding *The Sage* hostage, so if you want to enjoy sailing this summer you'd better rethink 'someday.'"

"I have nothing better to do than drive down here every weekend for a sailing threesome with you and Evan, so nice try with the blackmail."

She poured us both iced tea, and we made our way to the porch overlooking her large, wooded lot.

"Have you talked to him?" she asked hesitantly.

"By *him* I assume you mean Quinn, and no, I haven't. Elena has left me several messages, but I haven't called her. I sent her a few texts letting her know I'm fine and asking how she's doing."

"How she's doing? Nothing about Quinn?" Mac raised her eyebrows.

"I haven't asked about him, but she's offered more than I wanted to know."

"Such as?"

I sipped my tea and looked out the window at a spastic squirrel zigzagging around the back woods. "Such as he hasn't been sober a day since I left and he quit his physical therapy."

"I wondered."

"What do you mean by that?" I narrowed my eyes.

"Well, when I called him looking for you he was ..." The tight apprehension in her face was apparent, even though she had no reason to hide the truth.

"Drunk. Just say it. He was drunk."

Her nose wrinkled as she nodded.

"What'd he say to you?"

She didn't answer.

"Just tell me, I can handle it," I insisted as I put my glass on a coaster then twirled s few strands of my hair.

She sighed. "He said you ... crippled him and then dumped his ass and ..."

"And what?"

"Addy, what's the purpose of this? If it's over, then why do this to yourself?"

"Mac." I glared at her.

"He said he couldn't care less where you went."

Quinn was an awful drunk, but knowing that didn't lessen the sting.

"I bet you wish you never met him."

I winced. "No, I loved Quinn … I'll always love him. There was a moment in our relationship when I knew I'd given him so much of myself that I wasn't sure I'd survive without him. I did it anyway, because being with him was worth it." I bit my lips together for a few seconds. "I am … one day at a time, I'm surviving without him."

"I don't know how you do it. You're a much better person than I am. And you're definitely a better person than Quinn could ever hope to be. He doesn't deserve you." Mac spoke with an undercurrent of anger to her voice.

"Well, until I'm ready to face my past, and I mean *really* face my past, then I'm never going to have a lasting relationship. I try to convince myself that my past doesn't matter, but it does. It's part of who I am, and by not sharing it with Quinn I never let him know me, all of me."

A lone tear trailed down my cheek. "I may have deserved better than he gave me in our last few weeks together, but he deserved better too. He deserved the truth."

Mac stood and put her hands on her hips. "Well, this conversation has turned into a real downer, if you ask me. Let's call Evan and tell him to fake an illness, malaria or something, so we can go sailing."

I went from tears of sadness to tears of laughter.

"Malaria? Really? Has Evan been out of the country recently? I think he should go with something more believable, say ... rabies?" I tried to keep a straight face but failed miserably.

"Whatever, smarty pants." She rolled her eyes.

Mac had a lot of information stored in her brain; she was just very selective when it came to using it. We were a couple of oddballs. Mac was flighty by choice, and I was an unpretentious, walking zombie of "wasted potential."

LAKE MICHIGAN WAS calm and warmly inviting that day. Evan had just finished a big case the week before so he had some wiggle room in his schedule to hang out with us for the afternoon.

"What have you been up to in Milwaukee?" Evan asked.

I tried to corral my windblown hair into a ponytail as I gave him a generic answer. "Not much."

"Mac said you've been helping out at the Café. How does that go over with Jake?"

Oh yes, Jake.

"He's good with it. We've done a role reversal. I wait for his instructions and he's grateful to have another set of competent hands on busy days. I don't have to plan the menu, coordinate catering, or shop for food and supplies, and he doesn't have to pay me, except for a few free meals."

"You forgot to mention how much time you two have been spending together outside of work," Mac had to add.

She was aware we had become good friends and spent a lot of time together, but I hadn't told her about the kiss.

"Yes, we have a lot in common, so we've been hanging out." I replied with an even tone as I picked at my fingernails and searched for a new subject.

"That's great. He sounds like a good distraction from all you've been going through." Evan smiled.

Jake was definitely a *distraction*, but I wasn't sure yet if he was a *good* one.

"Jake's quite the hottie, and we both know he's had eyes for you since the first day he walked into the Café." Mac looked at me with a suggestive smile before giving Evan a reassuring kiss.

"He's ten years younger than I am, isn't that a little ... wrong?" I posed the question to myself as much as to Mac.

"Oh jeez, you're not old enough to be his mother, just a hot older woman. A cougar." A sly grin tugged at her lips while she made a growling sound.

"I'm not ready to jump into another relationship. You know that."

"Sex, Addy, just sex. Hot, sweaty, multiple-orgasm sex with a hot, young, firm, tattooed body. Dear God, I bet he's ready, willing, and oh-so-eager to please."

"Mackenzie! I'm standing right here," Evan protested.

"Oh sweetie, I'm just talking Jake up for Addy's benefit. You know you're my one and only hot sex machine," she baby-talked as she hugged him and grabbed his ass.

"Ugh, I think it's time to head back," I groaned.

CHAPTER SIX

Before I left for Chicago, I texted Jake to let him know I would be gone for a few days. His reply of "Okay, safe drive" was the last I'd heard from him. My nerves were frayed over seeing him again, but I refused to put off the inevitable.

I arrived a half an hour after the Café closed. The chicken part of me hoped Jake had left and I would have until morning to face him. Luck wasn't on my side. The lights were still on and his Harley was parked behind the building. I deposited my bags in my loft then went downstairs to see him.

"No rest for the weary?"

Jake was wiping down the counters but turned at the sound of my voice.

"Hey, sexy." He had his own version of a panty-dropping smile, and it wasn't too bad.

He wore faded blue jeans with various worn areas

exposing teasing glimpses of his muscular legs. His plain, white T-shirt hugged his chest and broad shoulders. The tattoos covering his arms accentuated his large, defined muscles.

I looked down at my feet to keep from staring at him, and to hide my blush from his greeting.

"Jake, don't say things like that," I spoke in a soft voice.

He moved closer to me, and with the back of his hand he pushed my hair off my shoulder. Then he traced my neck from my ear to my collar bone with the pad of his thumb. He leaned down and whispered in my ear. His breath on my skin awakened every muscle and nerve in my body.

"Don't say things like what?"

I stepped back until I made contact with the door. He followed my every move like we were doing a seductive dance.

"Jake, I can't." The rise and fall of my chest became more prominent as he inched closer to me.

"Can't, or won't?" He lowered his head and brushed his lips down my neck.

He smelled like lemons, mint, and rosemary. My mind screamed for him to stop, but my body melted involuntarily into his touch. I placed my hands on his chest to push him away, but when he looked into my eyes, I felt weak.

His ice blue eyes were filled with passion, but also innocence and kindness. I clenched my fingers, fisting his shirt, and pulled him into me. Our lips met and moved in a slow, synchronized rhythm. His kiss was soft and gentle. I felt the whisper touch of his hands threading though my hair and pulling me closer. His tongue briefly teased mine. He tasted as good as he smelled and that worried me. Releasing his shirt, I pushed against his solid chest.

"Jake, I don't think this is a good idea." I ran my tongue over my bottom lip, savoring his essence.

"Sorry, Addy. You just have no idea how long I've wanted to do that."

I detected a hint of blush spreading across his face.

"You've become such a good friend and that's a real feat in itself. It would be easy to drag you upstairs and happily tear off all your clothes—"

Jake's eyes bugged out as a huge grin spread over his face.

"But it wouldn't be fair to you. It would be purely physical because I'm emotionally unavailable right now." I breathed out an exasperated sigh. "I gave my heart to Quinn, and I don't know if I'll ever get it back ... I don't know if I want it back. The numbness I experience without it makes each passing day more bearable."

He remained silent for a few moments, chewing the inside of his cheek in a contemplative look that had me curious.

"So what you're saying is, you want to have your way with me, but you think I might be a clinger?"

I laughed. "Not exactly." Then I raised my eyebrows. "Are you a clinger?"

"Hmm, I'm not sure. I've never found anyone worth *clinging* to."

"That's just it. Relationships work best when both people want to stay and nobody has to hold on."

I pushed up on my toes and kissed him on the cheek. "We wouldn't work; I wouldn't stay. Goodnight, Jake."

Before he had time to respond, I opened the door to my loft then locked it behind me, taking the stairs two at a time.

I JOURNALED every day the year Mac and I spent abroad after the fire. It was therapeutic and I was in dire need of daily reminders that I did indeed have things to be grateful for. Some days I floundered around with no real purpose to my life. Other days felt like a downward spiral. I needed to find a purpose again. After Mac and I returned from our trip, I finished my PhD, then moved to Milwaukee to open The Sage Leaf Café.

Over the past year, Quinn had become my new purpose. The day I left him, I felt insignificant again. I was a pinball, bouncing around without ever finding the right fit. I needed to find gratitude again, and I needed perspective. I bought another journal, deciding it was time to start writing again.

My racing mind kept me awake most of the night. I

surfed the net, watched TV, read, and eventually lit a candle and meditated, just before sunrise. After clearing my mind, I fell into a peaceful sleep. Around noon I was awakened by my phone.

"Hello?" I tried to disguise my sleepy voice. After all, why would a thirty-two-year-old still be asleep at noon?

"Good morning, sunshine, or technically after-noon. You sound tired. Did I actually wake you?"

"Hi, Jake. No, you didn't wake me." I wasn't fooling anyone. "Okay, maybe you did. I didn't sleep well last night," I mumbled while yawning.

"I see, me neither. Were you thinking about me the way I was thinking about you?" His tone was mischievous.

"I was thinking about you some of the time, but I doubt the same way you were thinking about me."

Okay, maybe a little.

"Well, that's disappointing. Oh well, maybe next time. Are you planning on joining the living anytime soon?"

I flipped the covers off and stretched. "It's possible. Why do you ask?"

"Mendelssohn Winery is having their open house and I thought we should go."

"*We,* huh?"

"Did I stutter?"

I tapped my fingernail on my teeth. "What the hell, I don't have anything better to do."

"Wow. 'Gee, Jake, I'd love to go to the wine tasting

with such a devastatingly handsome guy as yourself. How considerate of you to think of me,'" he mimicked me in a high-pitched voice.

I laughed out loud and it felt good. "I'll be down in an hour."

Journal Day 1
Grateful for Jake.

Journal Day 2
Grateful for Jake and Mendelssohn Winery's silky red wine.

Journal Day 3
Grateful for Jake and his impersonation of Ron Burgundy in Anchorman.

Journal Day 4
Grateful for Jake, his to-die-for taco burger, and kale chips, and motorcycle rides at sunset.

FINDING my new purpose was a difficult challenge, but I enjoyed living in the moment with Jake, so my purpose could wait. We enjoyed being together and he made me laugh. There was nothing mature about our relationship, and that was what made it work. He was the biggest flirt I'd ever met. We held hands and he never missed a chance to kiss me goodnight, in spite of my constant reminders that our relationship had nowhere to go.

"Margarita night?" Jake asked as he closed up the Café.

I was busy wiping down the tables and counters. "What did you have in mind?"

"I'll make margarita pizza and you make margaritas. We'll flip a coin to see who chooses the movie tonight."

"It's a Wednesday night. I don't know if late night pizza, alcohol, and movies are such a great idea."

"You're right. It's not a great idea. It's a freakin' brilliant idea. As you like to remind me every day, I'm young, with twenty-something party stamina and you're old ... er. But since we both know you have nothing better to do than soak your dentures and sleep until noon, I see no reason not to eat, drink, and be merry tonight."

I snapped him on the butt with my towel. "I can't think straight when I'm around you. You're such a bad influence. I'll meet you upstairs. But I'm picking out the movie, so just keep your coin in your pocket, buddy."

Before I reached the door, Jake grabbed my arm and spun me around into him. "Maybe that's your problem ... you think too much."

He kissed me, then turned me back around, giving me a smack on my butt. "I'll grab the ingredients and be up soon."

I leaped up the stairs with a stupid grin on my face.

Jake was trouble, but I couldn't stay away from him. He was a delicious, physical temptation that became harder to resist with each passing day. I went years without sex before I met Quinn, but he apparently awakened the sex goddess in me and she wasn't ready to go back to sleep. In short, I was horny.

I set out my blender and glasses, picked a movie, and changed my clothes—three times. I settled on Daisy Duke cutoffs and a strapless, turquoise baby-doll blouse. I fingered through my hair and applied some lip gloss.

"Addy, what the hell are you doing?" I said to myself in the bathroom mirror.

I shut the light off and whispered back to myself as I walked out the door, "You're getting laid, that's what you're doing."

Two steps later, I was startled by a dark figure that stood up from my couch. I flipped the switch to the floor lamp and about lost consciousness.

"Quinn," I breathed out his name.

"Did I hear you say you were 'getting laid?' Interesting. How did you know I would be here?" His voice was slow and slurred.

He was drunk.

"How did you get in here?" I found my voice, but my words were laced with anger.

"Hmm, let's see, how would I get in here? Oh yeah, I used your ridiculously easy to remember code. God, Addy, you're too smart not to change your code more often."

He started to walk toward me, but his gait was clumsy.

He ran his finger over my bare shoulder and down my arm. My whole body froze at his touch.

"I like this, and those shorts are so fucking hot." His drunken gaze washed over my body and finally met mine. "You're right." He leaned into me, his liquor-laden breath fanning my face. "You are getting laid tonight."

My feet refused to move, but I turned my head to the side, wincing in disgust.

"You're drunk."

"Ya think?" He laughed.

"Why are you here, Quinn?" I asked in a calm, even tone.

"I'm here to take back what's mine." His voice had an edge to it.

"And what exactly do you think is yours?"

"You." He grabbed my arms and forced his lips to mine.

I moved my head away from him and tried to wriggle out of his grasp. "Quinn, stop!"

Before I had time to register what was happening, Quinn was being pulled off me and slammed up against the wall. Jake wedged his forearm under Quinn's chin, against his throat.

"You're not welcome here, so I suggest you leave while you're still breathing." The deep warning tone of Jake's voice was deadly. It was a side to Jake I'd never seen, not even in the ring.

Quinn tried to free himself, but he was weak and uncoordinated in his inebriated state.

"Take your fucking hands off me before I break them. You have no idea what I could do to you!" Quinn raged.

Jake didn't back down one inch; he simply shrugged his shoulders. "Maybe I don't, but what I do know is that I'm younger and sober and you couldn't land a punch tonight if the target was taped to your fist. So here's how this is going to go. I'm going to let go of you and you're going to walk your sorry ass out that door and leave town. Do I make myself clear?"

Quinn glared at Jake with no response and then his gaze fell to me. I looked away. Seeing him like that was torture. Jake slowly released him. Quinn rubbed his neck and headed toward the door with Jake right behind him. Then Quinn suddenly turned and threw a punch at Jake.

"Jake!" I screamed.

He easily dodged it, and before I could prevent it, Quinn was knocked out on the ground with a bloodied nose.

"Quinn!" My concern instantly shifted. I ran over and dropped to my knees beside him. "Quinn?" I yelled, grabbing his face.

Jake handed me a towel for Quinn's nose and a cold, wet washcloth to lay over his forehead. Quinn quickly came to again and sat up.

"Are you okay?" I asked in concern, taking the wet

cloth from his head as he grabbed the towel over his nose and pushed my hand away.

He stumbled to his feet and backed up toward the door, opening it with his free hand. "When you're fucking my fiancée later, don't be surprised if she calls out my name."

Even behind his busted nose, Quinn managed to leave with the last word and an arrogant grin on his face.

After the door closed, I washed the blood off my hands. I sensed Jake behind me, and when I turned to grab a clean towel, he leaned against the opposing counter with his tattooed arms crossed over his chest. His eyes held remorse.

"Addy I—"

My heart raced and my mind clouded with emotions as I grabbed his face and pulled it to mine, crashing my lips to his. He hesitated for a moment until I moved my tongue over his, deepening our kiss. A moment later he pulled back and cradled my face.

"We don't have to do this." His smile wavered.

"I know." I grabbed his hand and led him to my bedroom.

I STOOD at the foot of my bed facing Jake. My body was numb. I desperately needed to feel again. I removed my top, keeping my eyes on his. He lowered his eyes to my exposed breasts and his lips parted as he let out a slow breath. Then I unbuttoned my shorts and slid them down my legs. Continuing to stand motionless, he drank in my body covered only by a pair of white lace panties.

"Just sex. Okay, Jake? I want you to make me forget, if only for tonight."

He nodded as he unbuttoned his jeans, letting them fall to the floor. Then he removed his T-shirt in one smooth motion. Standing still, he waited for my lead. I traced my fingers over the collage of ink that covered his large muscular arms and chest. The mix of symbolism was mesmerizing: stars, feathers, branches, serpents, and Sanskrit. His muscles twitched as my fingers glided across them. My eyes occasionally glanced up to his. They were heated, and his firm gaze was fixed on me.

I sat down on the bed and inched back until my head found the pillow. His eyes raked down my body as he slid off his briefs. When his large erection sprung free, I couldn't stop looking at it. He bent down and retrieved a condom from his jeans. After sliding it on, he crawled up the bed and removed my panties. Then, spreading my legs, he kneeled between them and leaned over me until his lips were on mine. They didn't linger there very long before both his mouth and hands descended to my breasts, kneading and sucking them. I closed my eyes because all I wanted to do was forget about Quinn. But as soon as they were shut, he was all I could see.

It was his tongue over my nipples, his hands

squeezing and caressing them. I snapped them open as Jake sat back up on his knees and guided my hips up off the bed. I planted my feet firmly to the mattress and I pushed my hips up even further. He circled his thumb over my clitoris then slid a finger inside me. I bit my lower lip and released a soft moan. He pulled out and lined his sizable length up to my entrance. Grabbing my legs under my knees, he pulled me toward him then plunged inside me. He filled me completely. I closed my eyes and Quinn filled every inch of my mind.

Jake pulled back with a brief pause then plunged back into me. He repeated this over and over again. In my darkness, it was Quinn inside me. I felt our rhythm, our connection. I heard his voice calling my name as he came closer to finding his release. Jake picked up his pace and massaged my clit right over its most sensitive spot. I imagined it was Quinn's tongue bringing me to the verge of an explosive climax—the way he had done so many times before. As my orgasm melted through my core, I felt Quinn's name on my lips, until Jake's strained voice sounded in my ears.

"God, Addy. You're so sexy," he moaned as he came hard, reaching a hand over me to grab the iron railing at the head of my bed. He used it to steady himself as he slammed into me one last time before collapsing on my chest.

We were both breathless. I rested my chin on his shoulder, and looked at the eagle wings that spread across a back that was not Quinn's. A tear fell from my eye.

———

Journal Day 30
Grateful for friends with benefits, hot August days, and cold lemon sorbet ... on my sailboat.

AT THE END OF AUGUST, Mac and Evan left for Paris. They called it their last hurrah before starting a family. They knew Jake and I had become friends with benefits, but I wasn't ready to hang out as a couple. Jake and I were not a couple. We were simply good friends who had sex, lots of sex.

I hadn't seen or heard from Quinn since the night he left my loft with a bloodied nose. After my first night with Jake, I declared the tear I shed for Quinn to be my last. I also declared the next morning to be my first and last morning with Jake in my bed. Spending the night went beyond sex, and I was not interested in anything even remotely complicated. Over the next few weeks I managed to achieve the type of relationship with Jake that I had originally wanted with Quinn—sex only.

We escaped to Chicago for a long weekend since Mac and Evan were in Paris. After grocery shopping, we boarded _The Sage_ for four spectacular days. I loved sleeping on the boat and so did Jake. _The Sage_ was the only part of my life that screamed money. Everything about her was luxurious and over the top, the polar opposite of me. However, I couldn't imagine ever selling her, and I knew my parents would be happy to know I continued to enjoy her after everything that happened.

Our last night on the boat was perfect, the lake calm and the moon full. Since I had been selfishly taking advantage of Jake and his culinary skills over the past month, I decided to treat him to an Addy specialty. He waited patiently on deck while I worked on my top secret recipe. As soon as I brought our perfectly garnished meals up to the table, Jake started laughing.

"Mac and cheese? This is your top secret recipe?"

My attempt to glare at him failed because he had on board shorts and nothing else. His sun-kissed, tattooed skin was off the charts sexy. I pinched his nipple and twisted it hard.

"Ouch! I'm just kidding. You don't have to get rough."

I sat down across from him with my hot pink string bikini covering very little as well.

"It's macaroni with spicy cashew cheese sauce, roasted brussels sprouts, kale, and sun-dried tomatoes. The ultimate vegan comfort food."

"That's what I said. Mac and cheese." He grinned as he took a bite.

Without hesitation, I grabbed his bowl and tossed it over the side of the boat.

"Oh my God! What the hell?" he yelled in disbelief.

I took a bite of my food as if nothing had happened. "What? You disrespect my cooking, you disrespect me."

"What are you, the Culinary Mafia?"

He grabbed my bowl and started shoving the macaroni in his mouth using his hand as a spoon.

"Hey!" I yelled, jumping to my feet.

He stood and moved away from me, trying to keep his back to me so he could keep shoveling it in. I jumped on his back and we both fell to the padded L-shaped seating area.

"You shit." I laughed as I moved to straddle him.

He rested the bowl on his chest, but most of it was gone.

"Oh, I'm sorry. Here, did you want some too?" He grabbed what was left and shoved it toward my mouth, smearing it all over my face.

The bowl fell to the floor, luckily landing in one piece, as I leaned in and kissed him, making a point of rubbing my face over his so we were both a cheesy mess. He licked my lips and my cheeks.

"Mmm, I stand corrected. This is definitely one of your best recipes."

"What are you, five?" I smirked.

"Yeah, because I was the one who threw an entire bowl of mac and cheese, including the bowl, into the lake. Not very eco-friendly of you."

I scooted off him and grabbed the legs of his shorts. A couple of quick tugs and they were off and Jake was gloriously naked in front of me.

"We're done talking about this." I smiled.

He sat up and pulled me to him between his legs. I stared down at him, shamelessly admiring his young, beautiful body.

"Jake Matthews, you are sex personified."

He looked up at me and smiled as he untied my top.

"You're not so bad yourself."

He sucked in one of my nipples and grazed his teeth across it, before turning his attention to my bikini bottoms. Stepping out of them, I straddled his lap as his mouth found my breasts again. I eased onto his waiting erection until it filled me, his hands resting on my butt as he guided me up and down over it. My hands fisted his copper-blond hair that had finally grown enough to grasp in my hands. Pulling his head to my breasts, I arched my back.

Sex with Jake was raw and carnal. We didn't share emotional sentiments and rarely even shared words at all. We were bathed in moonlight and surrounded by the sounds of our flesh slapping together, our labored breathing, the occasional moaning, and the lapping of the waves.

I was surprised how easy it was for me to separate my feelings for Jake. We had worked together for three years and I cared about him as a friend, but when we had sex, it was purely physical for me. It was like I became a different person when he was inside me. I no longer thought of him as Jake my friend or owner of my Café. I experienced a total emotional detachment.

It made it easy for me to walk away the moment we were done. I had no desire to cuddle, spoon, or snuggle under the covers wrapped in his arms. I didn't miss him when my bed was empty in the morning, and I was never jealous when young beautiful girls flirted with him. He was my *distraction* ... he was my Olivia.

CHAPTER SEVEN

<u>Journal Day 35.</u>
Grateful for mac and cheese.

AFTER WE RETURNED to Milwaukee I received a call from Elena. It was great to hear her voice and talk with her again. It didn't matter that I ended it with Quinn. Elena felt like a surrogate mother to me, and I never intended for our relationship to end when mine and Quinn's did.

"Elena, so good to hear from you."

"Addy, how are you? I think about you all the time. I've wanted to call more. I've even wanted to come for a visit, but—"

"But Quinn is your son and you love him dearly so keeping in contact with me is awkward. Elena, I understand, I really do. I'm just happy to be speaking with you now."

"Oh, Addy, it wasn't just Quinn, it was you too. I felt

like my voice, my texts, my presence would have been too much of a reminder of what happened between the two of you, and I wanted to give you time to heal. Honestly, I wouldn't be calling you now, but I need your help." Her voice was sad.

"Name it."

The line went silent.

"Elena?"

"I'm here." There was another pause. "Addy, I need you to fly me back to Spain."

It was my turn to be at a loss for words.

"Um, sure." An uneasy wave of fear washed over me. "Is everything okay?"

"I'm sick, sweetie."

My heart sank and the lump in my throat swelled, words couldn't escape.

"It's pancreatic cancer. It's the real reason I left for Spain after Lucas died. Quinn and Alexis don't know anything about it. Alexis has young children and I couldn't burden her with my problem so quickly after losing her father. And Quinn had his plate full with Lucas' business matters. Chase and my sister agreed to help me through the chemotherapy and only contact Quinn and Alexis if I didn't improve. After eight weeks of chemotherapy, the doctors were optimistic. Then by the time you came for Quinn's birthday, I was in remission."

I wiped the streams of tears from my face and dug deep to gain some composure.

"It's back, Addy, but now it's spread to my liver."

"So you're going back to Spain for treatment?"

Her next few words were controlled and spoken with finality. "I'm going home, Addy. Valencia is my home ... I'm going home to die."

Oh. Dear. God.

It was like finding my parents murdered in their house all over again. I smelled the smoke and heard the screeching sound of the fire alarms coming from my house, walking around confused, my lungs burning from smoke inhalation after going back into the house when Malcolm didn't come out. The news that my whole life had been taken from me in a matter of minutes echoed in my head.

Then I heard it, and only it. *Th-thump, th-thump, th-thump.*

"Addy? Addy? Addy, are you still there? Sweetie, did you hear me? Addy?"

"Yes." My voice was flat, emotionless.

It was all I could manage to say. Elena had no idea what she was asking of me.

"Yes you heard me, or yes you'll take me back to Spain?"

The tears wouldn't stop. I licked the saltiness from my lips and closed my eyes, hoping they'd stop.

"Both. I'll get a flight out in the morning." I went to push the END button when Elena spoke.

"Addy, nobody else knows and I want to keep it that way. Okay?"

"Elena—"

"Nobody, Addy. It's how it has to be."

Journal Day 36
Grateful for perspective ... fucking perspective.

MY MOM USED to tell me that death put everything in perspective. She said without it the circle of life would be incomplete and the world would be out of balance. I often wondered if my mother was partaking in any sort of afterlife. If so, would she say the tragic deaths of everyone who mattered most to me were a necessary sacrifice to achieve balance?

If there was an up side to being an orphaned adult, it was lack of accountability. No official family, no official job, and very few friends, made it easy to leave town indefinitely. Both Mac and Jake trusted me enough to respect my need to leave for a while without much explanation. Mac was concerned at first, but I assured her I was fine and my secrecy was for someone else, not myself.

I arrived in New York by noon and hailed a cab to Elena's. The possibility of running into Quinn was extremely remote, but I couldn't help being a little on edge until we were safely boarded on a plane to Spain. When I arrived at Elena's, she was in the middle of sorting personal items into three boxes, labeled _Quinn, Chase,_ and _Alexis._

"Addy!" she yelled with genuine excitement.

Elena was a naturally thin lady, but she had lost weight, too much weight. Observing slightly yellowed skin, I imagined she was probably jaundiced. She sat at the kitchen table but made no attempt to get up. I leaned over and hugged her frail body.

"How are you feeling today?"

She dismissively waved her hand at me. "Ah, it's just another day. I've had better … I've had worse."

I pulled out a chair and sat down next to her as she continued to sort through some old photos. "What can I help you do?"

"I have an old jewelry box upstairs on my dresser. Could you go get it?"

I placed my hand over hers and squeezed it. "Sure, I'll be right back."

Her bedroom wasn't the one Quinn and I stayed in; hers had black and white photographs of her children and grandchildren covering almost every inch of the walls. The one that hung over her bed was a wedding photo of her and Lucas. It was a candid shot and they looked happy and blissful. The opposite wall had baby pictures of Quinn, Chase, and Alexis. All parents think their babies are beautiful, but Elena's really were. They all had dark hair and dark eyes with flawless skin. There was one picture where Elena was breastfeeding Alexis with Chase on one side of the chair and Quinn on the other. Chase looked at his baby sister with wide eyes while Quinn's dark eyes were fixed on his mother. My gaze drifted from one picture to the next. Each one portrayed a loving, nurturing mother, and her beautiful children. Tears raced down my face as I felt Elena's pain, what would be her children's pain, and the unearthed pain of my own past.

I stepped into her bathroom, taking a moment to wipe my eyes and nose, before I returned to the kitchen with her jewelry box.

"The photos that adorn the walls of your room are just so beautiful and intimate. You must feel surrounded by such love when you're in there."

She smiled as I handed her the jewelry box. "Yes, it's my favorite room in the house. As you probably noticed, it's not the master suite. When Lucas went through his ... rough patch, I made that room my own. I feel love in that room. I feel *loved* in those pictures. Motherhood is the ultimate expression of a woman's soul." She placed her hand on my leg. "Wouldn't you agree?"

Her comment and empathetic smile shook me to my core. My whole body tensed as I fought back the tears. I looked away from her gaze while giving a slight nod.

"Now, let's see what treasures I have to bestow upon my lovelies."

She wasn't going to let me cry. Like the flip of a switch, she was all smiles as she rummaged through her jewelry box. Most of the contents went in Alexis' box, but there were some men's watches and cufflinks that must have belonged to Lucas that she sorted into Chase and Quinn's boxes. She'd periodically hold up an item to share the history or sentimental value behind it.

My mind wandered to all my mom's jewelry, that was either packed away or in a safe-deposit box. Eight years later, and I still couldn't bring myself to go through their stuff. I had very few things that should have been of sentimental value, but what I did have was sentimental because someone wanted me to think of it that way. I still owned *The Sage* because I promised people I loved that I wouldn't sell it, not because of personal sentimental value. *Things* seemed more appealing to me when I had people to share them with. Since I'd lost those people, the materialistic things had turned into excess clutter with bittersweet memories.

"Here, my dear. I want you to have this." Elena held up a rosary. "This was my mother's Spanish colonial rosary with mother of pearl beads. I know you're not Catholic, but Quinn told me you meditate. Maybe you can use them for prayer or meditation beads."

"Elena, you don't have to—"

"Addy, I *want* you to have it. When I'm gone I want you to occasionally light a candle, hold these in your hands, and pray for my family. I want this to be a symbol of our connection ... nothing else, just you and me."

"Thank you." I held out my hands and she set the rosary in them then covered my hands with hers.

"Now, these boxes need to be taken to my closet. Nobody will think to go in there until after I'm—"

I saw her take a slow swallow as the sharp edge of reality cut into her and she stopped short of finishing.

"I've got them." I grabbed the first box and headed up the stairs.

We spent the rest of the afternoon sorting through personal items. Although I did all the foot work, Elena was still exhausted by dinner. She didn't eat much and insisted on going to bed right after she finished eating.

"Early flight in the morning, dear. Don't stay up too late."

"I won't." I gave her a warm hug.

She embraced me with love and whispered in my ear. "You know I'll never be able to repay you for what you're doing for me?"

"I don't expect anything," I whispered back.

Then she turned and slowly made her way up the stairs. "That's why I chose you."

Journal Day 37
Grateful for Elena.

WE LEFT EARLY the following morning, not on a private jet like I did with Quinn, but first-class commercial. I silently stood by and watched Elena leave her family home for the last time. I held her hand as the plane took off because I knew she was looking out the window and saying goodbye to America for the last time. She was saying goodbye to Quinn, Alexis, and her grandchildren. She was saying goodbye to Lucas, whose body was buried in a cemetery a few miles from their home. I imagined part of her thought, "See you soon."

We said very little on the flight to Valencia. I felt her pain in my bones. I never had the chance to say goodbye to my loved ones; Elena did, but chose not to. Goodbyes didn't ease the pain and they didn't give closure, at least not to the living. It was admirable of Elena to save her children from what was to come, but I also ached for their broken hearts that would be mistaken for anger. They would resent her for not telling them. They would long for the goodbye they never got to have.

When we arrived in Spain, I promised myself it was my last visit. The world was too big to spend time in a place that held so many painful memories. Spain represented the beginning of the end for me and Quinn. I knew when I left again it would hold new memories ... the memories of Elena's last days on Earth and the burden of guilt that I was the only one who shared those days with her.

Did Elena consider how her children would feel about me after finding out that I was the one to be with her? Maybe I was the scapegoat. If they hated me, it would only leave love for her. Honestly, I was fine with that. I loved Elena and I would willingly do that for her —for her children.

She arranged for transportation, but we didn't go to her sister's house. Instead, we ended up at a small beach villa with a breathtaking view of the Mediterranean.

"I assumed we'd be going to your sister's."

Elena eased her way out of the car with my help. "Addy, I told you nobody else. You're the only one that knows I'm dying, except my doctors and the at-home hospice nurse who will join us in a few weeks."

Her words cinched the massive knot in my gut.

"Are you sure? You said your sister and Chase helped you through this before. I'd imagine they'd want to be here too." I tried not to make it sound like a plea, but it was.

"That was different. They stood by me while I 'fought' the cancer. I'm not fighting it, Addy. They wouldn't watch me die if they thought there was even a remote chance I could do something to prolong my life, even if only a few months."

As we walked into the villa, she turned toward me. "They would think I was giving up, but I'm not."

I closed my eyes and nodded as the words fell from my lips as a whisper. "You're letting go."

Journal Day 38
Grateful for the beautiful view of the pristine aquamarine waters of the Mediterranean and of course, Elena.

Journal Day 39
Grateful for wicker rockers, hot tea, and Elena.

ELENA'S HEALTH quickly started to decline within the first couple of days after arriving at the villa. It was as if her body knew she had reached her final destination and it no longer had to be strong. Her back pain worsened by the day, and she vomited at night. Fruit was about the only thing that tasted good to her or that stayed down. By the end of our first week, she looked at least ten pounds lighter and an equal many years older. I made herbal teas to help with the nausea and to help her sleep.

Journal Day 44
Grateful for exhaustion and Elena.

Every day I suggested we call the hospice nurse to come stay with us, but Elena insisted she wasn't ready for that yet. The pain and nausea would eventually wear her out and she would collapse into a sleep. Every time she closed her eyes I wondered if it was for the last time. She never gave me instructions as to how she expected me to break the news to her family, so every time she opened her eyes a wave a relief came over me.

Journal Day 50
Grateful for hospice and Elena.

After twenty-four hours without sleep, Elena allowed me to call the hospice nurse. Within an hour of her arrival, Elena was medicated and sleeping.

Journal Day 51

Grateful for pain medication and Elena.

Elena seemed to rally after she awoke, but the nurse informed me that it wouldn't last long. Elena stayed in bed, propped up with extra pillows and a yellow and white floral quilt over her lap. I sat cross legged on the other side of the bed. We spent the afternoon talking, laughing, and crying. Before she agreed to more pain medication, she asked me to retrieve some envelopes from her bag. There were five: one for each of her kids, one for her sister, and one with my name on it.

"Please give those to my family," she said in a weak, raspy voice.

I looked at the one with my name on it.

"Don't open it, not until—" She looked out the window at the water for a few moments. "Tell me, Addy."

"Tell you what?"

"Tell me what happened to you."

I tilted my head and shrugged. "I don't understand what you mean."

She looked at me and reached her hand out to hold mine. "Yes, you do."

My tears came before my words, they always did, but I told her. I told her everything. It felt like reliving it, cutting me open and my heart bleeding out to her, as though I was dying with her. She said nothing, she did nothing, not one word, not one tear. My eyes were almost swollen shut by the time I finished. I felt her softly squeeze my hand. Then I wiped my eyes and opened them just as she was closing hers ... for the last time.

***

SOMEWHERE IN THE WORLD, Quinn was likely in a drunken stupor after putting in half a day's worth of work. Alexis might have been picking her kids up from school, and Chase was probably cruising home in his fancy sports car. With one phone call, their lives were forever altered.

"Hey, Chase."

"Addy, is that you?" he responded with hopeful enthusiasm.

"Yeah, it's me." I tried to bring life to my voice, but it was a futile attempt.

"You're the last person I expected to hear from. Don't get me wrong, I'm glad you called, but—"

"Chase," I interrupted.

"Yeah, what's up? You don't sound so good. Is everything okay?"

The hospice nurse had made arrangements to have Elena's body taken from the villa. I hadn't moved from the bed since she died. I ran my hand over the empty spot where she had lain just hours earlier. The familiar numbness spread through my body and the echoing rhythm of my lonely heart beating was all I could hear.

"Addy? Are you still there?"

"It's Elena, she—" The words choked me.

"Mom? What about her?" His voice was slow and cautious.

"Her ... um ... her cancer came back."

"What? How do you know? Who told you she had cancer? Why are *you* calling me? Where's my mom?" He sounded confused and overwhelmed.

"She called me several weeks ago and told me everything."

"Why'd she call you? I don't understand—"

"Chase! Please, just listen." We were both silent for a moment, then I took a deep breath.

Deep breath ... I am peaceful, I am strong.

"Her cancer came back, but this time it had spread to her liver. She didn't want to go through treatment and she knew you and her sister wouldn't understand. She asked me to bring her here."

"Here? My mom's in Milwaukee?"

"No, I brought her to ... Valencia."

"What? Addy where is she? This is bullshit. There's no way I'm going to let her die. The chemo worked before, it will work again. I'll do whatever it takes, but I'm not going to let her give up. I'm coming to get her. Where is she?" His words were desperate and frantic.

"Chase, she didn't want treatment, she just wanted to—"

"Doesn't! She *doesn't* want treatment, stop talking like she's already—"

"Chase ..."

"No! Don't you dare say it!" he yelled through his cracked voice.

His sobs sparked a new wave of tears trailing down my face. I didn't say anything, there was nothing left to say. I patiently waited for him to speak again.

"Where is she now?" he eventually asked.

"The undertaker took her about an hour ago. I'll text you the information."

"Addy?"

"Yes?"

"Did she suffer?" The weak, shaky tone to his voice was so fragile.

"No."

CHAPTER EIGHT

CHASE AGREED to call everyone else and explain what had happened. Later that night he drove to the villa. He wanted to see where his mom spent her last weeks. When he arrived he told me more about her first bout with cancer and the agony he went through keeping it from Quinn and Alexis. I told him about her last weeks at the villa and our conversations about her children. He wept in my arms like a little boy, and I hoped somehow he could feel his mother's love in my embrace.

I handed him the envelopes Elena had left for him, his aunt, and his siblings. He held them with a delicate touch, as if he didn't know what to do with them. I couldn't blame him. I still hadn't read the letter she left for me, and I had no idea how long it would take me to find the courage. Before leaving, he suggested I stay at his aunt's with him and his siblings until after the funeral, but I gratefully declined, opting to stay at the villa instead. It was going to take everything I had left in me to be near Quinn during the funeral. Staying under the same roof was not an option.

Journal Day 53.

Grateful for my beautiful mother, who brought me into this world 33 years ago today. I miss her every single day.

Grateful for Elena, who loved me like a daughter. I will miss her too, every day.

MOST DAYS I chose to believe in randomness. Otherwise, I would've been forced to believe that fate was cruel and karma vengeful. It was my birthday. I was supposed to be in Chicago with Mac and Evan. We'd planned a day of sailing, dinner at my favorite restaurant, and Mac's awesome carrot cake. Instead, I was slipping into a black sleeveless sheath dress with a belted waist and cowl-neck. I slid my feet into a pair of black heels and inspected myself in the mirror.

Too much black.

I debated putting my hair up in a tight bun, but decided to leave it down. As I put on lip gloss, my phone rang.

"Hey, Mac."

"Happy Birthday, my dear friend."

"Thanks."

"My heart goes out to you. I can't imagine how

you're managing to cope. Your birthdays will forever be bittersweet. Wish I were there with you."

Me too.

"I'll be fine. I dressed myself, so that's a start. Right?"

Mac practically had to dress me like a young child for my parents' funeral and then again after the fire.

"You've come a long way. What are you wearing?"

"I think my official funeral dress. It's pretty old, but as you know, I can't remember the details."

"Black sheath, sleeveless, belt?"

"Yep. Awfully pathetic, huh?"

"I don't think anyone will recognize it." She laughed, but then her voice fell serious again. "Can you do this?"

I sighed. "I can. I don't want to, but I can. Considering I flew my ex-fiancé's mother to Spain, watched her slowly die over the past few weeks, all while her kids were completely oblivious to her condition or even her location ... I think the funeral, in every sense of the word, is just an afterthought."

"You know that's not what I'm talking about."

"I know, you mean Quinn."

"He might not be too happy to see you ... you know, given the events of the past few weeks."

"The past few weeks? Try the past five months. It doesn't matter. It's not like I'm going to be sitting next to him, and when it's over I'm packing up and catching the first flight home."

"Why is Elena not being buried in New York next to Lucas?"

"Chase said Elena's parents had purchased plots for her and her sister next to theirs. I guess it's a family thing."

"Well, I love you. Promise me you'll do something that involves a small bit of indulgence on your birthday, okay?"

"I'd say I'm going to drown in a bottle of wine on the plane if I can get a flight out tonight. However, Quinn and his drinking problem have sort of ruined that fun for me."

"Oh, Addy. This too will pass. Safe travels, sweetie. We'll have a belated party when you get home."

"Thanks, Mac. See you soon."

THE SUN MADE an appearance that day in Valencia. The temperature was fair with a slight breeze. When the cab driver dropped me off in front of the Catholic cathedral, I was in awe. A massive architectural masterpiece with grandeur height, flying buttresses, and pointed archways. However, it wasn't the cathedral that had my attention, it was the enormous sea of people making their way inside. I started to think that maybe Elena was famous. The crowd was representative of something one might expect for a celebrity, royalty, or dignitary.

As more people continued to line up behind me, I

felt swallowed up by the crowd. Normally my claustrophobia would have consumed me, but feeling lost in the crowd comforted me. I felt hidden and protected. My shoulders relaxed and my fidgety hands stilled as a wave of relief washed over me and eased my anxiety about seeing Quinn. In fact, the chances of making any sort of eye contact with him seemed slim at best.

After I received my program, I was ushered to my seat. Maybe it was fate or divine intervention, but I owed some higher power a debt of gratitude for my seat, which was at the back and away from the aisle, surrounded by strangers and nicely hidden from the Cohen family.

I double-checked to make sure my phone was silenced and then read through the long program. Occasionally glancing up, I scanned the crowd to see if I recognized anyone. The front of the large cathedral felt like the distance of a football field away from where I sat. Checking my watch, I assumed the family would be seated soon, and my heart pounded in anticipation of seeing them—seeing *him*.

The organ sounded and everyone stood as the family made their way to the front of the church followed by the casket. Alexis and Mitch were first with Ethan and Ellen in tow. Next were Chase and Quinn. Chase was on my side of the aisle, partially blocking my view of Quinn. When I got a quick glimpse of his profile, I noticed his bearded face. He kept his head down, so I couldn't make out any expression on it before he passed, and then his back was to me until he fell out of view.

After we were seated, I reached into my purse and pulled out Elena's rosary and wrapped it around my hand.

Do you see this Elena? All of these people are here to say goodbye to you. You will forever be missed.

By the end of the opening rites, I was in my own meditative state. I couldn't recall what was said or who said it. My mind drifted to a place of comfort, a state of peace. Time vanished in what seemed like an instant. The next thing I recalled was the casket being carried out, followed by the family.

All I saw was Quinn. Then, as though he knew precisely where I was in the large crowd of hundreds of people, he looked up as he passed my row and his eyes met mine. It was only for a brief moment, but it was undeniable. He looked at me and only me.

I wanted out of Valencia.

I wanted out of Spain.

I wanted out of the misery of seeing Quinn and his family mourn the loss of Elena.

I stayed because I promised myself I would see this through out of respect for Elena. As I phoned for a cab, I laughed at myself. How many billionaires traveled by cab to funerals and burials? Probably just one ... me.

When I was pushed out the front doors by the crowd, I moved to the side and stood in a shaded area of grass, shifting my weight to my toes so my heels didn't sink into the ground. A large hand gripped my arm. I jumped and turned.

"Chase, jeez, you scared me!" I hugged him. "Hanging in there?"

He shrugged his shoulders. "I'll be better when this day is over. Anyway, where were you?"

"What do you mean?"

"During the service, you should have been seated up front with us."

"Uh … no. I'm not family."

"You're the person my mother chose to be with when she died. If that doesn't make you family, then I don't know what does. So let's go." He grabbed my hand and started to pull me with him.

I tugged on him to stop. "Go where?"

"The cemetery."

"I already called a cab."

"There is no way you're going to ride in a cab at the back of the processional to my mother's burial. Let's go."

I tugged again. "But Quinn and Alexis—"

"Alexis, Mitch, and the kids are riding together. It's just me and Quinn. *But* before you say anything, Quinn knows I came to find you, so don't worry about him. Besides, he's a bit preoccupied."

I surrendered, following him. "What do you mean by preoccupied?"

"Let's just say he has more than one flask hidden in his suit pockets."

THE WINDOWS to the Rolls Royce Limousine were heavily tinted, but I knew who waited on the inside, and my nerves were on edge. The driver opened the door and Chase motioned for me to get in first.

Deep breath ... I am peaceful, I am strong.

Quinn was on the far side facing the front, so I sat in the opposite corner facing the back. He peered out his window and didn't so much as look in my direction to acknowledge me. Chase sat next to him, opposite of me. He glanced over at Quinn then back at me. I smiled nervously then he leaned forward and squeezed my hand.

"*I'm* glad you're here. Okay?" He winked at me.

Unable to speak past the lump in my throat, I simply returned the hand squeeze and nodded.

The drive to the cemetery was agonizingly slow. I couldn't stop glancing over at Quinn as he kept his head turned away from me. He looked like a different person, with a full beard and longer hair. I had flashbacks of shaving his scruffy face in the bathtub after his accident. He wasn't speaking to me then either, but I felt responsible for him.

Those days were over. He was no longer my responsibility, but nothing could make me stop caring for him. In his right hand he held a stainless steel flask and the lid in his left. When we reached the cemetery, he tipped back the last of it and tossed the empty container on the floor. As the driver opened his door, Quinn spoke.

"Well, let's bury the dead so we can get the hell out of here." He looked at Chase. "You bringing my leftovers? I hear she puts out."

Chase pinned Quinn to the back of the seat by his neck.

"You shut the fuck up! If I hear you disrespect our mother or Addy again, I'll make sure you leave the country in worse shape than you did last time. So get your drunken ass out of the car and try and act like a semblance of the human being you used to be."

Chase released Quinn and both men adjusted their suit coats and ties before exiting the limo. Quinn shot me a quick glance as I stepped out, but I avoided his gaze as Chase put his arm around my waist and led me away.

When the service was over, Chase wanted a few minutes alone, so I went back to the limo. I opened the door and found Quinn sprawled out in his seat with his jacket off, tie loosened, and the top buttons of his shirt undone. He held another flask, and after tipping it back for a long pull, he scowled at me.

"You don't belong here," he growled out.

I ignored him because drunk Quinn was mean, cruel, and unworthy of my attention.

"I. Don't. Want. You. Here." He tried to provoke a response.

I continued to keep to myself. Turning on my phone, I checked for flight information to see if I could get a flight out that evening or if I would have to wait until morning.

After draining another flask, he threw it at my window. I jumped and looked at him just as the door opened and Chase got in. Seeing the startled look on my face, he squinted his eyes at Quinn.

"Is there a problem?"

Quinn shook his head then leaned back and closed his eyes. Chase looked at me. I shook my head and went back to searching for a flight out.

"There's a luncheon. Can you join us?" Chased asked, completely ignoring Quinn.

"Sorry, I can't, but thanks for the offer. I'm looking for a flight out tonight, and I want to be packed and ready in case something opens up. Could you just take me back to the villa?"

I expected Chase to try and persuade me to go with him to the luncheon, but to my surprise he simply nodded and instructed the driver.

We sat in silence the whole way. I wasn't sure if Quinn was asleep or passed out. When the driver opened the door I looked at him, but he didn't move. Chase got out and gave me a big hug.

"Thank you, for everything. I hope this isn't good-bye." He had an irresistible boyish charm.

I gave him a soft kiss on the cheek. "Milwaukee is a short drive from Chicago. The next time you're in the Midwest, look me up."

"Count on it. Later, then."

"Later, Chase."

I watched as the limo pulled away with the hollow shell of a man who still held my heart captive.

"Happy Birthday, Addy," I said to myself sarcastically. "However will you top this next year?"

I TRIED in vain to get a flight out that day. After succumbing to the reality that I wouldn't leave Spain until the morning, I rummaged through the refrigerator and found something to eat. I also found a bottle of wine that Elena and I never got the chance to open.

What the hell, it's my birthday.

After starting a fire in the pit out back, I settled into a patio recliner and watched the tide over a bottle of red wine. A few hours later, darkness surrounded me with the exception of a quarter moon and the few remaining embers in the pit. Standing with a slight wobble, the heavy numbness of the alcohol claimed my body. Looking down, I realized I was still in my dress.

"This is the worst dress ever. It reeks of death and misery," I slurred to myself.

I unzipped the dress and clumsily stepped out of it. Wearing only my black bra and matching lace panties, I marched out into the sand. As soon as I reached the water's edge, I tossed the dress into the endless sea. "Adiós!"

Turning around, I drudged through the sand back to the deck. I grabbed the wine bottle and went to pour more in my glass but noticed it was almost empty. I set the glass down, lifted the bottle, and tipped it back until the rest of the wine slid down my throat. With little regard for much of anything, I tossed the empty bottle in the sand and reached for the door. Instead of the knob, my hand grasped an arm.

"Holy shit!" I jumped back.

My heart raced as I worked to focus my intoxicated eyes on the dark figure standing in the doorway.

Quinn.

"What the hell are you doing here?" I shoved him aside as I stumbled through the doorway.

My eyes screamed in protest when I flipped on a light to find my way to the bedroom. I fumbled through my suitcase on the bed until I found my short pink satin robe. When I returned to the living room, Quinn was standing by the French doors looking at me. He still had on his black suit pants, but his tie was gone and his shirt was untucked with the sleeves rolled up to his elbows.

"You're drunk," he said. It wasn't a question because he knew the answer.

"You would know," I threw back in an irritated tone. "What do you want?"

"My fucker of a little brother locked me in the basement during the luncheon until I sobered up."

I grabbed a bottle of coconut water out of the refrigerator and unscrewed the top. "Kudos to him, but that still doesn't explain why you're here." I guzzled down half the bottle. "Especially since *I.*

Don't. Want. You. Here." I'd hoped the words would resonate with him, but from the look on his face I wasn't sure if he even remembered saying them to me earlier.

"I didn't have much of a choice. After I was released from the basement, Chase and Mitch threw me in the car and brought me here."

"Why?" I asked, not sure if he was being truthful.

He shrugged his shoulders. "Apparently, I didn't play nice with you earlier today. Chase thought I owed you a 'sober' apology."

I finished my bottle of coconut water and slammed the bottle down on the counter. "Fine, apologize, don't apologize, I don't give a rat's ass. Just say whatever you need to say and get the hell out of here!"

Not waiting for a response, I made my way to the bathroom, shutting and locking the door behind me. My bladder was about to explode, so Quinn and his forced apology had to wait. When I came out, he wasn't in the living room or kitchen. The hall leading to Elena's bedroom was illuminated. I tiptoed down the hall and found Quinn standing at the foot of the bed with his back to the door.

"Is this where she died?" His voice was emotionless.

"Yes."

"Why didn't you call me?"

"I promised her I wouldn't."

"I see. So if your mother were dying and she asked me not to tell you, then you'd be okay with that?"

The wine was slowly wearing off, but my ability and desire to show empathy was still numb.

"My mother was murdered and cut up into pieces by some psycho nine years ago. So if you're asking if I'd have been okay with her being injected with so much pain medication that she didn't feel a thing while she died on her own terms, then yes, I'd be okay with that."

"Jesus, Addy, I forgot how they—"

"How they what, Quinn? How they died? Good for you. Wish I could, but I can't. There hasn't been a single day in nine … whole … years that I haven't had the image of pools of blood soaking into the hardwood floors, grout, and wool rugs. I see it smeared on the walls, the banister, and the stairs. Then … then there are the images of their bodies, but not in one piece. No, they were cut up and strewn throughout the house the way a child scatters their toys!"

My heart thundered in my chest as my whole body shook.

"Get out, Quinn! Just leave." My chest heaved as my head spun.

"Whatever, I need a fucking drink anyway." He walked past me as I continued to stand in the doorway.

"Of course you do, just like your father did," I whispered.

He came to an abrupt halt and turned back toward me. "What did you say?"

I shut the light off and walked past him to the other bedroom because I was done talking.

"I asked you a question," he demanded as he followed me.

I lifted my suitcase off the bed and set it on the floor.

"I said you're just like your father," I growled at him.

He charged toward me until he had me backed up against the wall. He cocked his fist back and then sent it through the wall only a couple of inches from my face. I stood frozen in place, barely flinching. The alcohol had apparently paralyzed my reflexes.

"I'm not my goddamn father, so don't you ever fucking say it again!" he roared in my face.

I looked at him with no expression, no emotion. His warm breath brushed my face.

He pushed off the wall and took a few steps back. "I think I'd better leave before I say something I'll regret."

What?!

I raised my eyebrows in disbelief. "No! Don't you even think of leaving without finishing what you've started. I've been on the receiving end of the vengeful venom that comes from your drunken mouth. So please, don't spare me now."

He shook his head. "I'm done here." He opened the door and paused for a moment.

"You're such a pathetic coward," I said just loud enough for him to hear me.

He slammed the door shut again and turned around in another fit of rage.

"I'm a coward?" He laughed. "Oh, that's rich

coming from you, Addy. You're the one running from your past, not me. You're the reason I have steel plates and screws holding my pelvis together. You're the reason I can't make it through one day without a drink. And you're the reason my mother is—"

He stopped short, but I could see the bitterness eating away at him. The twitch in his jaw muscles told me he was biting back the words.

"Dead, right? That's what you mean. I'm the reason your mother is *dead*."

Nothing he said surprised me, but how it made me feel did. I knew they were the words he needed to say, and I thought I was prepared to hear them, but I wasn't.

He exhaled an exasperated breath. "I told you if I didn't leave I'd say something—"

"Stop! Just—" I pinched the bridge of my nose. "It's fine, Quinn. I know how it feels to have everything in your life falling apart around you. I know how it feels to desperately need someone to take the blame ... take the pain." I wiped away a few lonely tears before looking into his pained eyes. "I never found that person and so I just lived with the pain. But I ... I love you." I nodded my head and bit my upper lip as I tried to blink back the rest of my tears. "So I'll take it from you. I'll take the blame. I'll take your pain."

His eyes filled with tears as he shook his head. "Dammit, Addy! Don't say that." He bent over and rested his hands on his knees as a strangled sob escaped his chest. Then he fell to his knees and covered his face with his hands as months of emotions poured out.

"It hurts ... so ... bad," he cried.

Closing the distance between us, I pulled his head into me, resting it on my abdomen. He wrapped his arms around my legs like a young child and sobbed.

"I miss her so much," he gasped between sobs.

"Shh." I stroked his thick, dark hair as my own river of tears overflowed.

"It hurts too much, Addy. God, please make it stop," he pleaded.

He clung to me so tight it actually felt as if I was taking on his pain. Yet even amidst the pain, for a brief moment, his embrace made my heart feel whole again.

When I could no longer hear his sobs, I held his hand. He looked at me with red, swollen eyes. I bent down and kissed the tear-streaked skin on his face. He closed his eyes, as if just the touch of my lips lightened his heartache.

"Come with me," I whispered.

Without a word, he climbed back to his feet and followed me to the bedroom.

Standing beside the bed, I began unbuttoning his shirt. "What are you doing?" he asked in a weak, fragile voice.

"Taking it away." I looked up at him. "Just for tonight."

I finished removing his shirt, then his pants and briefs. He stood in front of me—motionless, suffering, broken. After shrugging my robe off, I removed my bra and panties. The moment was raw. After so much pain, anger, and heartbreak, we stood inches apart, bared to one another—physically and emotionally. I think we both knew it wasn't a surrender or the mending of our relationship, and it wasn't forgiveness. It was just coming up for a breath of air before being pulled under again.

The peace before the storm ended when I laid my hands on his bare chest. The connection was electric. His whole body quivered for an instant before he pulled me into his arms. His mouth attacked mine. The taste of him awakened a craving deep inside that I'd nearly forgotten. Every cell in my body screamed for his touch; the need to feel his flesh against mine was almost painful. We fell to the bed and our bodies entwined. Every move was frantic and desperate. My skin bruised under his fingers as they gripped my body. Pain, pleasure, hate, love—a tornado of emotions ripped through us.

Our eager and insatiable bodies lost all control. In that moment, I only needed to feel something, just a moment of reprieve from the numbness that had seized my body and emotions. My hands clenched and tugged at his thick hair with equal fervor. His mouth roughly explored my mouth, my neck, my breasts. It felt as if we were trying to physically consume each other. Lustful moans reverberated from his chest and mixed with sporadic whimpers that seeped from my emotionally-overwhelmed body.

"You're fucking killing me," he growled as he

hitched my leg up and sank into me. I wrapped my legs around him and took everything he had to give. Memories of him … of *us* after his accident, flooded my head as he relentlessly pounded into me. His face hovered above mine. I felt all his pain and all his anger. Then I closed my eyes and prayed for the tears to hold off.

As the intensity in my core started to build, I opened my eyes again to meet his. The sadness in his eyes, the exhaustion in his breath, and the anger that came with each unforgiving thrust pierced my heart. I saw the demons of my past: the loss, the grief, the love, and the pain. But more than anything, I saw anger. Then he closed his eyes, and every muscle in his face and neck contracted as he climaxed. The warmth of his orgasm flowed into me, his hand moving between us. He started to circle his fingers over my clit, but he stopped. A slap in the face. A reminder that it was about him.

The moment was over, and after he leaned down and pressed a chaste kiss to my cheek, so were we. Without a word, he pulled out. The physical loss was excruciating, but the severed emotions were beyond unbearable. He stood, and with his back to me, proceeded to put on his clothes.

"Quinn?"

CHAPTER NINE

Quinn

I KEPT my back to her as I buttoned my shirt. The sound of her broken voice saying my name fucking killed me.

All I needed was a drink.

I needed to get the hell out of there. She wormed her way under my skin, but I didn't want her there. My mind was such a fucked-up mess, I felt bewitched by everything about her: those blue eyes, her cherry lips, the way her long golden hair flowed down her back and over her fucking perfect breasts. Her smell, her touch, her voice ... it was too much. I had only one choice—to let her go. I had to get out from under her spell. She made me feel things I didn't want to feel. The truth was, I didn't want to feel anything.

"Quinn?"

"Just ... stop, Addy!" I yelled in frustration as I

shoved my feet into my shoes. Every nerve in my body was on edge. *I've got to get the hell out of here.*

"Quinn, look at me—"

"Goddammit! Just ... shut up. You won, okay? You brought me to my fucking knees, stripped me of my resolve, and left me with nothing. We're done."

All I needed was a drink.

I slammed the door and dialed up Chase.

"You apologize?" his smug voice answered.

"Just get your ass over here," I demanded.

"Did you apologize?" His stubbornness grated at my very last nerve.

"Fucking hell, Chase! Yes, she's completely satisfied. Now get your ass in the car and come get me!"

I ended our call before the little shit had a chance to say anything else. My mind was perplexed as to why I was the bad guy. Addy was the one with all the secrets. She was the reason I fell. She was the one who dealt out bits and pieces of her past to me like pins in a voodoo doll.

I was the one dealing with the shitstorm my father left behind. I was the one taking care of my family's needs while my sister tended to her own life and my brother kept his own little secrets about our mother. It was all bullshit. I would have loved to have seen Chase handle everything I did without the occasional drink. It didn't make me an alcoholic, and it sure as hell didn't make me my father.

All I needed was a drink.

I had to get her out of my head. She always had to

one-up me. She was smarter than me and had more money. At every turn she made some charitable contribution of both her time and money, while I was the selfish, materialistic bastard. I sent her thirty-two bouquets of flowers for her birthday and she surprised me with a trip to Spain for mine. My parents died, but hers were brutally murdered. Then for the finale, I treated her like shit after my mother died and she selflessly surrendered her body to me. She willingly accepted my pain while I took her for my pleasure ... on her birthday, that I refused to fucking acknowledge, but knew like the date was carved on my heart.

All I needed was a drink.

CHAPTER TEN

Addy

<u>*Journal Day 60*</u>
Grateful to be alive.

Some people cut themselves to get relief from pressure or emotional pain that's too overwhelming. To an emotionally stable person, this act seems insane. Not to me. I completely understood. In my own way, I had become a cutter, but Quinn was my blade and my scars were emotional.

I wasn't aware of just how alone and emotionally-stripped I felt after losing my family, until I met Quinn. He made me feel alive, equal parts pain and pleasure, but alive. I didn't just love him, I loved my addiction to him. I loved the life that flowed through my veins when I was with him. I loved that he made me laugh and cry. I loved that he made me scream in pleasure and pain. Every time he cut me, no matter how emotionally crippling it felt, relief rained down to remind me that I was in fact ... alive.

It had been one week since Elena's funeral, and I was back to looking for purpose in each day.

One day.

One hour.

One minute.

One second at a time was how I lived.

Mac drove to Milwaukee the day after I returned from Spain for another play-by-play of the fucked-up saga that I called my life. Then there was Jake ... *ah Jake*. He was the fleeting rainbow after the storm. It didn't matter how much debris was scattered from the storm, if you were looking at the rainbow, it meant you survived it. If there was one absolute truth in my life by that point, it was that I was a survivor.

After dodging him for that entire first week after I returned from Spain, he showed up at my door with dinner.

"Hey, gorgeous! Hungry?" His smile lit up the room and all I could see was the rainbow.

"Starving." I smiled and motioned for him to come in.

He set the sack down on the counter and snaked his arms around me in a warm embrace. "God, I missed you."

I waited for more but that's all he said. No "Where

were you?" or "Why didn't you call?" just an honest heartfelt sentiment. He pulled back and searched my eyes for a brief moment before his lips brushed mine. It was as if he was asking permission or testing the water between us. That small gesture of consideration was all it took for me to lean into his mouth. The kiss was soft and patient. He ghosted his hands over my arms and then interlaced our fingers before he ended our kiss.

"Shall we eat?" His smile was infectious.

"Absolutely. What's in the bag?"

He pulled out two covered bowls. "Ginger carrot soup."

I grabbed spoons and eased the lids off. "Mmm, smells amazing."

"I stole the recipe from this hot chef that used to mentor me."

Sipping a spoonful, I winked at him. "Oh my gosh, this tastes amazing. Your mentor must have been a culinary genius."

"Yeah, and real modest."

We enjoyed our dinner with casual conversation, mainly about the Café and some ideas Jake had for the holiday menu. Eventually my leave of absence became the elephant in the room.

"Jake, I can't tell you how much I appreciate your patience with me. Any other guy ... well, given our relationship over the past few months ... would have been knocking at my door, demanding answers. But you never called or messaged me while I was gone, and when I came home you waited a week when we both know you knew I was home. And even tonight, you have yet to ask—"

"It doesn't matter. I guess I assumed you were with ... him. But now you're back, alone, and—"

"His mom died."

A grimace spread across his face and his posture wilted.

"She had cancer and she asked me to take her home, to Spain. I stayed with her until she died."

The specific details weren't important, but he deserved to know why I left. Jake was a friend, and we had been intimate, but beyond that our relationship was undefined. He also deserved to know what happened the night before I left to come home.

"I'm so sorry. That must have been hard for you."

"It was. Elena was a wonderful woman and she will be missed." As I set our spoons in the sink, I felt two strong arms slide around my waist. I wrapped my arms around his and leaned my head back against his broad chest. Closing my eyes, I searched for the words that needed to be said. There really was no easy way to say it, so I went with the four words that said it all. "I slept with Quinn."

Jake's body was still pressed to the back of mine, and I expected some physical reaction, a flinch or his muscles tensing, but he didn't move. I waited until the silence was unbearable, then I turned to face him. His face was blank and completely void of emotion. "Say something," I pleaded, as I nervously picked at my fingernails.

"What do you want me to say?"

"I want you to tell me what you're feeling."

He turned and walked toward the windows, then put his hands behind his head with his fingers interlaced. "I don't know, Addy. What am I supposed to feel? After all, when our relationship got physical, you told me not to expect anything more than sex. So I didn't, at first." One of his hands dropped down to his side while the other clenched the back of his neck, as if trying to relieve some tension. "But then we started spending all of our free time together and ... well, I don't know, I guess in my mind, we were moving past the sex-only part without actually having an official talk about it."

"Jake, I care for you and it was never my intention to hurt you, but it was also never my intention for us to be anything more than ..." The words escaped me, or maybe they were never there.

"Never more than friends with benefits?" He finally turned to face me again.

I nodded, looking at the floor.

"Well, it doesn't matter now, since you're back with Quinn." He shrugged his shoulders.

Of course he would think I was back with Quinn. After all, I just told him I slept with him. "We're not back together," I said in a timid voice.

"What? I don't understand."

"We're not back together, it was ... or he was just ... God, I don't know!" I ran my fingers through my hair in frustration. Anger took over, but it had nothing to do with Jake. "He's a fucked-up drunk and I'm emotionally broken. It hurts to be with him and it hurts to be without him. Then there's you and you're so wonderful and—" Emotions uncontrollably flowed from my mouth, and I could barely keep up with my jumbled thoughts. Jake pulled me into his arms and the tears poured down my face.

"Shh, it's okay. This is quite the mess. Quinn's a drunk, you're emotionally broken, and I'm wonderful all right. I'm wonderfully in love with a woman who's given her heart to someone else."

No! No! No!

I pulled back to look him in the eyes as I shook my head. "No, Jake, you're not in love with me."

He held my face, wiping my tears with his thumbs. "I'm sorry, I know it's not the best timing, but I am."

Stepping back, I wiped the rest of my face with the backs of my fingers. "You deserve better than me."

"Why do people say that? I mean ... that's such a cliché. It's like you're implying that something is wrong with you, when what you mean is something is wrong with me."

"You're right, it is a cliché. What you think is implied usually is, but that's not what I mean. Quinn does have my heart and he always will, to some extent. And I don't know what the future holds for us, if there even is an *us*. Right now, I can't imagine having the same feelings for any other man, but honestly I never imagined having the feelings for him that I do. So when I say that you deserve better, I don't mean a better person, I mean a better love. You're young and you have a chance to find love and happiness now. I can't allow you to wait for me because I don't know if I can ever love you the way you love me."

I reached for his hands and held them in mine. "You deserve a love that consumes you, ignites an insatiable passion in your heart, and awakens a part of your soul that you never knew existed. A love shared so equal that you don't recognize where yours ends and hers begins. Everything about it will be undeniable, as if the fate of your love is stronger than any other force on Earth."

His face was unreadable, then his next words punched me in the gut so hard I almost couldn't breathe. "Then why are you here?"

Journal Day 70
Grateful for the courage to fight for my future.

YOUNG JAKE FLIPPED the switch for me. It was hypocritical of me to tell him to look for his one true love when I walked away from mine. Why was I there? What was I doing? The answer was simple. I was floundering.

The Café was no longer mine. My best friend was in Chicago, but I wasn't. I had a Ph.D. but wasn't using it. Unimaginable circumstances gave me the means to do absolutely anything I wanted. The words "wasted potential" came to mind as if my parents were sending me a message. My life needed to be more than hanging out at a café that was no longer mine and having casual sex with a great guy who would never own my heart. But my "wasted potential" could wait, my heart could not. Quinn and I had unfinished business. Our story was not over. It would never be over.

Journal Day 71
Grateful for the strength to let go of my safety net.

TIME WAS OF THE ESSENCE. My monkey brain was too unpredictable. Sitting idle in my loft contemplating my options was counterproductive. Before the Café opened I went to talk to Jake.

"Hey, Jake."

He was in the kitchen washing fruit in preparation for the breakfast juice rush. When he turned to me, my heart squeezed at the hint of sadness on his face. "Hey, yourself."

In that moment, I wanted Jake to be the one. My life would have been so much easier. He was the perfect mix of focused and carefree; he was kind, funny, giving, and he made me feel beautiful and special. However, just like the bird or whale that instinctually navigates thousands of miles to survive, I would have gone to Hell and back to be with Quinn. Being with him felt like my survival instinct.

"Listen, I thought about what you said and you were right. I shouldn't be here."

"Addy, that's not what I meant. I shouldn't have said that. I was just—"

"Honest. You were brutally honest, and I needed to hear it. Anyway, I wanted to let you know that I'm leaving."

He nodded and let out a deep breath. "For how long?"

"Indefinitely."

"Don't do this. You don't need to leave."

"I do. It's time. I belong with him and I'm going to do whatever it takes to make him realize it too. But, for you, my dear Jake, I want you to have my loft."

"What? No, I can't. What if you decide to come back?"

Tears stung my eyes as I bit my upper lip and shook my head. "I'm not coming back."

His brow furrowed as he pulled me into his chest. "I scared you off. I said too much."

"No! Don't ever think that. You woke me up. You reminded me that life should be lived to the fullest, without regret. I want you to do the same. The pain of heartbreak is worth it when you find the person who you were born to love."

I pulled back and pushed up on my toes and pressed my lips to the corner of his mouth. "You're the best detour I've ever taken."

He smiled as I turned to leave. "Addy?"

I stopped, but didn't turn back around. "Yeah?"

"If he hurts you ... I'll break every bone in his body."

The corners of my mouth curled up. "I know."

CHAPTER ELEVEN

<u>Journal Day 80</u>
Grateful for the piles of dry, crunchy leaves that have blan-
keted the ground and how they remind me of the best days
of my life. Grateful for the clarity of those beautiful memo-
ries that I will replay for the rest of my life.

It was destination Chicago, with a detour through New York. I officially emptied my entire loft and had my furnishings sent to Chicago to be put in storage. There was only one thing that stood between me and making my new home in the Windy City ... Quinn.

I carried around the unopened letter from Elena. Somehow I knew her words would be life changing for me, so I saved it for the day when I might need those words to take my next breath. My intuition led me to believe that day was coming soon. It had been almost a month since I'd seen Quinn. I had no illusions about what I might find in New York. Mac and Evan were eager to have me back in Chicago, but they were also onboard with my plans to get Quinn back no matter how long it took.

On the way to New York, my mind toiled through all the possibilities of what I might find when I arrived at Quinn's condo. The thought of him with someone else was gut-wrenching, but nonetheless a real possibility. There was also a high probability that he would be drunk and angry or downright cruel. Of course I hoped for the virtually impossible scenario: him sober, alone, and desperately missing me.

Eventually, I had to force myself to think of something else because planning for the unknown felt like a torturous emotional suicide. The radio was a perfect distraction. After all, a road trip wasn't official until the hippy Prius driver elicited at least a dozen crazy looks from other drivers mildly entertained by my lip-syncing to the radio. At least it looked like lip-syncing from their car, but on the inside of Karma I put on a Grammy-winning performance.

It was almost 9:00 p.m. by the time I made it to Manhattan. Standing outside of Quinn's door, the violent pounding of my heart made my chest feel on the verge of bursting.

Deep breath ... I am peaceful, I am strong.

I rang the doorbell and held my breath. Never in my life had I felt so nervous. I had to clench my teeth to keep them from chattering. My whole body was nothing short of a wreck. I felt like vomiting, fainting, and crying all at the same time.

Holy crap, Addy, get a grip!

Then the door opened. Quinn stood glassy-eyed, in charcoal pants, and a gray and white striped shirt, with the sleeves rolled up to his elbows and the top two buttons undone. The scenario of a sober, alone, and desperately-missing-me Quinn did not stand before me. He looked me up and down once with an angry scowl on his face.

"No," was all he said before he slammed the door in my face.

Round one goes to Quinn.

He got in the first punch, and I'll admit I was shook up a bit. I wasn't expecting such a quick rejection. Like any good fighter, I shook it off and knocked on the door.

No answer. Reaching in my bag for his key with my right hand, I tried the knob with my left. It was open.

Peeking around the corner, I saw him slouched in the corner of his couch with a rocks glass filled with ice and amber liquid in one hand, and his other draped over the arm. He was watching C-SPAN and didn't acknowledge my entrance. I dropped my bag to the floor and walked over to him. When he still refused to look at me, I positioned myself directly in front of him, blocking his view of the TV. He took a swig of his drink, then made eye contact with me.

"Get the fuck out." His voice was icy, but calm.

"No." I crossed my arms over my chest in defiance.

He stood, and our bodies were so close that his abdomen pressed against my crossed arms. I felt so small next to him. His dark, menacing eyes glowered down at me, but I held my own, refusing to budge one single inch.

"Then I'm leaving," he said, then threw back the rest of his drink and wiped the corner of his mouth with the back of his arm.

He grabbed his keys and headed toward the door.

"I'll be here when you get back," I called out in a surprisingly steady voice.

A cynical laugh escaped past his arrogant smirk. "I never took you for the type who liked to watch." Then he was out the door.

Deep breath ... I am peaceful, I am strong.

Time passed at an agonizingly slow rate over the next hour. The corner of my bottom lip was nearly raw from nervously working it between my teeth as I sat idle on his couch. A door opened, startling me from my anxious state. At first I thought it was déjà vu, but it wasn't. It was simply history repeating itself. Quinn was draped over some hussy, or maybe it was just some poor girl with daddy issues. This time the pain was more from seeing him self-destruct, versus seeing him with another woman. Neither one paid a bit of attention to me as they groped each other all the way up the stairs. I'd just stepped into a reality improv. Quinn was unpredictable, and I had no choice but to play off his every move.

I marched up the stairs after them, and just as his

bedroom door started to shut, I shoved it open. The unsuspecting brunette froze when she saw me. Quinn peeled his lips off her neck and turned in my direction. I crossed my arms over my chest again; it somehow gave me confidence, or maybe it symbolically shielded my heart. He glared at me with a hint of confusion in his eyes.

"You implied I could watch. So by all means, continue. Don't mind me."

Without hesitation, he turned his back to me and started undressing the young brunette as his mouth attacked her lips, neck, and chest. His porno was a horror movie to me, but I refused to look away. It would take more than a one-night floozy to make me give up. He pushed her back to the bed, and as he removed her bra, she looked over his shoulder at me. I smiled as her eyes stayed glued to mine.

"Quinn?" she said nervously as she tried to push him away.

He stopped and looked back at me. I delivered the same smile to him. No longer finding the humor in the situation, he walked toward me and grabbed my arms pushing me into the hall. "I changed my mind," was all he said before yet another door was slammed in my face. This time I heard the click of the lock, one I didn't have a key to open.

Deep breath ... I am peaceful, I am strong.

ROUND TWO GOES TO ADDY.

Life has to be the proverbial glass of water, just so everyone can choose to be the half-empty pessimist or the half-full optimist. I knew what the view looked like from both rims. Despite Quinn screwing someone else just feet from where I slept, I chose to see it half full. After all, when he shut the front door on me he could have locked it, but he didn't. When he kicked me out of his room he could have made me leave his condo, but he didn't. Most significantly, he could have fucked the brunette in front of me, leaving a visual that would be etched into my brain forever, but he didn't.

I left the door to the guest room across the hall from Quinn's open all night. There was no need to hide my presence from either one of them. It was a restless night of sleep. Truthfully, I didn't need a visual. I'd been with him in every way imaginable, so it was too easy to imagine him in all the same positions with someone else.

My modified mantra was "it's just sex, not love." Around five o'clock the next morning I was brought out of my light sleep by the sound of his door opening. Lying on my back, I propped myself up on my elbows and gazed out into the hall. My room was dark, so I'm not sure if he could see me, but I saw him walk out in running pants and a sweatshirt. He paused for a moment, looking into my room with an expressionless face, before he proceeded down the stairs. In light of the state he was in when I arrived, I was pleased to see he still exercised. It was a sign that he hadn't given up on himself—just me. I could work with that.

Not able to get back to sleep, I threw on some yoga clothes and went downstairs to push my body through an hour of physically demanding Ashtanga Yoga. Working up a good sweat through an intense workout was exactly what I needed to prepare myself for day two. As I cooled down in Butterfly pose, stretching my hips and lower back, the young brunette made the walk of shame down the stairs. She looked twenty, at best, and when she saw me she jumped.

"Oh shit, you scared me!" she breathed out in a panic.

I smiled and cocked my head to the side. "Can I get you some breakfast?"

Looking completely befuddled, she shook her head while scratching it. "Uh, no, I need to leave." She pointed to the door as she grabbed her purse from the floor, keeping her eyes on me like I was some sort of dangerous predator.

I put my palms together with my thumbs at my heart and my fingers spread out. "Namaste," I saluted and bowed forward. She was out the door in a flash.

Before I jumped in the shower, I scrounged through the kitchen and found plenty of fruit to throw together a fresh smoothie. It was a good sign that Helen, Quinn's housekeeper, still took care of him.

While I sipped my smoothie, I texted Mac to let her know I'd made it to New York and had initiated Operation Take Back My Man. Given that it was a Wednesday, I assumed Quinn was at work and I wouldn't see him until later. When I reached the top of the stairs, my curiosity pulled me into Quinn's room. Choosing to ignore the tangled sheets on his bed, I walked through the bathroom to his closet. When I flipped on the light, I froze. I couldn't believe what I saw.

The right side of the closet was still neatly lined with all the clothes I'd left behind. I slowed, stepping in farther, and opened the lower drawers. Sure enough, everything was just how I'd left it. A tear escaped one of my eyes, but I quickly wiped it away. It felt like a small victory, but I knew it would take more than that to win the war.

THAT EVENING, I made dinner. Soft music played in the background when Quinn came home. He tossed his keys on the entry table then loosened his tie as he spied me in the kitchen chopping red onions and carrots for the kale salad. My fitted black mini sweater dress hugged my curves and the V-neckline showed a nice amount of cleavage.

Glancing up, I smiled. "Hey, baby. How was your day?"

He walked over to the bar and poured himself a drink. As he sipped it, his eyes traveled down my dress to my bare legs and finally ended at my black high-heeled ankle boots. His mouth stayed neutral, but I detected appreciation in his heated eyes.

"What are you doing?" he asked with a hint of exasperation in his voice.

"Making dinner."

After taking another sip of his drink, he slammed his cup down on the bar. "That's not what I mean!" he growled.

Pausing to absorb the impact of his reaction, I took a deep breath and continued slicing the knife through the carrots. Keeping my eyes on the cutting board, I felt his body press to the back of mine. He grabbed my right wrist and squeezed it until I dropped the knife. My whole body tensed.

Closing my eyes, I willed myself to stay calm. I wasn't sure how much alcohol he'd had, but I knew he wouldn't hurt me. He moved forward another step until I was pinned against the counter. His hands moved to my hips, and then he slid them down to the hem of my dress.

"If you needed a quick fuck, all you had to do was say so. I'm sure you felt a little left out last night." His voice grated in my ear. Both hands fisted the hem of my dress, then as he pulled it up, completely exposing me.

My breath caught in my throat. He tried to scare me, but I knew the man who called me the love of his life and that's who I focused on as I closed my eyes and braced my hands on the counter. My teeth gritted together as he ripped my panties off. His hard cock straining against his pants rubbed into my backside.

"Is this what you want?" he seethed as I heard the

sound of his zipper. I was grateful that he couldn't see my face and the tears streaming down my cheeks. A moment later I felt the warm flesh of his erection at my entrance. He wanted to make me feel violated and used, so I did the only thing I could think of to turn the tables.

"I love you, Quinn." The words weren't a plea, they were a promise.

No matter how hard he tried to make me hate him, I never would. His body stilled. I waited to feel him push into me, but he didn't. Keeping my eyes closed, I felt the loss of all contact, but I remained static. A few moments later the front door slammed. I opened my eyes to find myself alone. After pushing my dress back down my body, I picked my shredded panties up off the floor and tossed them in the trash. Then I wiped my eyes and continued making dinner. There was no time for a pity party, no room for weakness, and no turning back.

Round three goes to Addy.

As EXPECTED, a few hours later Quinn came barging through the door, drunk, with a new flavor hanging all over him. Before they had the chance to get upstairs without acknowledging me, I clicked off the TV and strutted to the stairs like I owned the place. His guest glared at me.

"Who is she?" she sneered.

"I'm the love of his life," I said with a strong, confident voice as I walked upstairs in front of them. A few steps into the guest room I turned and caught Quinn's eyes as he paused a minute before he started to shut the door.

"I still love you." I held his steel gaze until the door closed. Sucking in a shaky breath, I collapsed on the bed and prayed for time to pass quickly. It didn't. I was cutting myself again with him—the man I loved was in that beautiful body ... somewhere.

Sleep didn't find me, so by four-thirty the next morning I was downstairs, doing yoga by the illumination of the city lights that came through the large windows. Each move grounded me, and with every breath I gained strength for another day.

By five o'clock I heard Quinn jog down the stairs. He was dressed to work out again. I paused only briefly when he turned the corner at the bottom of the stairs and met my eyes. The mix of anguish and contempt on his face made me wonder if this torture would ever end. The early-twenties Addy was gone forever, but I hated the thought of the Quinn who made love to me on the beach in the Canary Islands vanishing from existence. I just couldn't let him go.

"Good morning," I whispered with a warm smile.

He grabbed his keys and stared at them in his hand. "I fly out of town tonight. When I get back on Monday I expect you and all your shit to be out of here."

"No." I continued to the next pose.

"Dammit, Addy!" he yelled, crossing the room and standing at the end of my mat with a menacing scowl and twitching muscle in his jaw. He was on edge and I pushed him to his limit. "We are over. You need to *get that!*"

Standing up straight, I came toe-to-toe with him, refusing to back down. "We will *never* be over. *You* need to *get that*," I growled back through clenched teeth, before brushing past him. As I reached the top of the stairs, I heard the front door slam shut.

We were at the point in a fight where it was impossible to keep score; both contenders had bleeding cuts and wobbled to stay standing. It was no longer about tactics or outsmarting the opponent. The victory would be won by sheer determination and the stamina to go the distance. It had to be me. I didn't put my life on hold and drive fourteen hours to watch him fuck a new girl every night and verbally abuse me, just to tuck my tail between my legs and go home to Chicago empty handed.

THE REST of the day was uneventful. The hussy from the previous night made her walk of shame, I greeted her and offered her breakfast, she declined and left. I called Mac during lunch and shared a play-by-play of the saga. She was speechless, which was a first for her.

"Am I totally insane?" I knew the answer, but I needed to hear it from her.

"Yes, but in a completely diehard, romantic way. Seriously, who watches the person they love traipse a new woman to bed every night and then offers them breakfast in the morning?"

"What can I say, I like to think outside of the box."

"Outside of the box? Are you kidding me? We're talking not even in the same physical dimension. But I've got to hand it to you, Addy, you've got the biggest balls I've ever seen."

We both laughed for a moment, then a serious silence settled over the line. "What if it's not enough? What if I've already lost him?" My voice quavered.

"Stop, don't you dare think that. You'll get through, just don't—"

"Don't what?"

She hesitated. "Just don't lose yourself along the way. No man is worth that, okay?"

I didn't respond. I couldn't. My life felt like everything with him and nothing without him. Maybe I'd already lost myself in him. Maybe I wasn't just searching for the Quinn I remembered, maybe I was searching for the version of myself that only existed with him.

"No matter what, you're coming home for Thanksgiving, right?"

That was two weeks away and I'd honestly forgotten about it. Leaving Quinn was not an option, but in Mac's mind, neither was skipping out on Thanksgiving. That only left me with one option—I had to get through to him in the next fourteen days. It wasn't going to be easy, especially since he was leaving that night and I wouldn't be with him all weekend.

"Right, Thanksgiving ... no matter what."

"Great! See you in two weeks. Good luck, sweetie, and don't worry, he'll come around."

"Thanks." I wasn't so sure.

CHAPTER TWELVE

<u>Journal Day 85</u>.
Grateful for Quinn's return, even if the clock is ticking.

THE WEEKEND WAS lonely and boring. Wondering where Quinn was and with whom he was traveling wreaked havoc on my sanity. By Monday morning my nerves buzzed with anticipation. He usually came home after his trips, before going to his office, but my presence had changed his routine a bit, so I had no idea when to expect him.

I felt like the kid who waited out the countdown to punishment, still standing defiantly when the clock reached zero. He had made it clear that I was to be gone by the time he came home, but I wasn't. My "shit" was in the same place as it was when he left. I'd even gone with Helen on Friday afternoon to get groceries. She was a little confused about our new living arrangements, but I assured her it was temporary until we ironed things out. Helen was a woman of very few words, but the inquisitive look in her eyes told me the wheels in her head were constantly turning. I could only imagine what she thought about the mess between me and Quinn.

It was almost noon by the time Quinn came home. My time was up. The countdown was over. We were at zero. As promised, I stayed, but it was his play and I anxiously waited for his next move. After tossing his keys on the counter, he pegged me at the kitchen table and shook his head. "Have it your way," he mumbled as he carried his bags up the stairs.

It was only a matter of moments before I saw what "my way" was. Quinn paraded down the stairs with his arms full of my clothes from his closet. He opened the front door and tossed them into the hallway.

Shit!

Then he marched back up the stairs and repeated the same process until all of my belongings were strewn out in the hall. I didn't make any attempt to move the whole time, and he never looked in my direction.

When he finished he grabbed my handbag by the door and riffled through it. Eventually he pulled out the key to his condo. Then his eyes found mine again and he charged toward me as if I was a bug he was getting ready to squash. In those few seconds that it took for him to reach me, I felt like the child about to get spanked. There was no escape. My ass was glued to the kitchen chair, but not for long. He grabbed me and threw me over his shoulder.

"Time's up. Take your stubborn ass home and leave me the fuck alone!" With little regard for how I landed, he tossed me down on top of my stuff in the hall and slammed the door.

Round four goes to Quinn. Shit, shit, double shit!

Money can't buy happiness, true story. I had enough money to buy the entire building, yet there I sat on my ass amongst my "shit" in the hallway connecting multi-million dollar condominiums. *Well done, Addy.*

While I wallowed in self-pity, there was a brief moment when I thought the universe had delivered the official sign that I wasn't meant to be with Quinn. Then an angel of mercy appeared in the form of Quinn's neighbor, Mr. Grant. The tall, balding man was in his seventies and we had shared pleasantries numerous times when I had lived with Quinn. His wife was a cancer survivor who rarely left the building except to go on doctor's visits. He was heading out when the disaster in the hallway stopped him in his tracks.

"Addy?"

"Hey, Mr. Grant, how's it going?" I asked casually as if I didn't look like the most pathetic person in the world.

"I take it you and Mr. Cohen had a falling-out?" he

asked with raised eyebrows as he scanned my belongings.

I stood up and brushed off my jeans. "No, why would you think that?"

He tilted his head to the side and shot me a disapproving look.

I sighed. "Okay, yes, but it's just temporary."

"Well, good luck with that, dear. The missus and I are leaving for the winter, so you won't have to worry about your lover's feuds disturbing us." He started to walk toward the elevator.

"Wait!" I called as I hurried to him. "Do you have someone staying at your place while you're gone?"

He shook his head. "No need, we don't have plants or pets so—"

"Could I rent your condo from you for say ... the next month?" My puppy dog eyes pleaded with his as much as my soft but urgent voice.

It didn't look too promising from the apprehensive wrinkles in his nose, but I was desperate. "I'll pay you."

"How much?" He crossed his arms over his chest.

"Ten grand."

"Thirty," he countered.

"Twenty."

"Twenty-five, last chance," he deadpanned.

Quinn's door opened. He stepped over my "shit" and started toward the elevators where Mr. Grant and I stood.

"Fine," I whispered through gritted teeth, "but I move my stuff in today."

We both turned and smiled at Quinn as he approached. "Mr. Grant." He nodded his head in greeting while completely ignoring me. As he stepped into the elevator, Mr. Grant shared the news.

"Well, Mr. Cohen, looks like your lady friend will be staying at my condo for the next month."

The doors started to close as Quinn reached his hand out and stop them. "What the—" he started to yell, but his voice faded as the doors completely shut and the elevator descended.

Yep, round five goes to Addy.

THE GRANTS' condo was a similar floor plan to Quinn's, but the earthy tones, silk floral arrangements, and decor pillows gave it a homier feel. A woman's touch did that. I had the hall cleared by three o'clock, and I even arranged for the Grants' transportation to the airport. It was a fortunate change of events that I was able to stay next door to Quinn, but it still put me out of sight ... and maybe out of mind. The sad truth was I honestly had no idea what my next move would be. It seemed pretty unlikely that he would accept a neighborly dinner invite. He would be at work most of the time, and his evenings were unpredictable. I needed an in, but I had no idea what that was.

The next two days were uneventful. I didn't see Quinn once. The clock ticked and I had to step up my game, which wasn't hard when at that moment I wasn't even in the game. My first task was to elicit help tracking Quinn. I called Tom at the front desk and pleaded my case. All I needed was for him to alert me when he saw Quinn pull into the parking garage on the security cameras. He was apprehensive about it, even though I assumed he felt indebted to me after the gift I gave him on the security camera—the infamous girl hits Lamborghini, boy gets blow job in the parking garage incident. But like all the other greedy bastards in the building, Tom had his price too and once I found it, he was putty in my hands.

My phone rang with the heads-up call around 8:00 p.m. Tom also kindly warned me Quinn wasn't alone. No big surprise. There was no changing the fact that I'd fallen in love with an eternal playboy. I had been patiently waiting for hours, dressed in my shortest black cocktail dress and fuck-me heels. My makeup and long wavy hair looked like I was ready for a photo shoot. I grabbed my clutch purse and spied out the peephole until the elevator doors opened.

Deep breath ... I am peaceful, I am strong.

I threw back my shoulders and opened the door. As he stepped off the elevator with his bleach blonde easy lay for the night, he came to an abrupt halt, almost sending her face to the floor as she tripped over his feet. As I confidently strutted toward the elevator, his eyes raked over my body exactly how I knew they would.

My perfect, fake smile was appropriate for that

meeting. "Hello, Mr. Cohen and … friend, have a pleasant evening." I kept moving right past them into the elevator then turned around and pushed the button. Right as the doors started to close, Quinn shoved his foot into one side stopping them. He held up his finger and motioned for the girl to wait, then he stepped into the elevator mere inches from me as the doors closed behind him.

"What exactly do you think you're doing?" he asked in a slow, deep, agitated voice.

My heels put me up a few more inches on him allowing his alcohol-laden breath to drift over my face. "I'm going out."

"Alone … in this?" He nodded his head, motioning to my provocative attire.

I put my hands on my hips, "Yes, I'm going out alone, but I'm pretty sure because of *this…*" I ran my hands down my hips and pushed my chest farther in his direction "…I won't be coming home alone."

"What the fuck is that supposed to mean?" he growled inching even closer.

"It means while you have your head in your ass and your dick in some other girl, I'm going to find someone else to scratch my itch."

The elevator chimed as the doors opened. I stepped to the side and went to walk out when he grabbed my arm and turned me back into him.

"Nobody else is going to scratch your fucking—"

"Hands off!" I snapped as I stepped back out of the

elevator. "If we're over, then why the hell do you care who I'm under tonight?" He had nothing to say. "That's what I thought. Good night, Quinn." I hustled away, leaving him in the same pile of agony he'd been leaving me in since I arrived in New York. Mission accomplished for the night. The only kink in my plan was that I had no intention of bringing some stranger home. I found a hotel to stay at for the night and I made sure to get home the next morning right around 5:00 a.m. My makeup was a little smeared and my hair was in disarray, but wearing the same dress and carrying my high heels was a stroke of genius, or so I thought.

Quinn stood by the Grants' door wearing his jogging pants and a hoodie as I stepped off the elevator.

"Where the hell have you been?"

"Good morning to you too." I smiled as I nudged him aside so I could unlock the door. He followed me in and closed the door behind us.

"What do you want from me?" he asked, leaning against the door with his arms folded over his chest.

Dropping my shoes on the floor, I turned to face him. "I don't want anything from you. I just want you." A huge weight lifted from my chest. I was finally able to say the words I'd wanted to say from the moment I arrived.

"I can't be with you."

"Why not?"

"Because there's too much in the past I can't forget."

He was preaching to the choir, but that excuse wasn't going to work with me. "Yeah, well that's exactly why I'm here. There's too much in our past I can't forget, like the way you used to look at me and touch me. The sound of your voice when we'd talk for hours on the phone, or the way you'd rearrange your entire schedule to be with me for only a few hours. I miss the feel of your body holding me in the morning and the taste of your lips when you kissed me goodbye. I miss the smell of you on me and the way I didn't want to shower until I knew you were going to be home soon, because all of my senses craved you. I can't forget the way my whole body felt alive and living for only you when we made love, or how you stole every last piece of my heart and captured my soul when you called me the love of your life and asked me to be your wife." I laid my hands on his chest and looked up into his pained eyes. "It's *too much* for me to live without you."

He stood with his hands at his sides, completely still, ignoring my touch. Every cell in my body begged him to take me in his arms, but instead the rejection sent chills through me. Words were unnecessary. I could see it in his eyes, but he said it anyway. "I'm sorry, I can't." Then he turned and left.

Round six goes to Quinn.

Journal Day 88
Grateful for time.

THE IDEA WAS if I'm grateful for something it can't be my enemy. While most of the world worked hard to earn a living or make some worthwhile contribution to society, I brainstormed my next move. It was exhausting because not so long ago I was a worker and volunteer, making a difference. I had to resolve the situation soon and not just because of Thanksgiving, because Mac was right ... I was losing myself.

By the time I got the heads-up call from Tom that evening, I still had no idea what my next move was. Helpless and clueless, all I could do was spy out the peephole and wait to see his latest sacrificial lamb. As fights go, this was the moment I got knocked down and nearly knocked out. Up until that point, I believed Quinn still held a piece of us in his heart. I sensed his internal struggle, that what he said and what he felt were at conflict, but what met my eyes through the little hole in the door was a clear sign that he meant business. I blinked my eyes several times to make sure it wasn't an illusion, but it wasn't, *she* wasn't.

Hello, Olivia.

Quinn, alcohol, and Olivia. It was the worst possible combination. He looked completely wasted, far worse than I had seen him since I arrived in New York. She looked a little inebriated herself. I couldn't tell who held whom up. Hysteria boiled inside of me. I wanted to throw open the door and tear out her hair, and ironically his too. This was the definition of "low blow." The debilitating cocktail of emotions I felt the first night ripped through my body like a hurricane, only this time I couldn't hold them back.

I ran to the bathroom and expelled the contents of my stomach as tears trailed down my cheeks, the one thing that kept me from fainting was the close proximity of the cold tile floor.

Journal Day 89
Grateful for a place to call home. One week until Thanksgiving, I'll be there soon ... alone.

SOMETIMES SPENDING the night on the bathroom floor brings clarity to an otherwise cloudy situation. It was time to go home. I said what I needed to say and I did everything I could think of to bring Quinn back from his darkness, but sometimes even your best wasn't enough. I packed up my belongings and called Mac to give her my concession speech.

"Please tell me you've wrangled that Arabian horse of yours and you're coming home early." The excitement in her voice squeezed my heart to the point of pain.

"Well, you're right on one account. I'm coming home early."

"Oh, Addy, no," she whispered.

I held my breath hoping it would keep my emotions in check, but it didn't. The sobs came and they vibrated uncontrollably through my body. "It's—it's—over."

"Oh, sweetie, shh, calm down and tell me what happened." Her voice was soft and comforting, but too far away.

I told her everything and occasionally she offered soothing words of encouragement, but mostly she just listened. Shattered was the only word to describe how I felt.

"Sweetie, I know you're ready to come home and believe me, I am so ready to see you again, but I want to try something. Will you stay just a couple more days?"

"What? Why?"

"Just trust me, okay?"

I laughed. "Are you serious? Those are your famous last words before we end up in jail."

"Good point. Just do this for me, even if you don't trust me. How about that?"

I wiped my eyes and sniffled. "This better be good. I'm leaving this weekend no matter what."

"Oh it's going to be good, don't you worry about that. Now chin up, shoulders back, and remember you're a beautiful, brilliant, and ridiculously generous woman who will find happiness. It also doesn't hurt that you have the most amazingly awesome friend in the world. See you in a few days, love you."

"Love you too ... and, Mac?"

"Yeah?"

"I do trust you."

A pleasant hum came over the line. I imagined her smiling.

CHAPTER THIRTEEN

Journal Day 90
Grateful for Mac: my rock, my best friend, my family.

I STAYED LOCKED up in the Grants' condo for the next twenty-four hours, waiting for Mac's move. Of course I assumed she would show up soon, probably ready to knock down Quinn's door and give him the worst tongue lashing anyone had ever had.

There was no doubt in my mind that it would never work, but at that point I had nothing to lose. I understood she felt the need to try and help me. Allowing her to have a run at Quinn would give us both peace of mind that we had tried everything. With complete certainty, I knew in the end we would leave New York on Sunday without Quinn.

By noon I was going crazy, so I texted Mac.

Where are you?

Um … home, why?

> Are you kidding? What are you waiting for? I'm going insane, I thought you'd be here by now.

I'm not going to New York.

> Then what's this plan of yours and when is it taking place?

Patience. The verdict will be in by the time you go to sleep tonight.

> Verdict, what's that supposed to mean?

You'll see, now eat something so you don't pass out … and shave your legs.

> Ugh, you drive me bonkers!

Love you too!

Mac's plan went from predictable to a complete mystery which made me go from resigned and calm to extremely anxious. Eating wasn't so easy, but I managed half a sandwich and some carrots. By 5:00 p.m., I had a path worn on the Grants' wool rug in their great room. I couldn't stop pacing, waiting for the unknown. I imagined just about everything except what actually happened. Tom called up to let me know I had a guest.

"Who is it?" I asked, relieved that the wait was over.

"They requested I not say, just to tell you it's a gift from Mac."

"Send them ... or it up, thanks."

"My pleasure, Miss Brecken."

The suspense was unbearable so I went out the door and waited for the elevator. The elevator doors chimed and I was truly, unequivocally shocked.

"Surprise!"

No way!

He stepped off the elevator and I ran to him almost tackling him as I jumped up and wrapped my arms and legs around him. "Jake!" His name melted off my tongue like a verbal sigh of relief. I was overwhelmed with emotions as my eyes fought back tears and my heart leaped from my chest. There was no doubt that I was happy to see him, but it had only been a few weeks since I had essentially broken his heart. "Why are you here? How are you here?"

"Mac showed up at the Café and made me an offer I couldn't refuse." He grinned as I pulled back to look at him, still clinging to him like a koala bear.

"Wait, I just talked to Mac. She told me she's in Chicago."

"Well, you didn't expect her to be honest and ruin the surprise did you?"

Mac wasn't the best liar and had I called her, I would have known by the tone of her voice that she was lying. Lucky for her I texted. "What was the offer?"

"She said she'd watch the Café for a couple of days if I'd come visit you."

That didn't make much sense to me. "And?"

"Okay, she flew me out here first-class and told me there was a ninety percent chance I'd get to beat the living shit out of Quinn."

"So her plan to help me get Quinn back is for you to beat him into submission?"

"Not exactly—" He looked at me with a devilish grin.

"Then what?"

Before he had a chance to explain, the elevator chimed again. What felt like the worst timing in the world to me, made Jake smile from ear to ear. It was Quinn.

"Then this," Jake said a split second before he clenched his fist in my hair and pressed his mouth to mine. There was nothing friendly about his kiss or the way his other hand grasped my ass holding me tight to his body. My initial instinct was to pull back, but then the lightbulb went on.

Thank you, Mac!

I pressed my hands to his cheeks then ran my fingers up through his hair, fisting it to deepen our kiss. Jake carried me to the door I'd left open, making sure to keep his mouth on mine the whole way.

"God I've missed you," Jake moaned, breaking our kiss after we passed the threshold.

It was a jab to my heart because I didn't know if he said that for Quinn's sake or because he really meant it. The truth was, we had physical chemistry that required no acting. I prayed Jake didn't let the lines become too blurred. He reached for the hem of my shirt and pulled it over my head while he kicked the door with his foot, but the click of the door latching never sounded.

However, Quinn's thundering voice did. "Get your fucking hands off her before I break them off your goddamn arms!" he roared.

Jake's back was to Quinn, and he slid me down his body until I was on my feet, then he flashed me a sly smile and a wink. I wasn't sure if it meant I could take it from there because he'd done his part or if it meant he was finally going to take Quinn down like he'd been anxiously waiting to do for so long. I didn't wait to find out.

I stepped past Jake and walked to the door in my bra and skinny jeans. Quinn was explosive: his eyes looked nearly black, his jaw ticked from side to side, and his fists were clenched like he was ready to attack.

"Get out, Quinn. This doesn't concern you," I said in a slow, firm voice.

"The fucking hell it doesn't!" He didn't look at me. His death glare was aimed at Jake, whom I'd imagined by then was turned around and smirking at Quinn, just daring him to come closer.

I jabbed my finger into his chest. "The moment you traipsed that whore past my door and into your condo, you relinquished all rights to have so much as a casual opinion on who I see or what I do. So go find another pathetic bimbo to fuck because you were right, we are over!" I shoved his chest and he stepped back. "So now it's time for you to take *your* stubborn ass home and leave *me* the hell alone!"

My words even shocked myself as I stood there breathless. In that moment I wondered if Jake was there for Quinn's wake-up call or mine. Adler Sage Brecken was a survivor—a strong, intelligent, and independent woman. How had I turned into a doormat for a man who despised me more than he loved me?

Quinn grabbed my arms and pulled me a breath away from his face. "You. Are. Mine!" he seethed into my face.

Jake was on him in a heartbeat clutching his throat and pinning him to the wall. "She's not anymore," he gritted between his teeth.

I stepped back because the equivalent of two grenades were about to go off. Quinn grabbed Jake's arm and twisted out of his grip then landed a quick blow to Jake's ribs. Jake stood up and held his hands in a fighter's stance, like he did the time I watched him annihilate his opponent in the ring, Quinn's stance mirrored his. I recalled part of Quinn's workout regimen included advanced training in Brazilian Jiu-Jitsu, but I had never seen him use it.

"You don't deserve her, you worthless piece of shit," Jake goaded.

"Well, I'm sure as hell not going to let you have her," Quinn sneered back.

A cocky smile spread across Jake's face. "Too late, man, I've already had her."

That was all it took to officially pull the detonator

on Quinn, who then rammed into Jake drawing first blood. Then the two became a tangled tornado. Quinn shoved Jake into the wall shattering the glass of a large picture frame. Jake charged at Quinn slamming him into a bookcase, then he continued a relentless sequence of jabs to his abdomen and ribs until Quinn broke loose and tackled him to the ground.

I stood frozen and speechless as the fight continued. The dollars in damage to the Grants' condo continued to escalate as vases, coffee tables, picture frames, and sculptures were destroyed. Both of them had bloodied faces, but neither showed any signs of stopping. As they wrestled and fought their way closer to the large windows, I realized I had to put a stop to it before someone ended up crashing through the window and falling to their certain death.

"Stop it!" I yelled, but they didn't listen.

Jake punched Quinn and he fell backward against the window, causing it to crack. Fear overtook all rational thinking as I rushed to stop Jake. I tried to grab his arm as he cocked it down and back ready to give Quinn another blow to his abdomen, but his elbow found my eye and sent my body in the opposite direction and flat on my back.

"Addy!" Jake yelled as he turned around to see what he'd done to me.

"You motherfucker!" Quinn growled as he landed an uppercut to an unsuspecting Jake.

"Addy, oh God, are you okay?" Quinn picked me up amongst the debris and set me on the couch.

"Oh Jesus, Addy—" Jake rushed over to me.

"Back the fuck off!" Quinn yelled as he cupped my cheek with his hand and ghosted his finger over my throbbing eye.

"Just stop, please," I begged in a strained voice.

My eye felt like it was ready to explode. With a grimace on my face, I looked left to Jake, then right to Quinn. They both had pained expressions on their bloodied faces, but it had nothing to do with their pain, it was mine.

"I'll get some ice," Jake said as he stood and walked away.

"I'm so sorry, baby," Quinn whispered as he kneeled on the floor between my legs, still cupping my face.

"Go, just leave," I whispered back in a defeated voice.

I pushed his hand away from my face. "Jake may have hit me by accident, but you're the spiteful bastard who has completely broken me with your hateful words and manwhore ways. I'm not your possession and you can't claim me just because you don't want someone else to have me."

"Addy, I didn't—"

"Go!" I yelled as Jake came back with the ice.

Quinn stood, then he and Jake exchanged volatile scowls for a brief moment, both with clenched fists. Finally, Quinn glanced around the room at the aftermath and then to me once more before his eyes fell to the floor. "It wasn't what you think ... but it doesn't matter now," he said with a hardened expression that didn't match the quiet vulnerability to his voice.

He walked out of the condo closing the door behind him, and although I was uncertain of what he meant, he was right. It didn't matter.

JAKE HELD the icepack to my eye as he clenched his teeth with a grimacing smile.

"It's fine," I said as my eyes moved across his battered face, "you look much worse."

"This is nothing, just a few scrapes." He winked.

The deep cut by his eye did not look like just a scrape. "I should take you for some stitches."

He laughed. "If I'm still breathing and can stand on my own, then there is no need to take me anywhere. I should go clean up my face. I guarantee it looks worse than it is."

He pulled the ice away from my eye. "You, however, are going to have some swelling and nasty coloring for the next week or so."

Taking the ice from him, I shook my head. "I'll be fine. It's my fault anyway." A wave of emotional despair blanketed me, distracting me from the physical pain. My heart felt constricted as I struggled to meet his eyes. "I'm sorry, Jake. You shouldn't be here. Mac was wrong to send you."

"I'm the one who should be apologizing. I told you I'd break every bone in his body if he hurt you, and yet he walked out of here on his own two feet. You didn't mention he's had training in martial arts."

"Didn't I?" My face curled into a wry smile until the tensing of my facial muscles shot a jolt of pain to my eye. I sucked in a breath. "Ouch."

Pushing my hand with the ice in it back to my eye, he raised his bloodied eyebrow. "No you didn't. That's okay, rule number one in fighting: never underestimate your opponent." He scanned the room. "Do you want me to help clean up before I leave?"

"Where are you going?"

"Mac put me up in a nice room overlooking Times Square. She assumed you might have ... other plans tonight. But I can stay—"

"No, it's fine. As you can see I have some damage assessing to do before I write out a sizable check to the Grants."

"Are you sure? I'll stay if you want me to." He searched my eyes, maybe looking for some emotion that indicated I needed him, but it wasn't there.

"Go, enjoy your first-class accommodations. You've more than earned it."

He smiled. "Totally worth it ... I actually did it for you and nothing else. But since I'm in New York anyway—"

"Yeah, yeah, just go."

He stood and stepped over the rubble as he walked to the door.

"Jake?"

The soft, endearing look in his eyes as he turned erased some of the pain. "Yes?"

"Thank you."

He winked and eased the door shut behind him.

THE GRANTS' great room was in shambles. However, cleaning wasn't on my mind because my thoughts kept drifting to Quinn and his parting words. It began to eat at me until I knew I wouldn't be able to move on without knowing. I searched the rubble for my shirt then slipped it over my head before heading out and across the hall to knock on Quinn's door.

A few moments later he opened it. He still wore his bloodied, disheveled work suit minus the jacket. His face was mottled with red marks and dried blood and he held a bottle of Scotch in one hand.

"What aren't you telling me?" I demanded.

"It doesn't matter. You've made your choice." He turned and walked back inside letting the door start to close behind him.

Shoving the door back open, I marched in behind him. "What choice is that? Jake?"

He shrugged his shoulders with his back to me and lifted the bottle to his mouth.

"Why the nerve of you—" I growled as I stomped up to him and grabbed the bottle from his hand. Before he had time to react, I heaved it at the bar counter where it shattered everywhere. "You call me the love of your life and tell me you would lay the fucking world at my feet if I asked you to! Then, you have the nerve to nail me to the cross because of my past and blame me for doing exactly what your mother asked me to do. Then, when I still don't give up on us, you bring a string of whores into our bed and fuck them while I'm on the other side of the door!" My emotions exploded as I screamed at him, but he just stood there with a blank expression, numb to my words.

My chest heaved and adrenaline coursed through my veins, but he still said nothing. I was done, *we* were done. As I reached the door, I heard the faint sound of his voice.

"I didn't sleep with them."

Certain that I hadn't heard him correctly, I turned around. "What did you say?'

Shoulders slumped, he closed his eyes and took a deep breath. When he opened them, he captured my full attention. Dark watery eyes filled with ... *worry? Remorse?*

"Those women, I didn't sleep ... I didn't fuck any of them."

"Bullshit! I was here, I saw you—"

"You saw what I wanted you to see. There was no sex. I slept in the chair by the window, and they slept in the bed. Then in the morning I ... compensated them for their time."

Nothing made sense. My mind couldn't sort the insanity of his admission. I rubbed my temples trying to ease the tension in my head. "Let me get this straight. You paid those women to *not* sleep with you?"

He nodded.

I walked back toward him because I needed to look into his eyes. "Why?"

Taking a deep swallow, his dark eyes met mine. "I wanted you to feel my pain."

How did I miss it? Lost in the desert, all I focused on was a mirage of anger and contempt. Had I been able to see past the illusion, I would have found Quinn sinking into a dark hole of pain. I was his pain. The realization crushed me.

I reached for his face and he closed his eyes at my touch. "My God, what have I done to you?" Tears filled my eyes and I ran to the door. I had to get away from him. The shame of the pain I caused him was too suffocating.

As I reached for the door handle, his hand grabbed my arm and spun me around. "Where are you going?" He narrowed his eyes, shaking his head.

The emotions overflowed. "I can't take your pain away," I cried.

He leaned down and held my face in his hands as he rested his forehead to mine. "You're the *only* one who can take it away."

The feel of his lips kissing away my tears was like a ray of sunshine in the depths of Hell. Scooping me into his arms, he carried me upstairs to his bathroom. He set me down and turned on the water to fill the bathtub. When he turned back to me, I grabbed his shirt and pulled him closer. As I worked the buttons of his shirt, he brushed my hair back off my shoulders.

"Do you love him?"

Pausing, I stared at the button between my fingers for a brief moment. Then shaking my head, I continued.

"But you slept with him?"

I pushed his shirt off his shoulders and feathered my fingers over his bruised abdomen. "Yes."

"Why?" His voice was steady and calm despite the answers that had to sting.

"To take my mind off you."

I leaned in and pressed my lips to the middle of his chest then proceeded to unfasten his pants. As they dropped to the floor, he pulled my shirt over my head. I unbuttoned my jeans as he unclasped my bra. When it fell from my breasts, he brushed the pads of his thumbs over the swell of them with appreciation and desire gleaming in his eyes. Reaching over, he turned off the water then kneeled down to ease my jeans and panties over my hips and down my legs.

Holding his hand, I stepped out of them and into the tub of soothingly warm water. He followed me and sat down in the water before I sank down and positioned myself between his legs with my back to his chest. After grabbing a sponge, he dunked it in the water then squeezed it out over my shoulders and chest.

"Did it work?" he asked.

While I grazed my nails up and down his legs, I tried to figure out what he meant. "Did what work?"

"Did he take your mind off me?"

I sat up and turned around to face him, kneeling between his spread legs. Taking the sponge from him, I started blotting the dried blood from his face. "No."

"If I wouldn't have stopped you, were you going to sleep with him tonight?"

Keeping my eyes focused on his cuts, I smiled. "No." Then I looked into his eyes. "And I wouldn't have had to pay him to not sleep with me."

He dug his fingers into my sides making me squirm. "Do you think that's funny?"

Splashing water over the sides of the tub, I tried to wriggle out of his grasp. "Stop!" I squealed.

"Then stop laughing at me."

"I wasn't laughing, I was simply smiling."

"And what exactly were you smiling about?" He raised his eyebrow at me.

Leaning forward, I wrapped my hand around his firm length, then kissed his jaw, the corner of his eye, and every other place he had a bruise or cut. "I was smiling because after two grueling weeks I finally have you exactly where I want you."

"And where might that be?"

Moving my legs to straddle his, I lowered myself onto him, closing my eyes with the intensity of the fullness. "Right ... here."

His head fell back as he sucked in a tight breath through his teeth. I reached back and flipped the drain.

As the water level descended, I began to move up and down on him. He sat up and pulled me closer until his mouth captured my breast. My nipple hardened under the caress of his expert tongue. The head of his cock pressed against a bundle of nerves building the most exquisite climax. As I arched my back, I fisted his hair, pressing him harder into my breast.

"Oh God, Quinn, I'm so close," I whimpered on the verge of ecstasy.

Grabbing my hips, he guided me. The added force plunged the head of his erection so deep I exploded around him. He continued to move me on him, prolonging my orgasm as he climaxed, filling me with his warmth.

"God! You feel ... so ... fucking ... amazing," he panted into my chest as I released his hair from my fists and kissed his head in breathless exhaustion.

CHAPTER FOURTEEN

After our bath Quinn wrapped me up in his robe and put on some flannel pajama pants. He sat on the bed and let me rub arnica oil onto his cuts and bruises, then he rubbed a little around my eye.

"We look like hell." I laughed.

"Thanks to your attack dog."

"Yeah, well he didn't exactly leave unscathed either." I shifted my gaze to his as he finished with my eye.

"He's lucky he didn't leave on a stretcher."

"He thought the same about you."

"If I would have left on a stretcher, then he would have left in a body bag."

"Quinn!"

"I'm just saying—" He lay down on the bed and spooned me.

"I wouldn't be here with you if it weren't for him."

"Oh, so now he's a hero?"

"I'm right though, aren't I?" I turned my head back to see his face.

"I'm hungry. Do you want some popcorn?"

"Quinn! Are you really going to ignore my question?"

He sat up and brushed my lips with his finger. "Don't ruin the moment. Okay?" Then he walked out.

A WHILE LATER, he came back upstairs with a big bowl of popcorn, a glass of red wine, and a rocks glass filled with something clear.

I furrowed my brow at him as he handed me the wine.

"I thought you liked Merlot?" he said casually.

"I do, sometimes, but I don't want any tonight."

He grabbed it from me and set in on the nightstand. "Suit yourself."

Sitting next to me on the bed, he took a sip.

"What are you having?"

"Vodka tonic."

"Why?"

"Just to take the edge off." He shrugged his shoulders as he turned on the TV.

"Uh ... I thought what we just did in the bathtub took the edge off."

Turning toward me, he leaned in and kissed me. "It's just a drink. Don't make it into something it's not."

"Don't do this," I whispered.

He sighed and ran his fingers through his hair. "Do what?"

"Don't dismiss everything I say because you don't want to ruin the moment, and don't downplay your drinking problem."

"Drinking problem? Who said I have a drinking problem?"

"Are you kidding me? I don't expect you to magically cure yourself overnight, but you cannot be so blind as to not see that you have a drinking problem."

"Jesus, Addy! As I recall you had your fair share of wine that night we stayed at Mac and Evan's. The night you tried to have your drunken way with me but decided to masturbate after I said no. Does that mean you have a drinking problem?"

"Oh my God! Are you trying to compare your chronic binge drinking to one night that I had a few too many glasses of wine?"

He got out of bed and went downstairs without another word. A few minutes later I followed him only to find him refilling his glass with straight vodka.

In a much calmer voice, I tried a different approach. "I don't want to fight about this. I just want to help you."

"If you want to help me, then you'll stop treating me like a fucking alcoholic."

"Quinn, you were drunk at you mother's funeral."

"Yeah, my mother died. If ever there were a time to justify numbing the pain, wouldn't that qualify?"

"She wasn't just *your* mother, yet Chase and Alexis

managed to make it through without stockpiling flasks in their suit coat or purse."

"Not everyone deals with grief the same way." He finished his glass with several quick gulps then poured another.

We were getting nowhere and staying with an agitated drunk didn't seem like a good idea, so I went back upstairs and got dressed. When I came down he sat on the couch watching television with his liquid comfort.

"Goodnight," I said just loud enough that I knew he heard me. When he didn't respond, I fought the urge to say more and walked out the door.

Journal Day 91
Grateful that the words of The Serenity Prayer helped me sleep.

God, grant me the serenity to accept the things I
cannot change,
The courage to change the things I can,
And wisdom to know the difference

WITHOUT QUESTION, I was smart, but wisdom was a gift only granted by time. Sometimes I had trouble distinguishing which things in life I could change and which things I could not change. Quinn's behavior was one of those things.

My delusional thoughts about getting Quinn back and then helping him sober up weighed heavily on my mind. He had such contempt for his father because of his cowardly escape from reality through liquor. It was a monumentally incorrect assumption on my part that Quinn would be able to see himself doing the same thing.

In truth, I owed him nothing. But my guilty heart could not be convinced otherwise. There was no denying that I felt partially responsible for his problem. After all, he started drinking to cope with the physical and emotional pain he suffered after the climbing accident that had everything to do with me. Then the death of Elena exacerbated the problem, and part of me would forever question my decision to keep her secret from him. It might not have changed his drinking problem, but not knowing for sure made it hard for me to dismiss.

Admiring my shiner in the mirror early Saturday morning, I made a mental note of the things I needed to do that day. At the top of the list was checking on Quinn. Imagining how much he continued to drink after I left made my own stomach uneasy. Finding my way through the disaster, I didn't relish the thought of cleaning up the mess from the epic fight. Explaining it to the Grants would not be easy. When I opened the door, I was startled by the unexpectedness of someone standing right there.

"Quinn," I breathed out in surprise.

He leaned down and kissed me without so much as a word, then he brushed his lips over my black eye. "I'm sorry about the way I reacted last night. It was just a lot to take in and I wanted you to trust me, but I went about it all wrong. Can you forgive me?"

He looked irresistible in his black long-sleeved T-shirt and faded jeans. His narrowed eyes pleaded for forgiveness, which was almost impossible to deny as they were framed with cuts and bruises from the previous day's altercation. However, nothing he said sounded like an admission or acknowledgement of his drinking problem.

"What do you mean by trust you?" I questioned.

He pulled me into his body, and I willingly accepted his embrace as I rested the side of my face on his chest.

"I want you to trust me when I say I don't have a drinking problem." My body tensed and just as I started to say something he continued, "And, just to prove it to you I'm going to stop drinking for a while. Then you'll see I'm in complete control, and we'll no longer have this trust issue."

Quinn had nothing to prove to me. He was an alcoholic, and I knew it. However, since he was willing to make an effort, I couldn't say no. The lesson to be learned was his, not mine.

"Okay, but only if you fly to Chicago with me for Thanksgiving."

He squeezed me tighter. "Deal. We'll leave Wednesday afternoon."

"No, we'll leave tomorrow," I replied with a matter-of-fact confidence.

He pulled back to look at me. "Tomorrow is Sunday. I have work on Monday."

"Well, reschedule your meetings or call in sick. Do whatever you have to do. This is only going to work if there is some sort of accountability."

"You don't trust me to go to work and not drink?" He pulled back holding me at arms distance with a raised brow.

"Quinn, the whole point is to gain my trust. So I'm sorry, but I don't trust you to go to your office, where I know you have alcohol to offer your business associates, and abstain from drinking."

The firm look on his face conveyed some unspoken anger, but he said nothing. I slipped my hands up the back of his shirt and pulled him closer. "I'm not asking for the world, which you said you'd give me anyway. I'm just asking for this week."

Lacing his fingers through my hair, he pulled me to his lips. Our tongues united in a deep kiss as I exhaled a soft hum of satisfaction. With gentle restraint, I pressed my nails into his muscular back as my body heated from his touch. As my pulse started to accelerate, he broke our kiss.

"One week?" he confirmed.

I smiled with a nod.

We spent the rest of the morning cleaning up the Grants' condo. The final damage assessment bill would come later when they returned in the spring. After moving all my stuff back to Quinn's, we made lunch and rested on the couch.

"Will it just be the four of us for Thanksgiving?" he asked.

"Actually, Mac's parents will be joining us too." Quinn hadn't met Gwen and Richard. In fact, they didn't know much at all about Quinn, including how long we'd been together, our engagement, his accident, and the breakup.

"Are they okay with meeting me? After all, you were their daughter-in-law, and I'm sure in their minds no other man will ever live up to their son."

I moved over and straddled his lap, massaging his shoulders. "They'll be fine, it's just ..."

His hands moved to my feet and rubbed my insteps with firm pressure. "It's just what?"

"They don't really know that much about us." I wrinkled my nose and bit my lower lip.

"What do you mean?"

"I mean, they don't know how long I've been seeing you or that we were engaged."

He sucked his top lip in and worked it between his teeth for a moment. "I see. So what *do* they know about us?"

"Not a lot."

"Not a lot, or not anything?"

"Well, they know I'm planning on bringing you to Thanksgiving dinner and that we're kind of close."

"Kind of close, huh? Like how close?" He moved his hands up the inside of my shirt and cupped my breasts as his thumbs pushed their way under my bra to circle my nipples. "Like … this close?"

Biting my lower lip, I briefly closed my eyes. "Maybe," I breathed out.

He pulled off my shirt and removed my bra then captured one of my breasts in his mouth while his hand massaged the other, bringing my nipples to firm pebbles. "Like this close?" he murmured over my breast.

In no time my panties were drenched as my body melted under his touch. "Possibly," I said between labored breaths.

He flipped me over, my back pressed to the couch. Then he shrugged off his shirt with a slow, sexy motion. I could tell by his cocky grin he was acutely aware of just how much I loved seeing his naked, muscled torso. He grabbed my pants at the hips and pulled them off. Then his face moved between my legs and he inhaled my scent sending a jolt of sensation to my sex. It was so intense my pelvis jerked toward him. He hummed in appreciation as he hooked his finger around my panties and moved them to the side. "Like this close?"

His tongue grazed through my slit and over my clit. "Yes," I whimpered, "I mean no … I mean …" Two of his fingers slid into my channel as his tongue continued to circle my clit, "Oh God!" I moaned. I'd lost all ability to think, and he took advantage of the situation.

He pushed off of the couch and stood up. I drank in the sight of him unfastening his jeans and sliding them off with his briefs. He crawled over me again and attacked my mouth as he sank into me. Our fingers interlaced over my head, and I wrapped my legs around him as he plunged into me. His firm chest rubbed against my nipples while I tried to angle my hips. Finding just the right spot, he grazed my clit with each thrust until I shattered around him. Then he released into me with a final thrust and a vibrating moan escaping his chest.

"Like this close?" he whispered into my ear as he released my hands.

"Definitely not this close." I breathlessly laughed.

A few hours later, Quinn was in his office sending out emails to arrange for his extended Thanksgiving break.

"Hey, babe, can I get you anything?" I asked, peeking my head into his office.

"No, I'm fine!" he snapped. "I mean ... just give me a minute." His voice sounded strangled with agitation.

I walked further into the room and everything about him seemed off. He repeatedly clenched his fists over the keyboard of his computer, and when he released them his hands shook. His forehead looked moist as if he was hot and his overall demeanor seemed anxious.

And so it begins.

Leaving without saying anything, I went to the kitchen and squeezed him a mix of fresh fruit and vegetable juices high in vitamin C. Then I went upstairs and got him some B-complex and zinc from my bag and a couple of cayenne capsules. When I returned to his office, he was leaned back in his chair, rubbing his temples.

"Here, drink this and take these," I said, setting the vitamins and juice down on his desk.

He sat up and looked at them with squinted eyes. "Why?"

I walked around behind him and massaged his head. "You look like you're ... coming down with something. Just thought it might be best to load up on some vitamins, that's all."

That wasn't really all. He had classic alcohol withdrawal symptoms, but I refused to get anywhere near that topic. Offering him a beer to taper off slowly the old-fashioned way was not an option either since he was in denial that he had a problem.

"Thanks," he said as he popped the pills in his mouth and drank the juice. "What were the vitamins?"

"B-complex and zinc to boost your immune system and cayenne to fight off infection." *And decrease your withdrawal symptoms and cravings.*

He spun around in his chair and pulled me on his lap so I straddled him. "What would I do without you?"

I smiled as his nervous leg vibrated my whole body. *You would be drowning yourself in alcohol to relieve your symptoms.*

NOT SURPRISINGLY, Quinn didn't have much of an appetite for dinner. He drank more fresh juice and willingly swallowed whatever pills I put in front of him, which were quite a few. It was a rough night for the both of us as sleep evaded him at every turn.

If he didn't shake with tremors, he ran to the bathroom—luckily not to vomit—just to relieve his bladder of all the juice and water I'd been shoving down him. The herbs that I'd given him were also at work, detoxing his liver and cleansing his kidneys. By 4:00 a.m. he was sound asleep, thanks to a nice herbal concoction I'd given him an hour earlier. Equally exhausted, I curled up beside him and captured my own needed sleep.

I woke a little before ten Sunday morning. Quinn was still out and I didn't wake him. His body needed the rest to repair damage that had been done over months of abuse. He also needed sleep to reduce his anxiety and help prevent depression.

After easing out of bed, I went downstairs and called Mac to let her know we were going to stay in

New York a couple more days before flying to Chicago. It required more time to get Quinn in better shape. I cleaned up the juicing mess in the kitchen after I got off the phone with her.

Just as I finished, I heard the water running upstairs. As soon as I wiped off the counter, I grabbed a glass of water and carried it upstairs. Quinn sat on the edge of the bed with a towel around his waist and water from his freshly showered head dripping down his torso. Hunched over, he had his elbows on his knees. He stared at his shaky hands, fisting them several times then running them through his hair as he sighed. A moment later he looked up and jerked his head back with wide eyes, obviously surprised to see me standing there watching him.

Lowering his chin to his chest, he released a long, slow sigh. My heart clenched in pain. "It's not the flu, is it?" he asked in a thick voice.

I shook my head and set the glass of water on the end table. He pulled me between his legs and wrapped his arms around my waist so tight, I could barely breathe.

CHAPTER FIFTEEN

Quinn

How the fuck did I end up like my father? I was a self-made millionaire with razor-sharp instincts. I'd traveled the world in search of extreme adventures. I had worked my ass off to keep my body in top physical condition. I was envied by men and sought after by women. I was educated, disciplined, and focused. Yet, here I was, a complete fuck-up, clinging like a child to Addy. Fucking Addy. I loved her and hated her. She worshipped me like a sex god one minute and could turn around and completely emasculate me the next.

She had some nerve showing up at my door and making my life a living hell. I was perfectly content numbing my emotions with booze and then fucking the first girl who made my dick twitch. At least until she showed up. She was like a virus that consumed my whole being. Night after night I slept in the most uncomfortable goddamn chair while the woman I was supposed to be fucking slept in my bed because the girl I wanted to fuck was in the next room. Never in my life had I met someone as relentless as her. She never gave up on me and the scary part was, she knew me better than I knew myself.

Even after physically removing her from my condo, she managed to push all my buttons by inviting fucking Jake for a visit. I had no right to be jealous, but the thought of her under some other guy—making the noises of pleasure that belonged to me—made my fucking blood boil. Backing down was not an option. Nothing he did to me even came close to causing as much pain as her admission that she'd been with him. The hardest part to swallow was that she never would have been with him if I hadn't blamed her for everything, if I wouldn't have brought home some random girl in my drunken state and made her leave me.

She was broken when I met her, and I should have been her rock of support, but instead I was the rock that continued to crush her over and over again. I tried to let her go. She deserved someone better than me. But I needed her too much. She was giving and nurturing. Above all, she loved me ... she truly, no-holds-barred, one hundred percent loved me.

CHAPTER SIXTEEN

Addy

MY BROKEN MAN. My conscious, broken man. Quinn was no longer in denial, and while it broke my heart to see him in pain, it was necessary. I kissed his head and held him to me until he released me. It was what I always did; I held on until he released me.

"I'm my father," he whispered into my chest.

I cupped his face. "Look at me," I demanded. His glazed, defeated eyes found mine. "If you love me and fight to get better, then you are not your father. Do you hear me?"

He searched my eyes and I wondered what he saw. "I love you," was his answer.

I hadn't heard those three words from him in over five months. My tears fell.

"Oh, baby, no, what's wrong?" He pulled me down to sit on his lap.

I shook my head and wiped my face. "Nothing, it's just … nothing."

"Hey, you're crying. It's not nothing. Tell me."

"You haven't said those words to me in so long, and I didn't even realize how much I needed to hear them, until now."

"Addy, I know this may be hard to believe, but there hasn't been a single day, a single hour, a single minute, or a single second in the past year and a half that I haven't loved you." He kissed me fervently, melting away my insecurities.

As he released my lips, I smiled. "Even when I left New York?"

"Yes."

"Even when you came to Milwaukee and Jake handed you a beating?"

"I'd hardly call a sucker punch to a drunk man a 'beating,' but yes."

"Even when you were spitting venom at me on the way to your mother's burial?"

"Yes."

"Even when you kicked me and all my stuff to the curb?"

"Technically it was the hall, but yes, especially then."

"*Especially* then?"

"Yes. You are such a sexy fucking tease when you get all stubborn and bullheaded. I was so close to handcuffing you to my bed and introducing you to BDSM 101 for all the cockblocking you were doing. But

I love you, so I put some distance between us to protect you."

"Wow! I don't even know where to begin. You think *I* was the one being stubborn and bullheaded? And BDSM 101 for *cockblocking*? You brought home every girl on the street and locked me out of this very bedroom, night after night, and yet you felt cock-blocked?"

"Addy—"

"Who says that?"

"Addy—"

"And I am not a tease ..."

"Addy—"

"And we've had this BDSM discussion before, I will not be—"

"Addy!"

"What?" I finally snapped out of my tangent.

"I. Love. You. *Always*."

THE FOLLOWING two days were spent working through Quinn's withdrawal and detox symptoms. We were able to be more aggressive since there was no longer a need to pretend we were treating the flu. Herbalist Addy took over. Juice cleanse, herbal tinctures, coffee enemas, detox teas, sauna, massages, and acupuncture treatments kept Quinn not only on his way to a speedy recovery, but it also kept him busy and less irritable.

I had something for everything. Herbs to lessen the

cravings and reduce the withdrawal symptoms. Herbs to repair the damage to his liver, colon, esophagus, stomach, and intestines. Other tinctures were used to correct biochemical and neurological imbalances.

He was the perfect patient. The natural cleanse kept his libido intact, which is not the case with all recovering alcoholics. However, it was yet another activity to pass time and reward his hard-working nurse. We were far from recovery, but by the Wednesday before Thanksgiving, we were both looking forward to our trip to Chicago and a change of scenery. As we packed for the trip, I came across an envelope with Quinn's name on it. I immediately recognized it as the letter Elena left for him, and the seal hadn't been broken.

"You haven't opened this yet?" I asked as he set out his clothes on the bed.

"Nope."

"Why not?"

He sighed. "Well, to be honest, I didn't want to read her reasons or excuses for doing what she did. And, as you know, I was drunk and pissed at her and ..." he paused.

"Me," I whispered. "You were pissed at me."

He turned and looked at me with a sad smile. "Addy, I'm sorry. I was in a bad place at the time and—"

My wince mirrored his. "It's fine. I understand. For what it's worth, she left me a letter too, and I haven't read mine either."

"My mother left you a letter? Why would she do

that? You were with her when she died." He looked at me with narrowed eyes, head tilted.

I zipped up my bag and sat on the edge of the bed next to his pile of shirts. "That's part of the reason I haven't read it yet. I think it's meant for me to read in a time of desperation. I imagine the page is filled with words of wisdom that will pull me back into the light from the depths of Hell." I laughed. "Or maybe it's just a list of things I was supposed to do before leaving the beach house ... like take out the garbage, empty the refrigerator, and clean the toilet. If that's the case, then oops."

Quinn threaded his hangers through the opening in his garment bag. He traveled business-style—everything permanent-pressed, starched, and neatly on a hanger. I traveled like a teenage girl packing for a slumber party—everything wadded and shoved into a bag. Talk about yin and yang.

"If you were saving it for a desperate time in your life, then I can't believe you haven't read it yet. Surely over the past few weeks you've felt close to hitting rock bottom."

"Olivia accompanying you into your condo came close, but not quite." I smirked.

"Olivia? Are you serious? Not throwing you out, or my illusions of indiscretion, or the fight between me and Jake, or my substance abuse?"

"No, just Olivia. She's so vexatious. I'm the worst version of myself around her. She's an antagonist to my ego."

He plopped down beside me and pushed me back so he hovered over me. "You have no reason to be jealous."

"Jealous? You think I'm jealous?" I scoffed. "She may have finagled you a backstage pass to a few uppity fashion shows, but *I'm* the one who gave you step-by-step instructions on using an enema bag for your coffee enemas."

He fought to keep a serious face. "You're right. I don't recall the backstage security offering helpful tips such as properly lubricating the nozzle to prevent *rectal tearing* while entering the *anal sphincter*."

Fighting my own goofy smile, I returned with my best matter-of-fact reply. "Indispensable knowledge."

Journal Day 95.
Grateful for sober Quinn meeting the rest of my "family."

WE ARRIVED at Mac and Evan's by dinner Wednesday night. They welcomed Quinn with warm affection, as if our relationship hadn't just recovered from the most unpropitious circumstances. After dinner we relaxed in the living room by the fireplace. Dressed for comfort in a long sweater, leggings, and thick wool socks, I curled up on the sofa next to Quinn while Mac sat on Evan's lap in an oversized chair.

The wind gusted, producing an occasional screeching whistle around a few of the windows. We listened to a classical mix of piano music flowing through the surround sound. Mesmerized by the brilliant orange and red glow of the embers that illuminated the room, I yawned in exhaustion from a full tummy and a long day.

"Bed, babe," I whispered as I tilted my head back and kissed the corner of Quinn's mouth.

"Mmm," he hummed.

"You two skipping out on us?" Mac questioned.

"I think so. We were up pretty early this morning and it's eleven o'clock New York time," I answered, fighting back another yawn as Quinn stood and offered his hand to pull me up.

"We'll see you in the morning," Evan said with a smile.

"Goodnight," Quinn replied.

Mac scooted off Evan's lap and embraced me. "I'm so happy you're here, *both* of you," she whispered in my ear.

"Me too," I returned with a sincere smile.

I grabbed two tall glasses of water and followed Quinn to the guest room. He proceeded through his new nightly ritual of taking herbal pills and tinctures.

"These funky herbs are probably going to become my new addiction, trading one thing for another. I doubt I'd make it through customs with these."

I finished rinsing the toothpaste from my mouth. "They're non-addictive, non-funky herbs, not illicit drugs like marijuana. You'd make it through customs." I shook my head and rolled my eyes.

"I bet you were the nerdy girl in school who never wore makeup, brought natural peanut butter on cardboard-grain bread for lunch, and corrected your teachers by raising your hand and starting every phrase with 'actually.'" He laughed as he stripped down to his boxer briefs.

Slipping on a pink tank top I corrected him. "*Actually*, I was quite the slut in school. I wore a gaudy amount of makeup, miniskirts, and I went braless until college. And after the football games I gave head to the hottest beefcakes on the team."

I heard Quinn choking in the bathroom while he brushed his teeth. He walked around the corner wiping his mouth with a towel. "Beefcakes?" He raised his brows and smiled in complete amusement.

I pulled the covers up to my neck and rolled so my back was to him. "Yes, beefcakes."

He shut off the light and crawled under the covers facing me. I struggled to keep a straight face with his shrewd smirk just inches from me.

"Whatever you say, baby, but if you expect me to believe you, I'm going to need a demonstration of exactly what you did to the *beefcakes*." He palmed my butt and pulled me closer until his firm cock beneath his briefs pressed against me.

Checkmate, Quinn.

"Rise and shine, beautiful," the sexiest voice in the world whispered in my ear.

"Mmm, sounds like the hot beefcake from last night," I purred as I stretched my whole body awake.

"Everything about last night was hot, except you throwing around that word." He leaned over and kissed me.

Peeling open my eyes, I noticed he was showered and dressed. "How long have you been awake?"

"Long enough to go for a run, shower, and order breakfast."

"Where did you order breakfast from on Thanksgiving?"

"Mac. She said the kitchen didn't officially open until nine, so I preordered smoothies for us."

"What time is it?" I asked, trying to see over the pillows to the clock.

"Eight-thirty, why?"

I let my tongue wet my lower lip. "That gives me thirty minutes to show you just how *thankful* I am for you this morning."

His mouth was on mine in a flash. I tugged at his shirt until he broke our kiss. Crossing his arms, he pulled it off in one quick motion. "Thirty minutes? I can work with that."

Wasting no time, he discarded his pants as I shimmied out of my panties and peeled off my nightshirt. As he crawled over me, I pushed his chest until he flopped on his back beside me. I straddled his waist on my knees as he fisted his hard cock and rubbed it back and forth between my folds. The rest of my body started to feel warm and tingly as heat swelled around my sex. The teasing became unbearable, so I wrapped my hand over his to steady it as I prepared to sink onto him. I was desperate to feel the fullness of him buried in me.

"Addy? Are you out of the shower—" Mac's voice sounded as the door opened. "Oh holy hell, I'm—"

"Mac!" I squealed as I jumped off Quinn and frantically tried to pull the covers over our naked bodies.

She stood in the doorway holding a tall glass in each hand. "Pumpkin spiced smoothies," she said with a wrinkled face and partial grin.

My whole body flushed with blazing embarrassment. "Mac!" I gritted through my teeth with bugged out eyes while my hands fought with the sheets to cover us up.

She wouldn't stop staring at us. It was like we were animals at a zoo and she was observing our behavior with a casual passiveness and an appreciative grin on her face.

"Mackenzie!"

Startled out of her daze, she dragged her eyes from Quinn and looked at me. "Oh, yes, well ... I'll just put these in the kitchen for whenever you're done or ready or ..." With a polite nod and a tightlipped smile, she turned around and closed the door behind her.

I turned to look at Quinn, grinning from ear to ear with one arm bent behind his head, the other grasped around the sheet just barely covering his midsection. The dumb-ass smirk on his face pissed me off.

"What are you doing?" I asked as I elbowed him in the ribs.

He shrugged. "What do you mean? I'm not doing anything."

I grabbed a throw blanket off the end of the bed and wrapped it around myself as I stood. "That's my point. My best friend walked in on us having sex and you made no attempt to cover either one of us up, and the stupid grin on your face implies you enjoyed it."

Despite his effort to contain it, a laugh escaped his chest. "Oh come on, I didn't enjoy it. I just didn't see what the big deal was."

Halfway to the bathroom, I turned around and scowled at him. "The big deal is I'm not an exhibition-ist, and I'm not into public copulation!"

"Copulation?"

I continued into the bathroom. "Yes, copulation, coitus, intercourse, sex, fucking ... whatever!" Turning on the shower, I tossed the blanket out the door. Quinn caught it as he walked into the bathroom with his pants back on but not zipped yet. After I stepped into the shower, he leaned against the vanity and continued dressing.

"*Actually*, Addy, we weren't having sex yet. You were just getting ready to—"

Cracking the door open, I poked my wet head out. "I don't need a playback. I'm very well aware of what we were doing." I shut the door and continued to soap up.

"Let it go, baby. I'm sure she was just as embarrassed as you were. It's not like she's going to mention it again."

I shut off the water and wrung my hair out before opening the door and grabbing my towel. "What are you, crazy? I'll bet you a thousand dollars she insinuates it or uses some smart-ass innuendo at least a half a dozen times before the end of Thanksgiving dinner."

"You honestly think she's going to say something in front of her parents?"

"Yes. You don't know her like I do. Richard and Gwen up the ante in her mind. She's going to love watching me squirm."

He walked up behind me at the mirror as I combed through my hair. His hand slipped under my towel in the front. I closed my eyes and released a needy moan as his middle finger penetrated my folds and slipped inside me.

"Oh God," I breathed as I put my hand over his, urging him to keep going.

"Someone sounds quite desperate for a release," he whispered in my ear before he sucked in my lobe and grazed his teeth over it.

"Yes," I whimpered.

He inched his finger out of me then turned me around so I faced him. As predicted, he took his turn eliciting a blush from me when he slipped his finger into his mouth sucking off my wetness with a hum of satisfaction.

My heart rate doubled as my breathing became labored in frantic anticipation. Giving a gentle tug to the towel wrapped around me, it easily fell, leaving me bared to him. When his mouth captured mine, I could taste myself on his tongue and it was surprisingly an erotic turn-on. Grabbing my hips, he lifted me onto the vanity then pushed my legs up so they were resting on the edge. Dropping to his knees, I quickly felt the heat of his warm breath on my sex. I clenched my hands in his hair and pulled him to me without shame, just as the most irritating sound filled my ears.

"Let's go you two! Breakfast is waiting, and you should be *done* by now!"

Quinn stood and hugged me into his chest as he laughed. I, however, did not laugh. I was so sexually frustrated I nearly started crying.

"That's one," was all I could say in exasperation.

CHAPTER SEVENTEEN

Journal Day 96
Grateful for good friends, good food, and Quinn ... hot,
panty-scorching Quinn.

GWEN AND RICHARD were expected to arrive by noon. After breakfast, Mac played makeup artist to me and Quinn. My black eye was still colorful, as was Quinn's face in several areas. The last thing I needed was to try and explain to Gwen and Richard the fight that happened less than a week earlier.

The rest of the morning, Mac and I labored in the kitchen making everything except the turkey. Her parents agreed to bring the bird since neither Mac nor I wanted to prepare it or smell it cooking for hours in the oven. Evan and Quinn had disappeared to the man cave shortly after breakfast, but as soon as the front door opened, Mac called them upstairs.

"Mom, Dad!" she yelled from the kitchen. After

hanging up their coats, they rounded the corner just as Evan and Quinn got to the top of the stairs.

Richard set the covered turkey on the kitchen island then hugged Mac and me before greeting Evan with a handshake. Gwen was right behind him, gushing about how everything we had made looked and smelled so delicious.

It only took a few minutes before all eyes fell to Quinn. I looped my arm around his. "Gwen, Richard, this is Quinn Cohen. Quinn, Gwen and Richard Townsend."

"It's such pleasure to meet you both." Quinn wasted no time shaking Richard's hand and leaning in to kiss Gwen on the cheek. She blushed, as all women did in the presence of my Latin sex god.

"Very nice to meet you too," Gwen replied.

"Cohen, huh?" Richard questioned. "The name rings a bell." He squinted.

"Quinn's *into* everything. Right, Addy?" Mac smiled with a wink in my direction.

"That's two," I said between clenched teeth behind my smile so only Quinn could hear me.

He put his arm around my waist and squeezed my hip. "What Mac means is my business dealings are diversified. The Cohen name is fairly common around here."

"Well, let's eat so the vultures can dive into the bird carcass."

"Mackenzie!" Gwen scolded. "Must you be so crass in front of Addy's guest?"

"Oh, Mom, I don't think Quinn is easily offended. In fact, I think he's quite comfortable with my *obtrusiveness*. Addy, however, not so much."

Another wink and a smile.

As we all found a seat at the table, I held up three fingers to Quinn and mouthed, "That's three."

He shook his head then pulled out my chair before sitting next to me.

Richard offered the blessing, then we passed around the food.

"Tell us how you two met?" Gwen asked.

Quinn looked at me because it was my story to tell. Richard and Gwen were oblivious to my current affairs. They still thought I owned the Café and lived in Milwaukee. They were unaware that I'd spent so much of my time in New York with Quinn, and they definitely didn't know about our engagement and breakup.

The more I thought about everything they didn't know, the more I questioned my sanity for bringing Quinn to Thanksgiving dinner. I hated that the omission of important information felt like a lie, but it didn't feel like the right time to explain our complicated history. So trying to avoid a blatant lie, I kept my response vague.

"We met at an event I catered at a hotel Quinn owns in Milwaukee."

Mac passed the tray of turkey to Quinn, and he chose a small piece of dark meat.

"Funny, I pegged you for a white meat guy. Addy, did you know Quinn liked more *legs* and *thighs* than *breast* meat?" Mac cut in with one more wink and smile.

I tapped four fingers on Quinn's leg until he reached under the table and grabbed my hand. Somehow I had managed to get myself in the hot seat. Engaging with Mac in her attempt to fluster me was just as uncomfortable as fielding questions from Gwen about my history with Quinn. Lucky for me, Gwen was used to Mac's obnoxiousness, and ignoring her random comments was pretty typical.

"Are you originally from Milwaukee?" Gwen asked Quinn.

"I actually live in New York, not Milwaukee. I was just there checking in on my hotel when I met Addy."

"You live in New York?" Gwen clarified in surprise.

Quinn nodded as he chewed his food.

"That must be hard. Long distance relationships take so much dedication."

Somebody change the subject!

When Quinn looked at me, I had a flashback of almost a year earlier when I unexpectedly met Quinn's family for the first time on Christmas. The charade over dinner was emotionally exhausting, but in the end the truth came out. He owned our relationship and he acknowledged, in front of his whole family, that I was the girl he couldn't live without.

"Yeah, Addy, just how *hard* is it?" Mac smirked.

She had impeccable timing. While I stayed static at an emotional crossroad, contemplating a difficult deci-sion, Mac continued to use me as her comedic muse.

The corners of Quinn's mouth curled up ever so slightly as he inconspicuously drummed five fingers on the table.

"It's *harder* than you could ever imagine, Mac. So hard that sometimes if feels all consuming. It fills me with such intensity that I can barely breathe," I replied with a pensive face.

Quinn covered his mouth with his napkin as he choked on his food. Mac, however, was in no danger of choking because her food was practically falling back to her plate as she sat across the table stunned with her mouth agape. I'd just lost my thousand dollar bet, having officially silenced Mac on the event she witnessed earlier that morning. But I had more important issues to deal with, and she became too much of a distraction.

Focusing my attention back on Gwen, I took a deep breath.

Deep breath ... I am peaceful, I am strong.

"The truth is, I gifted the Café to Jake and since then I've been living in New York ... with Quinn."

The room fell silent. I reached over and interlaced my fingers with Quinn's. His expression was mine a year earlier, a mixture of sympathy, relief, gratitude, and love seen through his soft eyes and gentle smile.

"I don't understand. Why didn't you tell us?" Gwen's voice was pained.

My gaze fell to my plate. Gwen and Richard were family. They deserved better. Quinn squeezed my hand, and when I looked at him I found the courage to go on.

"Quinn didn't know about my past, about Malcolm. And I thought if I told you about us you would want to meet him, and I wasn't ready to rip open those wounds. Then our relationship hit some … bumpy spots, and we've been separated for the past six months. But now that we're together again, I want … I need you to know how much I love him. I'm sorry. I was such a coward, and while I fought so hard to protect myself, I ended up hurting everyone around me."

In that moment I felt more vulnerable than the dead bird on the table—the gap between my present and past waiting to be bridged. The pain in the gap felt crippling, but giving myself completely to Quinn was worth it. The truth needed to come out, but there was only one question in my mind. *Would it set me free?*

It was Richard's voice that broke the silence and sliced into me. "So Quinn knows about Sa—"

"I'm pregnant!" Mac yelled out.

The whiplash had everyone's heads spinning. All eyes were on Mac and Evan, who both beamed with joy and excitement. It was practically a race between me and Gwen to get to Mac and Evan. Like a loose ball in a football game, we descended upon them in a group hug filled with tears and laughter … everyone except Quinn. His tight eyes met mine as I tried to pull myself from the mob.

"I can't believe we're going to be grandparents again," Gwen squealed in excitement.

Quinn's eyes stayed fixed to mine as he pushed back in his chair then stood, tossing his napkin on the table.

As I started to go after him, Mac grabbed my arm. "Addy, I'm sorry—"

Turning back to her, I pressed my palms to her cheeks. "Don't. You have nothing to be sorry about." I forced a smile. "I am so happy for you and Evan. You are going to be a wonderful mom." The tears in her eyes were reflected in mine as she nodded.

When I reached the bedroom, Quinn's back was to me. His arms were crossed over his chest as he gazed out the window. I shut the door behind me and walked up behind him. He stiffened as I hugged his back. Then my tears came without reprieve.

"He tried to save her, Addy. There was too much smoke and not enough time. Oh God! I can't believe they're both gone. I'm so sorry—"

"Malcolm, I'm tired of having this conversation. It's called a family bed for Christ's sake. It's common practice throughout most of the world."

"Addy, watch your mouth!"

"Sorry ... for 'goodness' sake. Just because your parents put you in a crib and let you cry yourself to sleep doesn't mean we're going to do the same thing. If you make one

more stupid comment about her still being in our bed when she's a teenager, I'm going to kick your ass out of the bed because I'd rather sleep with her than you!"

"You're being unreasonable."

"Yeah, well you're being a prick."

My whole body shook as a new round of sobs surged through me. Clenching my fists into his shirt, I fought for control, but my knees gave out. The time had come to tell Quinn, but my voice was paralyzed with grief. He quickly turned and caught me in his arms.

"Oh God, it ..." my voice broke.

"Shh, don't speak. You don't have to say anything."

His loving voice should have been comforting, but it clenched my heart even harder. The physical pain matched my emotional anguish.

"It-hur-hurts-so-so bad," I sobbed in agony.

Cradling me in his arms like a child, he carried me to the bed. He hugged me, chest to chest. His heart carried the beat of mine. Then, when he tilted my chin up to kiss away my tears, it felt like he breathed life back into my burning, deflated lungs. A numbing wave of comfort blanketed my body, and my words found their voice.

"Sage was my daughter, the love of *my* life." I swallowed back the impending lump. "She had my blond wavy hair and Malcolm's green eyes." A warm smile born of fond memories graced my tear stained face. "She was going to be a real heartbreaker."

He squeezed me in loving acknowledgement. I

rested my ear against his chest and picked at an invisible piece of lint on his shirt.

"We hadn't been married that long when I got pregnant. I continued with school up until I had her. She wasn't planned ... but the best things in life never are." I turned my head just enough to kiss his chest. "Most people talk about the first time they lay eyes on their baby or hold them in their arms, but for me, it was the first little flutter I felt in my tummy."

I sniffled once and wiped at a few more tears. "Both of our parents were ecstatic, at least until I announced my plans to have a home birth. You'd have thought I was suggesting an abortion, as if all babies born at home were as good as dead. They questioned how someone with my intelligence could suggest something so 'careless.' But then, most likely starting with the word *actually* ..." We both released a small, tension relieving laugh. "I proceeded to present them with a sea of information on the safety of home birthing with a midwife, including: lower infant mortality rates, lower C-section rates, deceased risk of low birth weight, and lower premature labor rates. I also assured them I was young, healthy, and considered low risk for complications. Eventually, my debate team champion status was upheld, and one by one they jumped on board with my birthing plan. After only six hours of labor, in which I incorporated the HypnoBirthing technique, Sage was born in a birthing tub surrounded by people who already loved her and a very caring and competent nurse-midwife."

We held one another in silence for a while. Quinn's patience with me was beyond commendable. He still struggled with his addiction, and while the symptoms were much milder with the herbs he took, they weren't nonexistent. How he managed to suppress his urges and stay focused solely on my needs, forever remained a mystery. But, God, I loved him for it.

"Sage and I were inseparable. If she wasn't at my breast, she was nestled in my neck or held to my body in a wrap or carrier. She was my heart beating outside of my body, and I lived every second of every day for her and her alone."

More tears fell as my eyes bled with raw emotion. "I'm sure Malcolm had his own love story with her, as did his parents, my parents, and Mac. Everybody loved and adored her, but it was completely overshadowed by my love for her. At night I would watch her sleep, making sure that every time she took a breath the next one followed exactly when it was supposed to. By the time she was one, our families wondered when I was going to finish school. My parents had a mile long list of very expensive but highly qualified nannies. It sat on my desk untouched. Sage was my purpose. Malcolm made plenty of money. I didn't have to work.

At the same time I hated to rehash the same argument with my parents. I had agreed to get my PhD, but that was before Sage. She was a game changer. I spent the next year staving off arguments. My parents were on me about school, and Malcolm's new soapbox was our family bed issue. We had a crib, thanks to his parents spending a ridiculous amount of money on a decorator for our nursery. However, Sage never slept in her crib. I was an advocate of attachment parenting and co-sleeping, and the family bed was part of it.

That second year we spent countless hours arguing over the sleeping arrangement. Then, against my better judgment, a few weeks after she turned two, we moved her into her room. She cried every night, so I lay in her toddler bed with her until she fell asleep. Most nights Malcolm had to beg me to come back to bed because I was so reluctant to leave her. But eventually I did, I left her. That's—"

Tears swelled again in my eyes as the shattered pieces of my heart cut even deeper. "That's where she was the night of the fire. In her room—all-a-all a-lone." The memories shook me again as Quinn held me even tighter, using his body to absorb each gyrating sob that vibrated through me.

"Shh ... oh, baby, I am so very sorry," he soothingly whispered.

Shaking my head, I tried to push back slightly so I could finish. "There's more ... I'm not finished."

When he pressed me back into his chest and spoke, I could tell his own voice fought for control. "You are for today. You're finished for today. No more, okay?"

He offered me an out, a stay of execution, and I accepted it.

* * *

EXHAUSTED, I fell asleep. When I awoke it was almost 4:00 p.m. and Quinn still held me to him.

"Hey, beautiful," he whispered.

Squinting my sore swollen eyes, I smiled. "Not really where I saw the day going."

He kissed my puffy eyes then scooted out of bed. "I'll be right back."

A few minutes later he returned with sliced cucumbers in a bowl of water and ice.

"Spa treatment?" I laughed.

"Well, I can't have Richard and Gwen thinking I beat you up. Especially since the makeup Mac put over your eye has washed off and now you have two puffy eyes."

I closed my eyes as he pulled two slices from the bowl and rested them over my swollen lids.

"Nobody asked you why you were taking cucumbers from the veggie tray and putting them in ice water?"

"They might have, but they didn't because they're all passed out in the living room."

I laughed. "Tryptophan coma, or in Mac's case, first trimester coma."

He didn't respond to my remark, but I couldn't see his face. Was he apprehensive about pregnancy talk since my latest revelation?

"Quinn?"

"Yeah?"

"I'm fine. I'm better than fine. My best friend is pregnant. I'm going to be an aunt ... sort of. So as far as

I am concerned, for the next nine months the world revolves around Mac. Besides, I'm sick of being the center of attention, the elephant in the room, the fifth wheel, the—"

The warm sensation of his lips against mine came as a surprise. He dipped his tongue between them, soliciting a hum of satisfaction from my throat.

"Mac may be the center of your universe for the next nine months, but you will always be the center of mine."

"Stop! The goal here is to prevent me from crying. So enough with the sappy stuff."

"Sappy stuff? What do you expect me to say?"

"Guy stuff ... even Mac stuff."

He laughed. "You need to elaborate."

"You know something like, 'Mac may think she's the center of your universe, but I will be the only one with my lips at your hot melting core, rocking your world.'" Had I not had the cucumbers over my eyes I would not have been able to say those words, especially with such a deep manly tone. The look on Quinn's face would have stopped me in my tracks.

"Dear God, that was the worst impression of me ever. It barely qualified for corny phone sex." He laughed hysterically.

I peeled the cucumbers from my eyes and squinted at him. "Are you laughing at me? What's so damn funny?"

"'My lips at your hot core, rocking your world?'

Would that really do it for you?" he asked in wide-eyed amazement, still laughing.

Shrugging my shoulders, I tossed the cucumbers back in the bowl. "I'm embarrassed to admit this because it sounds so pathetic, but with you, Quinn, words are not necessary. All you have to do is show up and I'm yours."

Sitting up, I swung my legs off the side of the bed then eased onto my feet to head to the bathroom.

"Ditto, baby, ditto," he chimed behind me.

CHAPTER EIGHTEEN

Journal Day 97
Grateful for new life.

WE SPENT the rest of Thanksgiving grazing on the leftover food. The guys retreated to the basement for football while we gals talked everything baby. Mac wanted to be a mother since the first moment she laid eyes on Sage. She wasn't with Evan, or anyone else at the time, but with the tragedies that ensued over the following years, her plans to get married and start a family were delayed.

In many ways, I became her child. She looked out for me, helped me pursue my new dreams, and was always there for me in a moment's notice. Even when she met Evan, it was as if they had an understanding that Mac and her broken friend were a package deal. I knew she'd found "the one" when Evan didn't hesitate to open his arms to me. My intention was never to be a fifth wheel. Mac deserved someone as equally loving and unconditionally accepting as her.

Friday morning brought a sense of peace. I hadn't told Quinn everything, but at least he knew there was more. It no longer felt like I was keeping a secret; although I was aware the day would come when I'd have to share the rest. Opening those wounds again would be torturous, but with Quinn's love, the pain would eventually subside.

It was common knowledge that I was not a shopper, and Black Friday was the Olympics of shopping. Since I'd conceded that the world would revolve around Mac for nine months, I had to grant her the pleasure of my company in the massive chaos known as Black Friday in Chicago. Dragging my feet, I enjoyed an extra-long shower that morning while Quinn went for a run. Just as I started to shut off the water, the shower door opened.

"Going somewhere?" Quinn asked as he moved his naked sweat-glistening body closer.

"Don't even tease me. Just back off. Mac's going to be knocking on the door any minute, and I'm not going to spend another day walking around sexually frustrated," I warned, trying to maneuver my way out of the shower without touching him.

My attempt was unsuccessful. In a flash he had my body pinned to the shower wall. His erection brushed my abdomen as my nipples hardened against his chest.

"Quinn, please don't," I pleaded in a whiny voice.

He slid his hands up the curve of my hips and

continued to my breasts, cupping them while grazing the pads of his thumbs over my nipples. I tilted my head back and released a grateful moan.

"I told Mac to give you an extra thirty minutes." His deep voice vibrated around me. "She knows you won't be going anywhere today until she's heard you screaming my name."

Jerking my head upright, I gasped. "You didn't!"

He captured my mouth with such passion, I felt weak in the knees. Thanksgiving was an emotional roller coaster. My body had been teased almost to the breaking point over the past twenty-four hours, and I was desperate for him. Leaving me breathless, he squatted in front of me, clenching my butt with his hands.

"I did," he responded in a serious voice, before his mouth was at my sex.

I laced my fingers through his hair, then clenched them for support. He kissed with teasing motions, occasionally tracing the outside of my folds with his tongue, capturing ringlets of water melting down my body. The firm grip of his hands on my butt was such polarity to the gentle whisper of his lips and tongue.

I yanked his head back. "You're teasing me and I've had enough. I love you and the way you've been so gentle and understanding with me since we arrived. But right now I'm about to lose it. No foreplay, no teasing and caressing, I just need you to fuck me ... hard."

His mouth turned up into a wry smile, but his eyes were dark and serious. "Turn around then."

Without hesitation, I turned around and placed my hands on the tile wall. He tapped the inside of one of my ankles with his foot until I spread my legs more. He reached around to my front and slid his fingers over my sex with one hand for a brief moment until he positioned his cock at my entrance with his other. I gasped as he slammed into me. Pausing a few seconds to let my body acclimate to his fullness, he pulled out, then right back in, each time hard and unforgiving. One of his hands guided my hip while the other grabbed my shoulder.

"Is this how you want it?" he gritted through his teeth.

"Yes!" I yelled meeting him thrust for thrust.

He pulled out and turned me around. Grabbing my hips, he lifted me onto him as he pressed my back to the wall. Our mouths crashed together as we had my definition of wild monkey sex in the shower. It was exactly what I needed. His tongue warred with mine as his hands searched my body grabbing my butt, kneading my breasts, and pinching my nipples.

"Oh God, Quinn, I need this so bad," I moaned as my orgasm approached.

My words encouraged him until his pace was out of control. "Fuck, Addy!" he yelled as his warmth filled me.

He immediately snaked his hand between us and pressed his fingers to my clit.

"God, Quinn ... more!" I put my hand over his urging him to continue. "Don't stop, please!" I cried without restraint.

While circling my clit, he rocked into me one more time as I found my climax.

"Yes, yes, yes!" My grateful voice echoed through the bathroom.

My head fell to his shoulder, and I fought to find my breath.

"Satisfied?"

"You have no idea," I breathed out.

Easing me back on my feet, he kissed my forehead. "*Actually*, I think I do." He smacked me on the butt. "Now get going. I need to soap up, and you need to shop until you drop."

Our Black Friday shopping was tolerable. After just a few hours, Mac was tired so we stopped for a long lunch before hitting one more baby store. By the time we got home, Mac was ready for a nap.

"Hey, Addy?"

"Yeah?"

"I have an appointment with my midwife on Monday. Evan will be in court and my mom already has a commitment of her own. Would you consider staying an extra day to go with me?"

I loaded myself down with all of her bags from the back of the car. "Quinn won't be able to stay, which means I'll have to try and find a flight out Monday night, but I'm sure it will be fine."

"Thanks, sweetie. Oh did you need help with those?" she said with an innocent smile.

"Just get the door," I demanded, shaking my head.

"You can put them in the spare room next to yours. I'm going to crash for an hour or so until dinner," she mumbled over a big yawn.

"Sounds good."

After setting all the bags down, I pulled a soft baby blanket from one and hugged it to my chest while I closed my eyes.

"I bet you were the greatest mom."

I jumped and turned at the sound of Quinn's voice in the doorway.

"You scared me," I gasped as I folded the blanket and set it back in the bag.

"Sorry." He smiled as he walked into the room and wrapped his arms around me. "Do you want another baby?"

Squeezing him tight, I shrugged. I was afraid of overwhelming him with my honest answer. *Yes, being a mom was the most fulfilling job I've ever had. I always wanted to be a mom and I always will.*

"Why? Do you want a baby?" I asked looking up at him.

His eyes searched mine for a few moments, then he smiled and nodded his head before pressing his lips to mine. Carrying Quinn's baby was a thrilling thought, but we weren't ready yet. He still needed to work through his recovery. Then there was the issue of where we would live, a small topic I hadn't mentioned since our recent reconciliation. As much as I wanted him to give me back the ring, meet me at the altar, and give me a honeymoon baby, we needed to take a few steps back to make sure we didn't end up going down the same road again.

"Speaking of babies, Mac asked me to stay until Monday so I can go to the prenatal visit with the midwife. Her mom is busy and Evan will be in court."

"I need to get back."

"I know. I'll get a flight out Monday night."

"That sounds good. Listen, I talked with Alexis earlier and she'd like us to go to her house for brunch tomorrow."

No!

"Oh, I guess that's ... just fine."

He pulled back to look at me. "It'll be fine. She knows we're back together and she's agreed to be on her best behavior."

I gritted my teeth together and smiled a big, goofy smile with wide eyes. "All righty then, I'll be on my best behavior as well ... 'cause we're twelve, right?"

After he finished rolling his eyes at me, I turned, tilted my chin, threw back my shoulders, and walked out. "Besides, I'm much too intellectually advanced and socially refined to partake in something as petty and juvenile as a catfight."

In the background I heard a soft chuckle, but I

continued on to the kitchen without another acknowledgement.

***

<u>*Journal Day 98*</u>
Grateful for a ladies' truce.

THE INTERESTING THING about my relationship with
Alexis was we had not taken the time to know each
other well enough to have an accurate opinion about
the other. She seemed displeased with me simply
because I was not Olivia. I, on the other hand, reached
my point of exhaustion trying to befriend her before I
realized I never realistically had a chance.

We had little in common. Yes, she was a mother,
but her kids seemed like trophy kids—a concept I
would never understand. I liked yoga and good food;
she liked shopping and washing down her diet pills
with a glass of wine. I wore comfy, casual clothes with
minimal makeup; she wore tight designer dresses, high
heels, and a complete face painting every time she left
the house. She looked fake and acted fake. Even her
voice seemed fabricated for each specific occasion.
Essentially, we had two things in common: we both
had a vagina and we both loved Quinn.

"I have nothing to wear." I sighed in exasperation.

Quinn laughed. "I don't think I've ever heard those
words come out of your mouth."

He, of course, looked amazing, as if he'd just

finished a photo shoot for GQ magazine. He wore black pants and a black button-down shirt with thin grey pinstripes. His sleeves were casually rolled up to his elbows and the first three buttons of his shirt were open.

"Everything I packed is so casual," I whined as I rummaged through the mess in my suitcase. "I would have bought something yesterday if I had known that we were going to your sister's."

He sat on the edge of the bed to pull on his socks. "Addy, it's just going to be her, Mitch, and the kids. It's no big deal."

"That's easy for you to say. You look good all the time. Some of us actually have to try."

He grabbed my hips and tugged me between his legs. I had on my usual black lace boy shorts and matching bra.

"Baby, you could wear a white sheet and be the envy of everyone in the room. So just throw on some jeans and a top and let's go before I rip these sexy panties and bra right off you." Clenching the back of my thighs, he pulled me in so his face was nestled at my cleavage.

I grabbed his face and tilted it up to look at mine. "You're right. Intellectually advanced and socially refined people don't need to wear fancy outfits to mask their lack of the aforementioned." After a quick kiss, I grabbed my jeans from the previous day and a comfy but worn light blue sweater.

"Are you implying my sister is stupid and unsocialized?"

"No, of course not. I don't know her well enough, or at least I hope I don't know her well enough to make that judgment."

"I still don't get what you mean?"

I walked into the bathroom to apply some makeup as I continued to explain. "I guess I just wonder if she acts around you or Mitch and the kids the way she does around me. I've never seen her without her makeup perfectly applied or wearing anything but a tight dress and high heels. Even her voice sounds fake, like she's auditioning for the part of some uppity woman who was born into a wealthy family and has never been on the other side of the tracks, so to speak."

Quinn stood in the doorway to the bathroom with his hands shoved in his pockets. "Well, she *was* raised in a wealthy family."

I leaned in closer to the mirror to apply some mascara. "So was I."

He moved behind me and pulled my hair off my neck then kissed me below my ear lobe. "You, my beautifully grounded lady, are the exception. Maybe if we shipped Alexis off to India for a few months she might trade in her makeup and heels for yoga pants and incense."

"Hmm, sounds like the perfect Christmas gift. Maybe we could tell her it's a special spa retreat."

"My mother would go—" Stopping mid-sentence,

he bit his upper lip and looked at my reflection in the mirror with pain in his eyes.

Turning toward him, I caressed my palm over his cheek. "Yes, your mother would have gone with her and she would have loved it."

He nodded and blinked back the watery emotions that started to form in his eyes.

"Occasionally, I'd try to call my mom and dad after they died. I'd want to tell them something Sage did or said, and then I'd hear the recording that said their number was no longer in service. I felt guilty for forgetting something as significant as my parents being dead. Then I realized that it was in those absentminded moments that I was at peace. Their deaths weren't haunting me and I'd found a sense of normalcy in my life again."

"How do you do that?" he asked with a furrowed brow.

"Find a sense of normalcy?"

"No. How do you give me more of yourself than I deserve?"

I laughed. "Believe me, I don't try. It just happens. Maybe you're my true north."

MAC OFFERED to let us take her car, but Quinn had already made other arrangements. A familiar black Bentley pulled up in their driveway right on time.

Eddie got out, dressed in his usual black suit attire,

and opened the back door for me while Quinn got in on the other side.

"Miss Brecken."

"Eddie, nice to see you. Did you have a pleasant holiday?"

"Yes. Thank you for asking."

As soon as he closed the door, I turned to Quinn. "Okay, it's been almost a year and a half since I first met Eddie in Milwaukee. The weekend of Richard and Gwen's anniversary party, he told me he lived in Chicago and worked for you, and when you're not in town he follows your instructions. What exactly does that mean?"

"Hmm, wouldn't you like to know?"

"Let me guess. He drives around your Chicago mistresses or wait, maybe he takes care of your wife and kids or wait—"

"*Or* ... he takes my nephew and niece to school every day and picks them up. And maybe when he's not doing that, he drives my sister to all her pampering appointments. And when he's not doing that, maybe he provides airport transportation to my Chicago-based business clients."

He reached over and squeezed my leg while shaking his head.

"Maybe ... but my scenarios had more flair." I laced my fingers with his.

"I don't need any more flair. I have enough sitting right here next to me." He chuckled.

As we pulled up to their house, my nerves got the

best of me. Quinn squeezed my hand as he leaned over to kiss me.

"It'll be fine. I love you and they do too."

A nervous smile was all I had to give before Eddie opened my door. Quinn grabbed my hand again as we walked to the door. He didn't bother knocking before he opened it.

The moment we walked in, six-year-old Ellen charged at Quinn. He released my hand and scooped her up in his arms.

"Quinn!" she squealed.

"How's my favorite niece?"

"Good." She smiled while tilting her chin to her chest, rolling her eyes up to give me a shy gaze.

"Do you remember Addy?" he asked as her arms squeezed around his neck.

She nodded.

"Hi, Ellen. Did you have a fun Thanksgiving?" I asked.

Still staring at me with alien awe, she continued to nod without verbal response.

"Where's your brother?" Quinn asked as he set her down and took my coat.

"Kitchen," she softly replied before turning and running.

"Hey, man," Mitch called as he came down the stairs.

They shared a hand shake. Then, without hesitation, Mitch gave me a big hug. "It's about time Quinn got his head out of his ass and got back the best thing that's ever happened to him."

Pulling back, I wasted no time correcting him. "He didn't get me back. I went to New York for him, and he did not exactly welcome me with open arms. So, *actually*, he still has his head up his ass." I smiled.

Quinn grabbed my arm and pulled me into him. "Thanks, baby. You know it really hurts getting thrown under the bus like that."

"Yeah, well, it hurt getting thrown out of your condo on my ass."

"What?" Mitch asked with wide-eyed curiosity.

Nine-year-old Ethan bolted down the stairs. "Hey, Uncle Quinn."

"Hey, buddy. Thanks for saving me. Let's go find your mom." Quinn followed Ethan to the kitchen.

"Don't think you two are done with your little story," Mitch chided as I followed Quinn and Ethan.

"I'd better let Quinn tell you the rest. I'm sure he'll put a much more creative spin on it."

"I heard that," Quinn hollered.

Alexis was in the kitchen. Doing what? I wasn't sure. She was dressed for dinner with the Queen and had an apron on that looked brand new. There were numerous containers on the counter filled with food, but they looked like carryout containers from a restaurant. There weren't any pots or pans on the stove, and the oven was shut off. Then I caught sight of the light on in the microwave.

After she gave Quinn a big hug and asked Mitch to

open a bottle of wine, she plastered on her beauty queen smile and acknowledged my presence.

"Addy," was all she said before she removed the container from the microwave and exchanged it with the next one on the counter.

What the hell?

"Hello, Alexis. Is there … anything I can help you with?" I asked, dumbfounded by what I witnessed.

"I'm good, unless you want to grab some baby carrots from the refrigerator. The best restaurants in Chicago don't have much that's considered vegan, so I hope Quinn told you to eat before you came. There's dip in the fridge too, but I think it's a sour cream dip."

Quinn had already followed Mitch and the kids into the dining room, so he missed that little zinger.

"So, when did you get all this stuff?" I asked as I looked at the containers of meat and creamy side dishes.

"Last night after Quinn called and said you'd be coming. I had Mitch run and pick it up from that new French restaurant by his office. We did the same thing for his parents when they came for Thanksgiving: picked everything up the night before and popped it in the microwave the next day. I transferred everything to nice serving dishes for Thanksgiving, but I figured since Quinn's my brother and you're a vegan we could just serve them in the carryout containers."

Deep breath … I am peaceful, I am strong.

"That's fine, however, I'm not sure what my being a vegan has to do with it."

"Oh you know what I mean. Your kind just aren't ... oh what's the word I'm looking for?"

"Pretentious?"

"No."

"Ostentatious?"

"No."

"Vulgar, showy, stuck-up?"

"No, no, no. Hygienic. That's the word I'm looking for," she declared as she removed the final dish from the microwave.

"Hygienic? Do you even know what that means?" I questioned in disbelief.

She waved her hand in the air. "You know, clean ... well kept. Time to eat! Mitch, Quinn, come help carry the food into the dining room."

When the men made their way back to the kitchen Quinn raised a suspicious eyebrow at me.

"Is everything okay?" he mouthed as he grabbed two of the containers.

Biting my upper lip, *and tongue*, I nodded with big eyes that said otherwise. His forehead wrinkled in concern.

Alexis removed her apron, tossed it on the counter, and strutted into the dining room. "Don't forget your carrots, Addy," she called out.

Deep breath ... I am peaceful, I am strong.

After everyone was seated, Mitch gave the blessing. Then, as if we were at a late night office meeting, everyone started passing around the take-out containers. I set a handful of carrots on my plate, which surprisingly was an actual dinner plate.

"Is that all you're having?" Quinn whispered.

"Yes, because apparently you forgot to mention that I was supposed to eat before I came," I whispered between gritted teeth and a fake smile.

He furrowed his brow in confusion. "Alexis, why didn't you order anything for Addy?"

"I tried but they didn't have any vegan dishes." She shrugged and continued to eat.

"Then you should have ordered from someplace else," he returned in a firm voice.

"Alexis, when I asked you about it, you said you had something for Addy," Mitch added.

"Hello? Are you all blind? What do you think she's eating?"

"Mommy said you don't eat meat because you like to get all the attention," Ellen happily chimed in.

Quinn's whole body went rigid. "Ellen, Ethan, how would you two like to eat downstairs in front of the TV?"

"But we're not allowed to eat downstairs," Ethan protested.

Mitch got the hint and made his move. "Today is a special exception. Daddy will help carry your plates. Let's go."

Everyone waited in silence until the kids were downstairs.

"I don't need a lecture," Alexis announced breaking the silence.

"If Mother were here—"

Alexis cut him off. "Well she's not! Thanks to Addy, we will never see her again."

"Dammit, Alexis!" Quinn's hand slammed the table. "Addy didn't kill Mother. She didn't give her cancer, she didn't do anything wrong. She only did what Mother wanted her to do. So if you're going to be upset with someone, then be upset with Mother for not telling us. But Addy is off limits!"

"Don't you dare talk to me that way. You're nothing but a pathetic, drunken loser, just like Dad was. You fuck everything that moves and you have absolutely no respect for anyone but yourself. You two deserve each other. I'm sure it'll be a race to see if she can stab you in the back again before your stick your dick in someone else."

I stood and reached for Quinn's hand. "Let's go."

He didn't need any convincing. Without another word he marched off to get our coats.

"Going home to braid your armpit hair?" Alexis sneered as I turned to leave.

My ego dragged me backward until I stood next to her. "Wouldn't you like to know?" I grabbed a container of food and dumped it down the front of her white dress.

Her arms flailed to the side as she gasped in horror.

Then I repeated with another container of something that had a nice red wine sauce. "It's pretty pathetic that you spend time thinking about my armpits, because I guarantee you when I leave here I will no longer be thinking about that unsightly mustache on *your* lip. Better watch that, before long people will think you're a *vegan* with 'poor hygiene skills.'"

Her hand instinctively covered her lip. "You bitch!" she yelled as she stood up. "Do you have any idea how much this dress cost? Or how much money I spent on all this food?"

"Oh my God, the food, really? I guarantee you the French chef who made this last night would shit his pants at the thought of you serving it a day later out of the microwave."

Just as Alexis started to come at me, two strong arms wrapped around me from behind and carried me toward the door.

"What are you doing?" Quinn asked as he hurried us out.

"You'd better get out!" she yelled charging after us.

I tried to free myself, but his grip was too firm. "And who the fuck still microwaves their food anyway? Why don't you just let your kids smoke a pack of Marlboros for dinner?"

Eddie had the door to the Bentley wide open so Quinn could toss me in and shut it quickly. As soon as he was in the other side, Eddie wasted no time leaving the premises. I straightened myself after being manhandled into the car then crossed my arms over my chest.

Quinn raked his hands through his hair and

sighed. "That went well." He tried to hide his incredulous smirk but couldn't.

I looked out my window to hide the smile that crept across my own face. "I think so too."

My smile turned into an uncontrolled giggle, which made Quinn smile even bigger. "My mantra completely failed me."

"Yeah, I'd say so."

"How do you know about my mantra? I've never told you." I asked tilting my head to the side.

"Deep breath … I am peaceful, I am strong. You say it in your sleep. The first time I heard it was after our first night together. I thought it was some sort of sex mantra. I thought it was hot. But then I started noticing how you take a deep breath when you're upset, and I assume that's what you're saying to yourself."

Smar-ty-pants!

"Wow, babe! Your manly status just took a real hit with that confession."

"How so?"

"Now I know you're observant, and men are rarely observant."

"Well, then I might as well let you know that I observed everything at my sister's house. It was like a game of limbo, seeing which one of you two could stoop the lowest and not get hit."

"She started it."

"Real mature. What happened to my intellectually advanced and socially refined woman?'"

"She basically called me an unhygienic attention

hog who is not worthy of having food served on a plate, then she handed me a bag of baby carrots for brunch. And just so you know, I was also sticking up for you."

"Thanks, baby, but I've been pulling Alexis' hair, snapping the heads off her Barbie dolls, calling her names, and tormenting her boyfriends since she was old enough to walk. I'm pretty sure I can stick up for myself."

"Fine then, I was just trying to put the bitch in her place." I pouted.

"And … by bitch, you mean my sister?"

"And … by your sister, you mean bitch?" I retorted.

"I hesitate to ask, but I just can't help myself … microwaves and Marlboros?"

"Uh … yeah. It causes the formation of carcinogens in foods. Clinical studies conducted by Dr. Hertel showed significant changes in blood samples from test groups that consumed microwaved foods. Most notably in hemoglobin and leukocyte values, which went beyond normal daily deviations, suggesting pathogenic effects such as poisoning and cell damage."

Quinn looked at me like I'd just given birth to an alien baby. "I can't believe it—you're a conspiracy theorist."

"If by conspiracy theorist you mean someone smart enough to see the corruption and deception through the smoke and mirrors of our corporate-run government, then yes. I am a conspiracy theorist. Marlboros and microwaves, fluoride and Alzheimer's, mercury and autoimmune diseases, dairy and osteoporosis ... Choose your topic and I'll enlighten you."

His smile could not have been more exuberant. "Addy?"

"Hmm?"

"I love you."

CHAPTER NINETEEN

THE REST of our weekend in Chicago was uneventful, compared to brunch on Saturday. Quinn had to fly home Sunday afternoon. I was worried about how he would handle going back to work and meeting with clients while avoiding the temptation to drink. He had done it for years by choice without the cravings that come from addiction, but those days were gone and every day was going to be a challenge. A challenge that would get easier, but would most likely never be completely gone.

After Quinn said goodbye to Mac and Evan, I walked him to the door. He enveloped me in his arms and kissed the top of my head.

"It's going to be lonely in bed without you tonight."

"Well, at least you'll be in your bed and not the chair." I couldn't resist.

"Funny girl, huh? You're right. I'll be in my bed, but

not alone ... I'll have a big bag of *microwave* popcorn to keep me company."

"Real cheeky." I smirked with squinted eyes.

Our banter came so naturally. Everything about Quinn felt natural, fated ... perfect.

Squeezing him tighter, I said the words I'd been wanting to say since we left Alexis'. "Thank you for what you said yesterday."

He leaned back to look at me. "What did I say?"

"You said that it wasn't my fault your mom died. You've never said those words to me, and although I knew in your heart your felt them, it meant a lot for me to hear them."

"Baby, I've been a real jerk. There are so many wrongs that I'll never be able to right—so many things I've said and done that were cruel and, honestly, unforgivable. But what you did for my mother was amazing. I can't imagine what it must have been like to watch her die. You knew the consequences—the pain, the contempt—and yet you still said yes. I love you, and I've said before that if I were a better man, I'd let you go, because you deserve so much more."

Happiness is a choice, a state of mind. Thinking that Quinn made me happy would have implied he made my choices for me. That wasn't true. However, he made all the colors of my rainbow shine brighter, and I couldn't imagine deserving or needing more than that.

"You did let me go, more than once. And I came back, more than once. Oh God, what does that say about me? I just can't take a hint, can I? When we first met I accused you of stalking me, but look who's stalking now? How can I be so smart and yet so stu—"

His lips captured my mouth, and I felt hypnotized by his touch as my thoughts faded. The rest of the world ceased to exist when our bodies connected. After I fell limp in his embrace, he inched his head back and grazed his thumb over my then swollen lips.

"Stop analyzing. It's simple … you are brilliant and I am, and may always be, a fucking idiot. But I promise you, no one will ever love you as much as I do; thankfully, loving you *is* a no-brainer."

"Ah, babe, you will forever be my favorite ignoramus. Now get going before I have to explain to Mac why I'm dragging your sexy ass back to the bedroom."

Placing his hand on the back of my head, he pulled our foreheads together. "I'll see you later beautiful," he whispered.

"Goodbye, babe. Have a safe flight. I love you."

He grabbed his bag and turned back. "Never goodbye," he said with a wink.

My heart ached a little, as it always did, when we parted. Life was too unpredictable and definitely not "fair" in my book. The present was our only guarantee, which often filled the past with regret and the future with uncertainty.

Journal Day 100
Grateful for 100 days of life-changing perspective.

Monday morning Mac was just plain giddy. Her first official prenatal visit with the midwife went great. She found out she was further along than she originally thought, but with her irregular menstrual cycles we weren't surprised. The countdown was officially on, twenty-seven weeks until her due date.

"Addy, you have to get your ass relocated to my zip code. This is ridiculous! I hate to play the 'you owe me' card, but right now I have an excess of hormones raging through my body and I cannot be responsible for what comes out of my mouth."

"I know. As I recall I was the recipient of your hormonal and not-so-discrete vulgarity on Thanksgiving." I handed her a cup of raspberry leaf tea and sat next to the fireplace.

"Jesus Christ, Addy. Do you have any idea how crazy horny I was after walking in on you getting ready to mount your Arabian horse? I'm talking the. Best. Porn. Ever! I carried your smoothies back to the kitchen just as Evan was coming inside from taking out the garbage. I shoved down his running pants and sucked him off while I flicked my bean. The poor guy didn't know what came over me. The upside has been his eagerness to take out the garbage every morning since. This morning he woke me up at 6 a.m. to make sure I knew he hauled out the garbage."

The disgusted grimace on my face felt permanent. "Oh my gosh, Mac! TMI! And for the record, the BJ garbage story ... NOT the. Best. Porn. Ever!"

She sipped her tea and shrugged. "I guess it depends on what you're into."

I shook my head in rapid succession as if it were really possible to erase the visual in my head like an Etch A Sketch. "You know I'd love to stay and chat, but I have a plane to catch."

"Ah yes, you have to get back to New York and act out the happy ending to your epic love story, which of course ends in Chicago."

"Mmm, if it's truly epic, it will never end. Now go pee, and I'll meet you in the car."

***

I RETURNED to New York by dinner Monday night. After leaving several messages on Quinn's cell phone as well as half a dozen texts, all without response, I started to worry. The condo was dark and silent when I opened the door, however, it was odd that the alarm hadn't been set. When I flipped on the entry light, a dark shadowy figure on the couch nearly stopped my heart.

"Oh my God!" I gasped.

"Sorry, baby, it's just me."

I flipped on another set of lights. "Jeez, you scared me! What are you doing? I tried calling you and I sent you numerous texts."

"Sorry," was all he said in a somber voice.

An uneasy feeling rippled through my body in

chilling waves. Something was wrong. "Have you been drinking?"

"No," he said with a pained laugh. "I want one, so fucking bad, but I haven't had a single drop."

He sat with his elbows on his knees and his head cradled in his hands. I shrugged off my coat and knelt in front of him with my hands resting on his flexed biceps.

"Quinn, what happened?"

Taking a deep swallow, he shook his head as if the words were caught in his throat.

My mind started to roam in every direction. I thought about death, cancer, car accidents, business dealings gone wrong, but I didn't even once consider the words that came from his mouth.

"Olivia is pregnant."

Silence. Anguish. Heartache. Misery.

Deep breath ... I can't, I can't breathe ...

"No ... no ..." I shook my head as I sat back on my heels. Biting my bottom lip to keep it from quivering, I tried to blink back the tears ... but there were too many.

"I-I-don't understand. You said you didn't sleep with any of them, you told me you slept in the chair. This doesn't make any sense!"

"I wasn't lying, I didn't sleep with them ... when you were in New York. But before, when I was drinking—"

"STOP!" I screamed as I covered my face with my hands. "Just stop, I don't want to know."

"Addy, you were with Jake. How do you think that makes me feel when I think of him with you: touching you, kissing you, fucking you?"

"I get it, Quinn! It hurts, it hurts so ... damn ... bad!" I wiped my face and met his eyes. "But now tell me how it would feel if I told you today that I was carrying his baby? Tell me that it wouldn't fucking gut you. Tell me what you expect me to say, what you expect me to do?"

Leaning forward, he ran his fingers though my hair then held my head inches from his. "Stay. I *need* you to stay, as much as I need my next breath."

"Why are you doing this?" I sobbed. "Do you have any idea how desperate I was to hear those words from your mouth so many times before? And *now* you're asking me to stay ... and do what? Watch another woman carry your baby. The baby I was supposed to give you. It's not fair for you to ask me to do that."

"I know it's not, but I'm still asking. God, Addy, I'm begging you ... *please* don't go."

I wrapped my hands around his wrists as he continued to hold my head. His touch felt so vital to my existence. Then I cried, because my heart grieved for the life with Quinn that became more elusive every day. He picked me up and held me tight.

"It was supposed to be me—it was supposed to be me!" I cried out, as I pounded my fists against his chest. My shattered heart ached as my stomach wrenched. It was a dull pain that left me begging for reprieve.

"I'm so sorry, baby," he breathed in my ear.

An hour or so later I was still curled up on his lap. My tears ran dry and the all too familiar numb feeling blanketed my body. Quinn didn't speak; he didn't move. I think he would have held me there forever, if it would have meant I would stay. My ear rested against his chest and the sound of his heart reminded me of all the little pieces of mine that were still beating. That's the most amazing thing about the heart, even alone, each individual cell tells itself to rhythmically contract and relax. As much as I wanted to will mine to stop, it wouldn't.

"Why am I even here? It's like the world rejects me at every turn. I feel like I don't belong, but my soul is stuck in this stupid life. What the hell am I supposed to learn from all of this? I've tried so hard to be happy, content, and grateful, but it's too much ... I'm just too tired. I'm tired of existing."

"Me. You're here for me, to love me, live life with me, *be* with me. If you're too tired, I'll carry you through every day until you can walk on your own again. Just ... stay."

"I'll stay," I breathed out. Those two words came out so easily because, in that moment, I didn't care if I died. Honestly, I thought I'd already lost him and my only wish was to die in his arms.

IT TOOK me three days to get out of bed, with the exception of using the bathroom. I refused to eat, but I willingly drank water because I needed the tears. Quinn worked from home—specifically, from the bedroom. He only left my side to get food for himself or water for us. Fear was etched deep in his face. He was scared to leave me alone. I, on the other hand, feared *nothing.*

After seventy-two hours, I broke the silence. "You should go to work." My back was to him and my voice was weak.

"Only if you come with me."

I shook my head.

"Then I'm not going anywhere."

He sat in the infamous chair by the window, working on his computer. Closing his laptop, he moved to my side of the bed. Kneeling on the floor, he kissed my forehead. "I love you, and *you* will always be the love of my life."

He didn't know what that really meant. Olivia carried a piece of him that would change that. He would hold his little baby, look into its eyes, and see the reflection of his soul. The thought melted a few more tears from my eyes.

He kissed them away. "I'll be right back." He went into the bathroom and started the shower. A few minutes later he came back out with just a towel wrapped around his waist. "Let's go."

I shook my head.

"Then we'll do it the hard way, but you're taking a shower." He pulled down the sheets and stripped my clothes. Then he cradled me in his arms and carried me into the steamy shower. Multiple jets shot warm water out from the walls, while a massive square fixture poured rain-like water from the ceiling. He set me on my feet, and I closed my eyes as streams and rivulets raced down my body.

Starting on my back, I felt his soap-slicked hands slowly massaging my muscles. He took his time, giving every inch of my body his undivided attention. The tenderness and deep love I felt in his touch stirred the raw emotions that had festered for days. Grateful for the camouflage of the water, I let more toxic emotions flow from my closed eyes as he stood behind me, washing my hair.

Leaving me to stand with the warm water raining down on me, he quickly washed himself before shutting off the water. He wrapped me up in a long, thick, terrycloth robe and sat me on top of the vanity. After brushing my teeth, he dried my hair. More tears fell, as my mind drifted to memories of my mom. I used to love sitting at her vanity in a small gold chair with a white velvet seat while she used her soft-bristled brush on my long hair. She would look at my reflection in the mirror and tell me how I was everything perfect about her and my dad.

I wanted my mom so desperately. She would've known how to make everything better. As many times as I butted heads with her, I never doubted her love for me. I knew from experience, mothers were granted magical healing powers.

Did Quinn wish his mother were there to tell him

what to do … to magically make everything right in his world again?

When he finished drying my hair, he kissed away more tears, slipped on a pair of jeans, and carried me downstairs.

"You're losing weight, so either you eat, or I call Mac. What's it going to be?"

"Eat."

He peeled back a banana and handed it to me before getting one for himself. The interesting part about fasting is that by the third day, you're not hungry. It took me twenty minutes to finish my banana. Quinn made oatmeal with pecans, cinnamon, and coconut nectar. When he held a spoonful to my mouth I shook my head.

"You said you'd eat."

"I did." My response was monotone while my face remained expressionless. I tossed my banana peel on the counter in his direction, then I stood and went back upstairs.

CHAPTER TWENTY

Quinn

IF THERE WOULD HAVE BEEN a line of people waiting to spit on my father's grave, I would have been at the front. The truth was, he did more good in his life than bad. But ask any politician what stands out on Judgment Day and they'll all say it was the bribe they took, the prostitute they slept with once, or the pot they smoked in college. It doesn't take much to tarnish an Ivy League education, a thirty-year political career, a professional athlete's reputation, or even a Nobel Peace Prize.

My father came to America and built his companies from the ground up. He provided jobs for thousands of people and treated his employees with respect. He loved my mother and his three children more than life. He sacrificed so much to give us the life he never had. But in the end, it was the *one* poor business decision out of a million, a meaningless affair that lasted weeks compared to forty years of marriage, and a few years of addiction out of sixty years of sobriety that everyone remembered ... including me.

If fucked-up had a definition, it was what happened the night I let Olivia into my condo after I'd gotten home from work and numbed my misery with several hard drinks. Most nights I drank until I passed out, but she caught me a couple glasses shy of my goal. When she asked me how I was doing, all I could think about was Addy, my Addy, naked under Jake. Fucking Jake. I needed another drink, but what Olivia offered worked just as well. That was my mark. The night that tarnished everything else.

A baby. Olivia didn't even want kids. When she showed up at my office Monday, I knew she was pissed, but she tried to cover it with her fake enthusiasm. Asking her to have an abortion, which she would have done if it were any other guy's child, was not an option.

My mother didn't like Olivia, but she would have disowned me for suggesting or even allowing the termination of her grandchild. I think Olivia waited for me to drop down on one knee and promise her forever. That would never happen. There was no doubt that my child would not want for anything, but my feelings for Olivia would never go beyond simple respect for her being the mother of my child.

I told Addy I hadn't been drinking and that wasn't a lie. But I didn't tell her how many glasses of Scotch I poured at my office and shattered against the wall before I went home. Part of me knew I'd already lost her, so I figured why not start the numbing process. But when I arrived home with my brown bag of poison, I was drawn to the sealed envelope in my room, the letter from my mother. Before I removed the cap to my most certain demise, I tore open the letter. I felt confident that after reading it I would need the alcohol more than ever.

My Dearest Quinten,

You are such a beautiful expression of my soul. You were my first born ... and my first TRUE love. When I take my last breath, I will remember your first. When I held you in my arms, my whole purpose in life was realized. I lived to love you. You have to know, I died a million deaths after your climbing accident. The day you went in for surgery I promised God my life in exchange for yours. When I found out the cancer had returned, I knew it was time. I made a promise to God, and when he spared your life, I willingly followed when he called for mine. I'm ready. The chemotherapy nearly killed me the first time, and I can't do it again. Addy has offered to take me anywhere in the world, for any type of treatment. She'd spare no expense to save my life, to give you back your mother.

Everyone needs to know that Addy has been amazing. She's so broken—just shattered inside, yet she continually gives more of herself than she really has to give. I love her and I know you do too.

Forgive, my dear son. Forgive me for not saying goodbye. Forgive your father for his mistakes. Forgive Addy for everything ... always. Then forgive yourself. You don't have to be perfect to have the perfect life. Remember that, because had your father been able to grasp that, he would still be alive.

Love. Love yourself enough to hold on and love others enough to let go. I know you're so talented. Money and success have always come easy to you, but they're not worthy of your passion. Find your one true passion in life and follow it. Follow it until you take your last breath.

I will always be with you. Look for me in everything that makes you smile. Feel my loving arms around you when you're sad. And hear my voice in the wind and the ripple of the tides. Be well, my dear child. Thank you for the best thirty-five years of my life. Being your mother was truly the greatest gift!

All my love & all my life —Mom

I crumpled the paper in my hands and held it to my face. When I pulled it back, I noticed the smudged black ink from my tears. I raced to the sink to grab a towel. I blotted the letters before her words faded as quickly as she did. Then I put it in my safe at the back of my closet. When I returned to my bedroom, the brown sack of alcohol on my dresser taunted me. I grabbed it and frantically removed the cap before dumping the contents into the sink.

Addy sent me numerous texts and left multiple messages on my phone. I knew she was on her way. However, I needed all the time I could get to gain the courage it would to take to tell the love of my life that another woman was carrying my child. Addy believed in karma, but I wasn't as convinced until then. My cavalier and often reckless lifestyle caught up with me, and in that moment Olivia's pregnancy felt like karma.

Had I not read my mother's letter, I would have let Addy walk out my door forever, just like I tried to do so many times before. But one word kept racing through my mind, *passion*. Addy was my one true passion in life. I wanted her more than I wanted to breathe. I'd made up my mind that I would never give up on her. If she left me, I would spend the rest of my life, *until I took my last breath*, searching for her and begging for her forgiveness. I owed it to my mother. I owed it to myself.

Alcohol would have taken the edge off the emotional stab that came from breaking someone's heart. Telling Addy about Olivia—sober—was like slowly shoving a knife in her chest and simultaneously in mine as well. It was a raw, Shakespearean moment. She wanted to die in my arms and I in hers. I had to be strong for her, like she had been for me. But all I really wanted to do was lock out the rest of the world and never be separated from her again.

Being strong for her in one of my own weakest moments drained everything from me, but by some miracle, three days later we were both still hanging on. However, desperation continued to lurk at every corner. I needed to do something to jolt us out of our eternal misery.

CHAPTER TWENTY-ONE

Addy

LIFE IS full of peaks and valleys. Then there was my life. By Saturday morning I still felt like I was at the bottom of the valley, pinned under a massive boulder that crushed me. I could barely breathe and help was nowhere in sight. The previous day I spent in bed, even my water intake was down, which was fine because I was tired of crying.

Quinn spent the day either on the phone or downstairs answering the door. My curiosity had vanished, along with my appetite and will to live. I never asked him who was at the door or what the jumbled chatter was all about. I. Just. Didn't. Care.

Quinn cracked the blinds to the room, letting in just enough morning light for me to notice the snow falling. I squinted my eyes.

"Close them," I grumped before burying my face in the pillow.

"Not today, love. Today, you get out of bed." Quinn had a bit of hope in his voice that I hadn't heard since I arrived back in New York. He scooped me up in his arms and carried me out of the bedroom.

Taking one slow step at a time, he carried me down the stairs, and my lungs captured their first full breath of air since Monday. Everything, literally everything, was adorned with garland, lights, wreaths, ornaments, and ribbons. The air smelled like a delicious mix of cinnamon and pine. The harmony of The Christmas Song on the piano flowed from the surround sound. When we turned the corner at the bottom of the stairs, the sight before my eyes was grander than anything I had ever seen in my life.

Extravagant was inadequate, because there really were no words. The tree was a Griswold fantasy. The crystal star at the top nearly touched the double-height ceiling. There must have been a thousand ornaments hanging from the branches. It was Rockefeller Center meets Macy's, architecturally designed to perfection for Quinn's condo. Even his couch was covered in holiday decor pillows and two large poinsettias sat at each end. The kitchen island had red glass votives next to a plate of exquisitely decorated sugar cookies and two tall holiday mugs filled with hot apple cider.

He set me down on my feet and moved a step back, as if he wanted to give me a moment to absorb it all.

After several minutes my eyes found his again. I didn't see the alcoholic man I saved only a couple weeks earlier; or the father of Olivia's child; or the broken spirit that had clung to me just days earlier. All I could see was love. My whole body flooded with warmth, and my lungs welcomed the fresh air, as though I hadn't been breathing for days.

"This is ... I can't believe you ..."

Shaking his head, he flashed me his cocky grin and said the one word I needed to hear to bring a genuine smile to my face. "Elves."

Sometimes fighting hurts more than just surrendering. As much as I wanted our situation to be different, fighting reality was way too exhausting. What he did for me was the equivalent of Mac tackling me in the airport after the fire. It was my wake up call. I had to choose to live or die, but hanging on the precipice was no longer a choice.

"I love your elves."

"And me?"

I walked into his open arms. "You're okay."

AFTER I REHYDRATED with a large glass of water, we sat at the counter and sipped hot cider while the snow outside continued to fall.

"So what was your plan B?" I asked.

He wrinkled his brow and cocked his head to the side. "If this didn't work?"

I nodded with a smile.

"Fly you to the most remote place on Earth without telling anyone and never come back."

"I'm guessing it would have been less expensive than all this." I motioned to the room with my mug in hand.

"Probably, but who cares? I gave them your credit card, not mine." He kept a straight face as he lifted a frosted cookie to his mouth.

I shoved his hand, smashing his cookie into his face. "You shit."

He was undoubtedly caught off guard as he sucked in a deep breath, his eyes wide. I hopped onto his lap, straddling him, then wiped some frosting from the tip of his nose. I sucked it off my finger with a smile. "I knew you were just after my money."

"Mmm and this ..." He grabbed the back of my head and smashed his mouth against my lips. When his tongue slid next to mine, I could taste sweet vanilla and him. As he released me, we both laughed at the sight of the other's messy face. Then our eyes locked and our smiles faded. There was an almost palpable electricity between us. My heart raced as his chest rose and fell against mine. He curled a tendril of hair behind my ear and cupped my face with his hand.

I leaned into it and closed my eyes, "Quinn," I breathed out.

Dropping his head to my neck, he slid his tongue all the way to my ear. Sucking in my lobe, he grazed it with his teeth. "Addy," he whispered back.

My nipples pebbled under my thin white tank and heaviness filled my sex. He teased my bottom lip with his teeth and pulled on it, eliciting a moan from my throat. The bulge in his jeans pressed against my panties as I ran my fingers through his hair and arched my back, so my taut nipples pressed against his chest.

"Make love to me."

He stilled and looked into my eyes, then dragged his gaze to my lips for a moment before meeting my eyes again and nodding his head. Standing, he hiked me up on his waist as I interlaced my fingers behind his neck.

As he walked toward the stairs, I shook my head. "By the tree..." I grinned "...so the elves can watch."

He reached over and grabbed the plush, new, holiday blanket from the back of the couch and attempted to spread it on the massive rug by the tree. Then he kneeled down and laid me on the blanket. "Well, since I'm not sure if *you* left a big enough tip, maybe they do deserve a little show."

Kneeling between my bent legs, he removed his T-shirt. My shameless eyes admired every inch of his sculpted-to-perfection body. Each second with him was a gift. I continued to watch him remove the rest of his clothes, as well as my tank and panties, making sure I committed the moment to memory. That moment was everything, when our future seemed so grim. I never wanted to forget the way he looked completely exposed to me, but more than that, I never wanted to forget the way he looked at me.

Ghosting his lips over the swell of my breasts, he feathered his fingers up the curves of my hips to the sides of my breasts, finally pushing my arms above my head. As he interlaced our fingers, his tongue traced my nipple before sucking it into his mouth. My breath hitched as a jolt of sensation descended between my legs. When he moved to my other breast, he lowered his hips just enough for the tip of his hard cock to graze through the seam of my wet, swollen sex. My hips jerked up as the rest of my body writhed beneath him.

"Again," I moaned.

He licked a hot, wet path from my nipple to my mouth. Then as he plunged his tongue in to dance with mine, he angled his hips back and dipped forward, taking a deeper swipe between my folds and up across my clit.

"Again," I begged, pushing my hips completely off the floor.

Engulfing my mouth, he released my hands. One of his hands went straight to my breast, squeezing, tugging, and kneading it. The other snaked between my thighs. His fingertips softly brushed over my sex and just as I released a needy whimper, his middle finger penetrated my folds and slid up my channel. I squeezed his finger and nearly orgasmed. My breathing became erratic as I tried to control the building sensation that was ready to explode.

"Let it go," he whispered in my ear as his thumb circled my clit.

"Ung ... oh God!" Closing my eyes, I saw stars as I climaxed to his expert touch.

Before I came down, he slid his erection into me—completely. He paused as my muscles clenched around his delicious fullness. I waited for him to move, but he didn't. He pinned me to the floor with just his eyes. I rolled mine to the side and nervously chewed the inside of my cheek.

"Addy ... look at me."

I couldn't.

"Addy ..." He rested his forehead on mine as my damn tears came back. When I finally looked at him, he kissed them away.

"It was one night. I was drunk, but not passed out yet. I never even kissed her or looked into her eyes. I closed mine and thought of you ... with Jake." He brushed his lips against mine as he pulled back and pushed into me again and again. "It's you, only you, *always* you."

I wrapped my legs around his waist as he made love to me. It was no longer about a mind-blowing orgasm ... it was feeling connected to him in every way. Memories of the night he proposed to me on the beach played in my mind. I remembered the same feeling of need, anxiety, and desperation. Every inch of my skin craved his touch. Fisting his hair, I pulled him to my lips so hard I felt them bruising as they melded together. I didn't care. I surrendered my body to his as he breathed life back into me.

He stilled upon his release. "I love you ... I love you so fucking much it hurts," he groaned.

After he showered my face with soft kisses, he started to pull out.

"Don't ... not yet," I said, digging my heels into his firm butt.

He slid his arm under my back and lifted my body to his chest as he rolled to his back without breaking our connection. I rested my head against his chest, picking up the rhythm of his heart.

"I'm not trying to be needy it's just—"

"Shh, you don't have to explain. And for the record, I could live the rest of my life buried inside you like this. Besides, it speeds up the recovery time," he thrust his hips so I could feel how his shaft was already starting to stir again.

WE STAYED TANGLED TOGETHER on the floor by the tree for two more hours. I never wanted to leave our little bubble. We worshipped each other's bodies through leisurely caressing and tasting. His scent drove me crazy. It wasn't a cologne, lotion, or soap; it was those damn pheromones. I loved nuzzling my nose in his chest, hair, and the crook of his neck. He breathed me in just as often, and every time he did it sent chills down my spine. It felt like he could devour me; and in terms of crazy, insane, love addiction, nothing could be better.

Wrapped in the blanket, he had me tucked into his body, spooning my back.

"What are you going to do?" I asked in a soft voice.

He didn't answer right away, but I knew he heard me. "Whatever it takes."

Could you be any more vague?

Permanently landing in Chicago in twenty-seven weeks with Quinn was not going to happen. I would undoubtedly be there for Mac as her due date approached, but Quinn would be in New York, waiting for his own child to be born. The thought was crushing.

"Financially she doesn't need my help, but I'm sure she'll insist on it anyway. Other than money, there's not much I can do until the baby is older. Then I suppose it will be no different than shared custody in a divorce situation."

"God, Quinn ... could you be any more naive? You honestly don't think she's going to expect you to be at every prenatal appointment? What about the birth, will you be in the room with her? And what makes you think she's not going to expect you to have this child fifty-percent of the time from day one? Not every woman breastfeeds their baby. If she opts for formula, then it is quite possible you could be playing dad to a newborn. Bottles, diapers, late night feedings, crying, spitting up ... have you even considered this?"

"I'll hire a nanny."

"Who's here every night?"

"Of course, it's not exactly unheard of. Lots of

wealthy people hire nannies to basically raise their children."

Is he for real?

I sat up and pulled the blanket over my chest. "So if we had a baby and I died you would hire a stranger to raise our child?"

"No, of course not, that's not the same—" he ran his fingers through his hair in frustration.

"As much as it pains—no, as much as it *kills* me that she is pregnant with your child, it is in fact still *your* child. You can't treat this baby any differently than you would if it were our baby."

Shaking his head he exhaled. "That's just it ... it's not the same. No person wants to or should be told that they were a mistake, but what happened the night that child was conceived *was* a mistake. I can't love you the way I do and ever say otherwise. Don't you understand? It's just biology to me right now. I feel no more attachment to this child than a sperm donor would. But I don't have the option of anonymity and I fucking wish to hell I did!"

I jumped in his lap straddling him as I hugged him into me with a fierce intensity. "I'm sorry, I'm not trying to make you feel guilty, I'm just ... I don't know."

"I don't care if I sound like the biggest prick in the world, but even if I feel a connection or some sort of love toward this child, it will never compare to the way I would love our child. We would create something from us ... our love and part of my love for it would be that it was part of you ... the woman who *is* the love of my life. Can't you understand that?"

I did understand, and in that moment, I fell even deeper in love with him. Everyone has a dark side, those thoughts that enter our minds uninvited. Sometimes it is just a random "what if." What if I jerked the steering wheel to the right while going over a bridge and sent the car plummeting into the lake? What if I jabbed this knife through my chest?

Then there is the part of our dark side that's called *brutal honesty*. How does my hair look? Like a fucking poodle. Does this make my ass look big? Like the Titanic. Will you still respect me in the morning? I don't respect you now. The real truth is—honesty is rarely the best policy. Most nice people are liars and most jerks are honest.

Quinn was brutally honest. He would never feel absolute love for a child who, in his mind, was the result of the biggest mistake of his life.

I leaned back and cupped his scruffy jaw in my hands. "I do understand ... I really do. Now, let's change the subject."

He kissed me and tugged the blanket away from me. Then dropping his gaze to my naked body, he grinned. "We don't have to *talk* at all."

I leaned in and traced my tongue below his ear. "You're right, we don't," I whispered in a sexy voice, "we can ... *eat*." Grabbing the blanket again, I stood up and wrapped it around myself.

He groaned. "Tease."

L ATER THAT DAY I checked my phone and found fifteen missed calls from Mac. Guilt washed over me when I thought of her trying to reach me in an emergency.

"Fifteen, huh? And that doesn't count the five times I answered when she called," Quinn said, looking over my shoulder.

"You talked to her?"

"From the looks of things, I did a fourth of the time she called."

"What did you say?" I was worried he told her about me, about us. Mac was my go-to person, but pregnancy officially removed her from my call list. The last thing she needed was my problems.

"I told her you were under the weather."

"Crap, why'd you tell her that?"

"Um ... because I figured you'd be upset if I told her the truth."

"I would have, but you should not have said I was sick," I groaned as I scrolled through the dozen or more texts she sent too.

"What's the big deal?"

"The big deal is now she knows you were lying which means she either thinks I'm avoiding her or I've been abducted."

"How does she know I was lying?"

"Because I don't get sick."

"What do you mean you don't get sick ... ever?"

"Ever ... well, except food poisoning my senior year in high school and the occasional alcohol overdose."

"How is that possible?"

I shrugged. "Apparently I'm a freak of nature of sorts. Well, that and I eat a plant-based diet." After I finished reading her messages I sighed. "I think we're in the clear. The gist of her messages was she wants me to call her when you untie my naked, over-sexed body from the bed. Apparently, her pregnancy brain is stuck on one thought and one thought only ... sex. Anyway, she wants to know if we'll be returning to Chicago for Christmas. Well?"

When I looked back at Quinn he was in a daze looking at the tree while pinching the sides of his bottom lip together.

"Earth to Quinn ..."

He shook his head as if trying to clear his mind. "Sorry, I didn't hear anything past your naked, over-sexed body tied to my bed."

"Sadist. Yes or no to Chicago for Christmas?"

He looked around at our miniature North Pole and smiled.

Mine matched his. "We're staying here for Christmas?"

He winked with a slow, single nod.

CHAPTER TWENTY-TWO

QUINN STAYED HOME several more days to make sure I was off suicide watch. Then he reluctantly went back to the office Wednesday morning, but not before having his wicked way with me twice in bed and once in the shower. I sat, bundled in my robe, on a padded bench in the massive walk-in closet. I loved watching Quinn dress for work. I had a ridiculous weakness for him in a three-piece suit, and he knew it.

He smirked at me in the mirror as he finished tying his tie. "I need to go back to work today, but if you don't stop fucking me with those beautiful blue eyes, I'm going to be forced into *tying* you to the bed and torturing you with my tongue until the people standing across the street know my name."

"I think you're a little too full of yourself this morning. If you don't make it to work today, it won't be because of me, it will be because your big head won't fit through the door."

He tilted his chin up as he made a final adjustment to his tie. "A thousand dollars says you have a pool of hot, wet desire for me nearly ready to seep down your legs as we speak."

Cocky little shit!

Squeezing my legs together, I squinted at him. "I think you'd better just save your money for your venture capitalistic wagers at your stuffy, boring, financial geek job."

He walked over to me and bent down close to my ear. I caught a whiff of his aftershave wafting from his neck just inches from my lips. He slid his hand under my robe as I tried to tighten my legs together even more. My efforts were frivolous in such close proximity to him. His long finger easily slid between my folds into my drenched channel. My breath hitched. After moving back and forth a couple of times, he removed it.

"Cash is fine," his deep voice resounded in my ear.

As he stood straight, he stuck his wet finger in his mouth and sucked it. "Mmm, have a good day, my beautiful."

ALTHOUGH QUINN WAS AT WORK, it felt quite crowded in his condo with just me and all my thoughts. I never imagined the day would come that I would actually consider seeing a therapist again, but with my BFF being off limits for counseling, I considered finding someone in New York. I tried yoga and meditation, and maybe it was because I was in a place that held so many hurtful memories, but I couldn't clear my mind.

Everything ate at me, and I knew the longer it lingered in my mind festering, the worse things would get for both me and Quinn. I wasn't looking for someone to solve my problems or even validate my feelings. I simply needed a safe dumping ground for my garbage of emotions, a sounding board that wasn't pregnant or that didn't make me weak in the knees every time he looked at me.

Thankfully I had a few nice distractions, technically one every hour as my phone chimed with a text from Quinn.

What are you doing?

Not slitting my wrists if that's what you're wondering.

Not funny.

A little funny :)

An hour later ...

What are you doing?

Tying a noose.

Still NOT fucking funny!

Ahh ... now that was totally funny :)

Another hour later ...

> What are you doing ... and don't give
> me any shit this time!

> Smelling your shirt from yesterday and
> touching myself.

> What the fuck are you trying to do
> to me?

> Nothing yet ... I'm doing it all to
> myself ... gotta go ... actually not
> going ... I'm COMING!

That was pretty much the end of him checking up on me.

As the door opened later that afternoon, my body was transported back to its morning frenzy as my sex god walked through the door. I stole a moment to drink him in as he thumbed through the mail.

"Christmas cards from all your closest friends?"

He looked up just as I moved toward him. Tossing the mail and his keys aside, he wasted no time pulling me into his arms. "Fucking. Little. Tease."

Biting my lip to hide my grin, I worked on loosening his tie. "Did you touch yourself after we last *talked?*" I asked with a devilish grin.

Grabbing my ass, he yanked me closer until the bulge in his pants pressed into my abdomen. "I touched myself so much my fucking pecker is probably chafed," he growled.

"Poor baby," I said with pouty lips. "Do you need me to rub some lotion on it for you?"

He crashed his mouth to mine. Our tongues wantonly moved together as my fingers fumbled to unfasten his pants. I slid my hand under the waistband of his briefs and fisted his erection. He moaned into my mouth as he cupped my breast. Then his phone rang.

"Don't answer it," I mumbled into his mouth.

He ignored it as he pulled his suit coat back and shrugged it off his shoulders.

"God, I missed you today," he breathed out as he grabbed my hair and gently tugged it until I tilted my chin up. His lips, tongue, and teeth ravished my exposed throat. His phone rang again.

"Fuck!" he growled as he grabbed it from his pocket. His brows knitted in frustration as he glanced at the screen. "What?" he answered, bringing it to his ear. "What picture?"

I pulled my hand from his pants and stepped back. He held his phone back to look at the screen again. I peeked over the top of his hands to see what he was looking at. It was a photo of an ultrasound.

Back to reality.

I turned and walked to the kitchen. Throwing open the door to the refrigerator, I took out food to start dinner. I wasn't sure what was on the menu, I just needed the distraction.

Deep breath ... I am peaceful, I am strong.

Quinn tossed his phone by his keys and let out a deep breath. "Addy—"

"It's fine, don't ... say anything. It's just ... fine."

My body moved on instinct because my mind was in shambles. He came up behind me and pulled me against him. I paused.

"I'm sorry," he softly whispered.

I closed my eyes as a few tears fell down my cheeks. Biting my lips together, I nodded.

He turned me to face him and kissed my tear stained cheeks. "Tell me what you want me to do, and I'll do it. As long as I don't lose you, I'll do anything. Remember that time you asked me if I'd give it all up?"

I nodded.

"Well, I would. I'd give up everything for you. The money, my business ... the baby, I'd walk away from it all right now for you."

Swallowing back the huge lump in my throat, I smiled and wiped the lower lids of my eyes with the tips of my fingers. "I know you would." I laughed. "God, that's why I love you so much."

He hugged me to his chest and smoothed his hand down the back of my head. It was just one of many heartbreaking moments that would play out in our lives over the next year. I knew that I would need a little outside help to make it through.

AFTER DINNER we nestled on the couch and drank mint coconut milk hot chocolate in the midst of our very own winter wonderland.

"Have I mentioned today how much I love your elves?"

Quinn leaned in and licked some chocolate off my lips. "Nope."

"Well, I do. In fact, I don't want to leave this room until after Christmas."

"That's going to be pretty difficult. Have you seen our social calendar for the next few weeks?" He smiled.

"You mean *your* calendar because I can assure you I have absolutely nothing on mine, except fattening up on hot chocolate and cookies."

When I was younger my parents used to parade me around to every elite social event in Chicago. Charities, parties, political gatherings, social fundraisers—you name it, I'd been to it. Over the years I had managed to scale down my social calendar to a need-to-only list of events. Basically, birthday parties, weddings, and Gwen and Richard's anniversary party were all that occupied space on my calendar during the previous eight years.

Quinn rubbed his chin. "Hmm ... whoever then will I take with me to see the holiday shows at Radio City Music Hall and The Metropolitan Opera House? Or *A Christmas Story* at Madison Square Gardens, or *The Nutcracker* at Hammerstein Ballroom, or The New York Pops at Isaac Stern Auditorium. Or Andrea Bocelli at Barclays Center? Gosh it's such late notice, but I'm sure I can scrounge a date somewhere."

"You do not seriously have tickets to all those shows?" I asked, squinting with equal parts disbelief and excited anticipation.

He shrugged, sipping his drink. "What can I say? When I make very generous donations I receive the best seats to the best shows."

Struggling to hold back my incredibly goofy yet jubilant smile, I casually replied, "I suppose I could forego PJs and cocoa for a few evenings—"

"Nope, no way ... I will not have you sacrificing your holiday plans for mine," he goaded.

Grabbing his mug and setting it by mine, I crawled onto his lap and straddled his legs. I kissed him with ardent fervor then bit his lower lip. "I see what you're doing. You want me to beg, don't you?"

Pleasure danced in his eyes and his answer was obvious.

"That's fine, I'll beg now, but if I do ... I promise you'll be the one begging later," I whispered, inches from his lips, while I wiggled my hips over his growing arousal.

His whole face lit up, like I knew it would. Quinn was a competitor and never backed down from a challenge. My words were more of a playful threat, but he of course interpreted them as a challenge.

He had one response. "Beg me."

Game. On!

I put on my best whiny "Quinny" voice and showered him with compliments and gratitude for offering to take me to such wonderful shows. He reached the top of his pedestal and agreed to take me just seconds before I nearly vomited from the sound of my own pathetic voice. Then, like the sly devil he was, he threw in that his corporate holiday party was in two days as well.

Peachy!

The ball was officially in my court, which meant I had a headache and was too tired or "under the weather" for sex over the next couple of days.

By Saturday Quinn was on edge, but he'd have rather jabbed an icepick through his eye than admit it. It wasn't as if he hadn't gone a few days without sex before. When my monthly friend arrived, we took a break for the first two days. I would mope around all grumpy, wearing baggy clothes that said "stay the hell away," but usually by the third day my mood was better and he made a good case for shower sex that I rarely could refuse.

Going without sex, however, was completely different for him when I wasn't having my period and I wasn't wearing the equivalent of a potato sack. It was quite the opposite. I wore my tightest pants and shirts, the ones that showed the most cleavage, and that was just during the day. At night I dug out my sexiest lingerie, most of which either hadn't been worn or only worn once. Ironically, Quinn was also the cleanest guy in Manhattan by the weekend, having taken numerous cold showers throughout each evening. I took no pity on him because he was the king of his own palace, the controller of his own destiny. He could have had his way with me at any time, all he had to do was—beg me.

His holiday party wasn't until later that night. He spent extra time working out that morning. I didn't see him until well after lunch. When he arrived home he shot me a quick smile before heading upstairs.

"Where you going, babe?" I called out.

"Shower," was all he said without stopping.

I had an appointment scheduled at a spa and salon later that afternoon to get my hair and makeup done, as well as a mani and pedi. However, I *did* need a shower before leaving. Smiling to myself, I ran up the stairs, nearly tripping, and stripped off my clothes. When I entered the huge shower Quinn paused.

"Get out."

"I can't, sweetie. I need to get a quick shower before I head to the salon," I said in a fake-innocent voice while fluttering my eyelashes.

"Well, there are two other bathrooms," he blurted out, trying to stop me with his words.

Moving closer, I brushed in front of him allowing my nipples to graze against his chest as I reached for my shampoo. "I know, but all my stuff is in here," I replied, licking the water from my lips as I rolled my eyes up to meet his.

"I'm not falling for this," he sternly replied.

Stepping back, I squeezed the shampoo into my

hand and started lathering up my hair. His feral eyes slid over my body as I worked the soap down my neck and over my chest, slowly kneading my breasts. "Oh, I know you're not *falling* for this." I smiled. "*Actually*, just the opposite. In fact, I'd bet a thousand dollars you're *rising* to the occasion."

He turned his back to me and adjusted the water a few degrees cooler. *More like ten!* So I stepped up behind him, pressing my chest to his back. Then I slid my hands around and rubbed soap on his chest just briefly before moving my hand lower to his still firm cock. He jerked at my touch then tilted his head back slightly, releasing a tense moan as I stroked him a few times.

After standing under the water long enough for the soap to rinse off of my body, I released his erection and slapped him on the ass.

"Cash is fine."

Before I stepped out of the shower, I snuck one last glance over my shoulder at him. His back was still to me but his head was bowed with his chin at his chest. He had one hand on the wall bracing himself as the other adjusted the temperature—to straight cold.

CHAPTER TWENTY-THREE

When I arrived home from the spa, Quinn was already dressed in his tux. *Ho-ly. Shit.* Talk about spontaneous orgasm. Before he had a chance to comment on my hair or my schoolgirl reaction to him, I bolted to the closet and told him to stay out while I dressed.

After twenty minutes or so, his voice echoed from the bedroom. "How long does it take to put on a dress? I'll be downstairs."

Purchasing a new dress for the holiday party was not on my agenda ... until Quinn pulled me into a crazy standoff. I blamed it on him, but it was obvious my ego was just as bullheaded as his. The dress I picked out was a bit out of my comfort zone, but perfect for the night's mission. It was a full-length black dress with a plunging neckline that almost reached my navel. The back was exposed except for the two thin spaghetti straps that crisscrossed over it. The front of the mermaid silhouette skirt had a high slit. Quinn had seen me wear some fairly provocative dresses, much to his equal arousal and disapproval, but none quite compared to this.

After strapping on my ridiculously high heels, I took one more glance in the mirror. The stylist straightened my hair, which made it look much longer than it usually did. It was simple, sleek, and, according to everyone at the salon, "runway model sexy." Two words I didn't need to hear: runway model. Satisfied with the unfamiliar, yet kind of hot, reflection, I walked to the stairs and stopped at the top. Quinn's back was to me as he messed with his phone.

"Ahem ..."

He turned and the blood drained from his face. "No. Fucking. Way. Go change."

Lifting the skirt of my dress with one hand and holding the railing with my other, I carefully navigated down the stairs.

"Addy, I'm serious. There's no way I'm allowing you to wear that tonight."

Originally, I *had* thought the "No. Fucking. Way. Go. Change" was Quinn's backward potty-mouth compliment, but by the time I reached the bottom of the stairs, all the color had returned to his face, tenfold.

"*Allowing*? What are you, my dad?"

"I don't think you understand. This gala is a who's who of Manhattan's high society. I'm talking prominent businessmen, politicians, and even a few celebrities."

"*Gala*? You told me we were going to your corporate holiday party."

"It is … just a little more extravagant than what you're probably used to."

Oh really?

"How many presidents have you met?"

He looked at me confused. "One."

"I've met three. How many state dinners at the White House have you attended?"

"None."

"I've attended five. So I *don't* know what you think I'm used to, but I *do* know I'm not going to be awestruck by any businessman, politician, or celebrity at your little holiday shindig tonight. And I'm quite certain I don't give a damn if people like my dress."

"It's not about people liking your dress. It's about drawing unwanted attention," he growled.

Grabbing my wrap and clutch purse, I headed out the door. "Who said anything about not wanting attention?"

THE GALA WAS at one of Quinn's hotels in the Grand Ball Room on the top floor. As promised, there were plenty of famous faces in the crowd. Quinn may have not been the richest person in New York, but he sure was popular.

As we entered the hotel, he leaned down and whispered in my ear, "I'm going to request they turn the thermostat down, so you should leave on your wrap."

I smiled with a nice roll of my eyes as we entered

the elevator. "I'm feeling pretty *hot* tonight, so I don't foresee it being an issue."

"You're just trying to start a fight," he grumbled.

"Babe, I don't want to fight with you."

"I'm not talking about us. I'm talking about me and any guy who looks at you."

The elevator chimed at the top floor. "Don't get your panties in a bind, Mr. Cohen ... unless you're not wearing any, *like me.*"

"Mother Fuc—"

"There he is!" Zach called as we exited the elevator. He wrapped one arm over Quinn's shoulders. "Great party, man. You have the best planners in town."

"Thanks, my *elves* are the best." He smirked.

Zach let go of Quinn and stepped in front of us. "Holy shit, Addy! Your dress is—"

"Elegant? Completely appropriate for the occasion?" I gave Zach a tight smile.

His eyes went from my dress to Quinn's face and in an instant his smile was gone. "It's ... nice. You look lovely. I think I'm going to find Eden. I'll catch up with you later."

"Ease up with the death grip on my hand, caveman!" I gritted through my fake smile.

"Your fucking dress is going to ruin my night," he snapped back, his twitching jaw working overtime.

"Your pent up sexual frustration, being held hostage by your stubborn ego, is the only thing that's going to ruin your night. Now, I'm going to mingle and check out the food situation. When you decide you're ready to 'beg me,' you know where to find me. Just look for a crowd of men, I'll be in the middle."

Yanking my hand from his, I weaved my way through the massive sea of people. Had Quinn not insisted on taking the caveman approach, I would have told him how incredible everything looked. The glass elevator opened in the center of the Grand Ballroom to the most spectacular panoramic view of Manhattan. The room looked like a beautiful iced winter wonderland. Tables and chairs scattered throughout the room were dressed in silver and ice blue. Large glass vases were filled with blue glass Christmas ornaments and iced twig branches. The delicate crystal glassware sparkled from the hundreds of votives scattered on the tables.

There were at least a dozen Christmas trees with blue and white lights. The incandescent lighting was a mix of white and blue. Every pillar and every chair was wrapped in elaborate blue and silver ribbons and bows. Several large snowflake ice sculptures were illuminated with blue lights. A live band played holiday music, while servers filtered through the crowd with trays of champagne and hors d'oeuvres. The men were dressed in elegant tuxes and tailored suits while the women accented them in a rainbow of colored formal gowns and cocktail dresses.

Large men in suits with earpieces guarded every exit, keeping the room full of high society's elite safe from ... probably the middle class they screwed to get where they were. In some other life I would have been impressed by my surroundings, like Cinderella at the ball.

"Adler?"

I turned at the sound of my name. "Edward." I smiled warmly.

"Wow, look at you all grown up. What has it been, ten ... fifteen years?"

"Almost nine, it was at my parents' ..." I sucked in a deep breath, surprising even myself as to how difficult it was to say the words out loud.

"Funeral. Yes, I'm so sorry. You know your father was like a brother to me. I can't believe they never got a break in the case. It still angers me to this day that they called it a home invasion. Somebody knew something."

With a grim twist of my mouth, I somberly replied, "Yeah, somebody knows something, but justice or not, it won't bring them back."

A large warm hand rested on the small of my bare back as Edward's eyes focused behind me.

"Senator Carlson, glad you could make it." Quinn's deep voice filled my ears.

"Mr. Cohen, my pleasure."

The two men shook hands while Quinn's left hand stayed planted in a possessive claim on me.

"I see you've met Addy," Quinn said as his fingertips circled my skin, sending a rush of heat through my entire body.

"Actually, I've known Adler her whole life. I went to law school with her father."

Quinn's head flinched back as he narrowed his eyes. "Hmm, I thought your father was in investment banking?"

Before I could answer Edward continued, "He was, but only after eight years as a prosecuting attorney, followed by a twelve year term as an Illinois Supreme Court Justice. He decided to try his hand at banking like his father. He was a damn fine attorney but even better investment banker; nearly tripling his net worth in six months."

The gleam in Quinn's eyes and the satisfied smile on his face said he was impressed. "I had no idea. Addy doesn't talk much about money or her family's wealth."

"Well, it's not her family's wealth anymore. It's hers, all of it," he replied with a slow shake of his head. The subtle gesture was odd. It didn't have the sympathetic vibe with which he spoke just a few moments earlier, which made me wonder if it was more disbelief or maybe disapproval in the way I'd handled, or *ignored,* my inheritance.

"If you'll both excuse me, I'm feeling parched." I smiled politely while touching my hand to my throat.

"Of course, my dear." Edward nodded. "It was really lovely to see you again after so long."

"Thank you, the feeling is mutual." As I turned to leave, Quinn's hand slid from my back to my wrist.

"Enjoy the party, Senator, so glad you could make it."

Releasing his grip on my wrist, he slid his hand down to interlace our fingers as he pulled me into his arms. "Senator Carlson has known you for years, yet he made you uncomfortable. Why?"

"What makes you think he made me uncomfortable?"

"You're a beautiful, confident woman. When you're having a conversation with someone, you maintain eye contact with them. Your eyes wandered the whole time he was talking. Then there's your fingernails." He grabbed my other hand too and ran his thumb over my nails. "They're all rough and jagged because you've been picking the hell out of them, which you only do when you're uneasy about something."

"I bet your favorite childhood game was Clue. Am I right?"

"Monopoly, and you're avoiding my question."

"I bet you were the race car."

"Addy!"

"Yes, I was uncomfortable," I snapped back, feeling that way again because we were drawing attention to ourselves.

"Why?"

Glancing around uneasily at the people mingling by us, I squeezed his hands. "Not now, okay?"

"Addy—"

"It's too personal for a public display. Just *please* ... not now," I pleaded.

He nodded with a straight face. The concern in his eyes was evident and the thought of his concern for me warmed my heart. He stopped a server passing by and grabbed several fancy looking hors d'oeuvres from the tray.

"Vegan?" I asked suspiciously as he offered me one.

"It's all vegan." He grinned popping a small crostini with a wedge of grilled pineapple, cucumber sauce, and a mint leaf into his mouth.

I followed his lead and raised my eyebrows as my taste buds exploded with excitement. The sauce was amazing and the chef geek in me would spend the rest of the night trying to figure out what was in it.

"So good." I smiled, blotting my lips with the cocktail napkin. "I can't believe you had your posh holiday party catered vegan."

He winked and flashed me his signature cocky grin. "I heard plants are the new 'animal carcass' of gourmet cuisine. And there's this scorching hot vegan chef at my party who I'm trying to impress. I figured if I scored a few points now it might guarantee scoring with her later."

"Most nights I'd say your chances were pretty good, but rumor has it that hot babe you're talking about only puts out if you literally *beg* her." I circled my tongue around my lips, relishing the dark, heated look as he boldly undressed me with his eyes. "You should go schmooze with your guests. I have servers to stalk."

THE NEXT FEW hours played out like a game of cat and mouse. Quinn navigated the crowd with a close following of women on the prowl while I became more acquainted with his friends and business colleagues. Every time I scanned the crowd to find him, his eyes were on me.

If I was engaged in conversation with women, his look was playful and sexy, but when I found myself surrounded by a group of men, his look was filled with warning. He'd go from smiles and smirks to scowls and squints. It was only a matter of seconds before he inevitably found his way to my side with his arm around my waist, making his claim. He was, without question, the most handsome man at the party. Why he felt the need to claim me in front of every other guy was beyond my comprehension.

As the late night hours fell into early morning, the party continued going strong. However, the atmosphere and overall demeanor of the crowd transitioned from friendly formal to loudly inebriated. I hadn't had a drink since returning to New York to pull Quinn out of his spiraling demise. If he could live without drinking, so could I. The downside to being sober in the early morning hours was the hyperawareness of the handsy men who'd been served an excess of liquid courage. When it came to groping me, it was more like liquid stupidity.

Quinn was oblivious to the women grabbing his backside or tugging seductively on his tie because he was busy keeping frisky hands off me. His patience wore thin, especially when I agreed to dance with Chad, the young attorney he'd hired only a few months earlier to take over his real estate transactions. He was good-looking, in a Harvard-preppy boy sort of way. Without a doubt he was smart and probably graduated at the top of his class, but his choice in women, namely me, for the night was not his wisest decision. In the poor guy's defense, my dress made it impossible to dance with me without touching my bare skin.

I didn't need eyes in the back of my head to see Quinn coming. The look on Chad's face was all I needed.

"Mr. Cohen is closing in on us, isn't he?" I asked with a devious smirk.

"Uh ... yes," he nervously replied.

"Chad." Quinn's stern voice sounded behind me.

Chad's hands quickly fell from my bare back as he stumbled to distance himself from me. "Mr. Cohen, sir, uh—we were just—"

"Leaving, Chad, *you* were just leaving, right?" Quinn warned as he snaked his arms under mine and pulled my back against his chest with his hands firmly pressed to my abdomen.

Chad watched Quinn lay claim to me, and he nearly wet his pants. "I—uh—didn't realize she—Addy —uh Miss—"

Chad's confidence went from off the charts when he first asked me to dance, not realizing who I was, to negative fifty as party pooper Quinn put him in his place.

"Goodnight, Chad," Quinn dismissed him.

Turning around in his arms, I started swaying my

hips to the rhythm of the slow music. He obliged by moving his body in time with mine as his dark eyes seared into me melting everything south of my border.

"If you wanted to dance with anyone else but me, then you wore the wrong fucking dress." He looked like a caged animal teetering on the edge of control with his jaw firmly set and his eyes tightly fixed to mine.

"Chad? He's harmless. You hired him, so you must trust him. I figured I could, too. He came across as real … what's the word I'm looking for?" I pursed my lips and rolled my eyes to the side. "Eager, yes, that's it! I *felt* his young eagerness to *please*."

He released a feral growl as he pulled me so close, his erection firm to my abdomen. "Are you trying to get Chad fired or just seriously injured?"

Sliding my hands up the back of his jacket, I dragged my nails down over his shirt. "Will that really get you what you want?" I leaned up and whispered into his ear, still digging my nails into his back.

"What is it you think I want?" he asked, trying to stay in control.

I reached behind me and grabbed his hand, then taking a quick glance around us first, I slid it between us through the slit in my dress until his fingers grazed over my wet sex.

"Two words, babe: no underwear," I purred before removing his hand and walking away with a confident gait.

Torturing myself nearly as much as Quinn, I

headed for the ladies room to freshen up. Two drunk women stumbled out the door just as I entered. The ladies' lounge was like a fancy waiting room at a spa. Two modern charcoal grey sectionals occupied the center with multi-shaded grey decor pillows. White vanities and backlit mirrors lined the walls with grey velvet vanity chairs and complimentary makeup and hair care essentials. A single door in the corner led to the toilet stalls, and a row of sinks with modern, brushed steel fixtures and rectangular steel baskets filled with neatly-rolled hand towels.

Leaning into a vanity to check my hair and makeup in the mirror, I heard the echo of music fill the room as the door opened behind me.

Quinn.

Without a word, he made a quick survey of the room, including the stalls. Once he discovered we were alone, he locked the door. Still watching his reflection in the mirror, I continued to mess with my lip gloss.

"Unless you closed the open bar, it's not a good idea to lock people out of the restroom."

"There's another one on the opposite end," he murmured with a low, steady voice.

My whole body stilled as I noticed him shrugging off his jacket and loosening his tie. His gaze was alert and firmly fixed on me, and he proceeded to unbutton and remove his shirt with slow, calculated moves. My jaw fell lax as I drank in the sight of his torso. Taking an exaggerated swallow but refusing to turn around, I met his eyes in the mirror.

"We're not having sex in the bathroom. Not even if you beg me." My soft voice lacked the confidence I tried so desperately to exude.

He didn't respond. Instead, he continued to move toward me as he unfastened his pants; exposing his black boxer briefs stretched over his large bulge.

I could hear my own pulse as my breath quickened. "Quinn, no. I'm serious." I finally turned to face him as he got closer.

My close proximity to his bare chest sucked all the oxygen from my lungs. He had me cornered with nowhere to go.

"Baby, if you were *serious* then you wouldn't have worn this dress tonight." He ran his finger down the side of my face then pushed my hair back over my shoulder before continuing to trace his finger down my neck, across my chest, and down the exposed area of skin between my breasts to just above my navel.

"Besides, I think you've made your point. Do I like a good challenge? Yes. Have you been driving me crazy over the past few days? Yes. Do you want me to beg you? Fine. I'm *begging* you. Am I done watching you parade around my party in this fucking excuse for a dress? Yes."

Before I had a chance to formulate an answer, he fisted the material of my dress on both sides just below my breasts. Then he effortlessly ripped the sixteen or so inches of material holding my dress together in the front completely apart, exposing my naked body.

"Quinn! What the fuck!" I shrieked.

As his greedy eyes consumed my naked body, a bemused smile played across his face for an instant before his mouth attacked mine. My intentions of throwing a tantrum over my dress and his dominating aggression vanished when his bare chest pressed against mine. The stimulation of his skin brushing my nipples sent jolts of sensation to my hypersensitive sex.

I moaned into his mouth as his tongue reached past mine, consuming me. Every time with Quinn felt like the first night we were together. My body craved his, as if he hadn't touched me in every way so many times before.

Bracing my elbows on his shoulders, I weaved my fingers through his hair and pulled it hard until he released a raw animalistic growl. He wedged his leg between my legs, parting them just enough to slip two fingers through my slit and up into my drenched channel. Tearing my mouth from his, I let my head fall back as I sucked in a breath and released another deep moan.

"Quinn ..." I moaned, as he eased his fingers in and out of me, slowly at first. As tiny whimpers escaped my parted lips, he increased the pace.

"Look at me," he demanded.

Pulling my head back up, I forced my eyes to his. The harder and faster he pushed his fingers into me, the more intensely hungry his face became. My pulse continued to race as my orgasm approached. With his fingers fully plunged into me, he stopped moving them as he circled my clit with the pad of his thumb.

"Oh God!" I closed my eyes, no longer able to keep them focused on him as my trembling body shattered from his expert touch. He was so damn confident with manipulating my body to bring me unfathomable pleasure. As my breath came back, I opened my eyes to his cocky smirk.

"I fucking love watching you fall apart."

If I hadn't been so sated, his comment would have made me blush, but at that point I didn't give a damn. Any guy who could do that to a woman earned the right to say whatever he pleased.

He removed his fingers, pausing just long enough to spread my wetness around.

"I'm not done with you yet," he whispered in my ear as he hitched my legs up to his waist and carried me to the longer part of the sectional. After he set me down, I started to lean back as he removed his pants and briefs.

"Uh-uh ..." he smiled deviously as he circled his finger for me to turn over.

I turned over and leaned forward on my knees. There was never a need to spice up our sex life. Any time, any where, any way, was our unspoken motto. We made passionate slow love in bed. We had sensual intercourse in the tub and shower. We had playful sex on the couch or floor. Then there was the raw, primal fucking against a door or wall, in the kitchen, elevator, on the stairs, atop his desk, and of course ... in public restrooms. As much as I loved the beautiful way he made love to me, worshipping every inch of my body, sometimes I desired the carnal pleasure of sex that was desperate, possessive, and sometimes even a little rough.

Quinn had a bad-boy side to him that he hid under a three-piece suit all day. There was something erotic about him letting go of that control with me. I loved when he pushed me to my own limits of pleasure. Being sexually uninhibited with him was easy.

He kneeled behind me and tightly gripped my hip with one hand as he guided his erection into me with his other hand. I seethed at the fullness that always felt more intense from that angle. Without hesitation, he found a fast, hard rhythm, relentlessly surging into me until he reached his climax. Breathless, he leaned over my back, supporting his weight on one arm as he slid his other hand to my sex. Quinn never kept score when it came to orgasms; he usually gave me the first and let me have the last.

We left Quinn's holiday party in true style. He at least had on his shirt and pants; I wore heels and his suit coat that covered all necessary parts. We received a few interesting looks as we navigated our way from the ladies' lounge to the elevator. I kept my head down so my hair curtained my face while he warned off anyone who tried to approach us on our way out. *Note to self: remember to carry an extra set of clothes if Quinn feels sex-deprived.*

CHAPTER TWENTY-FOUR

As PROMISED, Quinn escorted me to see all the best shows during December. He shared his favorite musicals and concerts from when he was a child growing up in New York. I had seen some of the same ones in Chicago as a young girl. We also went ice skating at Rockefeller Center, snowboarding, Christmas shopping, and volunteered at various churches and shelters that opened their doors to the homeless.

The Quinn I originally knew would have preferred to write a check instead of giving his time, but that Quinn was gone. He was a more giving person in an intimate way that mattered, and he showed a genuine compassion for others. It was simply a bonus that with our time we also donated an insane amount of money. We arranged to have fresh produce delivered to the various locations all month long. Hunger wasn't the only issue. A lot of the homeless people had health problems, such as diabetes and heart disease. Many of the non-perishable food items available to the poor filled a caloric need, but often exacerbated other health issues.

We decided to stay in New York for Christmas. After all the planned events, I was excited to throw on some comfy clothes and stay locked in our condo for several days. Quinn snuck in a quick workout the morning of Christmas Eve. I did my yoga, showered, and went to work filling the place with the aroma of cookies and other baked goods. Holiday music filled every room, which was why I didn't hear Quinn come in as I rolled out cookie dough.

"How's Santa's naughty little helper?" he whispered in my ear.

With a startled jump, I turned around. "Shit! You scared me."

He pulled me into him. "Sorry, baby," he said with a sexy smile.

Dressed in black sweat pants, a gray, fitted Icebreaker thermal long-sleeved shirt, and a black beanie, I had to control my instincts to attack him. He looked young, playful, sexy, and hot as hell.

Pushing up on my tiptoes, I pressed my mouth to his and slipped my tongue between his lips. Grabbing my ass he pulled me in even closer as he released a deep sexy hum from his throat. "Come shower with me."

"Can't. I have cookies in the oven."

He ducked his head down to brush his lips down

my neck as he gently tugged my pigtails. "Shut off the oven," he murmured against my skin.

"It's not like a casserole. I can't just shut off the oven—they'll be ruined. When I'm done baking, you can do whatever you want with 'Santa's naughty little helper.'"

He stood up straight with raised eyebrows. "*Whatever* I want?"

I bit my lips together as I nodded. From the look on his face, it seemed as if Santa came early that year.

"Finish up then, and don't wipe off any of that flour that's all over your face ... I'll take care of that." He smirked.

As soon as he turned to leave the kitchen, I stopped him.

"Quinn?"

He turned back around just in time to catch me as I jumped up and wrapped my arms and legs around him. Kissing him with a fierce intensity, I pulled off his beanie and fisted at his hair. Just as quickly, I pulled back and looked into his sparkling eyes. "God, you're sexy," I breathed out with a huge smile.

I'd taken him by surprise. He stared at me without saying anything for a moment. Then the oven timer buzzed. "You'd better get your cookies before I decide to lay you across the counter and make you sing my favorite song."

I hopped down and grabbed the hot pads. "Your favorite song?" I questioned as he headed up the stairs.

"Yeah, it's a gospel piece called 'Oh God, Quinn!'" He chuckled the rest of the way upstairs.

Smart-ass.

By the time all the cookies were out of the oven and neatly placed in rows on the cooling racks, the view outside the large windows had transformed into a winter wonderland. Large snowflakes danced everywhere, the kind that almost looked fake because they were so big and airy. I couldn't help the smile that captured my lips. At thirty-three, I still felt like a kid at Christmas time. *Thank you,* I thought, feeling certain everyone I'd loved and lost before Quinn had called in a special favor with Mother Nature.

"Amazing, isn't it?"

Turning toward the voice that warmed my heart and healed my soul, I grinned. "It's a gift, that's for sure."

Quinn was showered, with his messy hair still wet. Dressed casually in jeans and a white fitted long-sleeved T-shirt, his sexy, bare feet padded toward me.

"May I have this dance?" he asked as he offered his hand.

"Really?" I asked, with a huge smile and wide eyes.

He didn't answer. Instead, he grabbed my hand and pulled me into him. With one hand on my back and the other gently holding my hand clasped in his, he led me around the room effortlessly staying in step to the slow rhythm of Nat King Cole singing "The Christmas Song."

"My Latin lover can dance too. I am one. Lucky. Girl."

"The Scottie dog," he said with a grin.

Tilting my head to the side, I narrowed my eyes.

"When I play Monopoly ... I'm not the race car, I'm the Scottie dog."

I couldn't hold back my laugh. "Okay, good to know."

"When I was five my parents or 'Santa' brought me a Scottie dog for Christmas. I hadn't thought about him for years until you asked me about Monopoly at my holiday party." He had a soft warm expression on his face.

The thought of Quinn reminiscing about his childhood melted my heart. "What did you name him?"

"Scott."

I giggled, which I usually only did when I'd had too much to drink, but in that moment I was drunk on Quinn. "Scott? You named your Scottie dog Scott?"

Spinning me around, then dipping me back with slow control and his face just inches from mine, he whispered, "I was *five*."

Lifting me back up, he embraced me in his arms and kissed me as the song ended. Ruining the moment, I giggled against his lips. "Scott ..." I laughed some more.

He pinched my sides until I squealed. "Stop! That tickles."

He bear-hugged me and dragged me to the couch where he plopped down with me in his lap. "Since you think everything's so funny, I'm going to at least give you something better to laugh about."

"Stop!" I squealed and squirmed some more. "I'm sorry, it's just so ..."

"So what?" he asked, finally giving me a reprieve.

I flipped around and straddled him, cupping his jaw in my hands and running my thumbs over his rough dark stubble. "It's just so endearing. You're such a sexy, confident, successful, and sometimes intimidating man. The thought of you as a little boy with your Scottie dog named Scott just makes me love you even more."

His mood sobered, as if he wanted to say something but didn't know how. Chewing the inside of his cheek he met my eyes.

"You never told me what you and Senator Carlson were talking about that bothered you."

Looking down, I pulled in a deep breath and slowly released it. "We were talking about my parents. I told you the case was unsolved and the police called it a home invasion. However, it was more complicated than that. My dad made some enemies over the years, during his time as a prosecuting attorney and Supreme Court justice. A few undisclosed sources believed the murders were retaliation for the conviction of a former police officer my dad prosecuted a decade earlier. The conviction was for narcotics, but the undisclosed sources believed the officer was connected to a few thugs who were wanted for some pretty heinous crimes.

"What I walked in on the day I found my parents was not your average home invasion. It was personal. Someone was sending a message. Concerned for my safety and that of my family, we were advised by some prominent people in law enforcement to let it go. There was an investigation to make everything official, but the case was left unsolved for reasons only a handful of people knew about. Edward, Senator Carlson, was not in the need-to-know group, which left him in the group of people who were angered by what they called a 'botched investigation.' So he makes me nervous because he'd love nothing more than to reopen the cold case. However, letting their deaths go and moving on has kept me alive. Nothing good can come of going after anyone at this point. It's the past and time has proven my silence is my safety. Let it be."

"You honestly don't believe you're danger?" he asked, with a grave look of concern.

I chuckled. "Not likely. I just said, as long as no one decides to shove the cold case in some prosecutor's face, demanding they continue to look into it, I'm not a threat to anyone. If they really wanted me, they would have left my body for my parents to find, not the other way around. Why? Is my big, strong man going to protect me?"

"You have no idea the extremes I would go to for you."

I couldn't hide my complete adoration for him. No man had ever made me feel so protected, so cherished, so loved.

With a big smile, I jumped off his lap. "I don't know what your holiday traditions were, but we opened one gift on Christmas Eve." I grabbed a large rectangular gift I had wrapped and set under the tree earlier that morning. "Open it," I said with giddy excitement as I handed it to him.

"Are you sure?" he asked with a goofy kid-like grin, "It's only four o'clock."

"Yes, yes ... open it."

Quinn was the epitome of the man who had everything. I'd had his gift long before I ever knew for sure if I'd get the chance to give it to him. I thought it would end up being mine as a reminder of a very emotional and heartfelt moment in my life. I spent a lot of money arranging and paying for it, but when I wrapped it for Quinn I knew it was worth it.

As soon as the paper fell to the floor, he froze, holding the sides and resting it on his knee. He took a deep swallow as tears swelled in his eyes.

"It's by a Spanish pencil artist. He's done pieces for celebrities and royalty. After seeing her on the beach the first day we arrived, I knew I wanted to capture her. As you know, everyone has a price. Luckily, I'm pretty frugal with my money, so I had enough spare change to track him down and bring him to the beach house. I wanted to remember her, and our time together, forever, but more than that, I wanted to give you a piece of her that you didn't get to see."

In his hands he held a pencil drawing of Elena in a lounge chair on the beach overlooking the Mediterranean. It looked like a professional black and white photo but even more exquisite. The attention to detail was stunning. It was a side view of her, with her eyes closed and head tilted back. A light breeze was softly flowing through her hair and a peaceful aura of contentment graced her face. It was sketched exactly one week before she died.

"Addy, I..." he choked on his words.

I kneeled down on the floor in front of him and gently pulled the framed sketch from him and rested it against the coffee table so he could still see it. Not taking his eyes off it, he shook his head and wiped the corners of his eyes with his palms. I didn't say anymore. I wanted to give him that moment. The sketch was so lifelike. It captured the essence of her soul. Looking at it made her presence felt. I crawled between his knees and hugged his torso. He combed his fingers through my hair and finally looked into my eyes.

"You're so fucking amazing. No one has ever done anything like this for me."

"Now we can both enjoy it as long as you don't try to kick me out again." I laughed, squeezing him tighter to lighten the mood.

"I will *never* and I mean *never* kick you out again. AND ... if you ever try and leave I will make it my life's goal to track you down."

Pulling back, I raised a single brow.

"A little creepy?" he asked.

Not saying anything, I held up my thumb and index finger about a half inch apart.

I MADE soup and seeded artisan bread for dinner while Quinn surprised me with his handyman skills. He brought a hammer, small level, and some picture hooks out from his office. Within minutes he had the framed sketch of Elena mounted to the wall above his fireplace.

He stopped in the kitchen and stood behind me, taking in a deep whiff of the soup aroma. I spooned some up with a long bamboo ladle, then blew on it before offering him a taste.

Taking a cautious sip of the steamy liquid, he hummed. "Mmm, damn woman, you sure can cook."

Glancing down at the tools in his hand, I responded, "Yeah, but my skills are limited. Not to sound condescending, but I never envisioned you with a toolbox hidden in your office. I underestimated you, babe."

He kissed me before walking back to his office. "*Never* underestimate me," he playfully shouted back.

It was almost more than one woman deserved. Latin sex god with a silky accent and a brilliant finance guy by day meets extreme sports jock with a to-die-for body who dons a tool belt on the weekends. *Panty sizzling.*

We ate dinner by candlelight. It was casual, yet

romantic. Our bubble was perfect. It may have been the calm before the storm, but I cherished every minute that didn't involve my past, or his future as a father to another woman's child.

"What's going on in that beautiful head of yours?" he asked while I methodically stirred my soup with a chunk of bread.

"You." I smiled as I glanced across the table at him.

"Mmm, clothed or naked?" he asked giving me a wink.

I replied with a soft chuckle, "Naked, of course. You're my all-time favorite sculpture, a modern day Michelangelo's David."

"Are you going to leave me if I turn fat and ugly someday?"

"Absolutely. Men don't grow babies or battle menopause. There's no good reason for you to be anything but eye candy."

"Eye candy, huh?"

Taking a sip of soup, I let the spoon linger at my lips as I winked back at him. "Speaking of ... I can't believe we've been home alone this long and I'm still waiting for you to have your way with me. Are you not feeling *up* to it?"

His sexy, crooked smirk taunted me almost as much as the rest of his sinful body. "Baby, I'm always *up* for you. I just like you so hot and bothered that you damn near self-combust from my slightest touch."

Squinting my eyes at him, I leaned back in my chair and crossed my arms over my chest. "Why must we always see who can hold out the longest? Maybe we should see who can *go* the longest, see who has the most stamina."

"You don't like it when I play hard to get?" he asked, looking all too confident with a gleam in his eyes and a teasing grin.

"Puh-lease ..." I huffed out as I stood up. After tossing my napkin on the table, I slipped off my leggings then removed my sweater in one swift motion.

"Sweet Jesus ... what are you doing?" he asked as his eyes greedily drank me in.

My *nice* comfy clothes were hiding my *naughty* lingerie, which consisted of a red see-through floral lace shelf bra with a white bow in the middle and matching thong panties. I straddled his lap then grazed my tongue along his jaw to his ear. "I'm just seeing if you like playing hard to get when I'm playing Santa's naughty helper." I unbuttoned his pants and rubbed the bulge straining against his briefs.

His breath hitched as he closed his eyes. "Addy ..."

"Quinn," I whispered over his mouth before I sucked in his bottom lip and teased it with my teeth.

He arched his back and dropped his head back. "Addy, I wanted to do something first." The higher pitch to his voice sounded like a desperate plea.

With his head still tilted back, I kissed his throat as my hand stroked his erection. "What could you possibly want..." I continued to suck and nibble at his neck. "...to do before *this*?"

His phone on the counter rang with the worst timing ever.

"Ugh! I hate your stupid phone … don't get it," I pleaded as my hand slipped under the waistband of his briefs. The deep moan from his throat fed my craving for more. Pushing his briefs down past his erection, I scooted up his body until my entrance rested at his wet tip. Pressing my mouth to his, I pulled the strap of my thong to the side and sank onto him, savoring the intensity of the fullness.

Surrendering, he thrust his tongue into my mouth and grabbed my ass.

His phone rang again.

He ignored it, focusing solely on me. Our mouths and hands were reckless, but our rhythm was seductively slow.

His phone rang again.

We both wanted to ignore it, but the loud ring was too distracting. The caller was relentless, which was unusual and therefore concerning on Christmas Eve. The romantic mood began to fizzle.

He grumbled in frustration as I crawled off his lap so he could answer his phone.

"Don't go anywhere," he demanded as he stood up and stumbled to the counter while tucking himself back into his briefs.

"This better be important," he answered in a clipped, firm voice. He was silent for several moments while he listened to whoever was on the other end of the line. "Okay, I'll be there soon."

He zipped his pants without a word or even a glance in my direction. His serious demeanor sent my nerves into overdrive. I was afraid to ask who called. Without hesitation, I slipped my clothes back on, and he made no attempt to stop me. Clearly distracted, he headed for the door and grabbed his keys and jacket. I couldn't wait any longer.

"Quinn?" I said with a soft hesitation.

He stilled, as if the sound of my voice startled him. Our eyes met for a brief moment. "I have to go."

His lack of explanation prevented me from asking anything else. We were about fifteen feet away from each other, but in that moment it felt like an ocean between us.

"Okay," was all I said. He was out the door. I was stunned. In such a short amount of time we went from sharing everything to sharing nothing. As I turned to blow out the candles on the table, I heard the door open.

Waving the trail of smoke away, I looked to the entry where Quinn stood.

"Come with me."

Nodding, I grabbed my purse, shoved my feet into my boots, and slipped my arms in the jacket he held open for me. He took my hand, lacing our fingers, while he led me out the door and to the parking garage. Always the gentleman, he opened my door and waited for me to buckle in, then he leaned in and kissed me.

"I love you," he said, with a wrinkle of concern

etched on his face. Before I could muster a response, he shut the door.

As we pulled out of the parking garage I found my voice. "Where are we going?"

"Hospital."

His lack of elaboration left a knot in my gut.

"What's going on, Quinn?"

Keeping his eyes on the road, he rubbed his forehead to ease some tension. "Olivia was having some cramping and bleeding."

We rode the rest of the way in silence. An overwhelming storm of emotions surged through me. Quinn was too quiet. I couldn't read him. Was he angry? Was he sad? Then there was my awkward presence. The girlfriend showing up at the hospital where the mother of his child was possibly miscarrying his baby. I could only be insult to her injury. My racing mind couldn't sort out why he brought me, unless it was for his emotional support ... but he wasn't saying anything. He parked and jumped out. I remained still, but not because I was waiting for him to be chivalrous, I simply had second thoughts about being there.

He opened the door, but I just sat there.

"Come on, baby," he said in a hurried voice.

"Quinn ... I don't think this is a good idea."

"Addy—" He blew out a long breath. "It's cold and snowing. You're not going to wait in the car."

"You shouldn't have brought me."

He reached in and unfastened my seatbelt. "Well, I

did because leaving you at home alone with your thoughts was not an option. Now let's go."

I wanted to scream at him. He didn't trust me, but it wasn't the time or place to have that discussion, so I hopped out. He grabbed my hand and led me to the entrance. When we reached the maternity floor, Quinn checked in at the nurses' station while I stayed back a few feet. One of the nurses gave him an update and offered to take him to see Olivia. Their voices were soft, but I heard her say they were monitoring Olivia and waiting for the doctor. As the nurse started walking down the corridor, Quinn looked back at me.

I shook my head. "Go, I'll wait out here."

He hesitated then offered me a weak smile and a nod before following the nurse. I was committed to our relationship. It wasn't going to be easy. The time had come to hunker down and wait out the storm.

Quinn sitting beside her bed holding her hand as they waited to find out the fate of their child ate at me like acid. I couldn't bear to see it, yet I went crazy wondering what was happening. He refused to leave me at home with my thoughts, and now I knew why. The mind was a powerful weapon. Imagination left to itself was more destructive than reality.

There were a few people in the waiting room, mostly older people, likely grandparents waiting for news of their new grandchildren. Grabbing a gossip magazine, I plopped down in a chair and absentmindedly thumbed through the pages. An hour later, I'd skimmed through every magazine and still no word.

My patience had worn off. After shooting off a text to Quinn, I rode the elevator down.

I needed fresh air, even if it was cold and snowy outside. The frigid air stung my face as the automatic entrance doors slid open. Reaching in my pockets, I felt around for my gloves, but they weren't there. I could not remember if I had them when we went inside. Quinn had the key to the Range Rover, but I decided to peek in the window to see if I'd left them on the seat. There was no need to go back inside to look for them if I never carried them in.

Shoving my hands in my pockets, I ducked my head and hunched my shoulders, trying to shield my skin from the biting wind. When I reached the Range Rover, I used the sleeve of my coat to dust the snow off the window, then cupped my hands over my eyes to see inside.

That was all I remembered.

CHAPTER TWENTY-FIVE

Quinn

WORST FUCKING CHRISTMAS EVE EVER! The day started out perfect with a good workout and then home to be with Addy. I had a one-track mind most days: get all my shit done and get home to Addy. She was stronger than any addiction I could have ever had. Work became work and play was no longer fun without her. I was undoubtedly the best possible version of myself around her, some days almost too much. I still had my man card, but it was tainted, like she somehow sprayed her jasmine oil on it and hid it in her goddamn pussy. The only time I knew for sure that I still had it was when I was buried balls deep inside her.

I had special plans for us that night. When she gave me the sketch of my mother something in our relationship shifted. I'd stood atop the summit of Everest, visited the pyramids of Egypt, climbed the Great Wall of China, and scuba dived the Great Blue Hole in Belize. None of those sights even came close to the beauty captured in the sketch of my mother. Addy gave me the last peaceful moment in my mother's life ... the essence of her being.

The picture was so lifelike, every detail immaculate and perfect. The tears came. I felt like a pathetic pussy. That woman was hell-bent on bringing me to my knees every single day, and the fucking crazy part about it was she had no idea what she did to me.

Dinner was amazing; Addy was Da Vinci in the kitchen. Then, without warning, she transformed into my every fantasy when she stripped down to some red hot, ball busting, cock-hardening lingerie. My plans slipped away. I had a goal for the night, and while it included her screaming my name in ecstasy, it wasn't everything. But she had her own agenda, and once again I was sidetracked, searching for my man card buried deep in her pussy. Deciding to go with the flow, and what a fucking amazing flow it was, I'd resigned to keep my surprise until later that night.

That's when the night turned into my own personal horror film. Fate stretched its vengeful hand from the sky and repeatedly stabbed a jagged blade into my happiness. Olivia called in a desperate panic on her way to the hospital. She was crying and totally losing it as she hysterically went on about painful cramping and bleeding. I couldn't think. My thoughts were as jumbled as Olivia's words. It wasn't until I was out the door that I realized leaving Addy alone with her thoughts and insecurities about my relationship with Olivia was the worst possible thing I could do. Taking her to the hospital was a close second, but I had no other option.

The whole way there, I fought back the urge to tell Addy everything. I wanted to tell her what was going through my mind, but I couldn't. She had been a mother, she loved all life ... hell, she nearly cried every time she saw me crack open a damn egg. Flies were shooed and spiders were gently escorted out the window with Addy around. But damn, for some reason unbeknownst even to myself, her quirkiness made me love her just that much more.

I didn't know what I really expected when we arrived at the hospital. Asking her to come with me to Olivia's room wasn't fair to her or Olivia, but I felt like a total ass for leaving her behind. Olivia was curled on her side in the bed. A nurse stared at a monitor that beeped with different numbers and lines on it. Olivia, although in a hospital gown, was in full makeup without a single hair out of place. The truth was, she needed it. With it she looked like a tall, thin model; without it, she looked like a lanky, pale woman with pointy hip bones and sunken eyes. She wasn't Addy. The love of my life was naturally beautiful. She stole my breath just the same with no makeup and six-in-the-morning messy hair as she did in heels, makeup, and an all-too-revealing evening gown.

Olivia was silent at first. The nurse told me my "wife" was doing fine, but the baby was being monitored. Much to Olivia's displeasure, as was evident by the scowl on her face, I corrected the nurse by telling her I was the father, not the husband. When I sat in the chair by the bed, she reached for my hand. Reluctantly, I offered it. She had tears in her eyes, but I had no words. There was nothing to say to the woman who was a recurrent mistake in my life. She represented the shallow, cold, man that existed before Addy. I did not miss that person. In fact, all I really wanted was for every reminder of him to vanish.

My cell phone vibrated and it was a text from Chase. It was officially Christmas in Spain and he wished us a Merry Christmas. The nurse caught me looking at my phone and told me I had to go to the waiting room with it or shut it off. As I went to stand, Olivia tightened her grip on my hand and begged me to stay. Grinding my teeth ... into my fucking tongue, I shut off my phone and sat back down.

Eventually, Olivia drifted off to sleep. The nurse told me they would continue to monitor the baby overnight. She was in the beginning stages of a miscarriage and normally they would send her home to be on bed rest, but since she lived alone they agreed to keep her overnight. Aka, the guy who knocked her up was a complete prick to leave her pregnant and alone over Christmas. The fate of the baby was uncertain. The nurse told me the doctor said it had about a fifty-fifty chance.

I seized the opportunity to check on Addy, but when I got to the waiting room she wasn't there.

Remembering I had turned off my phone, I powered it back up to check for missed calls or messages. There was a missed text from her about a half hour earlier. She said she needed some air and was going to take a walk around the building. It was cold outside, and I couldn't believe she was still out there. I texted her back to see where she was then waited.

After ten minutes with no reply, I tried calling her. It went straight to her voicemail, as if she had her phone shut off. Taking the elevator to the lower level, I tried her phone again. I searched the cafeteria, but she wasn't there. After impatiently pounding the elevator button without it descending to the lower level, I hurried to the stairs. Taking them two and three at a time, I sprinted to the entrance of the hospital. My coat was in Olivia's room, but I didn't care. I ran around the parameter of the hospital in an eager search for Addy. By the time I made it all the way around, I was breathless and frantic.

The only thing I could think of was her taking a cab home. She wanted to leave; being there and waiting for me was too much. I'd hurt her again. I had to get home to her and make things right. Jogging toward the Range Rover, I stopped as though my body had run into a wall. I realized my fucking key was in my coat pocket back in the room. The room where Olivia was most likely awake again. Fate's wrath rained down on me.

Just as I started to turn, I saw something in the distance, specifically next to my vehicle, which was a few rows straight ahead. The snow obscured my view as I squinted. One cautious step at a time, I walked ahead, trying to figure out what I was seeing, but as the image came into focus, I found myself in a full-out sprint.

"ADDY!" I yelled.

CHAPTER TWENTY-SIX

THE MOST BIZARRE dream had hold of me. I couldn't wake up, at least not completely. It was as if I was caught between two worlds. Flashes of light and unfamiliar voices faded in and out. Then there were moments of bliss. I was pregnant with just a little bump showing. A large hand splayed across my belly, feeling an occasional little jolt of movement as I cried. It was heartbreak and relief. I was excited yet scared. The voice behind me was familiar and comforting.

More flashes of white light blinded me as I struggled to recognize the voices and decipher the words that echoed around me.

"Addy?"

What?

"Can you hear me?"

Yes.

"Can you hear me? Do you know where you are?"

Yes ... and no.

My voice was lost. I struggled to speak and maybe I was, but nobody answered. Then I heard a familiar sound ... it was my own voice, but soft and slurred. As I focused on my tongue and my lips to make out the words, I realized my lips felt numb and swollen. Only a thin line of light appeared in my left eye and the pain started to radiate through my body. This was my reality. My face throbbed and I felt every beat of my heart in my face. I could move my left arm but my legs were shaking as my teeth began to chatter together. I tried to push my knees together but my feet were pressed against something, and it felt like someone was holding my legs open.

"No—" I heard my own voice again. It was stronger but still barely audible.

"Addy, you're going to be fine. You're safe now and we're doing everything we can to take care of you. I know you must be confused and uncomfortable, but we'll be done soon. Just stay with us, and try and relax your legs."

"No!" I said much louder. Then I let out a painful whimper as pain shot up my arm.

"Addy!" another familiar voice called from a distance.

"Sir, we're not finished. You need to wait outside and let the doctors do their job."

"I'm done waiting—"

"Sir, please, don't make me call security."

"Addy!"

Quinn ... Quinn ...

"Quinn ..." I managed when my mouth caught up with my brain.

"Mr. Cohen can stay," a man's voice responded.

"Addy, I'm here ... I'm so sorry, baby ..." his voice broke close to my ear.

Inching my head toward him, I saw part of his face level with mine. My neck was too stiff to turn any farther, and I could barely open my left eye. Raw pain and anger were etched across his face. He gritted his teeth but his eyes were soft. In the midst of all the chaos, there was only one thing that was unmistakable. I was in the hospital—injured. Everything else, including why I was injured, was still a vast sea of uncertainty.

"Was she?" Quinn's voice had an edge to it.

Was I what?

"There are no other signs. We'll move her to a room and keep her overnight for observation. The police are going to need to ask her some questions when she feels up to it."

"Thank you," Quinn breathed out, but not so much to the man who was talking; it was more like a sentiment of gratitude to a higher power, a verbal sigh of extreme relief.

My legs were removed from what I gathered by then to be stirrups, then I was covered with warm blankets. My good eye started to feel as heavy as my bad one, so I closed them both.

I awoke with a killer headache. In fact, everything ached. It became very obvious ... I'd been run over by a large truck. There was a heavy feeling over the top of my legs and the palm of my hand was pressed against something rough. My right eye managed to open, through protest, at the light that filtered through the partially opened shades. Quinn sat in a chair next to me, hunched over with his head on my bed. He had one arm draped over my legs while his other hand held mine next to his face. His eyes were shut and his lips were parted.

My fingers twitched against his cheek, and his groggy eyes opened. He turned his head and pressed his lips to my palm as he momentarily closed his eyes again. When he opened them back up, I saw the extent of my injuries reflected as pain in his eyes. He surveyed my face, and I could feel the sadness seeping from them.

"That bad?" My throat was dry and my voice was gravelly.

Meeting my gaze again he forced a pained smile. "You're beautiful ... always beautiful."

"Liar," I mumbled as I moved my tongue over my swollen upper lip. "What happened?"

He sat up and ran his hand over the blanket on top of my legs. Pursing his lips while he chewed on the inside of his cheek, he wrinkled his forehead in nervous apprehension. "You don't remember?"

I inched my head side to side.

"They're reviewing the security camera footage from the parking lot to see if anything was captured on tape, but there was quite a bit of snow blowing so they're not too optimistic."

"I remember going to look for my gloves in the Range Rover ... but that's all I can remember."

Quinn nodded his head and took a deep swallow. The lingering grimace on his face gripped my heart. "I found you..." he cleared his throat "...on the ground by the passenger door."

A nurse came in before I had a chance to question him more.

"Merry Christmas, Addy. My name is Christine and I'm going to take your vitals before Dr. Wilson comes in to check you over. If everything looks good you should be discharged within the hour."

I laughed despite the pain to my ribs. "If everything has to 'look good' for me to be discharged, then I'm quite certain I won't be leaving anytime soon."

Nurse Christine's eyes widened, then she looked at Quinn. "I didn't mean ..."

"She's just giving you crap. Welcome to my life. Her timing with her dry sense of humor is impeccable."

She smiled and her gaze lingered on my Latin sex god a little too long. I couldn't blame her. Even after a long night of sleeping in a chair, he looked deliciously sexy.

"I have this feeling that if I weren't laughing I'd be crying ... and it is Christmas so—"

"Well, your vitals are good. Blood pressure is normal and your temperature is back up. Dr. Wilson will be in shortly."

"Thank you," we both said in unison.

"Quinn?"

"Yeah, baby?"

"What happened with Olivia and the—"

"Merry Christmas. How's our patient doing this morning?"

"Hey, Todd." Quinn shook the doctor's hand.

"Good morning, Addy, I'm Dr. Wilson or Todd. Quinn and I run in the same maniac circle. It's nice to meet you. However, I wish it were under better circumstances."

"*Maniac circle?*" I questioned.

"Todd is a bit of an adventure buff like yours truly. We see each other quite a bit, especially on the slopes," Quinn replied.

"How are you feeling this morning?" Dr. Wilson asked as he looked at a computer monitor.

"I imagine not much better than I look. I ache everywhere, especially my head, left shoulder, and ribs."

"That sounds about right. I'm not sure what you've been told yet, but you sustained a concussion, dislocated left shoulder, and your ribs are bruised, but not fractured. You have numerous cuts and contusions, but those will heal quickly. Your eye received a pretty severe blow and we'll want to do a follow-up on it, but there doesn't appear to be any permanent damage.

However, if you still have blurred vision after it heals you should let us know. Now, the rape exam showed no signs of bruising, tearing, or sperm, so without further evidence, including your memory of the incident, we have no reason to believe you were raped. You're lucky Quinn found you when he did. You only suffered a mild case of hypothermia, but it could have been much worse given the adverse conditions."

Rape exam?!

My mind reeled. I was frantic, trying to remember something from the attack, but I couldn't remember anything. Rape? I couldn't imagine why they would suspect rape. Dr. Wilson did a thorough exam and talked with me about wearing a sling on the shoulder that had been dislocated. I had trouble concentrating, because all I could think about was the possibility of having been raped. I heard something about pain medication, and making an appointment with an ophthalmologist and gynecologist within the next few weeks, and even something about counseling, but it was all an echoing blur in my head.

"Addy?"

"Huh?" I startled from my daze.

"Todd asked you if you have any questions before he releases you," Quinn said.

"Uh ... no, I'm good."

Not good at all!

"Okay then, Quinn has my cell number if you need anything," he said as he shook Quinn's hand again and walked out.

"I'm going to go pull the Rover around to the entrance. Todd will have the nurse get you some scrubs to wear home. I'll be back up to help you get dressed. Okay?" He leaned in and kissed the top of my head.

"Where are my clothes?" I whispered.

He moved to the door as if he didn't hear me, but I know he did.

"Be right back." Then he was gone.

THE RIDE HOME WAS QUIET. I had so many questions, and Quinn wasn't offering much information. As we pulled into the parking garage, he broke the silence.

"A couple of detectives will be showing up soon to take your statement. I told them to make it quick."

"What am I supposed to tell them? I don't know anything. Hell, you know more than I do." I tried to hide the frustration in my voice, but I couldn't.

He parked and came around to my side. After he opened the door, he rested one hand on my leg and the other behind my head as he brushed his lips over mine with a gentle reverence. "I gave them my statement last night. You're the victim so they need to at least say they questioned you. It won't take long. Okay, baby?"

He helped me out as I winced from the pain when he touched my ribs. "What was your statement?" I asked as I tottered to the elevator.

"I'll tell you later. Let's just get you upstairs, showered, and in your own clothes before they show up."

Quinn dodged my questions quicker than I could think of them. I wasn't sure if it was to protect me or himself. What I did know was I needed the truth. When he got me upstairs, he started the shower then helped me out of the scrubs. After removing the sling, I protectively held my left arm to my body as we walked into the bathroom. Quinn disposed of his clothes and opened the shower door, but I continued past the shower to the mirror.

"Addy, don't!" he called, trying to stop me, but it was too late.

Shock. That was all I felt. The whole left side of my face and upper lip was swollen and bruised with numerous cuts. The right side had a few small cuts with bruising, but it was nothing compared to the left. I looked like a monster. Aside from my messy hair, I barely recognized myself. Then my eyes ventured down my reflection to my torso. It was mottled with bruises and cuts as well. Turning to the side, I got a small glimpse of my back and butt. I was a mess. From the look of the bruising, it was a miracle I didn't have multiple fractures.

Quinn stood behind me, and my gaze met his in the mirror. He looked so helpless with his sagging posture and eyes that struggled to focus on mine. I felt his pain nearly as much as my own.

"I think we should keep the holiday pictures to a minimum, don't you think?" I flashed him what was officially my ugly smile. Then I leaned forward toward the mirror and carefully pulled my lips apart. "At least I still have all my teeth."

"Jesus, Addy ... as I said, impeccable timing." He clasped my right hand in his and led me to the shower.

The hot water felt so good but stung a little as it trickled over my cuts. He squirted bath gel into his hands and soaped up my body. His movements were slow and cautious. As he worked his way down my torso, he knelt on the tile floor and gently worked the soap over my legs. After hesitating for a moment, he eased his fingers between my folds to gently cleanse that area. I pushed my fingers through his hair and he looked up at me. His tears faded into the water, but I still saw them bleeding from his crimson streaked eyes.

"I'm fine ... we're fine."

He finished washing me then wrapped his arms around my legs, clinging to me. It was a tender moment laced with heartbreaking anguish. All I wanted was to hold him in my arms, but everything above my waist was too bruised and sensitive.

"I love you, Quinn."

THE DETECTIVES ARRIVED AN HOUR LATER. Detective Andrews was a petite female with curly brunette hair pulled back into a bun and kind hazel eyes. She was the one who did most of the questioning. Detective Bartlett was a tall, thin guy with buzzed dark hair, blue eyes, and cute dimples. He jotted down notes and offered no more than a simple courteous greeting.

"Miss Brecken, can you tell us the last thing you remember before you were attacked?" she asked.

"I remember walking to the vehicle. I didn't have the key, but I was missing my gloves and I wanted to see if they were in there before I headed back inside to look for them. The windows were covered with snow so I brushed off the passenger's side and that's all I remember until I regained consciousness in the hospital."

"Do you remember seeing anyone around you on the way to your vehicle?"

"No."

"Did you hear anything?"

"Aside from the wind? No."

"We reviewed the security footage from the parking lot. The good news is your attack was caught on tape. The bad news is with the adverse weather conditions, we couldn't make out any distinguishable features of your attackers. They were dressed in black, including ski masks, and virtually no visible skin was showing. After they attacked you, they fled the parking lot on foot so we don't have a vehicle or any other lead so far. We will continue to question hospital employees who were close to the entrance last night and let you know if we find anything. Do you have anything else to add or any questions for us?"

Quinn scooted closer to me on the couch and eased

his arm around my waist. "I think that's all. Thank you," he answered in a quick cut-off response.

Just as the detectives stood to leave I stopped them. "Wait. What did the surveillance footage show?"

"Addy, she just said the weather was bad and they couldn't see that much." Quinn was eager to try and dismiss my question.

"I know they could not identify my attackers, but they can tell me what the attackers did."

I stared intently into Detective Andrews eyes, silently pleading with her, woman to woman, to tell me what she saw.

"The first blow, the one that knocked you unconscious, was to the left side of your head when you were looking in the vehicle's window. After you fell to the ground they proceeded to kick you until finally they stopped and removed your clothes ... all of them." She paused. I took a deep swallow and nodded for her to go on. "One of their heads jerked up like they saw or heard something then they quickly shoved your belongings into a black duffel bag, including your purse, and fled the scene. Approximately thirty-five minutes later the footage showed Mr. Cohen rushing into view where he picked you up and carried you toward the hospital entrance."

Of course they did a rape exam, I was left naked!

"Thank you," I whispered.

"You're welcome. And just to be clear, we see this type of thing all too often. Victims and their families try to make more out of it than they should. It's common to think you were somehow stalked and targeted and that your safety may still be in jeopardy. This is a big city and while we've made great strides to reduce random acts of violence, unfortunately they still happen. Be smart, but don't let this paralyze you from going places and doing things. Okay?"

I nodded. I heard every word, but something told me Quinn ignored them.

"We'll show ourselves out. If you need anything, here's my card."

Quinn grabbed it from her and stood to see them out anyway. As he came back to the couch, I watched him carefully. He avoided eye contact with me. Obviously, he was deeply troubled by what had happened. There was a huge difference between showing up at the hospital after something like this and actually being the one to find the victim. I was all too familiar with the discovery scenario.

"Look at me," I demanded, scooting to the side to face him.

His eyes met mine. My face was painful to see, as was hearing what I was about to say. "This was *not* your fault. Do you hear me?"

"But if I—"

"NO! No ifs ... no buts. I was in the wrong place at the wrong time. It was a random attack. Did you hear them say that? If it would not have been me, it would have been somebody else. Shit happens. It happens all the time. Every day we wake to see a new dawn is a goddamn miracle. I'm alive, and I know how terrifying it must have been to find me the way you did, but ... I'm alive. That's all that matters. You have to let this go or it will eat you up. It will destroy you ... it will destroy us."

I cupped his jaw with my hand and rested my forehead on his. "Just let it go," I whispered as he sucked in a shaky breath.

Could I have been raped had something or someone not have distracted my attackers? Possibly. I knew that's all Quinn thought about. I knew I would let it go long before he ever would.

CHAPTER TWENTY-SEVEN

QUINN CLEANED up the kitchen from dinner on Christmas Eve while I rested on the couch. He surprised me, once again, with his domestic skills.

"So you *do* know what the large cube is under the counter that I put dirty dishes in," I mocked as he poured detergent into the dishwasher.

"You're safe ... for now, but once you're better I'm going to teach that smart mouth of yours a lesson."

"God, I hope so." I laughed. "I'm starving. You haven't fed me today. Whatcha gonna make?"

"Since it's Christmas I thought turkey or even ham sounded good. I could whip up some potatoes drenched in butter, giblets stuffing, and gravy from the drippings and ground up neck meat."

"You're safe ... for now, but once I'm better I'm going to teach that smart mouth of yours a lesson."

He laughed. "God, I hope so." He brought me over a banana, peeled it back, and handed it to me. "It's not dinner time yet ... I have a surprise planned for that. In the meantime I'll do what you do to me."

"Which is?" I asked before taking a bite.

"Throw random pieces of fruit in your direction until you're not as hungry."

"I don't do that!"

"Bullshit! That's exactly what you do. 'Here, Quinn, have a banana. Here, Quinn, have an apple. Here, Quinn, eat these grapes. Here, Quinn, pineapple ... your favorite.'"

"Okay already, I'll eat some fruit, but tell me what we're having for dinner."

"What part of *surprise* don't you get?" he mocked me.

"Well, how long do I have to wait? It's already four o'clock."

"Maybe an hour, but in the meantime let me see those gorgeous feet of yours."

I turned sideways on the couch and rested my feet in his lap. He picked one up and started rubbing it.

"Babe?"

"Hmm?" he hummed with a smile.

"You never told me about Olivia and the baby. What happened?"

Still rubbing my foot, he looked ahead at the sketch of his mother on the wall. "After you were taken to your private room last night I got a call from her ... she miscarried."

He didn't look at me. His face was stoic. I had no idea what he was thinking or feeling.

"Did you go see her after you found out?"

"No, I wasn't going to leave you."

"Quinn she lost—"

"I *wasn't* going to leave you."

"She doesn't have anyone."

"Her parents were scheduled to arrive in town this morning. She's not alone."

"I'm sorry, I—"

"I'm not." His voice was cold.

"Quinn—"

He finally looked at me. "Don't, Addy. Don't make me out to be some insensitive bastard for feeling like the only thing that went right yesterday was Olivia miscarrying. I don't *want* to feel this way, but I do. I could tell you what you want to hear. That I'm broken up inside over the loss of my child. That I want to hold Olivia in my arms and make the pain go away because she lost her child too. But the ugly truth is ... *I don't.*"

He shook his head and closed his eyes as he released a quick breath. "I wish I were like you, I do. You have this Mother Teresa compassion for all life and I *love* that about you. But ... I don't feel that way. It's selfish. I know it's so fucking selfish that all I want is to be with you and everything else just ... doesn't matter."

"Quinn?" I whispered like I would to a child to calm him down.

"What?" he sighed.

"If your biggest fault is loving me too much, then I'd say I'm a pretty lucky girl."

All the tension visibly melted from his body, as a heartwarming boyish smile graced his beautiful face.

***

As PROMISED, within the hour I got my surprise. There was a knock at the door.

Quinn stood. "Promise to not be upset?"

"About?"

"Your surprise," he answered, biting his lower lip and smiling.

"Why would I be upset?"

He walked to the door and looking at me, he opened it.

"Merry Christmas!" Mac and Evan yelled in unison.

Quinn's eyes were still on mine, no doubt gauging my reaction.

"Addy, oh, sweetie ..." Mac gushed as she hurried over to me. "You look ..."

"Like shit." I smiled.

"Well, yes. You look like shit," she replied matter-of-fact as only she could do without hurting my feelings.

"What are you two doing here?" I asked, but my gaze was focused on Quinn as he took their jackets and set their luggage by the stairs.

"Quinn called last night. Don't be mad. He said you would be, but we are family and I would have been beyond pissed at the both of you had I not been called."

Quinn shrugged, feigning innocence.

"Are you … I mean were you …" She couldn't even finish. I could see by the grave look in her eyes that she wanted to know if I had been raped.

With my good hand, I grabbed hers and squeezed it. "No. The police saw the security footage. Apparently something distracted or spooked my attackers, and maybe they just wanted *all* my belongings anyway. It doesn't matter now. I was lucky. Had Quinn not found me, I might not be here." I sent a warm smile his way as he and Evan sat in the chairs adjacent to the couch.

"What were you two doing at the hospital on Christmas Eve anyway?" Mac questioned.

She and Evan knew nothing about Olivia being pregnant. They knew nothing about the extreme depression I suffered through after Quinn told me. Mac was pregnant and I couldn't risk her or her baby's well-being to help me deal with my problems. That was the reason Quinn was worried I'd be upset that he told them about the previous night. Mac was fine. She could handle the truth, but I did not want her to know this truth—ever. Olivia was no longer carrying Quinn's baby. It was in the past. I had forgiven Quinn and we were good. Telling them would only change the way they viewed him.

Quinn looked at me. He would deal with whatever I decided to tell them. He would never have asked me to lie to my best friend so he could save face.

"Quinn had a pregnant *friend* who was taken to the hospital. She ended up miscarrying. I needed some air ... you know how much I hate hospitals. Anyway, I went to look for my gloves in the Range Rover and that's when I was attacked."

Quinn looked at me as if to make sure I was okay with my lie. I gave a tight smile and winked at him. The man saved my life. The least I could do was have his back and choose not to throw him under the bus on Christmas.

"We're sorry to hear about your friend's loss," Evan said.

"Thanks," Quinn replied without any further elaboration.

"I'm starving," I announced, eager to change the subject. "I hope part of my surprise is dinner?"

"We're on it. I'm sure you had something spectacular planned, so tell me what to make and I'll whip these two boys into action," Mac declared as she headed to the kitchen.

CHRISTMAS DINNER WAS PERFECT, despite my swollen face, bruised ribs, and injured shoulder. We sipped hot drinks and fell into easy conversation by the mammoth Christmas tree. Mac was in complete awe of the extravagant holiday decorations. We hadn't revealed the circumstances that led to Quinn's grand surprise, so she naturally thought he was simply the most over-the-top romantic that ever lived. She would not have thought that if I would have told her it was his last ditch effort to bring me out of a life-threatening depression after he told me Olivia was carrying his baby.

"You know, Addy, you should look into taking a self-defense class," Mac suggested.

Quinn cleared his throat and smiled.

"Yeah, yeah, I've had that speech already. Quinn's personal trainer teaches self-defense so I'll be receiving private lessons as soon as my shoulder heals. It's not like I really had a chance to defend myself last night."

"Self-defense training is also about teaching awareness. The biggest part of self-defense for women is not putting themselves in vulnerable situations," Quinn explained as he squeezed my leg.

"Yes, dear," I mocked. "Changing the subject ... how long are you staying in New York?"

"I've taken off work through New Year's, so we can stay for a few days if you'll have us that long," Evan said.

"Absolutely. Stay as long as you'd like. All I ask is for you two trouble makers to stay out of jail this week." Quinn grinned, looking at Mac then me. Evan busted out laughing.

"Definitely. And don't forget, my lovely pregnant wife, your attorney is off this week," Evan added.

"Ha, ha. Well, this jailbird is going to bed. For some

reason my body feels achy and exhausted," I said while easing to my feet.

"Let me help you." Quinn jumped up to help support me with my good arm.

"The guest room is ready … but no hurry. Help yourselves to anything," Quinn told them as we headed to the stairs.

"Good night, and Merry Christmas … so glad you're here," I called back to them.

"Merry Christmas, so glad you're okay," Mac replied.

QUINN HELPED me into my not-so-sexy flannel pajamas which were pink, red, and white with reindeer and snowflakes. I went into the bathroom to brush my teeth and was once again reminded how the reflection in the mirror was a stranger.

"Ugh, I almost forgot how bad I look. It must have been a real treat for everyone to look at this disgusting face all evening."

"Jesus, Addy. You were brutally attacked less than twenty-four hours ago. You're lucky to be alive. Who gives a fuck what your face looks like. It's nothing that won't heal."

"You do realize I went thirty-three years without a black eye and I've had two now in six weeks' time."

"You're a real Laila Ali," Quinn added with a smirk as he shrugged off his shirt.

"I highly doubt her face ever looked this bad, maybe her opponent's."

"I'm going to take down all the mirrors in this place until you're completely healed," he murmured into my neck as he brushed his lips down over my injured shoulder.

"*You'd* still have to look at me."

"I'd still *get* to look at you. Tú eres mi belleza eterna." *You are my eternal beauty.*

"Don't stop," I mumbled over my toothbrush and mouthful of toothpaste.

"Tu amor me inspire, tu ternura me conmueve y tus besos me enloquecen." *Your love inspires me, your tenderness touches me, and your kisses drive me crazy.*

I spit and wiped my mouth. "Has that always worked for you?"

He clasped my good hand and guided me to bed. "What are you talking about?"

"Serenading women with the way Spanish rolls off your sexy tongue."

"You're the only woman other than my relatives to whom I've spoken in Spanish."

Oh ...

"Are you ready for your present?" he said with a grand smile.

"You got me a present?" I asked with wide eyes.

"It's Christmas. Of course I got you a present. What kind of schmuck do you take me for?"

"If it's chocolate, then I'm going to say my all-time favorite schmuck."

He went into the closet and came back out with a cube-shaped box wrapped in gold foiled paper and an elegant sheer lavender bow. "I'm not going to lie ... I thought this was a great gift until you gave me that sketch of my mother last night. Now, it doesn't seem so spectacular."

I held out my right hand and wiggled my fingers. "Gimme, gimme, gimme."

Quinn set it on my lap and I braced it between my legs so I could unwrap it with one hand. The box was too big for a ring ... my ring. I had assumed he would give me my engagement ring back or propose again, but he hadn't yet. It was possible that he was playing the box within a box trick on me, but that seemed a bit too cheesy for Quinn.

After removing the gold tissue paper on the inside, I was intrigued to find books inside, old books. The first one I pulled out was a signed first edition of Robert Frost poems. The second was a signed copy of Ken Kesey's *One Flew Over the Cuckoo's Nest*. The last book was a signed first edition of *The Cat in the Hat*. The three books were easily worth over fifty grand. The dollar figure wasn't what surprised me, it was the three distinctively different genre of books.

"My mother had them. I'm sure they're worth a fair amount of money, but that didn't matter to Chase and Alexis. They didn't want them. I thought of you, not because of the specific books, just because you like to read and I thought you'd appreciate the sentimentality that they had belonged to my mother."

"I don't know what to say ... I ... I love it."

He sat down on the bed beside me. "Here's the thing, I'm sure I fall into the 'what do you get the guy who has everything?' category, but you fall into the very rare 'what do you get the woman who wants nothing yet has very little?' category."

"I have you, babe. What more could I possibly want, need, or handle, for that matter?"

Gently, he kissed my lips. "You stole my line."

CHAPTER TWENTY-EIGHT

Evan and Mac stayed through New Year's. I was sad to see them leave, but it felt good to have Quinn all to myself again. Except, he too had to get back to work, or reality, as he called it. My face looked like a prism of colors and my ribs and shoulder were doing better, but I felt stiff and in need of physical activity. At my four-week doctor's visit, he gave me the go-ahead to start physical therapy. Stir craziness set in and I wanted to get out, even if only for therapy, but Quinn insisted we pay someone to come to me instead.

Calling Quinn overly protective and nervous about me going anywhere alone was a monumental under-statement. Instinctively, I wanted to fight him on it, but he carried around the horrific images of my naked, beaten, and for all intents and purposes, left-for-dead body in the parking lot, so I tried to be empathetic.

Time crawled as I fought to get better. Knowing I wouldn't see freedom again until I had recovered and taken the "required" self-defense classes was my incentive to work hard with my therapy. Then there was the other little annoyance, or rather big annoyance ... Quinn still thought I was too fragile for sex. By seven weeks post-attack my ribs were feeling much better, my shoulder had very little pain, and my face was healed.

Valentine's Day was upon us and I thought if that wasn't a free pass for sex, then I couldn't imagine what would be. Quinn made reservations at a posh vegan-friendly restaurant. I dug out the metallic red dress with the single long sleeve that I wore to the Broadway play the night Quinn fucked me in nothing but my platform heels at his mother's house. Since Christmas, he had been too calm and seemingly uninterested in sex. It was sweet and considerate for the first few weeks while I still felt stiff and uncomfortable, but then it started to drive me crazy. I started to feel a little rejected so Valentine's Day was supposed to be my sexual tension reprieve.

Quinn, as usual, was ready first and waiting for me downstairs. He watched me navigate the stairs with caution in my tight dress and ridiculously high heels. His face was indiscernible.

"Wow, Addy, you look amazing ... just sexy as hell. In fact, screw dinner I'm just going to take you back upstairs and do all sorts of hot, nasty stuff to you," I mocked since he wasn't saying anything.

His tight lips curled at the corners, but he said nothing.

"Cat got your tongue?" I purred as I slipped on my coat.

I tried to play it cool, but seeing Quinn in his suit and sexy, messy hair wrecked my composure.

Quinn held the door open for me. "After you, my beauty."

The frigid night air nipped at my bare legs, but New York hadn't seen snow for over two weeks. We took the Lamborghini and neither one of us could walk by the dent in the back fender without fighting a smirk. The drive to the restaurant was filled with casual conversation, at least on Quinn's part. I reached over and suggestively rubbed his leg.

"That feels good, a little more pressure. I've changed up my workout and my legs are pretty sore."

Not what I was going for ...

"Oh, by the way, I have to fly to Portland tomorrow, just for one night."

"Mmm, I could come with you and keep you *entertained* on the flight," I said while tugging the hair at the nap of his neck. Feeling a twinge of pain in my shoulder, I brought my arm back down and tried to discreetly rub it.

Quinn glanced over at me. "Your shoulder still bothering you?"

I scratched my nails across my skin. "No, just an itch." Looking straight ahead, I avoided eye contact because I could never lie to his face.

"Addy ..." he said disapprovingly.

"Quinn ..." I mimicked his tone.

"Did you do physical therapy today?"

"Yes, Doctor."

"Why the smart mouth tonight?"

I sighed. "Because I'm fine, but you keep treating me like I'm a china doll. You don't want me going anywhere by myself until I take self-defense classes, but I can't do that until I'm done with physical therapy."

"I told you, if you take—"

"I'm not taking a bodyguard with me in the middle of the day to the grocery store, or to yoga class, or to volunteer at the animal shelter. Do you have any idea how understanding I've been about what you saw the night I was attacked? I thought eventually you would lighten up and realize how impractical and frankly ridiculous it is to expect me to remain hostage in the condo until you get home.

Then there are the times that you've traveled. *'Sorry, baby, I'm going to sunny San Francisco for a few days, remember don't go anywhere.'* And I could have gone anywhere I damn well pleased, but I didn't because I respected your need to protect me after what happened. But it's been seven weeks and I can't do this anymore."

Quinn could have responded, but he chose to get out of the car and hand the keys to the valet then he walked around the back of the car. I hopped out unassisted, walked around the front of the car, grabbed the keys from the valet, hopped in the driver's seat, and sped off.

Glancing in the rearview mirror to adjust it, I noticed my completely irate lover standing in the street with his hands on his hips and what may have been steam seeping from his nostrils. Was I trying to upset him? Yes. His lack of attention to me, other than in a fatherly, protective way, had played on my last nerve. I felt like an errant child looking for attention. Exhilaration coursed through my body from the power of the insanely expensive piece of metal on wheels weaving in and out of traffic with uninhibited freedom. It was freedom from the condo, freedom from being held hostage from my daily life, and freedom from the guilt that ate at me when I worried Quinn. If I wasn't afraid, then neither should he have been.

The question was whether to go home or drive around for a while. Manhattan wasn't exactly the most exciting place to drive around, especially in a car that begged for speed. My point had been made the moment I drove off without him; there was no need to drag out the inevitable.

HAVING HAD A GOOD HEAD START, I made it home easily before Quinn. My appetite disappeared when he gave me the silent treatment, so I changed my clothes and crawled into bed. *So much for chocolates, flowers, and romance.*

The slam of the door downstairs startled me. My heart galloped and I held my breath waiting for Quinn to come upstairs. It was a standoff and I would not give in and go downstairs. Seven weeks of giving in and I was done. The surprising part was he never gave in either. At some point I fell asleep, and when I awoke in the morning I was alone in bed. His side hadn't been slept in, and it was already past seven, which meant he was gone. But not just gone to work, he was on his way to Portland.

I got up and looked around just in case I was wrong, but I wasn't. Not only was he gone, but there was no note or even a message left on my phone. Alone. I was all alone. The emotions came fast and furious as I crawled into a ball on the couch and cried. The anger felt like poison in my veins. We were not immature twenty-somethings void of relationship skills, we were mature adults who should have been able to have a grown-up conversation. Then the shame blanketed me because I had acted childish when I stormed off in his car. I blamed it on temporary insanity because I *was* going insane under house arrest.

However, the new day brought perspective to everything. It was too late to change the outcome of the previous night, but it wasn't too late to let go of my injured pride and call him. I wiped my tear-streaked face and grabbed my phone. When I called him it went straight to his voicemail.

"Hi ... I wanted to apologize for taking your car ... and um ... leaving you. I was just so frustrated and angry and hurt. You wouldn't say anything when I needed you to say *something* the most. Anyway, have a safe trip and we'll talk when you get home."

Wallowing around in self-pity got old, so I had a shower and got ready for physical therapy. I obsessively kept checking my phone, but there weren't any messages from Quinn. By the time I was done with physical therapy my patience had worn thin. Quinn still had not returned my call. Guided by thoughtless emotion, I called him again, and again it went to his voicemail.

"I'm sure you're busy with meetings or whatever, but I thought you'd at least have the courtesy to call me back or at least text me to let me know you arrived safely in Portland."

Five minutes later I called him again, this time he answered.

"Addy, I can't talk now. I'll call you later." His voice was short and he left no time for me to respond before he ended the call.

Bastard!

He might not have had time to talk to me, but he sure as hell would get a text whether he wanted it or not.

Thanks for hanging up on me, asshole!

The night I was attacked you refused to leave me home alone with my "thoughts," but now you're OK with it?

Want to know what "thoughts" I'm having?

I think you're the worst fucking communicator ever!

I think I'm sick of New York and this damn bachelor pad of a condo.

I think something changed the night I was attacked.

I think you look at me differently.

I think you're miserable having your ass anchored to me when you'd rather be living it up on the slopes or traveling with friends.

I think you're afraid of breaking me, physically by having sex with me or emotionally by admitting you don't want to have sex with me.

All these thoughts make me feel like crap.

I don't feel needed by you, I don't feel wanted by you.

I feel lonely and scared of losing you, and I hate myself for letting you be the damn gatekeeper to my self-esteem.

Last night I was so desperate for your touch. I needed to feel close to you, I wanted your touch so badly every cell in my body physically ached for it.

Don't you miss my touch? Don't you miss me ... or us?

Maybe you don't.

I sent the text without a second thought. Less than

a minute later my phone rang; it was him. Letting it go to voicemail, I decided to get out for a while. I no longer felt compelled to follow his orders. All I needed was a normal day, a chance to regain perspective.

I spent the rest of the afternoon at the animal shelter and soup kitchen. That was all it took to find myself again. The more I thought about myself, the more I lost myself. I had to reconnect with the part of me that mattered the most, which was the part I saw reflected in others.

BY EVENING I was in much better spirits. The text I sent Quinn was the worst version of myself ... all ego. However, I didn't regret sending it. He needed to see how much I depended on my freedom and communication with him to function with sanity. I started to feel like a zoo animal—trapped under the premise that it was for my own good. Sometimes it's better to die in the wild than suffer in captivity.

After I ate dinner, I downloaded a new romance novel. It was bittersweet though. Quinn and I had been living the romance and my need to escape the black and white monotony of reality had been replaced with a colorful spectrum of spontaneous lust, love, and romance. It seemed like the fireworks had fizzled, and I needed that rush of passion again, even if it was just a fictional fix.

By ten I was halfway through the book, snuggled

up on the couch in an oversized long-sleeved T-shirt and fuzzy wool socks. That was when I heard the click of the lock on the door. Motionless, I watched Quinn walk in and close the door behind him. He tossed his keys on the entry table, draped his hanging bag on the stair railing, and shrugged off his black wool overcoat. He was dressed in a charcoal suit with a white pinstriped shirt and a royal blue tie. With just his eyes, he pinned me to the couch as he walked toward me.

"What are you doing here?" I whispered, because he wasn't supposed to be home until the next day.

He removed his suit coat and tossed it on the chair, then he loosened his tie.

"What am I doing here?" he said slowly with a pensive expression. "Where did you expect me to be tonight? When the love of my fucking life tells me she's tired of living in New York … in my condo, where else would I be? When she tells me she feels like I look at her differently, or that my ass is anchored to her, or that she doesn't feel needed or wanted. Where in God's name did you honestly think I would be tonight?"

My teeth clenched and the lump in my throat strangled me. Refusing to blink my tear-filled eyes, I shrugged. Then, swallowing past that stupid lump of emotion, I fought for words. "Quinn—"

"No," he interrupted, shaking his head. "You've had your say, now I'm going to have mine. I left my meeting in Portland and rushed back here as fast as I could because you wanted me to say *something*, so here it is."

He knelt down on the floor as I sat up straight on

the couch. Reaching into his pocket he pulled out a ring ... my ring. Then he set it on the couch beside me before moving his hands up my bare legs until they squeezed the top of my thighs. His face was inches from mine, and his tense eyes and ticking jaw portrayed pure anguish.

"I had planned on proposing to you on Christmas Eve ... then you distracted me with your sexy little strip tease. Then Olivia called. Then I found you lying on the ground..." his jaw twitched as his eyes filled with tears "...I thought you were dead." His voice cracked. "Every time I look at you all I see is your cold, injured body in the parking lot. I notice every grimace as you hug your ribs when you laugh or sneeze. I know it takes you twice as long to do your hair because your arm quickly fatigues. You love yoga, but you haven't even attempted it since you were injured. So I've been carrying around this ring in my pocket looking for the right time to ask you to marry me. The time when I can take every inch of your body and claim it as mine again because I *do* miss your touch, I *do* need you, I *do* want you ... so much it's fucking killing me."

My heart ricocheted against my chest from his words, his smell, and his close proximity. I grabbed his loosened tie and pulled him into my lips. Our tongues mingled as I unknotted his tie and worked the buttons of his shirt. His hands gripped the top of my legs even tighter as he moaned into my mouth.

After undoing the final button, I splayed my hands over his chest. "Take me upstairs."

Bending his head down to kiss my neck and suck in my ear lobe, he slid his hands under my butt and lifted me as he stood up in an effortless motion. When he turned to walk to the stairs I stopped him.

"Wait!"

Pulling his head from my neck he groaned, "Wait? I hurried home to be with you, to touch you, to make love to you, and now you want me to wait?"

I grinned as I fidgeted with the collar of his open shirt. "I thought maybe there was ... uh ... something you wanted to *ask* me?"

"Are you having your period?"

I smacked his shoulder. "No, not that!"

Then I looked down at the couch and back to him again.

"Oh, that? Well, now you've ruined the moment. Maybe I should save it for another day so it can be a surprise," he said with a grin.

I grabbed his nipple and twisted it. "Ouch!" he yelled.

"*I've* ruined the moment?"

"Yeah, now it's not romantic. Now, last night, it was going to be romantic. You have no idea what I did to make last night perfect ... then you went on and on in the car about how miserable you've been and then for the grand finale you drove off ... IN MY CAR!"

Chewing the inside of my cheek, I squinted at him. "So ... you don't have anything you want to ask me?"

"Top or bottom?" he deadpanned, continuing his walk upstairs, leaving *my ring* on the sofa.

CHAPTER TWENTY-NINE

QUINN SET me on the bed then removed his shirt and pants. Working my bottom lip between my teeth, my eyes struggled to meet his.

"Addy?"

I forced my eyes up as I pulled my legs into lotus.

"I need you to be clear about something." He reached for the hem of my top and eased it over my head, being extra careful with my left arm. I was braless, and his close proximity had my nipples pebbling. "As long as I have a pulse, I will need you, want you, desire you..." he slipped off his black boxer briefs and squeezed his own hard glutes "...and this ass of mine will live in eternal ecstasy if it's anchored to you."

My grin was unstoppable. "Show me."

Tugging my wool socks off my feet, he uncrossed my legs and crawled on the bed between them as I leaned back. He lifted my feet up and rested them on his chest as he hooked my panties with his fingers and slid them off. Setting my feet back on the bed, he leaned over me and rested his weight on his forearms. Our kiss was slow at first as he sank into me. My muscles gripped him, welcoming every inch. Then, like the gradual progression of a storm, our hands, hips, and mouths gained momentum and raged out of control.

"God, I've missed you," he moaned as he kneaded my breast, his rhythm intensifying.

Pressing my nails into his flexed biceps, I wrapped my legs around his waist. He moved his hand from my breast to my butt and gripped it—hard. Approaching my climax, my soft moans turned into needy whimpers until I melted, nearly seeing stars.

With one last stroke he stilled, squeezed his eyes shut, and filled me with his warmth.

Breathless, he kissed me, humming in satisfaction. Without breaking our contact, he rolled onto his back, taking me with him. I wanted the feeling to last forever.

As I rested, sprawled out on his chest, he combed through my hair with his fingers. The feeling of him still inside me left me wanting more. I sat up on him, without breaking our connection. Just the heated look in his eyes had me ready for round two. When I suggestively wiggled my hips over his, he stirred inside me.

"God, I love how insatiable you can be," he said, wetting his lips with his tongue as he gripped my hips and guided my movements. Grinding over him, I closed my eyes, savoring the fullness of him hardening inside me. He recovered with sex-god speed and was ready to go. It wasn't going to take me long; the visual of his ripped sweaty torso under me brought me close. I still had to pinch myself sometimes. The fact that he was with me, and desired me, still seemed like a dream.

"I'm so close," I breathed out, as I continued to work my hips over him.

Gripping my right hip tighter with one hand, he moved his other to my abdomen and slid the pad of his thumb across my clit. Then, biting his lower lip, he rocked into me causing me to explode. He found his release at the same time, and I circled my hips and clenched him.

"Fuuuck!" he growled while his thumb continued to press into my clit, milking every last sensation from my body.

THE RHYTHMIC HARMONY of our breaths finding a steady pace again was the lone sound that filled the room. I was tired, but not ready to go to sleep. All I wanted was to feel our naked bodies spooned together all night.

"Do you have something you'd like to ask me?" I questioned in my sweetest, I-just-gave-you-two-amazing-orgasms voice.

"Do you want to go again?" he asked, with a cocky, teasing edge to his voice.

Dumb-ass!

"Fine, then, at least tell me what plans I ruined last night," I mumbled.

"Oh, you mean the restaurant I rented out just for the two of us at the price tag of ... a small fortune? The grand piano that was brought in to be played by a well-known pianist whose name I will never reveal? Or do you mean the mountains of flowers, daisies, and of course lavender roses that were scattered throughout the entire dining area. Oh, and by the way ... I gifted your organic vegan truffles to the waitstaff."

"You'd better be kidding me," I said in disbelief, yet the stabbing sensation to my heart told me he was serious. He had planned the most romantic proposal on the most romantic night of the year and I annihilated his plans. "Then why did you act so distant in the car? Why did you ignore me and let me get all worked up?"

"I wanted to throw you off a bit, so it would be a bigger surprise. I love getting you all worked up, then shocking the hell out of you. Unfortunately, you turned the tables on me last night."

"Jeez, you must have been pissed, *incredibly* pissed." I felt punched in the gut.

"It was the first time I slept in the guest bed, so yes, a little pissed."

I turned to face him, going for the innocent doe eyes. "Will you ever forgive me?"

"Eventually." He smiled. His expression turned

serious. "So you're miserable living in New York with me?"

Exhaling, I focused on his chest as I traced his muscles. "Definitely not you, just here. Don't get me wrong, I'd live in a cardboard box on the street with you if that's where I had to live to be with you. I miss Chicago or maybe I just miss the feeling of home. I dream about a wooded acreage just outside of the city with wildlife, lots of privacy, and a small meadow of wildflowers. I dream about porch swings in the morning and a fire pit for roasting marshmallows in the evening. I imagine bird houses, wind chimes, and large blooming lilac bushes in the spring."

"And how many kids do you see running around in your meadow of wildflowers?"

He completely surprised me with his question.

Glancing up at him, I shrugged and smiled. "If they're yours, then at least a dozen."

"If they're mine?" he said in a firm voice. "Who else's would they be?"

Giggling, I kissed his chest. "You never know ... Tom from the front desk has been giving me the eye since I gave you head in the parking garage."

"Christ! What is Tom ... sixty, seventy years old?"

"Some women like older men ... they're more mature and *experienced*." I laughed, admittedly crossing over into the ridiculous realm.

"Yeah, Tom's *experienced* with taking his medications three times a day and pissing every ten minutes because his prostate is the size of a grapefruit."

I laughed until the moment passed. We held each other in silence for a while, and just as I started to drift off to sleep Quinn spoke.

"Do you ever wonder if your attack had anything to do with your parents?"

"No," I answered while I yawned.

"How can you be sure?"

"Because I'm still alive."

"Yeah but—" he tried to argue.

"But nothing ... my parents were targeted because of what my dad did many years ago. If that person wanted me dead, I'd be dead. It was an act of revenge and they got it. If anyone truly believed I was in danger, I would have been put into witness protection by now. You need to let what happened to my parents go. I have. And as for my attack ... it was random, some idiots, probably high and in need of money for more drugs. This is New York City, after all." I reached around and clenched his firm butt. "I hope after tonight when you look at me you can envision me naked on top of you instead of left for dead in the snow."

He peeked under the sheets. "I think I can conjure up a few new images."

I WOKE up early the next morning. Surprisingly, Quinn was still in bed.

It was fate.

The ring was mine.

I slithered out of bed—holding my breath—and tiptoed downstairs. When I turned on the light, the ring called my name. The poor, lonely symbol of eternity was all alone on the couch just where Quinn had abandoned it. I picked it up and started to slide it on my finger.

"Don't even think about it."

"Shit! You startled me," I screeched as I whipped around, feeling guilty.

Quinn walked toward me wearing only his black boxer briefs. Grabbing the ring, he slid it onto his pinky finger. It didn't even fit past his first knuckle.

"Are you serious? You no longer want to marry me?" I asked in disbelief.

He chuckled as he slid his arms inside my robe, pulling me into him. "Oh, I'm going to marry you. I'm just not going to reward your bad behavior."

"So what exactly do you call last night?"

"Courting." He smirked as his hand slipped into the back of my panties.

"Oh, so now you're courting me?"

"Hell no! I'm letting you court me."

I grabbed his wrist and pulled his hand out of my panties. "I am *not* courting you," I huffed as I marched into the kitchen.

"Maybe you should ask *me* to marry *you*," he suggested with a sly smile.

Turning on my heel, I fisted my hands on my hips and lifted my shoulders. "Fine. Will you marry me?"

He clenched his hand on the back of his neck and rubbed it as he pursed his lips and looked up at the ceiling. "I'll think about it."

I squinted at him before turning and grabbing the electric teapot. "You're a real shit," I grumbled.

Quinn's phone rang before he could respond. He grabbed it off the counter. "Yes?"

He was silent for several minutes. Whoever called had a lot to say.

"Fucking unbelievable. God! I wish this would just go away."

I grabbed two glass tea cups from the cabinet.

"Set up another meeting with Cove's attorneys."

The sound of glass shattering stopped his conversation.

"I'll have to call you back," he clipped. "Don't move, baby. What happened?"

Shards of glass were scattered at my bare feet. Quinn hopped up on the island and grabbed me, lifting me from the mess.

"Sit here," he said as my feet dangled from the counter. He slipped on his shoes and grabbed the broom. "How'd you drop both glasses?" he asked while sweeping up the mess.

"Uh, I don't know ... they just ... I just ..."

After he finished sweeping up the glass, he scooted my legs around so my feet were over the sink.

"Let me wash off your feet in case you have any small slivers of glass on you."

I nodded.

He dried my feet then helped me off the counter.

"Baby, what's wrong? You look like you just saw a ghost or something."

Rubbing my hands over my face, I shook my head. "No, I'm fine. I guess I just startled myself when they slipped out of my hands. Uh ... who was on the phone?"

"It was my dad's business partner. Remember I told you about the legal issues my dad was dealing with?"

I nodded.

"Well, his partner is still trying to keep their investments and reputation untarnished, even though it's way too late for that. My dad knew it years ago, that's why he's no longer living."

"You said Cove's attorneys. What is Cove?"

"The name of their corporation, it's the abbreviation for Cohen-Vessey. I hate to rush out, but I need to get showered and head into the office." He kissed my cheek and jogged up the stairs.

Grabbing my stomach, I rushed to the hall bathroom and vomited. My whole body shook. Then, reaching for the sink, I pulled myself up and splashed cold water on my face.

Deep breath ... I am peaceful, I am strong.

Easing the toilet seat down, I turned and sat on it with my elbows on my knees and my head resting in my hands. I don't know how long I sat there, but when I heard the tap of Quinn's shoes on the stairs I shut the door and locked it.

A few minutes later he knocked on it. "I'm leaving, baby. You okay?"

Taking a deep breath, I fought to steady my voice. "Yeah."

"I'll call you later. Maybe we can go to dinner," he called as his voice faded the farther he moved from the door.

"K," was all I managed.

CHAPTER THIRTY

Quinn

I CALLED Addy later that afternoon to see if she was up for dinner, but she never answered her phone. I must have messaged her a hundred times with no response. Finally, I left work early because I couldn't shake the feeling that something was wrong. She seemed off earlier that morning, like something was bothering her. I kicked myself for leaving her as I managed to hit every fucking red light. When I finally pulled into the parking garage, I was relieved to see Karma was still there. On the way up in the elevator I tried to calm myself down. She loved listening to her rock music, so I figured that was why she didn't hear her phone. When I opened the door to the condo everything was quiet, no music, no vacuum, no TV, no Addy.

"Addy?" I yelled as I did a quick sweep of the first floor.

No answer.

Running up the stairs, I continued to call out her name, but everything was silent. "Fuck!" I yelled as I ran my hands through my hair. Then I checked the closet, all her stuff was there, nothing looked different from that morning. Looking around for a note, I came across her phone on the kitchen counter. The screen showed all my missed calls and messages. I clicked on her calendar to see if she had an appointment I didn't know about, but there was nothing for that day. It wasn't like her to leave without her phone, but it was possible. I would go crazy. I couldn't just wait so I called down to Tom.

"Mr. Cohen, how can I be of assistance?"

"Tom, did you see Addy leave the building today?"

"Yes, probably around ten this morning."

"Did she say where she was going?"

"No, sir, she actually seemed unusually quiet or distracted."

Fuck, fuck, fuck!

"Did she take a cab?"

"No, sir, she walked ... heading south if I remember correctly."

"And you haven't seen her since?"

"No, sir."

"Call me as soon as you see her again."

"Yes, sir."

I was known for my calm, controlled, business-like demeanor, but with Addy I was a fucking shaky finger on a hair trigger. It was how I knew I had fallen in love with her. My need to protect her trumped all concern for myself and everyone else in my life. It was the reason I barely held it together after I found her on the ground, naked, beaten, and unconscious. She was mine to love and protect, and I fucking failed her in every way that night. Those blue doe eyes of hers looked at me as if I was some kind of hero for saving her life, but it was bullshit. She was too blind to see that had it not been for my epic fuck-up she would never have been "in the wrong place at the wrong time," as she liked to say.

An hour later, I decided to go look for her. It would be dark soon, and I couldn't sit around at home doing nothing. Tom had instructions to call me as soon as she came back, so I jumped in my car and drove to all the possible places I thought she might be. After two hours of driving everywhere I could think of, I still hadn't found her and Tom hadn't called either.

When I got back to my condo I called the police, but of course they gave me the whole spiel about twenty-four hours ... missing persons report ... reasonable belief that something had happened ... fucking blah blah blah. They said that since she was seen leaving on her own accord that abduction didn't seem likely. I couldn't even begin to imagine where she would have been going on foot in such cold weather. The more I thought about it, the more the image of her knocked out in the snow kept popping into my head.

I must have brought Mac's number up on my phone a dozen times after I got back, but I never pressed *send* because I knew how much Addy hated to worry her pregnant friend, and I felt like an ass of a fuck-up for even having to consider making another call about how I failed to protect Addy.

By ten I was in need of a drink. I'd gone from worried to pissed, back to worried, and then to fucking outraged. I replayed our morning over and over, but I couldn't come up with any reason why she'd leave. We'd had some playful banter about her ring and the proposal, but Addy knew me. She knew it was just a stupid game and in the end she would bring me to one knee. The desperation to find a reason why she might be mad was agonizing because I knew if she wasn't mad, then something was wrong and she was in danger, or injured, or worse ...

SLEEP EVADED me and by five in the morning I couldn't wait any longer. Since I had five more hours until I could file a missing person's report, I decided it was time to call Mac.

"Quinn," was all she said in a groggy voice.

"Sorry to wake you but ..." I had trouble saying the words.

"But Addy's gone," she said knowingly.

"Fucking hell! You've heard from her?"

"We need to talk."

"Mac, where is she? Is she okay? When did—"

"Quinn! We. Need. To. Talk."

"So talk." I was irritated and impatient.

"Not on the phone."

I never even let her finish. Instead, I was on her doorstep in just under two and a half hours. She answered the door in her robe with her hair pulled back in a bun.

"Quinn."

"Mac." I stepped in and she took my coat.

"Can I get you some coffee?" she asked.

"I'm fine. Where's Addy?"

"I don't know. Come have a seat."

"What? You don't know? Then why the hell am I here?"

Evan came down the hall. "Quinn," was all he said as he kissed Mac, then her tummy, and grabbed his briefcase.

"Bye, honey, I love you," she said as he walked out the door to the garage.

She plopped down on the couch and I sat in the chair across from her.

"She's gone." Her face wrinkled with pain.

"What the fuck does that mean? Gone where?"

"I don't know. She wouldn't say and I didn't ask."

"Why the hell not?"

"Because she didn't want me to have to lie to you when you came looking for her."

"I don't understand ..." My head was a cluster-fuck; nothing Mac said made any sense.

"Do you know how the fire started?"

Whoa, whiplash! The new direction was unexpected. "Yes ... well, no ... I mean she said it was a lightning strike."

Mac nodded her head then sipped her tea. "How did your dad's business get into 'legal trouble?'"

"What does that have to do with anything?"

She wouldn't answer. Instead, she just kept that pathetic, pained look on her face.

I sighed. "One of his companies manufactured a product that allegedly caused some injuries."

"What was the product?"

The truth was I never paid that much attention to the specifics of the lawsuits against my father's company, at least the product specifics. Even after he died and I took over his business affairs, it was all about the money and legal mediation to reach settlements before they went to court. It wasn't my company. It was an inherited thorn in my side.

Rubbing my temples, I tried to remember the specifics. "Some natural gas or propane tubing."

"What was the issue with it?"

"Fuck, Mac! What does this have to do with anything?" I gritted between my teeth. I swore her damn pregnancy hormones were messing with her brain.

She took a deep breath then began to speak. "They manufactured corrugated stainless steel tubing which was a new type of gas line that was installed in homes. The problem or defect in the product was that even a nearby lightning strike could cause the line to become electrically energized. Then that power surge had the potential to puncture a hole in the line and cause a *fire*."

The whole damn room spun. I tried to formulate a sentence, but I couldn't.

"Addy wasn't in a good place after the fire. In fact, she wasn't around here at all. We left the country for a year while my dad handled all the legal aspects of things. Addy never cared about the lawsuit; she knew it wouldn't change anything. My father had a different opinion and since it was his family too that died in the fire, he took it upon himself to ... make the responsible parties pay."

Still confused, I shook my head. "It ... it wasn't my company."

"It doesn't matter. COVE was the name she connected to the fire ... now she has a face to go with the name."

Letting my head fall to the back of the chair, I closed my eyes. "Where is she?"

"Quinn, I *really* don't know."

"Well, then I'll just have to find her," I said with certainty as I pushed myself to my feet.

"You won't find her."

"You don't know what kind of resources I have." I couldn't believe she doubted me.

"Doesn't matter. Addy is infinitely more intelligent than both of us combined, and she has unlimited resources. So I don't care if you're the fucking FBI or head of Homeland Security ... you won't find her until she's ready to be found."

"So you're not worried about her?" I asked with my arms crossed over my chest.

"Of course ... I'll always worry about Addy." She rubbed her hands over the little bump of her belly. "But I have to prioritize now, and Addy knows it."

I walked to the couch, bent down, and kissed Mac on the cheek. "Thank you and ... I'm sorry."

As I walked to the door she called out, "What are you sorry about?"

"Your brother and Sage ... they were your family too," I replied as I buttoned my coat.

"Quinn?"

"Yeah?"

She paused for a moment, contemplating her next words. "Nothing, have a safe flight home."

Nodding, I forced a smile then left.

ADDY OWNED ME. She once asked me if I'd give it all up for her. At the time I couldn't answer her hypothetical question, because it seemed so ridiculous. By the time I arrived back in New York to the silence of my condo ... my empty, Addy-less condo, I knew the answer. Yes. Positively, absolutely, unquestionably, one hundred percent, without a fraction of a doubt, yes. I would give it all up for her. I, too, would live with her in a cardboard box.

The sensible part of me knew that Mac was right. Addy probably couldn't be found unless she wanted to be, but I had to try. I wasn't the FBI or head of Homeland Security, but I knew people who were connected to both. I would spend every dime I'd ever made to find her. She either would come back to me or I would spend the rest of my life searching for her. In my mother's words: "Find your one true passion in life and follow it. Follow it until you take your last breath."

It only required a few phone calls to get things going. A buddy of mine, Harrison, had been in the Army's Special Forces, and after he got out he started his own private investigation business. He was perfect for the job because he had a lot of connections and mad, raw instinct.

Once I had the right people lined up to search for Addy, I focused on COVE's connection to the fire. It wasn't an easy task, either. Since the onset of lawsuits that had started nearly a decade earlier, massive amounts of information had been confiscated from the company. With the fucking mess of lawyers and their attorney-client privileges, almost everything was labeled "confidential," aka off-limits, to the son of the company's dead cofounder.

What I did find out were the specifics on the product. More than one company manufactured that type of flexible tubing, and my father's company was not the only one dealing with lawsuits. The manufacturers blamed the installers and vice versa. Very few cases made it to court; most were settled through mediation. In the end, the manufacturers had a hard time making a case for themselves because patents were being filed and new lines of lightning-resistant tubing were already in production.

The obvious question by wrongful death attorneys at that point was, "If there was nothing wrong with the original product, why the revisions?" The more I looked into things, the easier it became to see why my father's life ended the way it did. Living with the guilt of innocent lives lost because of something he funded was emotional suicide. Then there was the nightmare of figuring out how to keep a company going after such a huge financial hit. He employed hundreds of people and they needed their jobs. They depended on their stock in the company, health insurance, and retirement. When business is good, there's no better view than from the top. But when something as catastrophic as a major class action lawsuit happens, the CEOs start to feel like they are crushed at the bottom of the heap, not just financially, but emotionally, too. Success doesn't come without risk.

Addy was aware that I inherited a mess from my father. I was certain she did not blame me. However, I was not so certain she could ever look at me again and not see my father's failures. I wasn't sure if I could either.

DAYS TURNED into weeks and still no word from Addy. Harrison hit dead ends in all directions he tried to track her. I was a fucking mess. Sobriety was effortless when Addy was with me; she was my focus, my purpose, my addiction. Not knowing where she was or if I'd ever see her again weakened my willpower. Some days I exercised before and after work to stay focused on anything but taking a drink. Some days I'd stop and pick up some Scotch on the way home, read my Mother's letter, stare at her picture, then slam the full bottle into the wall. But most days I worked my ass off to move my company's headquarters to Chicago. That was where Addy called home and I had to believe that she would return *home*.

By the end of March, I had purchased a new building space for my corporate headquarters and a beautiful wooded lot outside of Chicago. Then I found the best architect who specialized in eco-friendly design. He happened to know a great interior decorator, who I hired to find all the right mismatched pieces of salvaged and eco-friendly furnishings that would make our home feel, as she quoted, "warm, inviting, and environmentally sound" and most importantly, Addy-approved.

Transitioning my business to Chicago took longer than I expected. Most of my employees were very willing to make the transfer, especially after I promised that all their moving expenses would be handled by the company. However, as I anticipated, there were a few who didn't want to uproot their families to make the move, and for those I personally made sure they found comparable positions with other companies in New York.

The "big move" was by far the craziest thing I had ever done in my life ... which said a lot for a self-professed adrenaline junky. Packing up my personal and professional life and moving 800 miles, on the slim chance that the love of my life would come back to me, seemed crazy to my friends, family, and business associates. But I had no other choice. Addy had my heart, and I could barely breathe without her.

I surged ahead without looking back or slowing down. If I paused long enough to think *what if*, the bottle became my greatest temptation. *What if*, meant no Addy, no future, and as far as I was concerned, no reason to piss my time away on a wasted life ... which was how every day felt without her.

When my birthday came around, it was yet another painful reminder of how much I missed her. Both Chase and Zach wanted to come visit me in Chicago, but I insisted they wait until after I was settled. Our house took shape, and I no longer split my time between New York and Chicago. I rented an apartment two blocks from my new corporate headquarters. There were several choices in the area, but I chose the cheaper, more conservative one that was just under ten grand a month. I was certain Addy would be proud of my frugality.

I kept in contact with Mac and Evan. They knew about my relocation, but I swore them to secrecy. Mac seemed like the weak link in my plan. She promised not to say anything if Addy contacted her. However, I questioned all promises made by a woman who was in her last month of pregnancy. Evan said she was the most unpredictable ticking time bomb. That was fine with me, as long as she kept her mouth shut if Addy called. I needed her to *want* to come back to Chicago, and if she didn't want to see me then the knowledge of my presence there would have certainly kept her away. Mac knew that too, so I had no choice but to trust her. She wanted Addy home as much as I did. We all agreed upon one thing ... if Addy was going to return, it was mostly likely going to happen in the next month. When we first found out Mac was pregnant, she promised to be there for the birth.

BY THE TIME Mac was 37 weeks, I made the assumption Addy was back in Chicago, but Mac swore she hadn't heard from her. I checked the hotel she stayed at when she was in town for Richard and Gwen's anniversary party, but there was no record of her there. Then I decided to look up the address of her parents' house. I couldn't recall her ever mentioning anything about it, and I wondered if she still owned it.

After hours of research and several phone calls, I hadn't found anything. Something wasn't adding up. Not only could I not find their house, I couldn't find record of any Brecken who had ever been an Illinois Supreme Court Justice, or attorney, or a well-known businessman.

Digging deeper, I also couldn't find an Adler Sage

Brecken listed as a graduate of the University of Chicago. Then I tried Adler Sage Townsend, but I couldn't find her under that name either. However, I did find Mackenzie Townsend and Malcolm Townsend listed as graduates. Finally, I called Mac because nothing made sense and I became obsessed with figuring out Addy's past.

"Hey, Quinn. No, I'm not in labor, and no, I haven't heard from Addy."

"Believe it or not, that's not why I'm calling. But, how are you doing?"

"I'm fat and puffy. I can't sleep, everything makes me feel bloated, and my boobs are leaking."

Sorry I asked.

"I'm ... uh ... not sure what to say," I replied. I was genuinely interested in how she was doing, but the leaking boobs comment had me tongue-tied.

"There's nothing to say. You asked, so I told you." She laughed, which was a relief because I was *way* out of my comfort zone.

"So what are you calling about?"

"I was wondering where Addy's parents used to live, but I couldn't find any information."

"Addy sold the place. A young family lives there now. I can give you the address if you're curious and want to drive by there."

"No, it was just wishful thinking on my part that maybe she still owned it and was staying there."

"Holy crap ... trust me, if she still owned it she would *never*, I repeat *never* stay there."

"I figured it was a long shot."

"Though I'm surprised you didn't find out the address. They were very well-known and the news of their murders was in every paper," she responded in disbelief.

"That's the fucking craziest part. I can't find any information on them. It's as if Supreme Court Justice Brecken never existed."

"What do you mean *Brecken*?"

"Townsend was her married name, so I assumed Brecken had to be her maiden name that she went back to after Malcolm died."

There was an awkward pause. "So ... Addy never told you her parents' names?"

I felt like a complete dumb-ass. How it never came up in conversation all of a sudden seemed ridiculous. True, she never wanted to talk about her past, but I should have been a little more inquisitive. *Fuck!* I sighed. "No, apparently she didn't."

"Her parents were Benjamin and Mabel Ellery."

"Ellery?" Addy had never mentioned that name. "Holy shit ... the *Ellery murders* ..." The infamous murder of the Ellerys never registered with me because my mind was stuck on the name Brecken. "Jesus, I remember that. It was all over the news and in every paper. The Ellerys were her parents?" It just wouldn't sink in, probably because I was stunned that I'd known Addy for nearly two years but *never* knew who her parents were. "So why'd she change her name to Brecken?"

"For several different reasons, anonymity for one—"

"Security?"

Mac hummed. "Mmm, maybe, but mostly it was a sentimental name. She wanted to carry a piece of her past with her forever."

I wanted to smash my fucking phone against the ground. Just when things started to make sense, Mac added another piece of information that didn't fit.

"What is so sentimental about Brecken?"

"It's not really my place to say."

"Jesus Christ, Mac! The whole reason Addy left is because we both somehow failed to disclose everything about our pasts. I'm not doing this shit anymore. I need to know everything so—out with it already!"

"Addy was four and a half months pregnant at the time of the fire."

Fucking hell!

"She went into labor right after the fire. They never knew if it was related to Addy's smoke inhalation, stress, or just an unfortunate event that would have happened anyway. If the baby would have had a couple more weeks of development, it might have had a chance, but—"

I was pissed, but not at Addy. She tried to tell me everything the day she told me about Sage, but I wouldn't let her finish. It was killing her and I couldn't stand to see her hurt anymore. I was pissed at the world and the total shit hand of cards Addy was dealt. She didn't deserve any of it. At least a case could be made for the bad things that happened in my life. I had been less than innocent over the years, and I figured eventually I would have to "pay the piper." Addy, however, was like a prison inmate serving a life sentence for a crime in which she was wrongly accused and convicted.

"It was a boy ..." Mac continued, "... and she named him Brecken."

CHAPTER THIRTY-ONE

Addy

AUCKLAND, New Zealand is known as the "City of Sails," and it's the gateway to some of the most beautiful islands with windswept beaches and tropical forests. It wasn't *The Sage*, but the yacht I chartered gracefully floated adrift with the south-westerly winds. February, March, and April still fell into peak season for sailing off the coast of Auckland. Sometimes sailing simply let me forget; other times it put things into perspective.

Maybe it was the vast infinity of ocean that made me feel like a single period in a novel, something so insignificant, yet its absence made something else incomplete. I'd suffered, but I had also survived. My story wasn't the Holocaust or other atrocious genocides like the Bosnians, Armenians, Aborigines, or Native Americans. My story still had an untold ending that was mine to decide. The only thing holding me captive was my past.

The day I left Quinn, I grabbed two things: my purse and Elena's letter. I walked to the coffee shop down the street before hailing a cab. Quinn was too resourceful, and I figured he would have Tom review the security cameras. I wasn't leaving any trail for Quinn because I did not want to be found. The cab drove me to the airport and from there I called Mac. She was surprisingly calm and understanding of my need to leave. I was no longer her first priority, nor did I want to be. Knowing she had Evan and a baby on the way made it easy to leave. It gave me peace of mind, which wasn't easy to come by those days.

Quinn, on the other hand, was a grave concern for me. He was constantly one drink away from falling to pieces again. When we were together he was strong, even through the difficulties that ensued after my attack. He was rock solid and precisely what I needed, even if I hadn't recognized it at the time.

However, I needed more. I needed him to be strong without me. Playing the hero was exhausting. I had always been the giver. I moved to New York. I went with Elena to Spain. I picked myself up and survived when the drunk, angry version of Quinn no longer wanted me around. I survived his wrath when he kept trying to kick me out of his life. I sobered his ass up, and I forgave his monumental indiscretion with Olivia.

Those days were gone. I had to start thinking about myself. If we were to have even the slightest chance at a future, he had to hold it together and be strong without me. I did not *expect* him to wait an eternity for me, but I *wanted* him to.

COVE was his father's company. That I understood. Quinn didn't kill Malcolm, Sage, or Brecken. His dad didn't either. That, too, I understood. Nevertheless, his connection to the most tragic event of my life was hard to swallow. I wasn't sure if Quinn's face would represent the past that broke me or the future that would heal me.

Then there was his side to consider. The ramifications of the lawsuits destroyed his parents' marriage and eventually led to Lucas killing himself. It was not fair to ignore the possibility that Quinn's feelings toward me might forever be tainted. There was a very real chance that my face would be a reminder of the worst time in his life.

I intentionally left my phone behind. Burner phones were the safest bet to keep Quinn off my track. Mac understood I couldn't give her any way of contacting me, but I promised to check in every few weeks. She never once asked where I was. She never asked if or when I was coming home. And she never told me that everything would work out. The few times I called her she spent most of the time telling me about her pregnancy, but she never asked how I was doing. I never told her either. It signified such an important turning point in our relationship. I had to learn to walk on my own, to figure things out, to prove I had the strength to overcome whatever life handed me. Mac had to let me go; in some ways she had been my enabler, always there to coddle me whenever anything went wrong. It was time for her priorities to shift, and I was so proud of her for recognizing it.

OUT OF ALL THE emotions that dictated my life, guilt was the hardest one to let go. Over time, the pain eased and the anger faded, but the guilt wouldn't budge. It took nearly nine years to forgive Malcolm for Sage's death. Had she been in our bed, we would have all made it out of the house. I knew it wasn't fair to blame him, but somehow it lessened my grief. If my mind was preoccupied with blaming him, then it was easier to not let my heart grieve for him.

Nearly nine years after his death, on a yacht in the Pacific Ocean, I forgave Malcolm. Then I grieved his death. He was my husband and the father of my two children, and I did love him. Letting go of the anger let the pain creep back in. Instead of trying to push it away or bury it, I felt it. I welcomed it. I owned it.

The other part of my guilt wasn't as easy to release. If I blamed Malcolm for Sage's death, then I blamed myself for Brecken's. The "what ifs" were agonizing.

What if I would have gotten out of the house sooner instead of arguing with Malcolm?

What if I wouldn't have gone back in to look for them?

What if after the fire I would have focused all my

energy on the little baby inside of me instead of wishing my heart would stop beating so I could be with my precious little Sage?

The biggest "what if" was in the present moment. What if I didn't learn from my past? I couldn't be that person, so before I docked back in Auckland, I said the hardest yet most necessary words. "I forgive myself."

On the plane ride back to the States, I took care of one last piece of unfinished business, Elena's letter. I loved her like a mother, and as I prepared to follow the path that had been laid before me, I knew the time had come to open the sealed envelope. As I unfolded the letter, the first three words sucked all the air from my lungs.

Adler Sage Ellery,

To the beautiful daughter of Benjamin and Mabel Ellery, the wife of Malcolm Townsend, and the mother of Sage and a little boy I have to assume was named Brecken, I'm so deeply sorry for your loss. When you walked into Quinn's apartment on Christmas, I instantly recognized your sea blue eyes. Your family was the first wrongful death lawsuit filed against Lucas' company. His partner never wanted to know the personal details of the lawsuits; to him it was all about the money. Not for Lucas. He wanted to put a face to every name. We had a folder filled with photos of the victims and their surviving family members. Honestly, it bothered me to see Lucas thumb through the photos every night as I watched him fall apart physically and emotionally. Some mornings I awoke to find him passed out on the couch with an empty bottle of Jack Daniels still clenched in his hand and the photos spread out over the coffee table. I wanted to burn them. I wanted to save my husband, but I didn't ... I couldn't. Instead, I let him self-destruct one day at a time. Other mornings I awoke to an empty house. The man who cheated on me wasn't the man with whom I fell in love. I lost him way before he took his own life. Lucas could never forgive himself, and I don't expect you to forgive him either. I just wanted you to know that the deaths of your husband and children were not only recognized by Lucas, but that he too mourned their loss.

Quinn never knew about you, your family, or the photos. He assumed his dad was just being reckless and cowardly. Lucas was so ashamed of what had happened with his company, and he was ashamed of what happened to our marriage. He couldn't bear to share all the details with his children. He chose to die a coward and a cheater in their eyes instead of a murderer. Someday, I hope they can see him for what he really was, an honest businessman and a loving family man who lost his way in an ocean of guilt and remorse.

As a mother who loves her son, I want to beg you to never give up on Quinn. However, I also love you like a daughter, which means my instinct to protect you weighs against my desire to have my son find happiness. So, here's all that I have left ...

Find peace wherever it may be in this world. Love and be loved. I give to you my heart-felt gratitude for what you have done for me. You owed me nothing, yet you gave me every-thing. Your presence in my life came to be such an unexpected, yet extraordinary gift. Take of mine what you wish, but please give me yours. Give me your past, all your pain, all your anger, all your guilt. Release it to me, and I will be a safe harbor for the life you need to leave behind.

Know that by now, I've already thanked your family for the sacrifice they made so that my family could know and love you, our Addy.

Have a beautiful life,
Elena

ELENA ASKED me to tell her everything about my past right before she died, and I did. I told her about Malcolm and my parents. I told her about the fire. Then I told her about Sage and Brecken. The biography of my life read like a horror story. As the tears bled from my eyes, I felt my soul being ripped from my body. I nearly died with her. Then she took her last breath and with it she took my past. I just didn't realize it until I read her letter. A letter that I had been carrying around for close to nine months.

Timing *is* everything. Had I read Elena's letter right after she died, I would have packed my bags and flown back to Chicago before the funeral. Mac would have played the usual role of consoler, and she and Evan might not have conceived their child. I would not have gone back to Quinn, and he most likely would have continued down his path of self-destruction. But nine months after Elena's death, I read her letter through a different mental lens. While shocking at first, by the end of it I had a clarity that had eluded me for nearly a decade. It was time, my time.

CHAPTER THIRTY-TWO

Quinn

Apparently, Mac's baby was in no hurry to make an entrance into the world because it wasn't until the first week in June that I got the call from Evan early in the morning.

"She's in labor. The doula is here and the midwife is on her way." Evan sounded nervous.

"And Addy?"

"Uh ... yeah, she's here too."

"When did she get there? Why didn't you call me?"

"Girl code. Well, Addy and Mac code anyway. Don't be pissed at me. If my overdue pregnant wife tells me to keep a secret or else she's going to rip my nuts off and throw them in the garbage disposal, then I don't have a choice. She said I could call you when she went into labor, but you can't come over."

"So help me God, if you let her leave town before I get—"

"Listen man, she's not leaving without ... well let's just say she wants to see you ... to talk. She'll call you, okay?"

"Fine ... actually I'm going to text you an address and whenever she's ready just have her go there."

"Okay."

"Oh, and Evan?"

"Yeah?"

"Congratulations. Give Mac a big hug and kiss."

"Thanks, Quinn. That means a lot."

I left my apartment and headed to the house. It was officially finished, thanks to the massive number of workers that had been working relentlessly over the previous few months. I hadn't stayed there yet because I refused to sleep in our new bed alone. I was hopeful, nervous, excited, and still a little fearful.

Evan said, "She's not leaving *without* ..." without what, I wondered? Did that mean she was leaving? Maybe she was finally ready to say goodbye.

Never goodbye!

Just the thought had me wanting to punch something, or drink something. I had to stay focused; it was my last chance. If she saw the house, the lot, if she saw me and still wanted to leave, then I knew it would be forever. I gave her everything I had to give, and all I could do at that point was hope it was enough.

The day dragged on and it fucking killed me to not

call Evan. Finally, around six that evening, I heard the sound of a car pull up outside. When I looked out the window, my heart nearly pounded out of my damn chest.

Addy.

She had never looked more beautiful. Her blue blouse flowed over her khaki capris and matched those mesmerizing eyes. I expected her to come toward the porch, but she didn't. She wiped her eyes and walked toward the woods. When she fell out of sight, I went out to look for her. Her back was to me as I approached with caution. She hugged her arms to her body as she stared at a large oak tree. I gave her space, as though she were a fragile, frightened animal. She had to know I was there, but I waited for her to speak first. I would have waited a lifetime just to hear her voice.

"Why here?" she softly spoke.

"It made me think of you. The location, the trees, the meadow … just the *feel* of it. The price tag … not so much," I said with a slight chuckle.

Still not turning around, she responded curiously. "Oh?"

"My realtor friend told me about the property. He said the house that was here went through demolition years ago and since then it's just been sitting vacant. He put me in touch with the land trustee who said the property wasn't for sale. I made an offer anyway. He flat-out refused until I tripled my offer, then he just laughed at me. Surprisingly, the next day I received a call from him. He said the land unexpectedly was for sale, of course conveniently for the insanely high price I offered him the day before. But it didn't matter, I wanted it for you … I wanted it for us."

CHAPTER THIRTY-THREE

Addy

MAC GAVE birth at home to a beautiful baby boy she named Brecken. Then Evan handed me an address where Quinn wanted me to meet him. I asked why *that* address, but he just shrugged. A half-hour later, I pulled down a private drive with large trees bordering both sides that formed an enchanted archway. The most spectacular view came into sight—a large, three-tiered home with clean lines sat atop a small hill, with trees on three sides and a beautiful meadow just beyond the drive. Hanging from the covered front porch was a modern-looking teak and brushed aluminum swing. The top tier of the house was covered in solar panels, the middle tier was a beautiful roof-top garden, and the lower tier looked like a private balcony with an outdoor fireplace. All three floors had custom floor-to-ceiling windows and the graduated landscaping at the front incorporated native grasses, edible flowers, and ... lilac bushes.

Quinn's Lamborghini was parked in the driveway. When I got out of the car, the floodgates opened. It was so much more emotional than I ever imagined it could be. Like a magnet, I was drawn toward a large oak tree on the edge of the woods. That was when I heard the rustle of footsteps in the brush behind me. Fate, undeniably, was the most powerful force in the universe. Tears continued to trickle down my face as I asked him, "Why here?"

While I listened to his answer, I thought back to the epiphany I had about letting go. While docked at shore that day, I called Edwin Cooper. He was an old family friend and the trustee not only to my parents' estate, but mine and Malcolm's as well. He handled everything when I could barely take care of myself. I told him to sell. He laughed and told me that the stars must have been aligned because just the day before he had received a ridiculously over-priced offer on the land.

CHAPTER THIRTY-FOUR

Quinn

ADDY SHOOK her head and sniffled. Then she walked closer to the tree and slowly lifted her hand to the trunk. I started to close the distance between us, but stopped when I saw what she was doing. Her finger traced initials carved into the trunk.

MJT

AST

SET

"Oh my God, Addy," I whispered. "This is where you—" I couldn't finish and I didn't have to.

She nodded. "Malcolm Joseph Townsend, Adler Sage Townsend, and Sage Eleanor Townsend."

"Addy I ... I didn't know ... about any of it. I didn't know how the fire started. I didn't know it was my father's company. I didn't know about your son, and I promise you I didn't know it was here."

"I know you didn't." She paused for a moment. "It's amazing though, isn't it?"

I couldn't answer. I was still in shock and I had no idea to what she was referring.

"It's amazing how many different roads we can take, but they all lead home."

Taking a deep breath, I fought back my own tears as I choked out the words I was so afraid to ask.

"Are you ... are you home?"

Her body stood motionless as my heart clenched in my chest. In what felt like an eternity, she released a slow, steady breath, as if she was letting go of every breath she had taken up until that moment. Then ... she nodded.

The relief nearly brought me to my knees. I stepped forward until there was no more distance between us. I kissed the top of her head then rested my cheek on it.

"I will love you forever," I whispered.

As I wrapped my arms around her, she placed her hands over the top of mine and slid them down to her *little ... round ... belly*.

Leaning her head back on my chest, she whispered with the most heartfelt emotion, "Do you have anything you'd like to ask me?"

EPILOGUE

ON THAT FATEFUL day underneath the large oak tree that symbolized the strength and courage of my journey back home, Quinn fell to one knee, and with tears streaming down his beautiful face, he asked me to spend forever with him. Then he kissed my little belly and whispered words of love to our unborn child in Spanish.

Apparently, while the doctor was doing my exam after the attack, he noticed a slight displacement of my IUD, so he removed it. Somehow, we both missed that important bit of information. It didn't matter, because Quinn was ecstatic and I was, too. In our two years together, and apart, we both experienced love, pain, sorrow, compassion, honesty … but mostly, forgiveness.

In the weeks that followed, we each shared our letters from Elena, and an ocean of tears. Quinn learned the truth about his father, and with that came the healing and closure he needed. We also made amends with Alexis. When we told her about my past she nearly sobbed. I saw a side to her I hadn't ever seen before. It was a tenderness, that came as much from Lucas as it did from Elena.

We went to my storage unit and found my firesafe. In it were some of the few precious things that survived the fire, including discs filled with digital photos. Quinn experienced my life in pictures. There were photos of my parents, my graduation from undergraduate school, my wedding photos, and of course, lots and lots of photos of Sage. I shed many tears that day, but never once did I feel guilt or regret for the path my life had taken. They weren't decisions I'd made, they were uncontrollable circumstances. In other words ... life.

Our house, well ... it was beautiful. It was us. The neat modern lines of the design and the sheer size of it were Quinn, but the eco-friendly furnishings with tasteful splashes of warm color were all me. I loved everything about it, but mostly, I loved the new memories we made.

Two months after Quinn proposed to me under the big oak tree, we were married in the exact same spot, surrounded by close friends and family. He suggested we find a new spot to carve our initials into the tree. I suggested we leave the poor oak tree alone. It had been Malcolm's idea to carve our initials; I called it tree graffiti. Instead, we planted more trees on our five-acre property. One for each soul that left our lives too early.

We honeymooned on *The Sage* around the Great Lakes for two weeks. Quinn refused to put his pregnant wife on a plane, and I refused to stay home. We set sail on the first of what would be many compromises in our marriage. We had two weeks of beautiful weather. I was in heaven, soaking up the sun and breeze in my little bikini with my baby belly bared to all ... *all* being just Quinn. He was in his own heaven. Nothing about my pregnancy turned him off. He couldn't get enough of my full belly and plump, firm breasts; while I couldn't get enough of him touching, teasing, and kissing every inch of my engorged and highly sensitive nipples. And sex. Never enough sex. But nothing compared to the view of his dark eyes gleaming at mine while his lips kissed every inch of my belly. It was pure love and adoration.

THE CALENDAR FLIPPED to November and my belly had reached capacity. I was still doing yoga every day, and when Quinn came home he took *us* for a walk down our private drive. By the time we reached the house, I was exhausted and in need of a foot rub.

Then, late one night, I felt my contractions start. Quinn put on a calm supportive act, but I could tell he was beside himself with nerves, anxiety, and excitement. I was quite calm; I'd done this before ... sort of. Then by five o'clock the next morning I called my doula and midwife. While we waited for them to show up, I seized the opportunity to say something to Quinn that I had wanted to say since I first found out I was pregnant.

He rubbed my lower back as I sat on an exercise ball, circling my hips. "Babe?"

"Yeah," he said.

"Thank you."

"For what?"

Tears pooled in my eyes as I looked into Quinn's. "A life."

He knelt down in front of me and rested his forehead on mine. When the first tear escaped, he kissed it away. "I'm *truly* honored," he whispered.

Three hours later we welcomed Benjamin Lucas Cohen, five pounds, eight ounces. Then, seven minutes after that, we welcomed Elena Mabel Cohen, five pounds, two ounces.

***

QUINN WAS a natural at parenting and completely smitten with his son and daughter. I occasionally tandem-nursed Ben and Elena, but most of the time he insisted on holding one while I nursed the other. He wore jeans and no shirt every day so he could be skin-to-skin with them, cuddled under a warm blanket. I always had the camera nearby to snap candid shots of my big, strong man holding our tiny babies to his chest. I fell in love with Quinn all over again.

On Christmas, the twins were six weeks old. Chase arrived at our house Christmas Eve and I nearly had to fight with him and Quinn to get my babies back, just to feed them. The rest of the family came over Christmas morning. Brecken, Mac and Evan's son, was almost seven months old. He rolled everywhere, full of smiles, giggles, and enthusiastic squeals. Mac glowed in her role as mother.

"So when is that husband of yours going to get back to work so we can have some mommy-baby play dates?" she asked just loud enough for Quinn to hear.

"When they start school," he piped in, carrying Elena toward the rocking chair where I nursed Ben. "Switch?" he questioned, as Elena started to fuss.

Much to his displeasure, Gwen swooped in and snatched Ben as he handed me Elena. "Sorry, Daddy, you're going to have to share today." She smiled as she carried Ben toward the kitchen.

Quinn shook his head with a fake scowl.

"See, Quinn, there's plenty of help. Time for you to get back to your day job," Mac prodded.

He grabbed Brecken from her lap and nuzzled his belly until he was in a giggling fit. "Tell your mommy I don't want to go back to work," he said in a goofy voice.

After dinner, Alexis and Mitch took Ethan and Ellen home to play with their new gifts. Mac and Evan left with Brecken, as well. Chase was in a food coma on the couch, while Gwen and Richard held the twins. Quinn helped me clean up in the kitchen.

"Come here," he whispered as he clasped my hand and pulled me out of the kitchen toward the stairs.

"Where are we going?"

"My babies are sleeping *and* supervised," he said with a devilish grin, as he led me up the stairs.

"You mean *my* babies are sleeping, right?"

"No, that's not what I mean, but we can argue that point later."

"There's no point to argue because I carried them nine mon—"

Quinn's lips pressed to mine as he scooped me up in his arms and carried me the rest of the way to our bedroom. He laid me on the bed then began to remove his clothes.

"What are you doing?" I whispered as I tried to listen for noises downstairs.

"It's been over two months since I've made love to my beautiful wife. So before we bring up our little prince and princess, who sleep so peacefully between us every night, I'm going to have my way with you, Mrs. Cohen."

I pushed down my leggings then pulled off my sweater. "They've been asleep for a while, we'll have to hurry."

He slid off my panties as I unfastened my bra. "Baby, it's been *two months*," he said seductively as he crawled between my legs. "As much as I'd love to take my sweet time with you, I'm never gonna last that long."

I wrapped my legs around him as he sank into me with a slow, appreciative moan. Then I pressed my palms to his face. Our connected bodies stilled as he rested his forehead to mine. "Eres el amor de mi vida y te amaré por toda la eternidad." *You are the love of my life and I will love you for eternity.*

A SERENDIPITOUS ENCOUNTER in the front of my Café brought Quinn into my life. I offered him my body, filled with a shattered heart and a wounded soul. He offered me hope. Some people spend their whole lives searching for the unknown or trying to achieve the impossible. Quinn did both in two and a half years. He found a part of me that I never knew existed, and he completely mended my broken heart with two beautiful babies and his eternal love.

On our one-year anniversary, I gave him a framed, black and white photo of us on *The Sage* during our honeymoon. It was my pregnant belly, with his hand on one side and his cheek resting against the other side. His eyes were closed, but his facial expression was pure bliss. I'd written a special dedication to him at the bottom.

> Quinn, my love,
> You are my hope. It wasn't until you let me go that I knew my only hope was holding you.

My heart beats for you and the most precious and beautifully-fated life we share together. Thank you for loving me ... thank you for releasing me. ~ Addy

The End

ACKNOWLEDGMENTS

Readers – Wow! Thank you so much for clicking the purchase button for Jewel E. Ann Who? I'm blown away by the feedback. I've connected with some wonderful people around the world through Facebook, Twitter, and Goodreads. It's crazy and amazing! You're the reason I write.

Bloggers – Your generosity and willingness to help connect Indie authors like myself with enthusiastic readers is incredible. You are truly a lifeline. Caitlyn from Made for You Book Reviews, thanks for my first official "Yes." Sandy from The Reading Café, I'm grateful for the interview opportunity to let readers know more about me. The Rock Stars of Romance, what can I say? You rock! Lisa, you spoon-fed me New Author 101 with saintly patience. A huge thanks to you!

Max, from The Polished Pen – Thank you for going above and beyond editing my manuscript. Your invaluable suggestions have made me a better author!

Kiezha with Librum Artis, thank you for the re-edit after my much needed revisions two years after publishing. You're a delight to work with.

Jyl – Just when I thought a thirty-year friendship couldn't get any better ... it did!

Jennifer – One Vinyasa at a time, you ground me and help me find sanity in the midst of chaos. I love that we jumped off a cliff into the unknown together!

Beta Readers – Thank you for your honesty and helping me see my story outside of my head.

To my mom and sister – Thank you for raking through my manuscript over and over again. I'm touched and brought to tears every time I think of all you've done.

Last, but never ever least, my "boys" (hubby & three sons) – I may write for my readers but I write because of you. There will never be the right words to thank you for allowing me to follow my dreams. You are every beat of my heart and the love I feel for you is my greatest inspiration!"

ALSO BY JEWEL E. ANN

<u>*Standalone Novels*</u>

Idle Bloom

Undeniably You

Naked Love

Only Trick

Perfectly Adequate

Look The Part

When Life Happened

A Place Without You

Jersey Six

Scarlet Stone

Not What I Expected

For Lucy

What Lovers Do

Before Us

If This Is Love

Right Guy, Wrong Word

The Fisherman Series

The Naked Fisherman

The Lost Fisherman

Jack & Jill Series

End of Day

Middle of Knight

Dawn of Forever

One (*standalone*)

Out of Love (*standalone*)

Because of Her (*standalone*)

Holding You Series

Holding You

Releasing Me

Transcend Series

Transcend

Epoch

Fortuity (*standalone*)

The Life Series

The Life That Mattered

The Life You Stole

Pieces of a Life

Memories of a Life

ABOUT THE AUTHOR

Jewel E. Ann is a *Wall Street Journal* and *USA Today* bestselling author. She's written over thirty novels, including LOOK THE PART, a contemporary romance, the JACK & JILL TRILOGY, a romantic suspense series; and BEFORE US, an emotional women's fiction story. With 10 years of flossing lectures under her belt, she took early retirement from her dental hygiene career to write mind-bending love stories. She's living her best life in Iowa with her husband, three boys, and a Goldendoodle.

Receive a FREE book and stay informed of new releases, sales, and exclusive stories:
https://www.jeweleann.com/free-booksubscribe

www.ingramcontent.com/pod-product-compliance
Lightning Source LLC
Chambersburg PA
CBHW070233200726
48293CB00005B/1600